"Multifaceted c
strong sense of
romance."   —*Book Reviews & More by Kathy*

"Funny, heart-wrenching and just downright swoon-worthy . . . I highly recommend."
                                   —*Scorching Book Reviews*

"A very compelling read . . . I am thoroughly hooked on the Silver Creek series and the characters in the area."
                                   —*The Book Pushers*

"The tension and the chemistry . . . were off the charts . . . The plot was original and provided some strong emotional moments between hero and heroine."   —*The Season*

UNEXPECTED

"A sensual, emotional story . . . Thoroughly enjoyable and satisfying."   —*Ramblings From This Chick*

"An enjoyable romance . . . I really appreciated the twists that Yates took with her particular tropes because her story stayed fresh while I was reading."   —*The Book Pushers*

"A great start to what I'm sure will be a wonderfully brilliant new series."   —*Harlequin Junkies*

"The humor and the secondary characters, along with the romance, helped to make this an entertaining read."
                                   —*The Book Binge*

continued . . .

UNBUTTONED

"I loved *Unbuttoned* by Maisey Yates in a big way . . . I love a feisty heroine and a charismatic hero, especially when they clash. The scenes where they duked it out verbally, all the while undressing each other mentally, were so delicious . . . Lots of fun."
　　　　　　　　　　　　　　—*Smart Bitches, Trashy Books*

"A sexy, compelling read . . . It's a great start to what looks to be a promising new small-town contemporary series and has introduced me to a new-to-me author who writes enjoyable characters with great emotional depth, witty dialogue and steamy love scenes."　　　—*Ramblings From This Chick*

"A lot of fun to read . . . I look forward to reading the next installment. She provided humor, tension, smexy-times, twisted family dynamics and a re-enjoyment of life."
　　　　　　　　　　　　　　　　　—*The Book Pushers*

"Maisey Yates is a very talented author and has created the perfect small-town romance about two people that found love once they learned to take a leap of faith . . . I can't wait to see what is in store for the residents of Silver Creek."
　　　　　　　　　　　　　　　　　—*Books-N-Kisses*

*U*NBROKEN

MAISEY YATES

BERKLEY SENSATION, NEW YORK

THE BERKLEY PUBLISHING GROUP
Published by the Penguin Group
Penguin Group (USA) LLC
375 Hudson Street, New York, New York 10014

USA • Canada • UK • Ireland • Australia • New Zealand • India • South Africa • China

penguin.com

A Penguin Random House Company

UNBROKEN

A Berkley Sensation Book / published by arrangement with the author

Berkley Sensation Books are published by The Berkley Publishing Group.
BERKLEY SENSATION® is a registered trademark of Penguin Group (USA) LLC.
The "B" design is a trademark of Penguin Group (USA) LLC.

For information, address: The Berkley Publishing Group,
a division of Penguin Group (USA) LLC,
375 Hudson Street, New York, New York 10014.

ISBN: 978-0-425-27369-2

PUBLISHING HISTORY
Berkley Sensation mass-market edition / August 2014

PRINTED IN THE UNITED STATES OF AMERICA

10 9 8 7 6 5 4 3 2 1

Cover art by Anna Kmet.
Cover design by Diana Kolsky.
Interior text design by Kristin del Rosario.

To my husband, Haven.
The friend I couldn't help but fall in love with.

ACKNOWLEDGMENTS

So many hands go into making my books what they are. And I have a whole lot of thank-yous to hand out. To my wonderful agent, Helen Breitwieser, for her endless support and all the hard work she does for me. My fabulous editor, Katherine Pelz, for believing in these characters, and letting me bring this town to life. My mom and dad, for taking care of me, even now that I'm an adult. My husband, for being the best man on the whole planet. My kids, for keeping me grounded by making sure I rarely leave the house without food on at least one item of clothing. Jackie Ashenden, critique partner extraordinaire, who never lets me get away with pulling my punches. And of course, coffee, the reason I wake up each morning. Seriously, without coffee, I would never wake up in the morning.

One

"It's bad form to get drunk at your sister's wedding, right?"

"Since when has that ever stopped you, Cade?"

Amber Jameson leaned back in the folding chair and then checked to make sure the little purple bow tied to the back hadn't fallen off and onto the grass. She'd spent too many damn hours tying those things on yesterday.

They were finicky. Finicky flipping ribbons. Almost as finicky as the bride, who, while cute as a button under normal circumstances, had had a bridezilla flare-up while they'd been decorating yesterday, turning Elk Haven Stables into a country-fairy-princess dream, and had gone around micromanaging said ribbon-tying.

And placement.

She'd demanded ribbon curls in lengths that were impossible for mere mortals to achieve. If Lark weren't the little sister Amber had always wanted, she would never have gone along with all of it. Not without attacking her with the scissors she was using to curl ribbons, at least.

But then, Lark's life had been short on frills, being that

she had been raised by two brothers and a dad. So Amber supposed she was entitled.

But then, Amber's life had been short on this kind of thing too, and she didn't feel at all yearny for it. Nope. Marriage and men and bleah. Not her thing. Not these days.

"It doesn't usually," Cade said, leaning back in his chair so that they were sitting at the same angle. "But I thought, since this is for Lark, maybe I should behave."

She looked at her friend's profile. Strong, handsome. Square jaw, roughened with dark stubble. Brown eyes that always had a glint of naughty in them. And today, he was wearing a suit jacket and a tie, along with a black cowboy hat.

Damn, damn, *damn,* he was fine. Sometimes it hit her, like a shit-ton of bricks, that her best friend was the best-looking guy in a five-hundred-mile radius. Or possibly the world. And it made her feel . . . things she didn't want to feel.

Then he turned to face her head-on and offered her his very best smart-ass Cade smile, and the moment faded out as soon as it hit. Like driving on one of Silver Creek's fir-lined highways and seeing a sunbeam peek through the trees. A brilliant shaft of light that colored the world gold for just a moment before racing back behind the dark green branches. Just a glimpse; an impression of something she didn't want to explore.

Like, ever.

"When did she grow up?" Amber asked, looking over at the dance floor, where Lark was currently holding on to her new husband, both of them swaying to the music without displaying any particular dancing skills. Quinn was a rough-and-tumble cowboy type, though he seemed to have a little more rhythm than his new bride. "It makes me feel old," she continued. "Like an old cliché. Sitting here at her reception looking at this grown-up woman in a wedding gown and thinking . . . how is she not eight years old still?"

"Imagine how I feel," Cade said, his voice rough.

"Yeah, I know."

The Mitchells were a part of Amber's cobbled-together family. She didn't have a lot in the way of people who loved her, so when she found people who were willing to accept her, she clung to them as best as she could.

In her younger years that clinging amounted to some very poor decisions, but she'd matured past that. Especially after she'd realized that her grandma and grandpa weren't going to just ship her straight back into the system. That they were going to let her stay in Silver Creek.

That she could stay, with them, in their home.

Since then, she'd built herself a solid foundation for her life. And Cade was the cornerstone. Had been since she was fourteen years old. She would never, ever do anything to jeopardize that.

Though, there was nothing wrong with infrequent, secret ogling.

"Are you having empty-nest syndrome, Mitchell?" she asked, nudging him with her elbow.

"Me? Oh, hell no. This nest isn't getting emptier. Maddy runs around like hell on pudgy feet. That little beast cut holes in one of my work shirts the other day with those little plastic-handled scissors. And now Cole and Kelsey have the other baby coming in January. Nope, it's just filling up over here."

"But Lark's gone."

"She's been gone. She's been shacking up with that asshole I now call a brother-in-law for a year."

She patted his thigh and pretended not to notice how hard and hot and muscular it was beneath those thin dress pants. "I know. But now it's official."

"Yep."

"Emotions don't bite, Cade. Don't run from your feels," she said dryly.

"That's pretty rich coming from you, missy."

She made a face at him and earned a smile. "I don't have to take advice to give it. I'm emotionally stunted and I know it."

"That's why we get along so well."

"I thought it was because I'm such a good pool player," she said, lifting her beer up from the table and taking a long drink.

"That's not it. I'm a lot better than you are."

"Uh-huh."

"What do you think?" he asked. "Wanna dance?"

She eyed Cade. More specifically, his leg. The one she hadn't just patted. "Um . . . really?"

He lifted a shoulder. "Okay, maybe not." The grooves around his mouth deepened, and Amber felt an answering chasm deepen around her heart.

She hated that he couldn't dance anymore. Hated that the man she knew as being so totally vital and energetic was hobbled because of a rodeo accident four years ago.

For a long time they'd all blamed Quinn, Lark's husband, but they found out they'd been mistaken—which was hard for Cade to process, as evidenced by the fact that he frequently referred to his new brother-in-law as an asshole.

They were getting there, but they weren't exactly best friends yet.

The dude-bonding process was not yet complete.

Now they didn't quite know who to blame, except for a poor kid who'd been paid to sabotage the ride. The spike he'd put beneath Cade's horse's saddle had only been intended to end the ride faster, not send Cade to the hospital and cause life-changing, career-ending injuries. Getting hung up on your horse was never a good thing, but when the horse was that spooked? You didn't walk away. You got carted away on a stretcher.

Quinn got to move on from it all. His name was cleared. He was reinstated into competitions. And the question of who'd sabotaged Cade was left unanswered.

And Cade would never be fixed. Even if they did find out who was behind it, Cade wouldn't magically be healed, damage undone by justice. That hurt her. Always. Every day.

Because whenever she had a problem Cade was there. He was always trying to fix things for her. Had been since they were in high school. But there was no fixing this for him. And she'd give her own leg to do it, so he could go back to doing what he loved.

She only used her legs to wait tables and help around her grandparents' ranch.

She didn't do anything like Cade had been doing. Watching

him ride? It had always sent a flash of light down her spine. A spark that lit her up everywhere and sent tingles to *places*.

It was art with him: athletic grace and sheer masculine willpower. Straining muscles, gritted teeth, dirt, sweat and mud flying in the air.

Yeah, that flipped her switches like whoa.

Cade Mitchell on the back of a bucking horse was a truly orgasmic experience.

When he was through with a ride, he always shook. From his hands down to his boots. Adrenaline, he said. She shook too though, and it wasn't always from adrenaline.

He scared the hell out of her. Watching his accident during the Vegas championships, on TV in her living room, had been the single most painful moment of her life.

Her best friend, her family, dragged around the arena like a rag doll, white as death and knocking on that door.

In those moments, she'd gotten a look at life without Cade. And it had been a yawning vacuum of empty cold. She'd always known he was important. Right then, she'd realized just how important.

Ironically, she would still give just about anything to get him back in the saddle, so to speak. Because he loved it. Even though she knew that after that accident she'd sweat off three pounds during those precious seconds he was on the back of one of those beasts.

Small price to pay for allowing him to have his passion. For giving him back the ability to dance, however badly, so they could go out on that wooden floor together on his sister's wedding day.

But there was no going out on the dance floor for Cade. So they'd sat at the table and drank beer until the sky turned purple and the candles, strung over the tables in mason jars, lit everything with a pale yellow glow.

"Last dance," Amber said, knowing that Quinn and Lark would be leaving soon, off on their honeymoon. "Wanna get out of here?" she asked.

"Are you hitting on me?"

"Hay-ell yeah. What do people come to weddings for but

to hook up? Certainly not to see their BFF's little sister tie
the knot with a ridiculously handsome cowboy."

"You think he's handsome?" Cade asked, eyes narrowed.

She looked back at Quinn and Lark, who were still
twined around each other like vines. "Uh, yeah. Have you
checked that tat he has on his shoulder? Me-*ow*."

"Hey, he's my sister's husband," he said, grimacing
slightly when he said the words.

"Don't worry, I'm out of the game."

"I thought we were gonna hook up."

"Did I say hook up? I meant 'Let's get out of here so I
can whup your ass at pool.' How about that?"

"Sounds like more fun anyway."

More fun than watching his little sister ride off into the
sunset with a guy that Cade still had a tough time with in
some ways. He didn't say that, but Amber could read Cade's
subtext pretty well. Most often, said subtext was *cheeseburger*
or *breasts*. But every so often it was a real, deep emotion that
he was never, ever going to show to the public.

Or even to himself.

Which was when she made sure she was on hand to help
him out.

"Yep. I'll even buy you a beer because you look so damn
purty," she said, tweaking his hat.

"Well, shucks," he said, that lopsided grin tilting to the
left, tilting her stomach along with it. "Let's get on with
it . . . Can you play pool in that dress?" he asked, indicating
her very abnormally feminine attire.

"If you can play in a tie."

He reached up and grabbed the knot at the base of his
throat and loosened it. "I think I can handle it."

"But can you handle me?" she asked, quirking her brow.

"I guess we'll see."

The Saloon, so named because it had been around since that
was the usual name for a place where drinking and carousing
occurred, was packed. Not so much because it was a Sunday

night, but because there was no other nightlife in Silver Creek. Nothing beyond a music festival that ran through the summer and attracted mainly the gray-hairs who only lived in town seasonally.

Not that Cade needed much of a nightlife. Not considering he hadn't done any real "going out" since his accident. Not considering that, even if he did, he couldn't dance.

He didn't know why he'd asked Amber to dance at Lark's wedding.

Ah, shit. Lark was married. That made him feel . . . well, it made him feel. And that was just something he hadn't been prepared for.

But she was his baby sister, and dammit, no matter how unsentimental he wanted to be about it, he and Cole had practically raised her. Which really made Amber closer to the truth than he wanted to admit.

He had empty-nest syndrome. A thirty-two-year-old single man with commitment issues . . . and empty-nest syndrome. As if he wasn't enough of a dysfunctional gimp-bag already.

He wandered up to the bar behind Amber and settled in next to her, his forearms resting on the wooden surface, which was scarred from years of use and misuse. Bottles broken in brawls and Lord knew what else.

There was a story on the menus about a shoot-out between a sheriff and an outlaw that had resulted in the outlaw giving up the ghost on that very bar top.

The Saloon was filled with history. And Cade had spent too many nights in it over the past four years, just soaking in the alcohol haze and absorbing the hormones of those more up to the challenge of getting laid than he was.

He'd become pathetic. And he didn't have it in him to change it.

"Two Buds, please," Amber said, leaning over the counter and catching the bartender's attention a lot quicker than Cade would have.

"I wanted a hard cider," he said. In truth, he would really like to have something that would knock him on his ass, but he tried to save the pitiful drunk trick for the privacy of his own home. In case he got maudlin.

"Too bad," she said.

He was glad she was here. Because there was nothing she hadn't been there for. Every hard thing he'd ever had to cope with. Finding out about his father's affair, his mother's death, his father's death . . . his accident. Lark's wedding.

Amber Jameson had been there for every-damn-thing.

"Beer me," he said once she had the bottles in hand.

"Try again. I don't speak frat bro."

"Amber," he said, giving her his very best plaintive look.

"Fine. I pity you. Drown your sorrows in the way society has dictated men ought. Much healthier than expressing genuine emotion."

"Can I interest you in a friendly game of pool wherein I use your sad, pathetic skills at stick-handling to make me feel more like a man?"

She arched a brow. "Sure, honey, if you think hitting balls into a pocket will make you feel more like a man."

"I do," he said, getting up from the bar and heading to the table.

Amber picked up a cue and started chalking the end. "Your balls are mine, Mitchell," she said, the light in her eyes utterly wicked.

"Whose balls haven't been yours?"

That taunt didn't come from Cade's mouth, and it had him on edge instantly.

Mike Steele. Standard Grade A douche who worked at the mill. They'd all gone to high school together, but he'd never been too big of an ass. He was drunk tonight though, and hanging out with two other guys from high school who fell on the wrong side of the jerk spectrum.

And for some reason, they were interested in letting their asswipe flags fly tonight.

Cade opened his mouth to tell them to back down, but Amber had already whirled around, the end of the pool cue smacking sharply on the floor, the tip held up by her face.

"Can I help you, Mike?" she asked.

"Just saying, is all," he said, his words slurred.

"Maybe you should just say a little clearer," she said, "because I didn't quite take your meaning."

"He's just sayin'," douche number two said, "you're like the town mare. We've all had a ride."

Cade saw red. Death and destruction flashed before his eyes, but Amber barely blinked.

"Come on now," Amber said, her tone completely cool, "official rules say there's no score if the cowboy can't stay on for a full eight seconds. And if I recall right . . . you didn't."

"You stupid slut—"

And then Cade did step in, his fist connecting with the side of the other man's jaw. And damn, it felt good. He hadn't punched anyone since . . . well, since he'd broken his brother-in-law's nose a year ago.

He was worried the other two goons might round on him, but they were too drunk to maintain a thought that went in a straight line, so they didn't seem to key in to the fact that Cade had just laid their buddy out flat.

"Hey!" Allen, the bartender, shouted. "Cade, could you not bust faces in my bar?"

"Tell these assholes not to run their misogynistic mouths in your bar." He looked around at all the people who were staring at him, agape. "Yeah. Ten-dollar word, I just raised the IQ of the entire room," Cade shouted.

"Oh, Cade, for heaven's sake," Amber said. "Knock it off."

"He said—"

"Like I haven't heard it before?"

"I'm not going to listen to it."

"There's no point. And I don't need you to step in and save me. I just wanted to play pool. Now you punched him and we have to go so he doesn't call the cops on you."

"I know the cops."

"So what? Now I'm a spectacle, so thanks."

"Are you . . . are you pissed at me for punching a guy who called you a—"

"Yes! I am pissed at you! Outside," she said. "Now."

They walked out the swinging front door of the bar and

into the dirt and gravel parking lot. Dust hung in the air, clinging to the smell of hose water and hay, all mingling together to create their own unique scent of summer.

"What did I do? He was the one—"

She turned to face him, her cheeks red, her blue eyes glittering. "He's not worth it. He's got half a brain and a tiny peen. And all you needed to do was just let it go. I don't need attention called to shit like that, Cade."

"What do you mean 'shit like that'? As in, it happens frequently?"

"Yes."

"I've never . . ."

"Because they're normally too sober to do it in front of you. Why do you think I have no friends other than you?"

"Because I'm all you need?" he asked, knowing full well that wasn't true.

"Because I came into town with a bang, no pun intended, sixteen years ago, and no one can forget it. Because a lot of the guys from high school and I . . . and now as far as the women are concerned, I'm that skank their husband screwed under the bleachers during free period."

The blood was pounding in his ears, his heart racing. "I don't think of you that way."

"I know. But I didn't have sex with your husband."

A laugh rushed out of him, awkward and angry. "Obviously that will never be a problem I have with you. And it's not like you slept with their husbands after they were married."

"Granted. But it doesn't seem to matter."

"Who cares about that high school BS, anyway?"

"Everyone," she said. "Everyone but you. Which is why we're friends."

"I did a lot of stupid things in high school. Nobody gives me crap."

"That's because you were never naked with them. Guys are dumb about that stuff," she said, the lines around her mouth curving downward. "Anyway, it doesn't matter, Cade."

"It does."

"No. It doesn't. And don't go punching people for me anymore."

"Come on . . . you liked it a little."

The previously noted grooves at the corners of her lips turned up a bit. "Fine. A little bit. But only because he *so* had it coming."

"He really did."

"I wonder if any of your former flames are going to come up and accuse you of being a man-whore."

"Nah," he said, "they won't. But only because they don't want anyone to know they slept with me. That guy's just pissed cuz he's not going there again."

"I'm going to go ahead and take that as a compliment."

"I would never mean it as anything else."

"I know," she said, looking down at her thumbnail. "I'm not the same person I was then."

"Sure you are. You're just more emotionally well-adjusted."

That earned him a smile. "Is that what you call this? Shooting pool, drinking beer, bar fights?"

"If it's not well-adjusted then we're both screwed."

"I think we're screwed."

"Good thing we're screwed together then." He slung his arm over her shoulder and they started walking back to her truck, the gravel shifting underneath his boots with each step.

"I guess so." She pulled away from him and rounded to the driver's side, climbing up inside the cab and turning the engine over.

He got in behind her, slowly. Pissed that just climbing into a truck made him conscious of his limitations. Made him see the bad kind of stars—not the orgasmic kind, but lightning bolts of pain shooting up his thigh and crawling up his back, stabbing right at the center of his spine.

He settled into the seat and let out a long breath. For a second there he'd felt ten foot tall and bulletproof, punching that jackass in the face.

He didn't want to know what that said about him. But

maybe it didn't matter, since he was back to feeling roughly six foot three and vulnerable to being trampled on by a horse.

Which he was.

He held on to the handle just above the passenger window and leaned out, shutting the heavy truck door.

"Do you feel like a man now?" she asked, maneuvering the truck out of the lot and onto the cracked two-lane road that led back to Elk Haven Stables.

"I'm riding bitch in your Ford, how much of a man could I possibly feel like?"

"Would you like me to throw you a raw steak when we get back to your place?"

"No. Tuck me in and read me a bedtime story."

"Aw, poor baby." She leaned over and put her hand on his thigh. Second time that night. Weird, but he seemed to be keeping a ticker on "number of times her fingers come into contact with him" that evening.

"She's married and off on her honeymoon," he said, resting his elbow out the truck window.

"Yeah. What do you think they're doing right now?"

He whipped his head around to face her. "Playing Scrabble."

"Is that what the kids are calling it these days?"

He had no frickin' idea what the kids were calling it these days. He hadn't had it for four years. Four. *Years*. He half expected the League of Men to come and confiscate his dick after so much time off.

He grimaced. His thoughts had taken an unsanctioned turn. He didn't like to think about his celibacy. His sister on her honeymoon was honestly preferable.

"Word games. In flannel pajamas," he growled.

"Fine, Cade, whatever works for you." She cleared her throat. "I bet Quinn got a triple word score."

"No!" he said. "I punched a guy for you; don't torment me."

"You deserve it. You've given her enough hell."

"I have not," he said. "I've been a steadying and wonderful influence. Godlike, in many ways."

"In what ways?"

"I have to think of examples."

"No, I believe you."

"She turned out in spite of me," he said, letting out a heavy breath. "I'm well aware of that. Kind of amazing that Cole and I were able to turn her into a functional human being. Or maybe she just did . . . anyway."

"Either way, you should be proud."

"Damn. I am an empty-nester."

"As you pointed out, you still have Cole."

"Oh, yes." Never mind that living in his older brother's domain was suffocating as hell. Cole was a great guy, but when it came to the ranch, which they all owned equal stake in, he could be a control freak.

And Cade was usually happy to be in the backseat on decisions, because he liked to be a silent investor, so to speak. He'd put money into the ranch from his wins on the circuit, reaped profit in return, had a place to crash at when he was home, and mainly got to live on the road.

But now he was home. All the time. And having a brother who thought of himself as his boss didn't really do a lot to help with their sibling rivalry.

Cade had been fine for a while, playing the dumbass and in general drifting along with whatever Cole said.

But now that this was starting to look like it was going to be his life . . . like he was never getting back in the saddle in a serious way . . . well, now he was starting to realize he was going to have to make a new success for himself.

Otherwise his glory days would be perpetually behind him. And never in front of him. Ever again.

What a nice thought that was.

"I only drank half a beer and I'm starting to get philosophical and shit," he said.

"Uh-oh, better get you home then. I wouldn't want to embarrass either of us by being present for this."

"You really are a good friend," he said.

She looked at him and smiled. "The best."

"Pretty much the only one I have."

"Because you're surly."

"Am I?" he asked.

"You just punched a guy in the face for offending you, so yeah, I'd say so."

"I think it was noble of me," he said.

"Noble and godlike in one conversation. If this is your version of being a sad drunk then I'd hate to be exposed to your ego when you're feeling sober and upbeat."

"You'll be around me in that state tomorrow. Because now I owe you a game of pool."

"I don't know. I think I owe you for defending my honor. I didn't need it defended, but nonetheless, I appreciate you risking bruised knuckles for me."

"Anything for you," he said. "You know that."

"Oooh, dangerous promise, Cade Mitchell. You never know what I might ask of you."

"I've known you for sixteen years and you haven't shocked me yet."

"That smacks of a challenge," she said, giving him an impish smile. "You know I can't resist a challenge."

When Cade got home, Cole was sitting in the swing on the front porch his wife, Kelsey, leaning against him, half-asleep.

Maddy was undoubtedly upstairs in bed. Most of the guests were probably back in their cabins. A wedding at the ranch during busy season had everyone amped-up and exhausted. Lark had invited everyone staying at Elk Haven to the big day, and nearly all of them had taken her up on the invite.

Which probably accounted for the quiet now. Too much dancing. Too much drinking. And now, lights out by ten.

"Where have you been?" Cole asked.

"I went out with Amber."

"You went out instead of seeing Lark off?" he asked, shifting Kelsey's head to his shoulder.

"I figured she was in good hands. She didn't notice, did she?"

"She didn't say. I'm sure she didn't really."

"Yeah, so I figured I'd go have a beer."

"We had beer," Kelsey said, her voice sleepy. "And I couldn't drink any, cuz, bump"—she put her hand on her stomach—"so there was plenty for you."

"I just wanted to get some space," he said. "I didn't really want to watch her leave."

"With Quinn," Cole said. "Aren't you over that?"

"I'm as over it as I can be. But I spent three years blaming him for what's happened to me. And while I mainly think of him as a decent guy, I would sort of hate anyone who ended up with Lark on principle. For a while, at least."

"Well, it's too late to hate him. They're married now."

"Well, get off my back, asshole," Cade said, walking up the steps and toward the front door.

"What's your deal, Cade?" Cole asked.

"My deal is that I feel like I just came home after curfew and Mom and Dad caught me. I'm a little old to be dealing with judgment from you on how I chose to spend my evening."

"I don't normally care what you do. Go snort some bath salts and have an orgy with the entire staff of Delia's Kitchen for all I care, as long as you get your work done the next day. But half-assing Lark's wedding? I'll call you out on that."

"I was there," he said, gritting his teeth.

And he hadn't been able to dance with his sister, or his best friend, and he'd run out on it because it had hurt. Because it had made him feel, again, like he was half a human being.

He would rather have his balls dipped in honey and stuffed in an anthill than admit that, but it was the truth.

He wasn't telling Cole because . . . Scrotum. Honey. Ant-hill.

He didn't owe Cole an explanation anyway.

"Whatever, Cade, I shouldn't be that surprised at this point."

"Boys, do I have to turn on a hose and spray you down?" Kelsey asked.

"Maybe just remind your husband of his place," Cade said, pushing the front door open and walking into the main area of the cabin.

The front room was huge, with an L-shaped staircase that led to a mezzanine floor, vaulted ceilings and a wall of windows that overlooked the back pasture and the mountains that encircled the ranch. There was also a counter where they kept rolls, muffins, donuts, a single-serving coffee brewer and hot chocolate packets.

They were a motherfuckin' hotel.

He stomped over to the bar and started running hot water through the coffeemaker before adding hot chocolate to it. He didn't need more booze.

The front door opened and Cole and Kelsey walked inside. Kelsey scurried up the stairs and Cole stood there in the entryway, his arms crossed over his chest. Cade leaned against the counter, partly to affect an "I don't give a shit" posture. And partly because his leg felt like it was being chewed on by rabid badgers.

He needed a hot bath with Epsom salt. And a horse tranquilizer.

Not a lecture. But it seemed he was about to get a lecture.

"Look, man, I'm sorry," Cole said.

"You're sorry? What the hell?" he said, letting his body form to the back of the granite countertop, taking as much of the weight off of his back and spine as possible.

"You're right. Not my business. You make your choices about what you want to do with your life. Or not do with it. It's not my business."

"That is the worst damn apology I've ever heard. It was wrapped in an insult."

"I'm not trying to insult you. I'm just saying, I have to stop expecting you to make the choices I would."

"Back up. Explain."

"You don't have motivation."

Cade slammed his mug down on the counter. "That's bullshit."

"Is it? Because I'm pretty sure that you've been living in the big house and working as a ranch hand for the past four years."

He bent and grabbed ahold of his leg. "Oh, I'm sorry, did you want me to go and start running marathons in the name of Elk Haven Stables?"

"That's not it."

"You know what, Cole? This is pretty surprising considering I did have some ideas for you and you shot them down."

"Cade, I don't have room for bison. We're focusing on the cabins, the lodge and the rodeo contracts, and you know that. We don't have the funds for a venture like that."

"We do."

"No, we have Dad's debt, Cade, or did you forget?"

"I didn't forget. In fact, if you recall, I found out just how screwed we were a couple of years ago because I was going over our fucking finances, so don't give me this 'you don't do anything' shit."

The worst thing about Cole's accusations was the ring of truth to them. It was the fact that it was how Cade felt about his life.

Because he'd had his dream—success that he'd fantasized about from the time he was a little kid. Traveling, riding a horse for money. Doing the kind of dangerous stuff his mother had always said was giving her gray hair.

That had been his job. And it was gone now. Then he'd had to learn to walk like a baby, all over again, and now he was starting over.

The worst version ever of being born again.

To top it off, there was no resolution to it. Anger at Quinn had been concrete. He'd had someone to blame, and as small as it had been . . . there had been comfort in it. Now he had nothing. No clue who'd messed him up. No clue who'd ruined his life and stolen his career. And no lead on it either.

It made him feel aimless. It made his anger directionless.

Though right now, it was a little directed at Cole.

"That's not it . . ." Cole put his hands in his pockets. "Okay, fine, I am sorry. I'm just a little messed up about Lark getting married."

"You'd think that given we had a year to adjust to it we'd be fine. She hasn't even been living here." He was echoing the conversation with Amber, as if that might make it all true and fine.

"Yeah, but now it's permanent. Now it's just us," he said.

"She still owns a third of the ranch."

"Yeah, but she won't do as much here."

Cade cleared his throat. "I liked it better when you were being a jackass."

"Feelings aren't really my favorite thing either."

"You're more well-adjusted with them these days."

"Eh. Wife. She makes me talk about them . . . You know, acknowledge that I have them, so . . ."

"Thank God I don't have a wife."

"They aren't so bad," Cole said, one side of his mouth turning up.

"I'll let you have that joy all to yourself. I will be the favorite uncle to all your children and Lark's children and maintain the lifestyle to which I have become accustomed."

"Eating Doritos, alone in bed, in your childhood home?"

"That nacho cheese flavor is worth sharing the sheets with crumbs."

"As opposed to . . . a woman?"

Cade took a sip of his hot chocolate. "You're not allowed to comment on my sex life."

"You're standing in the living room drinking a cocoa before bed. I think we can safely assume you currently don't have one."

Cade shifted so that his middle finger was resting on the handle of the mug. A not-so-subtle suggestion for his brother. Who was right. Asshole.

"We're not talking about that," he said. He took a deep breath. "Reconsider the bison, Cole. I think we'll make money doing it. A lot of restaurants are offering it as an alternative to beef, and I think we could really start something here."

Bison had never been his dream. Riding saddle broncs, with the dirt kicking up around him, the crowd cheering and the cameras and lights on him? That was his dream. But it was gone, and he felt desperate to put his mark on something.

To have something that was his idea. Success he created.

"It's too risky," Cole said. "And it requires changes to fencing, a lot of space . . . I don't think we're in the position to do it. We don't want to diversify too much too early."

"Maybe you don't but I do. And last time I checked, you weren't the be-all and end-all here."

"Maybe not. But I'm the one who spent his whole life here. This is my dream, Cade. This is what I've spent every moment working on. Since before dad died, and especially after. You went off and did the circuit, and that was fine. You've supported things financially, and yeah, technically you and I have equal ownership here. But the thing is? I'm the one who's put in the physical work. I'm the one who knows how to run it. I'm not trying to be a dick, but I am the one who understands the way this place works, inside and out, better than anyone else."

Cade tightened his grip on his mug. Sure, Cole knew the ranch. But Cade had known, always, about the truth of their life. About his dad's debts. About what really needed to be earned to keep the place running.

Cole knew the ranch. But he'd only known half the story about what was happening beyond that.

"Fair enough, I get that, and yeah, I can concede that you know the place better than me," Cade said. "But not if the end result is just going to be you acting like you're the boss and I'm the laborer, and not part owner."

"The problem is, I don't think we're ever going to want to do things the same. Two mules pulling the wagon in a different direction. It doesn't work."

"Nice analogy," Cade said. "So that's it? We can't have two leaders so by default you call the shots?"

"Not by default. My sweat is in this place."

"Mine too."

"Not as much."

"Are we going to measure? Try and see who has the most sweat? Maybe we should hurl logs and see who can throw them the farthest."

"It's late," Cole said. "And I have more than Dorito crumbs waiting for me in bed, so I'm going to go."

"And then we don't have to solve the problem. Brilliant. Perfectly like us."

"We'll solve it. I'm sorry I was an insulting prick, okay?"

"It's okay. You can't help it."

He shrugged. "The older brother thing dies hard."

Cade thought about Lark, all grown up and married. "Yeah, trust me, I know. But that doesn't make it any more fun for the person on the receiving end of it."

"Let's just put the bison on hold," Cole said. "We'll discuss it again in a year maybe? After we get through the busy seasons. After we have being a guest ranch down to a more well-oiled system. After we get the horse breeding program a little bit more solidified. That doesn't seem too authoritarian of me."

"No," Cade said, setting his mug on the countertop. "Fine."

Cole nodded and turned, heading up the stairs toward his room. Toward his crumb-free bed.

It was easy for Cole to put it on hold, because he had a life. Because he had a wife and a kid, and a ranch that he called the shots on.

Cade wasn't sure he wanted any of that, ever, but he sure as hell needed something.

A year before they even broached the subject of the bison. A year before his only idea on contributing would be considered.

Another year in holding-pattern hell.

He wasn't sure he could deal with it. But he wasn't sure what to do about it either.

He was a take-charge kind of a guy. A doer, not a thinker, much to his mother's chagrin all through his teenage years.

But his injury had taken his control. It had taken the charge right from him. He couldn't do what he chose to anymore, and he had no idea what the hell he actually wanted to do.

Except sleep. Hell yeah, he was pathetic.

He would go to sleep. And tomorrow would be the same as every day that had come before it for the past two years.

Just. Fucking. Perfect.

Amber groaned and shuffled the stack of bills from the table to the counter. She sighed. Then she pondered putting them in the shredder.

But she couldn't do that. Damned adulthood.

She wasn't sure when she'd be able to pay them either. Maybe if she picked up another shift at the restaurant she could do it. But the medical bills from her grandma's illness, the funeral fees, and the taxes her grandfather had forgotten to pay—they weren't much on the fixed income, but two years of that was from when the farm had been producing decent income, and getting slapped with a back-tax bill at a self-employed rate was killer.

It was just dire.

She shuffled to the coffeemaker and picked up the carafe. Thankfully, it was on a timer, so she didn't have to worry about making it while she was this bleary. She always tried to wake up before her grandpa, which meant getting up before the sun, so that she could bring him coffee and breakfast and get him set for the day before she went off to wait on strangers.

Waiting on her grandpa was definitely preferable.

She loved the old man more than anyone else. Except for maybe Cade.

She moved to the stove and fired up the gas range. The pan was greased and waiting for her already. Her grandfather was a man of habits.

Every morning she made him whole wheat toast, two fried eggs, hash browns—pre-shredded at the beginning of the week because she was not doing that at five thirty a.m.—and two strips of bacon.

Amber didn't indulge in quite the lumberjack breakfast he did. Though he didn't seem to have suffered for it. He was still lean as could be, though he had definitely aged since she'd first arrived.

He'd been old from the first moment she'd met him.

Fourteen, angry, terrified. Because she'd been uprooted, not just from the home she was living in—that was normal—but from her city, from the people she'd called friends.

Taken from Portland and brought out to the little pile of bricks rising out of the wilderness known as Silver Creek.

At first, she'd wanted to get sent back. Back to where she

had access to her friends. To drugs and alcohol and all of the crutches she'd been using to deal with the pain in her life.

So she'd done her best to make them hate her too. Since she was sure it would happen anyway. Like her mother had. Like every foster family had from the moment she'd darkened their door. Angry, sullen . . . crazy, as one foster mom had called her.

But her grandparents hadn't let her do it.

In their mid-sixties, wrinkled and gray, the oldest people she'd ever been exposed to, they'd also been the toughest. They'd expected her to work. To collect eggs. To be home when they said and to dress like they told her.

And they'd never, ever given up on her. They'd opened their home up to her. They'd given her their name.

Eventually she'd stopped trying to get sent away. Eventually, she'd decided to pour everything into being the best granddaughter she could be, because they'd given up their quiet, drama-free years to deal with the child their wayward son had never even met.

Their love, and Cade's friendship, was the thing that had pulled her off the path to what would have probably been an early grave, and she couldn't even begin to show the full depth of her gratitude.

Though bacon-making was a nice, physical representation of that gratitude. As was getting up before dawn to make breakfast, and working extra shifts to make sure the ranch didn't get seized by the government or a bank or something.

She would never allow that to happen. This was her home. The only place that had ever felt like home. The only place she'd lived for longer than a couple of months.

Sixteen years of her life had been spent here, and she wasn't going to let anyone else take it.

She hummed while she prepared breakfast and did her best not to think about the bills. Then she piled all the food onto a plate and set it on the table just as her grandpa walked in.

His gait had slowed, and his brain didn't quite hold on to everything the way it once had, but he still got up and about.

Still made sure he walked around the property and checked on everything.

They didn't have much beyond a small vegetable patch and some chickens anymore, but it was still her grandpa's pride and joy.

"Morning," she said, going back over to the stove to retrieve her egg, toast and coffee.

He sat slowly, a smile on his face as he surveyed the food she'd laid out for him. "Morning," he said, his hand trembling as he raised his coffee cup to his lips.

"I've got an early shift today," she said. "And I probably won't be home until late. You think you'll be okay?"

He put his cup down and waved his hand. "You know I'm fine. You act like a worried hen. Just like your grandma."

"Well, I can't help it," she said, sitting in her spot across from him. "I need to make sure you don't feel like I'm abandoning you out here while I work."

"The other option is putting me in a home," he said. "And I'd rather be alone than deal with scheduled board game nights."

She laughed. He might be slowing down a little bit, but Ray Jameson still had the same curmudgeonly sparkle Amber had always found so endearing. He was a gruff old guy, but she liked that.

"Like being in hell, I'm sure," she said.

"They do that, uh . . . what do you call the thing where they sing to the lyrics?"

"Karaoke."

"Yeah, they do that at those places."

"It makes a good case for not going there," she said, dragging her toast through her runny yolk and taking a bite.

"I'm old and wise," he said.

"Yes, you are."

There was a knock on the front door. Amber jumped in her chair and looked out the window. The sun was just starting to rise above the ridge of the mountains, a golden line illuminating the tops of the dark green trees. The air was still blue, night hanging on until the bitter end.

And no one should be knocking on the door just yet.

"I'll get it," she said, walking out of the kitchen and into the little entryway.

She looked out the top window of the door and saw a man's brown hair, and nothing else. She knew it wasn't Cade because he would call before coming over. At this hour at least.

She tucked her hair behind her ear and opened the door.

The man standing on the step was about her age, tall and decent-looking, a cowboy hat in his hand and a smile on his face.

She distrusted him. Instantly.

Mostly because not trusting someone was her default setting until they proved she had reason to do otherwise. But also because he was at the door at six in the morning, and he was smiling.

She just hoped he wasn't from the IRS.

"Can I help you?" she asked, putting a hand on her hip and mentally calculating the location of the nearest rifle in the house.

"Sorry to come by so early," he said.

"Then why did you?" she asked.

She'd never been one to play games. She wasn't shy, bashful or easily shamed. And she would happily take the upper hand of this situation, thank you very much.

He, whoever he was, no doubt thought that showing up to do his business early and unexpectedly would put her on the wrong foot.

Too bad for him, that wasn't possible with her.

"I was given the impression, by Ray Jameson, that it would be all right. This is Ray Jameson's place?"

She felt her hackles lower a bit. "Uh. Yes. May I ask what your business is here and who you are?"

"Jim Davis." His name rang some bells, but she couldn't quite place him. Not this early. Two cups of coffee would be required before she was feeling that sharp. "I spoke to the bank earlier this week about the standing of Ray's loan."

"Why the hell was the bank giving you information on my grandfather's loan?"

"I'm an investor. Well, part-time, anyway."

"What are you the other part of the time?" she asked, leaning into the doorframe, making sure that he knew he wasn't welcome inside—not just yet.

"A cowboy," he said.

She could have rolled her eyes. "Interesting. Now what are you doing here?"

"You the typical welcome committee?" he asked, obviously getting annoyed with her now.

"Yessir, I am. If you've got a problem with that? I don't have a comment card for you to fill out, so it's just too damn bad. State your business."

"I'd rather speak to Ray."

"I'm the executor of Ray's estate," she said.

Once she'd discovered her grandfather's forgetfulness with the taxes and several other bills, she'd gone and handled all that so that she could take care of all of the finer details of his life.

"Then you're the person I want to see," he said, smile broadening.

"I thought I might be."

She still didn't give an inch, still kept him on the porch.

She had a good sense for people. She'd been exposed to a lot of them growing up. And most of them hadn't wanted anything good, in her experience. People in general wanted to use you to elevate them. That was about it.

Cynical, maybe, but she was better insulated against douche bags than most.

"I'm here to make an offer on the ranch," he said.

"What?"

"I want to offer on the ranch. The bank said you'd been in default, and that there were some other issues . . ."

"They had no right to disclose that information!"

"Regardless, I'd like to help out."

"Mr. Davis, nobody just wants to help out. Everybody wants something, and it isn't to help. So you want to buy all this?" she said, looking around.

"I do."

"Well, too damn bad. I don't want to sell it."

"You haven't heard what I'm offering."

She thought of the bills on the counter, and all of the stress. And then she thought of what it had always meant to come back to this place.

"Doesn't matter."

"You say that because you have no idea what you're turning down."

"You could be offering me magic beans and a goose that lays gold freakin' eggs and I wouldn't say yes. This is our home. Our legacy. We aren't going to sell."

"Did I step into a heartwarming family film when I wasn't looking?" he asked, arching a dark brow.

"Nope. You just stepped onto my porch. Now step off. We don't need any more visits from you. Okay. Thanks, bye."

She shut the door and bolted it, then went back into the kitchen.

"Who was that?" her grandpa asked.

"Damn vacuum cleaner salesman," she said.

"Did you tell him we didn't want any?"

"I told him we had a vacuum that worked just fine." Their vacuum was possibly older than Amber, but her grandma had always insisted that nothing new was made as good as the old, reliable appliances that were made out of solid hunks of metal.

If it had really been a vacuum cleaner salesman she probably would have taken what he had on offer. She could really use an eight pound wonder instead of that forty pound beast that always sounded like it had just sucked up a cat.

"I thought maybe it was a boyfriend of yours," her grandpa said.

She rolled her eyes and pulled her purse and sweater off of the counter. "I don't have time for boyfriends."

"I wish you did."

She leaned down and kissed his cheek. "I know you do. But trust me, I don't."

"And when I die, who's going to take care of you?" he asked, his tone gruff as ever, but with tenderness running beneath it.

"I'm going to take care of me," she said. "But you're not allowed to die," she said, her throat getting tight, "for at least another thirty years."

"I'll be eating bacon from a tube by then. Best you let me go before that."

"It's too early to be this morbid," she said. "And I have tables to wait. So if you'll excuse me . . ."

"Have a nice day."

"I will," she said.

She dug her keys out of her purse before she went outside, just in case Mr. Jim Davis was still loitering. Happily, he wasn't.

Then she got into the truck and started it. And her thoughts shot to Cade. Maybe because they'd just ridden together last night, and maybe because when he'd stumbled out of the truck last night at his house, something in her stomach had tugged hard, low and tight.

Because she knew he wasn't in a good space, and she hated that.

And part of her had felt like maybe she should follow him in and hang out for a while, but . . . early morning and waiting tables and all.

She took a deep breath and shot him a quick *good morning, how ya doin?* text before throwing the truck into reverse and heading out toward town.

In spite of the weird start, she hoped the day would end up being normal.

CHAPTER

Three

The lunchtime rush was just starting to slow when Cade walked into Delia's and spotted Amber, rushing around between tables.

She hostessed during the dinner hour, when they opened up the back of the building, but during the day she just ran herself off her feet serving three-egg breakfasts and giant burgers.

He seated himself on the red, glittery, vinyl-covered bar stools at the formica counter and waited.

"I'm here to see Amber," he said, when one of the other waitresses paused near him.

She smiled and winked. "Sure, Cade, she'll only be a minute."

Everyone knew that he and Amber were best friends. He had a feeling a lot of people misconstrued the nature of their relationship, and he couldn't exactly blame them. He and Amber had both cultivated a bit of reputation around town, and even though both of them had calmed down considerably since their teenage years, they'd earned the label of town hellions, and they'd done it with style.

He felt a hand on his shoulder, and he turned to see Amber standing there. "What's your poison, handsome?"

"Burger. You don't happen to have buffalo burger, do you?"

She wrinkled her nose. "No. And you know we don't."

"It's better for you."

"And that matters to you?" she asked.

He patted his stomach, which was flat and hard thanks to the workouts he did to keep the muscles in his back as strong as possible. He'd always been into fitness. A strong core was essential to keeping your ass on a horse. But he'd had to really work at it since his accident.

It was the only thing that kept him mobile. If he put on weight and didn't have the muscle tone to support himself, there would be no getting around at all.

"I'm a total health nut," he said. "Now bring me a beer, extra french fries and a hamburger."

She rolled her eyes. "Are you sure they didn't hollow out your leg during one of your surgeries?"

"Pretty sure all they did was leave a bunch of metal behind."

"Well, either way, I'll get your food. Just a second."

"Do you have a break coming up?"

The bell above the door sounded and they both turned as a group of people walked in. "Probably not. I'll just end up eating a sandwich over the counter in the back."

"They have to give you a break," he said.

"I know, but I need the tips. I don't want to skip a table. And if you stiff me, Mitchell, so help me, I'll stab your thigh with a butter knife."

"I'm not going to stiff you," he said, watching her walk to the door to greet the large party that had just come in. He turned back to the counter, his stomach growling.

It smelled like griddle grease, bacon and beef in here, and he was starving.

The bell above the door sounded again, and a man walked in wearing a cowboy hat. A man that Cade knew.

He slid off the stool and stood. "Jim," he said, just loud enough to get his former competitor's attention.

Jim saw him and his expression shifted from flat to a wide smile. "Cade Mitchell." He walked over to the counter and extended his hand. "How you been?"

"I lean slightly to the left now, but other than that, pretty good."

"You seem to have recovered pretty well."

"Yeah. Pretty well." In that permanently damaged way. "You eating?"

"Hell yeah." He sat on the stool next to Cade and put his hat on the counter.

"Great."

"Actually, it's interesting I ran into you."

"Is it?" Cade asked.

"Yeah. I'm moving to town. Or rather, I'm looking into it."

"Really?" Cade had never had a lot of thoughts about Jim Davis one way or the other. He was fierce competition, that was for sure. But he was quiet, and he'd always been respectful.

He didn't have that brash swagger that Quinn Parker—and in truth that undoubtedly Cade himself—possessed.

Cade had always liked him in a passive way. As much as you could like the guy you were trying to beat at everything.

"Yes, really. Thinking of starting a ranch."

"Is there any land for sale?" Cade asked.

"Not at the moment. But something's bound to come up."

Amber came back just then with a basket of fries and a bottle of beer. She froze when she saw Jim. "Hi there," she said, blinking rapidly. Then she turned to Cade and offered him a look that held a thousand words. Not necessarily words that Cade could easily translate, but they were there for sure.

"This is Jim Davis," he said. "We used to compete on the circuit."

"Jim . . . oh," she said. "That's why I recognized you earlier."

"Earlier?"

"Yeah . . . Jim came by to pay me a visit this morning," she said.

"I did. And I'm actually here to pay you a visit too."

Amber's dark brows shot upward. "How did you find out where I worked?"

"Just did a little asking around."

Everything in Cade stood up, took notice, and got ready to bust skulls. He didn't like this. Didn't like that Jim was here and nosing around Amber. And he especially didn't like the stiff line in Amber's neck.

He knew her as well as he knew himself. Probably he was actually better in touch with her emotions than his own, if he were honest.

"Who have you been asking?" Amber asked, her voice brittle.

"Not a big deal, darlin'," he said. "I wouldn't worry about it."

"Did he just 'darlin'' me?" she asked Cade.

Jim continued as if she hadn't spoke, and Cade's passive liking of the other man started a rapid descent into active disliking. "I'm willing to buy you out for half a million."

Amber about got whiplash. "Are you kidding me? What the hell kind of lowball offer is that? And no."

"I have to warn you, baby, I don't take no very well."

She looked at Cade. "Did he 'baby' me?"

"I'm going to keep asking," Jim said.

"You're going to get tired of me real quick," she said, crossing her arms under her breasts.

He looked her up and down. "I doubt that."

"Hey," Cade said, standing and putting his arm around her waist before he could fully think the action through, "she said she didn't want to talk about it. We aren't talking about it. And if she tells me that you're bothering her, I won't be responsible for my actions."

"Thank you, Cade," she said stiffly. "I have to go and get your burger." She turned to Jim. "Can I get you something?"

"Not now," he said, picking his hat up from the counter and putting it back on his head. "I'll see you later," he added, nodding toward Cade.

"You better make sure I'm happy to see you then. Maybe find a new topic," Cade said as Davis walked back out.

"Tell me the story," Cade said, turning back to Amber.

She shook her head. "I don't have time. Later, okay?"

"When do you get off?"

"Dinnertime. I have to bring leftovers home to Grandpa."

"Can I meet you over there?"

"Yeah, sure. I'm just hoping he'll still be awake when I get there. Do you want me to grab you something for dinner too?"

He nodded. "Yeah, that'd be good."

She smiled, then scurried back toward the kitchen, disappearing for a second, then reappearing with his burger on a plate. "Later," she said.

"Yeah."

He watched her wait tables while he ate, and pretty quickly he realized some of the regulars were watching him watch her. And he realized that his protectiveness could easily be misconstrued by old busybodies who had nothing better to do than speculate on the lives of the people around them.

It was fine if Davis wanted to make assumptions. Cade sort of hoped he would.

He took a bite of his hamburger and kept his eyes on Amber. She was the best view the room had to offer anyway. And he didn't have anything to prove or disprove to these people.

And if they did spread some rumors, maybe it would help to discourage Jim Davis from showing his face at Amber's place again.

"Meatloaf," Amber said, putting the casserole dish in front of Cade. "Yum. And Grandpa went to bed before I came home, so it's all for us."

She was in the habit of bringing plates from home so that she could transport leftover food to and from the restaurant. Delia was great like that. Nothing went to waste. It all went to employees or to the homeless shelter, but everything got eaten.

"I'm actually excited about Delia's meatloaf," Cade said, looking too broad and too masculine for the little wooden chair he was sitting in.

"She's pretty awesome," Amber said, sitting down across from Cade and handing him a fork.

He smiled and took a bite straight out of the casserole dish, and she did the same.

"I agree. So explain the douche bag to me," he said.

"Uh . . . you're the one who knows him," she said. "Explain him to me."

"I don't really *know* him, know him. I competed against him. He wasn't real offensive or anything."

"He wasn't Quinn, in other words?"

"No. Actually, the fact that he is a douche bag is sort of a surprise to me. So tell me the story."

"Well, he showed up at my house this morning at freaking six a.m., asking to buy the place. I told him where to shove it."

"You didn't even listen to the offer?"

"Hells no. I'm not moving from here. Ever."

"What if you could get him to give you a good offer?" he asked.

Leave it to freaking Cade to play devil's advocate. Freaking Cade.

"It doesn't matter. Money is not as important as a home."

"Some would argue that money is essential to buying a house. So . . . money is important to home ownership."

"Shut up. I'm not talking house. I'm talking home. I've lived in a lot of houses, Cade. A lot of freaking houses. I had to have a small enough amount of stuff that I was easy to move. Everything I ever had fit into a plastic bag. One plastic Albertson's grocery bag. Blue and white, depressing as hell. I hate moving," she said, squeezing her eyes tight, trying to ignore the moisture that was building in them, the sting that was growing stronger back behind them. "This house . . . It's the first place that ever had people in it that seemed to want to keep me. You like moving around. You seek it out. I don't think you can understand my attachment to it."

He frowned. "In a way I can. Yeah, I like to stay mobile, but I always know the ranch is there. I always know I can go back to it. So whether or not I live in it, I do have my stability.

And I have more than what fits in a plastic bag. I won't even pretend to understand that kind of trauma."

"Like you didn't have your own," she said, taking another bite of meatloaf.

"Yeah, well, we all have our crosses to bear, right?"

"You and I seem to be carrying more than one. At least I think so," she said.

"I won't argue."

She sighed. "We're in debt, though."

"What? Why didn't you tell me?"

"For this exact reason," she said, frowning and stabbing at the top crust of the meatloaf.

"What reason? Because meatloaf?"

She scowled at him. "No, because your posture immediately went Superman. Stiff shoulders, puffed-out chest. I can practically see your cape billowing in the wind."

"What's wrong with that?"

"I'm not yours to save, Cade Mitchell. I have my own life and I have to figure things out. And I don't want you giving me money, because heaven knows there's no surer way to kill a friendship."

"It wouldn't kill ours."

"That's what they all say. Anyway, it's not that dire. I'm going to fix it. It would help if this was a producing farm, of course."

"Have you ever thought about leasing pasture space?"

"Uh . . . I hadn't, actually. I don't really have the rancher gene, so sometimes these things just don't occur to me. I should work at getting the rancher gene though, unless I want to be a waitress for the rest of my life. Which is fine, but it's not really what I want to do."

"What do you want to do?"

She lifted a shoulder. "Dunno. I'll figure it out eventually. But on my own time. Anyway, what do you want to do?"

One corner of his mouth lifted. "I don't know either. I didn't know there would be a quiz with my meatloaf."

"There is no such thing as a free meal, Mitchell. Meatloaf special, navel-gazing required."

"I don't navel-gaze. I drink."

"Drinking makes you navel-gazey. Trust me. I was just with you last night while it was happening."

"Don't let me do it two nights in a row."

"Maybe your new calling has to go with singing 'Kumbaya' and talking about your feelings?"

He laughed. "Nobody wants to hear me sing. Ever."

"I've heard it. If you recall, I've been around you when you were so drunk you could hardly stand, much less navel-gaze. But dear Lord, you can certainly sing Tim McGraw when you're drunk. Or at least you think you can."

"You're very lucky to have been present at a limited-edition Cade Mitchell concert."

"I raised my lighter in salute."

"Was it that long ago? Back in our lighter days?"

"Yeah, I think you were like eighteen. We went down to the tracks that ran by the river and smoked until we reeked, then busted out the cheap beer you stole off your dad."

They both knew just when that had been. When his mom died. She remembered it a lot better than she wanted to. The accident that had ripped through his family and torn at Cade in ways that no one else would ever know.

Cade's guilt wasn't like anyone else's. Because Cade was the one who knew about the affair his father had been having. The affair that had resulted in a child.

And he'd kept it secret. Then it was too late to decide to tell. Too late to right any wrongs, if his decision had been wrong.

That day she'd held Cade Mitchell while he cried. A lanky, skinny kid who'd been there for her when she'd needed him most, broken and bleeding his pain all over her shirt as he cried like a little boy who would never hug his mother again.

Which is exactly what he'd been.

And then they'd sat on dark, coarse sand littered with round rocks, washed smooth by the water, filling the air with enough secondhand smoke to cover up the damp, earthy smells of the riverbank. After that there had been a lot of drinking on Cade's part.

More tears.

Then the singing. And laughing. And they'd both just lain there until it was dark. Until the dampness from the sand sank through to their clothes.

Not the best memory. Except it was the perfect example for just how solid their friendship was. It wasn't a friendship forged in good times. It was a friendship made from loneliness and pain so deep, they never shared them with anyone else.

The kind of friendship that meant you could sit at a kitchen table and eat meatloaf out of a casserole dish together and never think anything was weird about it.

"I remember that," he said, his voice rough, and she knew he'd just shared in the whole memory.

"I'm shocked. Completely shocked that you remember it. You were hammered."

"Parts of it are fuzzy."

"I'm sure. Actually, it seems to me like your entire senior year should be fuzzy."

"How's yours?" he asked.

"Parts of high school I wish like hell were a lot fuzzier."

"Such as?"

She made a face. "Such as Mike, the jackass from the bar. I wish I didn't remember what he looked like without clothes."

"In contrast, I'm sure he cherishes the image of you naked," Cade said, his smile turning wicked.

For some reason, hearing Cade say the word "naked" in reference to her body made her feel hot. And her throat felt tight. And she felt . . . sticky.

She looked down into the casserole dish and cleared her throat. Meatloaf would provide clarity. It was homey. And well-behaved. Much like she was. Seeing as she was reformed and all, and not looking to get . . . unreformed.

She took another bite and found it did help to make her throat feel less tight.

"Well," she said, talking around her bite, "obviously he has some issues with those memories."

"And now he'll hopefully remember to keep his mouth shut," Cade said, lifting his fist and drawing his fingers over his knuckles.

"See?" she asked, this little show making her feel decidedly less warm. "Superman stance. Cade Mitchell to the rescue."

"It's better than just ignoring your plight."

"Fair point," she said, raising her fork and waving it in his direction. "But you don't need to fix everything in my life."

He grabbed her fork and tugged it out of her hand, his smile positively naughty now. "Okay."

"You have my fork."

"Not my problem. I don't have to fix it."

"I'll get another one out of the drawer. Because I am my own savior, asshole."

"Go on, save yourself."

She stuck her tongue out at him and went and retrieved another fork from the silverware drawer. "See? I have saved myself from abject fork poverty."

"Inspiring. When they make the Lifetime movie I hope it stars someone good."

"*A Paucity of Forks: The Amber Jameson Story.*"

"You're so brave."

"I am," she said, sitting back down across from him and letting the silence settle between them.

She couldn't let go of this. Not ever. This house. This life. This friend.

She'd lost her grandmother already, one of the cornerstones of her existence. And she knew she didn't have that many years left with her grandpa.

When they were gone, this house and Cade would be all that was left. And she would do everything in her power to make sure she kept both of them.

Cade whistled as he walked up to Amber's front door, her keys in hand. He'd popped into the diner for lunch again, just to make sure that Davis wasn't back skulking around, and she'd sent him on a mission to bring her grandpa some pulled pork and slaw.

He knocked twice and then unlocked the door, pushing it open and heading inside. "Ray?" he called.

"Is that the Mitchell boy?" Cade heard Ray's voice coming from the direction of the living room. Cade would always be the Mitchell boy to Ray. He'd been around since he was sixteen, and at first Ray and Ava had been understandably wary of the young guy sticking so close to their granddaughter. But at some point, they both accepted the extremely platonic and protective nature of his relationship with Amber.

"Yep," he said. "It's the Mitchell boy, and I brought food from Amber."

He heard the sound of Ray's recliner as the old man put the footrest down.

"No need to get up, Ray," Cade said. "I'm a full-service deliveryman. It's coming up. Along with a beer, if you're interested."

"Abso-damn-lutely" was the reply.

"Hang tight." Cade went into the kitchen that was nearly as familiar as his own and got a plate and a bottle of beer. Then he popped the beer top on the counter and headed to the living room.

Ray had the TV on mute, and he was settled in the orange recliner he spent a good portion of every day in. He'd owned that thing since Cade and Amber were in high school. Cade imagined that, like most of the things in this house, Ray didn't see the use in parting with it unless it was completely nonfunctional.

If it was still repairable, either with tools or duct tape, it didn't leave the house.

There was a knock on the front door, and Cade set the food and drink on the table beside the chair. "I'll get that," he said.

He turned, walked to the entryway and jerked the door open, freezing when he saw Jim Davis standing there on the step.

Davis frowned. "What are you doing here?"

"I spend a lot of time here," Cade said. "I think, actually, that I'm the one who should be asking what *you're* doing here."

"Can I come in?"

"Why?"

"I want to speak to Ray. Last I checked, it was his name on the mortgage documents."

"His and Amber's." Cade crossed his arms. "And Amber said she didn't want to talk to you about this."

"Well, she's not the only one who gets a say, and that's a fact. I want to talk to Ray."

"If this property ever goes up for sale, you'll know by the sign at the end of the driveway, and you can pick up a flyer like everyone else."

"I don't really see how this concerns you."

"You don't?" Cade asked, and for a second, he didn't either, so it was difficult to say exactly where he was going with all of this. He had no legal claim on anything. No call to kick him off the property. He wasn't Amber's family, or her husband or her lover. He was her friend, and he had nothing to back up what he was saying.

But he knew he didn't like Jim Davis being here, even if he didn't know quite why it bothered him so much.

And he knew he didn't want him coming back. Not while Ray was here alone. Not while Amber was here alone.

But he had no idea what he was supposed to do about that. How he would protect them both if Jim wanted to come again. And again and again. Because in Cade's mind, it was all starting to look a little bit like harassment.

The words that came out next came without him thinking at all. "I'm moving in soon. Which means there really isn't a hope of you buying it."

"She sold to you?" he asked.

"No," Cade said, trying to sort through the different solutions wiggling around in his brain, trying to figure out just where he'd been going with it. He knew that he wanted Jim to understand the fact that if Cade had to, he'd stand in the gap. Between him and Ray. Between him and Amber. Ownership, someone like Jim would understand. Proprietary, male, territorial, chest-beating, that's-my-woman stuff.

"Because, Amber's mine," he said, the words almost a growl. And that much he knew was true. She'd been his from the moment he'd first seen her in the halls at school, and every day since. She had been there for every bad thing. And he would damn sure be here for this, even if it wasn't a big deal. Even if the kick in his gut that made him feel so uneasy about all this was an overreaction, he would just make sure. Because he had to. That made thinking of the rest of the sentence easy. "I'm her boyfriend, and I'm moving in with her."

Jim drew back, obviously shocked by the revelation.

Cade heard the crunch of gravel and the sound of a truck engine, and he looked over Jim's shoulder to see Amber's truck rolling up to the house; then he heard the sound of Ray's armchair.

Oh, dammit all to hell.

"What's going on?" Ray asked, coming into the entryway. "And who's this? Who's moving in?"

"Sorry, Ray," Cade said. He had to brazen it out now. Shit. "We didn't have time to talk to you about it yet."

"You're planning on living in sin here with my granddaughter. And me?"

"Not sin, per se. Depends on your particular . . . definition of . . . This isn't the ideal moment to reveal all of that," Cade said. "And I meant to tell you differently."

"What's going on here?" Amber was standing at the bottom of the porch looking confused and angry and ready to jump on Jim Davis and take his throat out with her teeth.

"I was just here to speak to your grandfather," Jim said. "He's a grown man, and I don't think it's fair for you to be keeping business matters from him."

"You don't have a business matter with us, Mr. Davis," she said tightly.

"I just told him as much," Cade said, standing firm in the door.

"And he mentioned some other things too," Ray said from behind Cade. "Why didn't you tell me you were moving in together?"

CHAPTER

Four

Amber felt like she had stepped into some alternate, testosterone-fueled universe. From the man on her porch to the man at her door, and the older man behind him, she could feel the masculine indignation in the air.

And then her grandpa was talking about . . . someone moving in?

"This man," she said, pointing at Jim Davis, "is a stranger. He is not moving in here." She wondered if somehow her grandpa had gotten some of the things Jim had said about buying the place twisted.

"Not him. The Mitchell boy."

She blinked.

Jim Davis turned to face her. "Apparently I can't buy because the almighty Cade Mitchell is moving in and taking control of your life? Didn't realize she was yours." He directed the last part at Cade.

That she was . . . his? That she was Cade's? Cade was moving in?

She caught Cade's eye and his expression stopped any words that were tempted to escape. Obviously she was supposed to roll with this. Cade was in Superman posture, whether he wanted to admit it or not, and her grandpa looked . . . Well, she wasn't really sure what to call the expression on his face. And Jim Davis looked pissed.

Frankly, she wanted to keep him looking pissed. Because since he was the enemy, him being angry had to be good for her.

"Yeah," she said, putting a hand on her hip. "Cade is my boyfriend. And he's moving in. To share my room and put his toothbrush on my sink."

Just saying those words made her stomach knot up, and she had no freaking idea why. Except that she'd never shared a sink with anyone. She'd never even shared a bed with anyone, in the stay-all-night-and-cuddle-me sense. She'd had sex, sure, but in the we're-young-and-horny-and-you're-desperate-and-I'm-emotionally-unstable way.

But that was a far cry from toothbrush cohabitation. And with Cade, no less.

"So . . ." Cade said. "As you can see, things are settled here. And there are no financial issues. And you dare come around again, it's me you're going to be dealing with."

"Well, and me," Amber said, shooting Cade a dirty look. "I'm not . . . moving out when you move in."

Cade ignored her and turned to face Davis again. "As I said, you'll be speaking to me next time you come by. So if I were you, I'd skip it. I could damn sure beat your ass on the circuit, and I'll beat it here too."

"Seems to me," Ray said, stepping past Cade and onto the porch, "that you're bothering my granddaughter. And . . . Cade," her grandfather said, stumbling over Cade's name, "and as they both live here—or are about to—seems like you might be trespassing. And I'd hate to have to call the authorities. But I will, son, make no mistake."

Jim backed away from the door. "Now, there's no need to start calling the authorities. All of this is simply being blown out of proportion. I'm not a danger to anyone; I'm just a businessman. And a very interested buyer. So if y'all

change your minds"—he shrugged—"I'm not going anywhere for quite a while."

He turned on his heel and walked out to his truck, having the ever-loving gall to tip his hat at her as he got in, then
gunned the engine and started to back out of the driveway.

And that left the three of them standing there. Not having
a clue about what to say. She looked at Cade, then at her
grandpa, who was looking at Cade, who was looking at her.

"I—" she started, then the words just sort of died. The
look on her grandpa's face wasn't angry. It was something
else, and she couldn't even place it.

"So when are you moving in?" he asked Cade.

"I don't exactly have an exact date. Exactly."

Never, she screamed inside her head. *Never!* But Cade
wasn't saying never. He wasn't correcting things at all.

He was still going with it. Like it was a thing. A thing
that was happening. And her mouth still wasn't working,
and her brain was sort of out of sync with everything and
all she could do was manage another vague "I . . ."

"I'm glad to hear it," Ray said. "This place has gone to
seed. Honest to God, I haven't known what to do about it.
But if you have some ideas . . . it's all yours. I'm sure you
can make it produce again. Lord knows Amber's been
stressed about money."

"I could do something on the property, Grandpa," she
said.

"It's not the kind of thing women like to do."

"Bull! Grandma did tons of things around the ranch."

"Yes, she did. But it was never her full-time work. Are
you going to tell me that's what you want to do? Find a way
to make this place successful again on your own and manage
a crew? I'm not going to turn over ownership to him, but
the control of what happens with the fields that are just
empty now? Hell yeah, I'll give that to him. I don't know
what else to do, Amber, and if you do, then say so."

"I . . . I don't have ideas."

"And we don't have the means to do anything."

Cade was looking abashed at least. Like an abashed,

meddling asshole, but abashed nonetheless, and it pleased Amber to a degree. "Whatever I can do to help," he said, "I will."

"You can start with some-a the junk that needs fixing around here," Ray said.

"Of course," Cade said.

"And you"—her grandpa directed his focus onto her—"you said you didn't have time for a boyfriend." He walked down the stairs and toward her, and all she could do was look at him. "I'm glad you weren't telling the truth this time," he said. "Because I worry an awful lot, you know. About what will happen to you when I'm gone. About you not having anyone to take care of you."

She started to say that she would take care of herself. It was what she'd done for the first fourteen years of her life, after all.

But the words stuck in her throat. Because yes, she had taken care of herself for the first fourteen years of her life. And it had been horrible.

Yes, she took care of herself now, in many ways. And her grandpa. But she wasn't alone. He was here. He loved her. He made this house a home, gave it a heartbeat, and a sweet kind of comfort. And when he was gone, the warmth would be too. Her grandma was already gone, and when her grandpa went . . . there would be her.

And it would be just like going back to that place. That dark, horrible place she'd lived in, where everything had been so lonely. And unless she was on something or in someone's arms, she'd had trouble breathing, because outside of all that, outside of being drunk or high or having sex, there had been nothing good. There had been no one.

She never wanted to go back to that, and she wasn't sure she had a choice. Sure, she had a choice in how she handled it. Because she was a thirty-year-old woman and she didn't have to handle her pain that way. Not anymore.

But that didn't mean the pain wouldn't exist.

That was what kept the words—those very important words of denial—from coming out of her mouth.

"She won't be alone," Cade said, walking out onto the porch. "She'll always have a place with my family. With me."

She didn't doubt those words. They were like balm to her soul. Except . . . well, except part of her did doubt them. Not Cade's belief in them, because she was certain he believed in them one hundred percent.

Her doubt stemmed from the fact that he would replace her in his life someday. He would get married. And he would have a wife, and fat babies, and he wouldn't need her around. More than that, his wife probably wouldn't want her around, because, based on past experience with Cade's girlfriends, non-related-female friends didn't usually go over well.

And if not for that reason, simply because he wouldn't have time for her anymore.

This was one long line of depressing thought.

"The water heater is old," her grandpa said. "If you use it all up every morning in the shower I'm not going to be happy. Now, I need to go back in and sit."

He turned and walked slowly back up the stairs.

Leaving nothing between Amber and Cade but the yawning expanse of porch and a whole lot of awkwardness.

"So . . . well," she said. "That was . . . why the hell did you end up lying about that?"

He walked down the steps, casting the house a backward glance.

"Oh, he can't hear," she said. "He can hardly hear it when you knock on the damn door. What just happened?"

"Davis showed up, and he made it real clear that he means to harass you into giving him his way. And if he has to go through Ray to do it, he will. I happened to be here, and so I helped in the only way I could think to help."

"The only way you could think to help was to lie about us moving in together? Is this how you offer help to everyone?"

"No. You're a special case."

"Well, what the hell do I do now? Grandpa thinks you're moving in. And moreover . . . he's happy about it. Davis thinks you're moving in, and if he comes back, then . . ."

"Then he better find me here. Look, we can be adult about this and figure it out."

"Are you going to live with me until my grandfather dies?"

"No . . ."

"Then what's the point?"

"I'll fix some things. I'll stay until Davis leaves you alone. It's not going to be that hard."

"Except he's not going to expect to have us sleeping in twin beds like Lucy and Ricky," she said.

"No. But he's not going to come into your room either, is he?"

"No."

"I can probably get by mainly sleeping in a guest bedroom. Your grandfather doesn't do much in any room but the living room and his room, right?"

"Yes."

"He sleeps at the opposite end of the house. It will be fine. I bet he'd even prefer it if he knew I was sleeping in the guest room," Cade said.

Amber let out a sound that was somewhere between a growl and a gargle. "Sure, he'd like that, but he's not an idiot, Cade. He knows that if you move in, you move in for one thing."

"Give me your wisdom on that subject, Amber."

"You move in for companionship, and late-night movies and warm fuzzy feelings. *Not.* You move in for sex, jackass, and you know that as well as I do."

"I have had sex plenty of times, and never once had to move in for it. Hell, I've barely ever had to stay the night for it."

She lifted a shoulder. "I don't see the point either. Getting laid doesn't have much to do with cohabitation in my mind."

Cade arched a brow, a questioning look on his face. Yeah, fine, let him question. Her sex life was dormant, and by virtue of the fact that Cade was normally around, he was probably pretty sure he knew that. But let him wonder.

"But," she continued, "moving in provides full access to the nooky. And even my grandpa knows that."

"What happened to old-fashioned values?" Cade asked.

"Which old-fashioned values are you after? The kind that saw brothels opened in the main strip of town? The old-fashioned values of Henry the Eighth? King Solomon and the concubines, perhaps?"

"Point taken. People and sex, right?"

She snorted. "Yeah. People are having the sex, now and always." She cleared her throat, trying to ignore the weird, tense feeling in her chest. "So, anyway, this is weird."

"It doesn't have to be weird."

"It doesn't? My best friend is going to be living with me, whilst pretending to be sleeping with me. Shenanigans, Cade. Shenanigans."

"I'll also be fixing up the place for your grandpa. That's helpful, right?"

"What about Elk Haven? And Cole?"

"I don't really care about that right now. It's not like I get paid hourly to work there. I get a portion of the profits that are brought in because I own part of it. And because I invested a certain amount of my earnings and my settlement money into the place. I can take some time off." He cleared his throat. "You may also be interested to learn that I did some smart investing."

"You did investments?"

"Yeah, I have a friend who is into that stuff."

"Not me, obviously."

"I have more than one friend."

She narrowed her eyes. "Do you?"

"You don't know everything about me. I met people while traveling. Anyway, I've made a little bit. And I have . . . Your grandpa wants something done with the ranch and I do have some ideas about what I might like to do."

"Really?" she asked, crossing her arms under her breasts.

"Yeah. You know about them. You encouraged me to talk to Cole about the bison thing. And . . . now that I think about it . . . this really is perfect. Whether I'm here or not, this could be where I base my operation from."

"You want to put buffalo in my field?"

"Bison. I mean, the start-up isn't cheap, but I do have the money. I could re-fence everything, we could buy a certain number of animals."

"You want to put mothereffing buffalo in my fields?"

"Bison. And you don't have anything but weeds in them, Amber, so what does it matter?"

"Cade Mitchell, why the hell do you suddenly think you can claim space in my home? My bedroom—"

"Guest bedroom."

"Whatever. My bedroom, my field . . ."

"There isn't anything happening here. Nothing making you any money. And this way I won't be giving you a handout. You can get a percentage of the profits."

"And if it fails?"

"We'll have lean protein to last us through the long winter months. And possibly some very unconventional fur coats."

"Did you just think all this up on the fly?"

He put his hands on his lean hips. "Basically."

"I'd be impressed if I wasn't so irritated by your hijacking of my life."

"I'm not doing it to bother you," he said. "I'm doing it to help you. So instead of being so damn stubborn for the sake of being damn stubborn, maybe you should just say . . . I don't know . . . 'Thank you, Cade, for a lifetime of covering my ass.' "

"But I don't need—"

"Amber," he said, "there's no one out here. There are no points for pretending you don't need anyone. Because no one else is here to see, and I think your act is just that. A buncha bullshit."

"I've had to count on me, Cade, because in my experience, things happen and it's only you that's left standing with you."

"Have I ever not been there? Has your grandpa ever not been there?"

"My grandma's not here now."

"But she would be."

"Abandonment doesn't always have to be because a

person quit caring. The effect is the same. No, it's even worse. Because no matter what, I'll never pass her on a street. I can never look her up online and find her phone number and yell at her for going away. I could do that with my mom, you know? She's alive still, even though she's moved to Chicago. I could still find her. I have found her. I could call and give her a piece of my mind. Scream myself hoarse. Because she's still here. Grandma isn't. Grandpa won't be. As much as we hate talking about it, Cade, you almost weren't. So yeah, I don't count on life handing me fresh-squeezed lemonade and warm fuzzies. I count on having lemons thrown at my head while I dodge spiderwebs, flaming spears and other awful things, because that is my life, okay?"

He crossed his arms across his chest and leaned back on his heels. "You think you have the monopoly on loss here?"

She looked away from him. "No. I know I don't."

"Then don't talk to me about it like I don't understand. I do. But what the hell is the point of living like everyone's already dead? Then I might as well be six feet under and not here offering you support. I'm trying to help. Could you make an attempt at being a little less emotionally crippled for ten minutes or so and try to think it through with logic?"

That was one of the downsides to having a friend you knew so well. And who knew you. They didn't sugarcoat things. She would really like some sugarcoated *poor babies*, but Cade wasn't going to hand them out today. He was set, his jaw fixed and determined, his dark eyes blazing with that epic Mitchell stubbornness that she knew so well.

Cade seemed like a laid-back, affable kind of guy. And in many ways, he was. But then, that was his secret. He didn't seem like the competitor in the rodeo who was taking it all deadly serious, and that was why he won. He made a career out of people underestimating him.

But Amber knew better. She knew that when that man set his mind to something, changing his mind was like beating your head against a brick wall. Fortunately for her, she had a hard head.

And she'd used it many times with him over the past few years.

"If you're staying here, you're making breakfast in the mornings."

"It's the gentlemanly thing to do. Since, in theory, I'll have been keeping you up all night banging your headboard against the wall."

Stinging heat flooded her face, centering on the apples of her cheeks. Bastard. She hadn't blushed in . . . she wasn't sure she'd ever blushed in her whole life, and here she was blushing like some innocent kid.

"A night of headboard-banging is worth at least four strips of bacon. I'll have to keep up my stamina. A short stack of pancakes wouldn't go amiss either."

"What do you think people do in the bedroom, Amber? Run laps around the bed?"

"Oh, no, I just thought you might need to have the woman on top. All things considered." As soon as the words left her mouth, she wanted to call them back.

Cade was the first person to make fun of his injuries. Most of it was a defense mechanism, and she knew it. She doubted Cade knew it, but she did. And sometimes she poked fun at him too.

But right when she said those words, she knew she'd gone over a line. Insulting his sexual prowess was one too far. Even for her.

He arched a dark brow and took a step toward her. There was very little change in his expression, his posture still casual, his weight still distributed unevenly to help relieve the pain in his leg. But she could feel the change in him. Could feel his anger, a wave of heat that surrounded his body and radiated outward. Could see it in the depths of his dark eyes.

"You have to be careful saying things like that," he said.

She tried to say something, anything, to smooth it over because, hello, she was a bitch and she was most particularly a bitch because Cade was trying to help her and she was being a jerk because her pride was acting up like a bad case of hives. But she couldn't speak, her throat totally closed up for some reason.

Maybe because she'd never had Cade's anger directed at her, not like this. Not in this very male, very predatory kind of way that seemed dangerous in a—dare she think it?—sexy way.

"Because," he continued, "some people might think you were asking for a demonstration."

She nearly choked. "I'm not."

"Like I said, be careful. Now, be a dear and show me to my room."

Her jaw dropped and she forgot to feel guilty for her bitchiness. "Don't make me fire up the forge and brand your ass, Mitchell."

She turned and walked back toward the house, and Cade followed. Close. She could feel his heat at her back, could feel a weird crackle of tension between them.

They walked inside and he closed the door behind them. "Just a second," she said. She looked into the living room and saw her grandfather asleep in the chair in front of the TV. "All right, follow me."

She headed up the stairs, their feet clunking on the hollow wood steps and, somehow, adding to the awkwardness. Since when was there awkwardness between her and Cade? She blamed him for this. For his stupid plan. His stupid Save the Amber plan.

Like she was a snowy plover, sitting on a beach and being all endangered, and he was some kind of magnanimous park ranger keeping people off her dune.

She could defend her own dune.

Except now, he was all up on her dune. Meddling and shit.

"Okay, Cadence," she said, because when she used the childhood nickname given to him by Lark she could not think about him having sex—either on the bottom or the top. "Are you sure you're up for this?"

She pushed open the faded wooden door at the end of the hallway and made a grand, sweeping gesture toward the twin bed with a rustic metal frame, covered by a faded and threadbare quilt her grandma had made around the time Hitler had invaded France.

There was a round tatted rug on the floor, also the handiwork of her grandmother. Also from a time that predated the Internet.

There was an old-fashioned alarm clock on a doily, on a rickety old nightstand. And in the closet, Amber happened to know, was a collection of her grandma's old winter coats. Which smelled heavily of mothballs.

They didn't often put guests in the guest room, so it was, frankly, not entirely guest-ready.

But Cade had volunteered. So he could suck it.

"Here it is," she said. "All the comforts of home. If you happen to be the Swiss Family Robinson."

"I've spent nights sleeping in horse trailers; do you really think this bothers me?"

"Your family home is pretty swank."

"Yeah, and I'm not in it very often. At least, I spent a lot of years not being in it very often. Besides, Amber, I'm not backing out on this. Not now. It has to last for at least as long as Davis is sniffing around. I'd be bunking with you even without your grandpa counting on it."

"I don't want to lie to him," she said. "Not Davis. My grandpa."

"Yeah, I got that. And I don't want to lie to him either. And I didn't mean to. But he overheard what I said—which was not premeditated, by the way."

"Which gets you a reduced sentence, but doesn't absolve you entirely," she said, glaring pointedly.

"I wanted to help. Which I think should get me pie and cookies, and not your laser eyes of doom."

"I have my pride," she said, sitting on the edge of the bed and wincing when a coiled-up spring dug into her butt. She bounced lightly on the lumpy mattress. "You really are going to be cursing my name after a couple of nights of this."

"You don't give me enough credit, Jameson."

"You haven't sat on the bed yet."

He walked across the room, his gait more uneven now than before they'd climbed the stairs. It made her chest hurt, made her regret her brattiness even more. He sat down next to her, his fingers curved around the edge of the mattress.

He bounced up and down like she'd done and cast her a sideways glance. "Yeah, this sucks. Did your grandma put her enemies up on this bed?"

Amber laughed. "They don't normally have guests. I think my bedroom was the good guest room, but they moved me into it and . . . I don't think we've had anyone stay here since. Surly teenager put a cramp in their social life, I guess."

"You were pretty surly. *Are* pretty surly."

"Shush," she said, pinching his bicep and not managing to grab hold of much. He didn't have pinchable flesh, that man. He was too rock-solid.

Suddenly she became very aware of the fact that they were sitting on a bed together. And it was hard to breathe again. Particularly with his words from earlier hanging between them still, like an unwanted cobweb that needed to be swept away.

Some people might think you were asking for a demonstration.

No. She didn't want a demonstration. Though, for some reason, she was having a hard time looking away from his mouth. His mouth was one of the most beautiful things on earth, in her humble opinion. Those lips, curved into a smile, had always meant that her day was going to get better, just because he was there. Pressed into a firm line, they presented a challenge to get them to curve upward.

And then, just aesthetically speaking, they were a sight to behold. The lower lip was fuller, the upper lip dipping down in the middle, making the kind of dent she was sure some women fantasized about sticking their tongues in.

Not her. Because he was her BFF and ew.

Yes. Ew. That was her official stance on tonguing Cade's lip dip.

"You're certainly prickly," he said. "Like a porcupine."

"Don't forget it. I'm a badass mofo. If I get you with my spines you're going to be filled with regret and woe."

"I think I got hit by one already."

She frowned, a sharp pain lancing her chest. Man, she felt like a bitch. "Sorry. I'm too pointy sometimes. I know."

"Not usually with me."

"I know. But you've been Super Cade more times in a row than I'm used to."

"You've been in jeopardy more often than normal."

"Until Lex Luthor ties me up in a warehouse somewhere, I don't think you have to worry too much."

"If I'm ever in jeopardy, you have my full permission to save me," he said. "How's that for equality?"

"You'll never admit to needing me," she said.

"You never admit to needing me either."

"No. You're a master at unsolicited help."

His expression sobered. "In all honesty, Amber, you've done a lot for me. I don't like to talk about when my mom died. And I didn't want to be around anyone when it happened because . . ."

She nodded and bit the inside of her cheek. She knew why. Because he'd been raw in a way no eighteen-year-old guy wanted to be in front of anyone. Because his grief had been a living monster that had picked him up in its jaws and shaken him like a rag doll.

And he hadn't wanted anyone to see. But he'd let her see.

"Yeah, well," she said, clearing her throat. "I'm a judgment-free zone when it comes to emotional disasters because I'm such a mess."

"A surly mess," Cade said, that delicious—but not to her—mouth of his curling up into a smile.

"Rawr," she said, standing up because really, sitting next to him was starting to make the whole left side of her body feel like there were little caterpillars crawling over her skin.

"I have to go home and . . . tell Cole that we're moving in together."

"You're going to tell him though, right?"

"About?"

"About the . . . us not banging?"

"Why?" Cade asked, standing. "It's not his business. He

doesn't share everything with me. Like that time he banked his sperm and accidentally knocked up someone he'd never met."

"He told you."

"After a couple of months."

"This is different."

"No. For the sake of authenticity, I think that we need to keep the details on the down low. All he needs to know is that I'm moving in with you. It's not like it's going to shock anyone."

She crossed her arms and shifted her weight. "Really? You don't think everyone is going to be shocked by the fact that after sixteen years of friend . . . oh."

"Yeah. *Oh.* I'm willing to bet half of everyone thinks we've been *banging*, as you put it, for years."

She let out a snarly sigh. "Fine. You're probably right. But . . . but I have to face this guy afterward."

"He won't care."

"What if he thinks I broke your heart?" she asked.

Cade laughed. "Cole probably doesn't think I have a heart to break. I think he assumes all my feelings originate from my dick." Cade lifted a shoulder. "He's not . . . wrong, per se."

"Oh please, Cade, spare me."

"I'm just saying. Fine feelings have sort of been beaten out of me. Cruelly. Life carries a big stick."

"Yeah, I've met life's beating stick on more than one occasion."

"Can you honestly say you believe in love?"

She nodded slowly. "Yes. I do. Because my grandpa never loved another woman but my grandma for fifty-five years. And that's pretty amazing. That's love. Or even something deeper."

"But do you think it's common? I mean, do you think that's normal?"

"No."

"Right. Exactly. I mean, I think Kelsey and Cole really have something, and by God, if Quinn does anything to Lark, I will tie a fricking rock to his neck and throw him over Mill Creek Falls. So he better believe in love. But as for the rest of us? I don't know. I don't even think I want to try. After finding out what a bastard my dad was . . . it's not worth it. And look at your parents."

"I would, but they aren't around."

"There is that."

"No," she said, "I'm with you. Firmly in a grinchlike state on the topic of love. Firmly."

"So, there you have it."

"Why would Cole even believe that you were moving in with me, then?"

"Because it's you."

His words made a kind of warm, melting feeling spread through her.

"And because if I tell him your breasts are even better out of a t-shirt than they look in one, he'll totally buy it."

"Oh . . ." The warm feeling faded sharply. "Cade . . ."

"It's something I would say."

"I know," she bit out. "So go. Go build your disgusting case for our relationship being real and then . . . I can't believe I'm saying this, but go ahead and move in."

"I'll be in tomorrow night," he said, smiling and walking out the bedroom door.

She waited for him to disappear around the corner, until she could hear the sounds of his boots on the stairs, and then she collapsed onto the bed with her arm over her eyes.

Stupid Cade and his stupid ideas. Stupid Cade and his stupid ideas that really would be quite helpful because she was in over her head, getting harassed by a jackass and about to lose the farm like some cliché old movie.

This was temporary anyway, and resentment aside, Cade was one of her favorite people on the entire planet, so having him stay with her was really a good thing.

She let out a long, slow breath. Nothing was going to go wrong.

CHAPTER

Five

Nicole Peterson wasn't sure why she'd decided to come to Silver Creek. Well, no, that was a lie; she knew exactly why she was here. Maybe the truth was she didn't know what she expected to get out of this little family-finding experience.

She'd spoken to Cole Mitchell, the man she'd found out was her half brother, on the phone, and he'd never seemed that interested in having her out to the ranch. Not that he was rude . . . just hesitant.

It was the last phone call she'd made to Elk Haven that had spurred her to make the trip. It wasn't Cole she'd talked to, but his wife, Kelsey.

She'd been able to hear their little girl in the background. And Kelsey had said they were expecting another baby. And she'd been so sweet.

And she'd said there was plenty of room and that she should come. And Nicole's faint protest of "What about Cole?" had been met with: "Let me worry about him."

So here she was, letting Kelsey worry about it. Except she was worrying about it too. Loitering in the mercantile and touching things she had no desire to purchase. Or even look at.

Mainly she wanted to get in her car and go back to Portland. And why not? She had a very nice cubicle there waiting for her. With a new swivel chair. And she had her apartment. And a fixed-gear bike. Yeah. Life was sweet in Portlandia.

Yet still, she was here.

She sighed and ran her fingers along a line of little die-cast tractors that lined the top row of one of the shelves.

"Can I help you?"

She turned around and all the breath shot out of her lungs. The guy was . . . well, holy hell, they did not grow them like that in Portland. He was tall, broad and muscular with a beard and a flannel shirt that was pushed midway up his rather delicious-looking forearms. Flannel and beards were a common enough Portland attraction, but he was wearing neither ironically. Unlike most of the men she knew, this guy actually could be a lumberjack.

"Um . . . I'm just . . . in the market for a new tractor," she said, picking up one of the miniatures. "This one will do. Red. I like it."

He shook his head, dark brows knitted together. "Nah. You need a Deere." He picked up a small green tractor, then took the red one from between her thumb and forefinger, set it back on the shelf, and handed her the one he'd chosen.

"I like red," she said.

"You look like a city girl to me," he said.

"Do I?" she asked.

"Yes. Judging by the tattoo," he said, indicating the sleeve that ran from her shoulder down to her wrist. "And the hat," he added, looking at her beanie.

"Stereotyping," she said. "You're assuming I'm not a mini-tractor mechanic."

"*Are* you a mini-tractor mechanic?"

"Uh, no. Can't say that I am. I am in the tax preparation business, which is . . . not nearly as exciting. Or greasy."

"So what brings you to town? Tax crisis?"

"Uh, no," she said, pushing a strand of hair behind her ear. "Family stuff. Kind of."

"I see."

"Eh. You don't, but that's okay. It was a nice try."

"How long will you be here?"

She shoved her hands in the pockets of her jeans and lifted her shoulders. "I'm not really sure, actually. It's . . . open-ended family stuff."

"Well, if you end up needing a drink, and I know with my family I always do, we could always go and get one. Together."

She laughed. "Are you hitting on me?"

"Trying to. Women don't usually have to ask for clarification—did I do something wrong?"

"No, it's just . . . unusual."

"Bullshit."

"Guys always think I'm going to shank them. Or tell them they owe the fed a bunch on this year's return."

"Cowards," he said.

"I'm useless with pickup lines."

"Try me," he said.

She put her hand on her hip. "I can help you find additional deductions," she said, wiggling her brows.

"As I'm a small-business owner, you have no idea how hot that sounds to me." He smiled and her stomach did a flip thing. Which was stupid because her stomach shouldn't be flipping with anything but nerves right now. She shouldn't be thinking about anything but meeting her half brothers and half sister for the first time.

And then a horrifying thought occurred to her.

"You aren't a Mitchell, are you?" she asked.

He frowned. "No."

"Are you related to them, even distantly?"

"Not that I'm aware of, but you know, people do have their secrets."

She could have howled with laughter if the whole thing weren't so close to home. "Uh, yes, they do. Actually"—she let out a long breath—"that reminds me of something."

"What's that?" he asked.

"That I have somewhere to be."

"Just a second." He walked back over to the counter and picked up a business card, then brought it back to where she was standing and held it out. She took it and smiled. "Thanks."

She turned the green tractor over one more time, then set it back on the shelf.

"Keep it," he said. "Free of charge. Because you need a reliable tractor if you're going to hang out here in the country."

She sucked a breath of air through her teeth. "Eh. I'm not worth giving stock to. I'm probably never going to have that drink with you. And if I did, you'd be out a drink and a small tractor, with nothing in return. At least not what I think you might be looking for."

"It's a gift," he said. "Free of obligation."

Nicole lifted the tractor back up from the shelf and looked at it, then back at the super gorgeous, epically stunning man that she had no time or emotional energy to pursue. She was here on a mission. Sleeping with some random dude didn't come into it. It would only complicate things.

"Thank you," she said. "I'll hang on to it."

"Why did you want to know if I was a Mitchell?" he asked. "You aren't pregnant with one of their babies, are you? Because I seem to have a track record for hitting on women who are pregnant with Mitchell progeny."

"No, my, uh . . . my uterus is currently vacant. Also, *what*?"

"Long story. Or . . . not. I made a pass at Cole Mitchell's wife before she was his wife."

"Oh. Okay." That was an oddly relieving explanation. Or maybe not odd at all. It was just nice to know that her brother . . . that was a weird way to think of him—wasn't also spreading illegitimate spawn across the state. Like their father had done.

"Did I put my foot in my mouth?" he asked. "I do that a lot."

"No. It's . . . I'm going to take my tractor and go now."

"Okay. John. My name is John."

"Nicole," she said. "So . . . nice to meet you and . . . bye."

"I'll see you around."

She scrunched her nose. "I don't think so."

He chuckled, and the sound poured a shot of heat down through her body, all the way to her toes. "In a town this size?" He shook his head. "Yeah, I'll see you around."

"I'm moving out," Cade said, twisting the bottle of beer in his hand, the water droplets leaving cold moisture on his palm.

"What?" Cole looked up from the fridge.

"I'm moving out."

"I heard you. So I guess what I really meant was: Why in the hell would you do that? You work here. We need you here. Your family is here."

"Because," he said, shifting his weight to his right side, trying to relieve the ache that was pounding in his leg like a sonofabitch. "I'm moving in with Amber."

That earned him a facial expression that was almost comically still. "Moving in with her?"

"Yes."

"What happened to . . . her breasts being the only breasts you weren't trying to grab?"

Cade frowned. "Did I say that?"

"Something to that effect."

His frown deepened. "I'm an asshole."

"Yeah, but that's beside the point."

Cade took a sip of his beer. "It's been a long time since I groped random breasts, you know. Or even tried to."

"I know," Cole said. "Doritos. And hot chocolate, remember?"

Cade grunted. "Yeah. But you don't know everything. Obviously. Amber and I are moving in together."

"Because you're sleeping with her?"

The thought made Cade's throat feel tight. Made him feel like he might need to peel off his skin because it suddenly felt too damn hot. "Yes," he said. "I mean, obviously. Frequently. Athletically. Why else would I move into that farmhouse she lives in and take on all those projects. Sex. And bacon. You can't overlook the bacon."

"When did this happen?"

"Is this what marriage does to people, Cole? Turns them into women? Are you honestly asking me for romantic details? There was a day when sex and cured meat would have been enough of an answer for you."

"You've been best friends with her since you were teenagers and I've never seen you look at her like she was anything other than a friend. Not even once. You make eye contact when you talk to her."

"Yeah, well, things changed."

"Does this have anything to do with you being pissed at me?"

"No," Cade said. It was the truth. It was a bonus that he would be getting some distance from Cole, but it wasn't the driving reason, or even the reason at all, that he'd ended up in this situation.

He just wanted to protect Amber. And some distance from Elk Haven? That was all fine with him, but it hadn't entered his mind at all when he'd pushed her to let him actually move in. Well, it almost hadn't entered his mind. Much.

But then the idea of getting a start on the bison initiative was sort of tempting too. And proving that he was right. There was that.

"Like I would make this kind of decision based on you," he added for good measure. "This is about me. And Amber. Us. The us that is me and Amber. And her breasts, which I like." That was about as convincing as . . . nothing. But it was weird to talk about her like this.

"Good for you. Both of you," Cole said, his expression oddly stiff. "But you'll still be working here, right?"

Cade braced himself for the storm that would surely follow his next statement. "No. I'm not going to be working here. I'm going to be working on the Jameson property."

"What the hell, Cade? You aren't a Jameson. You're a Mitchell, and we need you here."

"Hire someone, Cole."

"This is your legacy."

"No, it's damn well not," he said, anger pouring out that he hadn't entirely realized he'd had. Annoyance, sure, but he hadn't known he was this damn ragey about the whole thing. "It's *your* legacy, Cole. You've made that abundantly clear. Until I have equal say in it, until it's just as much mine as yours, it won't be. I have a chance to take a piece of land and make it mine. This is dad's. It's yours. It won't ever be mine, and maybe that's okay, but only as long as you stop acting like I should be as invested as you when it's not my vision. And frankly, I didn't give a rat's ass when I was traveling cross-country all the time, but that's not my life now. I have to settle down or I have to . . . get a job at a bar. Except I can't even do that because I would have to stand for too long on a hard floor so . . . my options are limited here."

"And how are you going to work the Jameson ranch?"

"Hire people."

"You'll do that by . . . ?"

"Spending a shitload of my money."

"You don't have money."

"I actually have more than you think. Stock market windfall combined with the percentage I personally am entitled to for arranging the rodeo contracts—and I sold my sports car. So, yeah . . . I have the money to do this. So I'm going to."

"You are doing this because you're pissed at me," Cole said.

"No. Because not everything in life is about you, or everyone's relationship to you. If your wife hasn't beaten that out of your head by now, I guess there's no hope."

"I guess not," Cole said, crossing his arms over his chest.

"Bottom line, this is for me. This is for Amber." Cade was starting to fear it was in that order. But what did it matter as long as Amber was protected?

"We'll miss you."

"No, you won't."

"Kelsey will. Maddy will."

"Yeah, well, I'll miss them."

"Are you going to stay and eat your fucking dinner or are you not eating dinner here anymore either?" Cole asked.

"I'll eat," Cade growled.

"Fine."

"Don't poison my food." Cade started walking out of the kitchen and into the main area of the house.

"Don't be a damned child," Cole said.

Cade bit back his intended response, which was going to be something alone the lines of *I know you are but what am I*, when he saw a petite brunette standing by the drink area in the lobby.

"Can I help you?"

Her blue eyes were huge in her pale face as she looked from Cole to Cade and back again. "I was hoping Kelsey would be around."

"She drove over to the next town to do some shopping," Cole said. "Can I help you?"

"It was Kelsey that I talked to, so I was hoping to . . . see her. I should have . . . called or something. I can go. I actually made a reservation in town—"

"Is everything okay?" Cade asked, because he didn't like to see a woman look that jumpy. It made him suspicious of things he didn't really want to be suspicious of.

"Fine. Yes. No, not fine, not fine at all. Are either of you a Mitchell?"

"Both of us."

If Cade hadn't been completely certain he a) had never slept with this woman and b) hadn't had sex in four years, he might have been thrown into a slight paternity panic. But as it was, he was sure that whatever the sin, it wasn't that.

"I'm Nicole. Nicole Peterson. I think . . . we might share genetic material."

"By that," Cole said slowly, "you mean you're our half sister."

"Sure, yeah," she said, clearing her throat, "if you want to say the 'sister' word. Which seems . . . weird, all things considered."

Cade looked at Nicole Peterson, the woman who was at

the center of one of the darkest, shittiest moments of his life. And he knew it wasn't her fault. He knew she had no responsibility for any of it. And that it wasn't a choice of hers that had caused that moment.

And he still couldn't deal with it.

"I'm going to Amber's," he said. "For . . . you know. Nice to meet you," he said to Nicole, then turned and walked out the door, leaving Cole to deal with the woman who was the physical evidence of just how imperfect their dad had been.

Cade knew it was the wrong thing to do. He knew it was weak, and terrible, and he still couldn't bring himself to stop it.

Because nobody knew the situation like Cade did. Nobody knew just how weak their dad had been.

But Dave Mitchell had made damn sure Cade knew. He hadn't even bothered to hide it, not when Cade had overheard a phone call between his dad and his dad's mistress. Dave had known Cade would keep his secrets. Because Cade was just like him.

Not Cole, not the responsible one that Cade knew had worked so hard to emulate a man who hadn't ever existed.

No, Dave Mitchell had known just which son was cut from the same cloth.

Cade hated it. Hated it more than anything. Because he'd been forced to keep secrets that had tried to eat him alive. Because he'd known things that he knew would destroy his mother and had kept them to himself until it was too late to do anything different.

Because he knew his dad was right. At the end of the day, Cole was good. Faithful to a fault. Loyal and responsible.

And Cade was just like their father.

When Cade showed up at the door, Amber knew, immediately, that something was wrong. She'd like to say it was the mystical friendship connection. But really it was because she'd seen Cade go through enough hideous shit to know when it had just hit the fan.

"Can I come in?" he asked.

"Well, you live here now, right?" she said, moving to the side and allowing him entrance.

"I guess so," he said. "And damn good timing."

"What happened? Did you and Cole have a fight?"

"Cole and I always have fights," Cade grunted, moving into the kitchen and opening the fridge, digging around for a while before resurfacing with a beer, which he promptly braced against the kitchen counter and popped open.

"So what's up then?"

"Nicole Peterson."

"Did you knock someone up?" she asked. And she didn't know why, but the idea filled her with more than the normal, friendship-ish horror that one might feel over the thought of an accidental pregnancy.

"Fuck no," he said. "And why is that always the assumption?"

"Who else assumed that?"

"My subconscious. Which is bullshit, because my subconscious, my primary conscious, and . . . all my damned consciousnesses know full well I have not had sex in four fucking years!"

The words about knocked Amber backward. "You . . . what?"

Cade took a long drink of beer, his eyes locked with hers, furious. He lowered the bottle, but his glare remained in place. "That's not really the point."

Except it was the point that was sticking in her mind. Which was juvenile, but honestly, Cade got around. She'd known the guy since he was a virgin. And she'd known that he *was* a virgin, which spoke to just how young they'd been. And then she'd been privy to the loss of said virginity, and conquests thereafter, which was only fair, because she told him about hers.

At least until she'd stopped having them. She'd had to get her crap together, and once she'd realized that every time she'd ever let a guy put his hand under her shirt it was just a desperate bid for a feeling of connection . . . well, it had started to seem sad.

She could remember, clearly, the last guy she'd slept with. The craving she'd been driven by to feel rooted to someone, rooted to the world, for just a moment, and how his touch just hadn't done it. How he'd been inside of her and she'd felt like he was a thousand miles away because she'd become too aware of what her behavior meant.

There had been a time when she'd been able to squeeze her eyes shut and pretend that skin-to-skin meant she was close to someone. But then, right then, with this guy on top of her, she'd had a kind of weird, personal revelation and it was like seeing herself clearly for the first time. Like sitting above the sexual activity, watching it and wondering what that sad girl thought she was getting out of all this.

When sex wasn't about love, or even desire, it all seemed a little bit tragic. It was like she was living out a depressing art film. Complete with mediocre climaxes and a distinct feeling of disconnect and malaise.

Well, no more.

She was still a massive ball of dysfunction, but she was a massive ball of dysfunction alone in bed with her clothes on. So . . . win.

Though she hadn't been aware that Cade was on the celibacy train. Because there was a certain point where they'd started to keep their sex lives to themselves—that was what adulthood did, after all, took giggly over-sharing away from you—and she'd started very consciously turning a blind eye to his shenanigans, because it was a little like being on a diet and watching someone eat chocolate cake. And éclairs. And donuts. Over and over and over.

"Sorry, it's the point I came away with," she said. Because when you were on a diet, even if you didn't want to see someone eat cake, it was nice to know that other people could still enjoy cake.

Dirty, sexy, naked cake.

And apparently Cade had not been having . . . cake.

Weird, now she was hungry. And a little horny.

"Well, it's not the point. Because she's not pregnant. Because I'm celibate as a priest and also she's my sister."

"Oh."

"My half sister."

"No, well, obviously." She knew about Nicole, though she hadn't known her by name. Knew about the affair Cade's father had had, and that it had resulted in a love child, debts and a whole lot of angst for Cade.

"She's here."

"Really?"

"Yes. Like . . . like she has a right to be here," he said, stalking back to the fridge and pulling out a block of cheese, then setting it on the counter, bracing one palm against the Formica surface, the other on top of the cheese.

"Doesn't she?" Amber asked.

"Yes," Cade growled, turning back to face her, the cheese still in his hand, his fingers curling tightly around it.

"Well . . . for heaven's sake, Cade, what did the dairy do to you?" She leaned forward, took the cheese out of his hand and opened the fridge, putting it back inside.

When she turned back to face Cade he was scowling at her like she'd taken his best friend away, and not a block of cheddar.

"What?" she asked.

"I was going to eat that."

"You were going to squish it. Anyway, she does have a right to be here, doesn't she?"

"My dad didn't make any provision for her in the will," Cade said, his voice rough.

"And that means she doesn't have a right to anything that was his?"

Cade put his hands on his lean hips and let out a long, slow breath. "No. I know she does. But I don't know how to deal with this. I don't know how to just embrace her like a long-lost sister and I feel like her showing up here . . . Like she and Cole are asking me to do that, and I can't. Maybe Cole can because he found out in a different way. Maybe because he believed dad was a superhero until after he kicked the bucket, Cole can separate everything. But I can't. I had to keep this a secret from everyone. I had to . . . I knew. I knew he'd been screwing with other women. I knew that Nicole existed and I wasn't allowed to tell anyone."

"Except me," Amber said. "We keep each other's horrible secrets. It's what we do."

They had been a dysfunctional petri dish of angst in high school. The keepers of every secret pain, every secret longing. Best friends in a way she could never have been with another girl, for fear of judgment. For fear of not seeming normal. And she knew it went the other way for Cade. He couldn't have talked to another guy about what he was going through. Because it was all about feelings. And pain. Things guys just didn't like to talk about.

The very reason their friendship probably seemed unlikely to weather adulthood and the crap that came with it was the very reason it had. No one else could provide what they gave to each other.

"Yeah," Cade said, "it is. And in the spirit of horrible secrets . . . I don't want her here. I don't want to bring her into the family. I don't want her to be part of us, because I want to forget that . . ."

"I know," she said. She opened up the fridge again and retrieved her own beer, then tugged on the back of one of the wooden chairs. "Set a spell, Mitchell boy."

He gave her a withering look, but sat, and she did the same.

"So this sucks," she said.

"Yeah, it sucks. And I'm too emotionally crippled to deal with it."

She frowned. "Poor choice of words."

"Why? Because I'm physically crippled too?"

"Well, I wasn't going to say anything."

"Except you did," he said, a reluctant smile toying with the corners of his mouth.

"Yeah, well, count on me to say the inappropriate. Like I'm about to now. *Four years?*" It didn't beat her dry spell, but even so.

"There's a reason I've never mentioned this."

"It's too late. You did now. And you know how I am." Desperate to take his mind off of his problems, and also hopelessly fascinated by this new bit of information. What the hell was wrong with her?

"Infantile?" he asked.

"Yuh-huh. That."

"You said it yourself," he said.

"I said what? That I'm infantile?"

"No, I mean, you summed up the issue earlier today. Do I need the woman to be on top? I think that was your question."

She felt her face get hot. How was it they were talking about sex again in such a short succession? Oh, well, *her.* That was why. Because for some reason she kept bringing it up. She was kind of wallowing in morbid, sexual Cade curiosity. Which, in many ways, wasn't wholly unusual, but she usually kept it all under wraps a little better than she was at the moment.

"Oh, yes, that question. Which we should probably forget. For the betterment of our friendship. Because it was bitchy." She added the last part quickly, because she didn't want him to get confused and think she meant it was because she was actively thinking about what sort of sex he could have.

She *was* wondering that, but she didn't want him to know it. Hell, *she* didn't want to know it.

"Yeah, it was bitchy. But I suppose I deserved it," he said.

"For moving in with me and protecting me from the big bad man?"

"Yeah, that. Well, either I deserved you to insult my virility and masculinity or I deserve a medal of honor." He leaned back in his chair, then abruptly leaned forward. "And to be clear, it's not a question of whether or not I could have sex. It's that the women I might approach may have a similar concern about my ability."

Her face stung, heat lashing her cheeks. Okay, now she felt like a Grade A dick. Because she'd really stabbed him in an insecure point, and she hadn't meant to. Not quite that unerringly. It was the best-friend curse. Almost like a sister, she knew just which places to punch, even if she wasn't trying to go for a weakness.

Though, unlike a sister, she'd gone on to picture a woman riding Cade like he was the horse and she was the cowgirl . . .

She coughed and looked away from him.

"I have no physical problems in that area," he said.

"Great! I get it," she said, holding her hand up. Good Lord, she was going to have the vapors. She didn't even know what the vapors were, except that her grandma had sometimes said something shocking had given them to her.

And while she didn't know what they might do, or feel like, Amber was certain she was on the verge of them.

"I'm just saying, because I feel like I have to defend myself here."

"I'm about to cover my ears and hum." For everyone's safety.

"Fine, we'll talk about something else. Something that is not my damn family's own personal secret baby scandal. And something that is also not whether or not I have full use of bodily functions—and I do."

"Great. Like what?"

"Like the fact that I'm going to bed, and in the morning, I have an appointment to talk to a rancher, because in a few weeks, I'm thinking bison."

"Bah! Bison."

"You doubt me, but I promise you, I can help. Leasing the land to me, and having me pay to fix it up, is going to help you dig out of debt, and then that asshole Davis isn't going to have a leg to stand on. He'll lean to one side worse than I do."

"Har har."

"Think about it. We'll get this place going and it will solve your financial woes, plus it will be a working ranch again."

"You're scheming. You're like Pollyanna when you scheme. All heart and optimism. It's fricking nauseating, Cade, I hope you know that."

"Part of my charm," he said.

"Feh." She waved her hand.

He let out a long sigh. "Ready for bed?"

Her heart skittered up into her throat like a cat up a tree. "What?"

"Ready to go to bed? I have an early morning ahead of me now. I assume you do too."

Oh, right. Yes. She'd overreacted. And her brain had jumped straight to . . . well, to sex again. *Bad Amber! Bad!*

"Oh . . ." she said, hoping she didn't sound as breathless as she felt, "like to go to sleep."

He looked at her like she'd grown a second head. "Yes. To go to sleep."

"Yeah, I'm exhausted." And embarrassed, because her

mind was completely in the gutter tonight. She needed some alone time. And by that she meant . . . time with her oscillating showerhead. But if she did it tonight, with Cade down the hall . . .

Gah.

Sleep was what she needed. The rest would have to wait. She was a pro at just ignoring physical lust. It was what she did now. Mainly because she'd never felt like she was in a place where she could have a relationship that was even halfway functional.

Usually, she didn't miss it. Every now and then she did. This was one of those times, apparently. Which was strange, because sex had never been that good. In that it wasn't better than what she could accomplish on her own, or with the aid of her shower massager.

Cade took one last drink of his beer and walked over to the sink, setting the bottle next to it. "I'll put it in recycling in the morning. Got a toothbrush I can use?"

"Ew, no, Cade I am not swapping spit with you."

"I'm having a flashback." He arched a brow. "I think I recall you saying that to me in high school."

Her face got hot again. Damn all these unintentional double entendres and sexy thoughts! "Actually, I don't recall ever having to say it to you. Because you were basically the only guy who never asked."

"Guys at school treated you like shit. I hated it."

"And that's why you and I are friends," she said.

"Apparently not good enough friends to share a toothbrush."

"I would give you blood. Hell, I would give you a lesser internal organ that wasn't required for survival, or that I have more than one of. But I'm not letting you use my toothbrush. Sleep tight. With beer breath. Go get your toothbrush in the morning."

"He left because of me, didn't he?"

Nicole could tell that neither of her half siblings, Lark or Cole, or their respective spouses, Quinn and Kelsey, wanted to confirm her statement. But she could tell, just as easily, that it was true.

"Well," Cole said, rubbing his hand over the back of his neck. "Well."

"He did," Nicole said. "It's okay. I'm kind of used to people skipping bail on me. Sorry. But I am."

"Our dad . . ." Lark started.

"Hey, it's not a thing, Lark," Nicole said. "We all had a crappy time, okay?"

Her poor half sister had just rolled in from her honeymoon, of all things, to find Nicole here at Elk Haven, with no sign of Cade.

Cole had done his best to explain it all and smooth it all over. Or rather, Kelsey had, since she was the one who'd said that Nicole could come.

And Nicole was figuring out pretty quickly that either no

one could get mad at Kelsey, or no one could argue with her. Or maybe both.

"No," Lark said. "It is a thing. And don't feel like you have to act like it isn't. We're realistic about what Dad's actions meant. And yeah, it was hard. For me, for all of us, but we're dealing with it. You aren't the bad part."

"Exactly," Cole said. "The disappointment of Dad not being who he was is a few years old for me. And it was a hard thing to come to terms with. For a while I made some bad choices about it. Trying to protect Lark from the truth, which kept you away too. And I do regret that. Because a piece of this place should be yours. Even if it's just the option to come up on holidays or for free vacations. I mean, hopefully it will mean more than that someday, but . . . until then."

Nicole shifted in her seat, her fingers curled around her coffee cup like it was her lifeline to the earth. "Cole . . ."

They all startled when the front door opened and one heavy step hit the wood floor. Nicole's head whipped in the direction of the entry, and she saw Cade standing there, looking like someone had just forced him to chew a handful of bees.

"Mornin'," he said, walking into the room, his hands jammed in his pockets. "I'm here for my toothbrush."

"Just your toothbrush?" Kelsey stood up and crossed her arms. "Lark is back. And Quinn. And Nicole is here."

Cade nodded his head once. "Lark. Good to see you."

Nicole noticed he didn't greet her or Quinn.

Well then.

"Have a cup of coffee," Kelsey said.

And because no one argued with Kelsey, Cade crossed the expansive living area and took a cup off the bar, holding it beneath the coffee urn and dispensing some of the dark liquid into his cup.

He stayed there, leaning against the counter, clearly there against his will.

"How was the honeymoon, Lark?" he asked.

"Blissful," Lark said, one eyebrow arched. "We swam with dolphins. Flippin' dolphins!"

That pulled a smile from Cade. "Wow. You got away from the Wi-Fi."

"I didn't log in to the Internet once in the villa we rented."

"What did you do with your time?"

This earned him a more intense eyebrow arch, and a very male, very cocky half smile from Quinn.

Cade's scowl returned. "You're taking this revenge against me for a few off-color jokes very seriously."

"All the dirty Cade jokes, all the time, for twenty-two years of my life. Hell yeah, I'm retaliating and enjoying it. Deal."

Nicole couldn't really imagine Cade making jokes, dirty or otherwise, because she'd only seen him looking . . . sour.

He slugged his coffee back and winced. "Toothbrush. And then I have to get off to work."

Cade turned away from the little happy family gathering, or whatever the hell they were trying to pass that knot of awkward off as, and headed up the stairs.

Yeah, he was kind of being a prick. But honestly, at the moment he didn't care. The inside of his mouth felt like it was lined with Astroturf, the evidence of his father's failings was down in the living room, and he'd slept like absolute hell on Amber's evil mattress.

He'd half expected to find a pea under it this morning and discover he was a motherfucking princess.

He had to see a man about some bison today. So he didn't really have time to feel like an arthritic old geezer thanks to a crappy mattress, and he really didn't have time to confront his feelings and deep inner fears about his moral character.

He pushed open the door to his bedroom and stalked inside, throwing open the closet and cursing a blue streak when a sharp pain shot through his leg and up his spine.

He did not have time for this shit. Today or ever. And it was his life.

He growled and threw a duffel bag onto his bed.

"What crawled up your butt and died?"

Cade turned and saw Lark standing in the door, her arms crossed, tugging the Superman *S* on her t-shirt into a weird shape.

"Well, nice to see you too," he said.

"You were a jackass to Quinn. And to Nicole."

"When am I not a jackass to Quinn? And as for Nicole, I haven't decided how I'm going to deal with her yet."

"How about like what she is. As much of a victim of this as any of us. You know? No. She's more of a victim than we are, Cade. We have this house. We had Mom and Dad. We had all kinds of amazing things that she just didn't have, and now you're punishing her too. For what? Being born? I think she's had enough of that."

"I'm not faking it, okay? It's not her. I'm not mad at her, I'm not sorry she's alive, but I don't know how I feel about any of it, and I'm not going to sit down there and smile sweet while inside I have no idea what to think about it. Do we want another sibling?"

"The question is moot, Cadence. We have one."

"Don't call me that. This is why I don't especially want another sister. My hands are full with the one I have."

Lark lifted one shoulder. "Well, honestly, I doubt she'll feel like a sister in the same way I feel like one. You didn't grow up with her. You never put anti-itch cream in her toothpaste tube. And no one is asking you to feel that way about her. Not now, and maybe not ever, but the fact remains, she's our half sister and she deserves . . . something. From us. From Dad. From Dad most especially, and he died before he could ever give it. So that means it's up to us."

Cade let out a sigh, the crushing pressure in his chest annoying him. Because it meant he knew she was right. "When did you get so damn smart?"

"I've found clarity and serenity thanks to Quinn's mighty lovin'."

Cade curled his lip. "That's a step too far, Mrs. Parker."

She smiled at that. "Mrs. Parker. It has a nice ring to it. But you really do need to figure out how to be nice to my husband. I'm keeping him."

"Old habits."

"You know he didn't have anything to do with your injury."

Cade nodded slowly, his leg giving him a nice jolt of pain right on time. "I know. But I hated him for a lot of years."

"You don't hate him now though."

"Only for taking you away," Cade said, his chest still tight. "But I'm glad for you too."

Lark's brown eyes went glossy. "Oh, Cade. That was . . . sweet."

"Yeah, don't get used to it. I didn't get to talk to you after the wedding, but you were the prettiest bride I've ever seen."

"You're only saying that because you've never had your own bride."

He laughed, short and harsh. "And I won't."

"Never?"

"Not in the cards."

"What about Amber?" Lark asked, her eyebrows knitting together. "Cole said . . ."

Ah, damn Cole. And damn him for forgetting about the Amber ruse. "Cole has a big mouth. But come on, Lark, you should know there's a difference between a little bit of sex, and marriage."

"Sure. That was my intent with Quinn, after all." He did his best not to wince. "But look, here I am, leg-shackled to him for the rest of my life, in sickness and health, blah blah blah. Plus, it's Amber. I figured if you ever got around to sleeping with her it would be 'cause you loved her."

Cade shifted, trying to balance his weight so that his leg wouldn't scream at him quite so loudly. There was no way for him to have this conversation without sounding like a first-class heel.

Because Lark was right. He did love Amber. Oh, not in the way she meant, but he did.

And that meant there was no way in all the world he'd ever use her to soothe the savage beast of his sexual appetite. So trying to convince her he would . . .

It was inauthentic, and there was no way for him to come out of it smelling like anything other than bull pucky.

"Look," he said, already knowing he'd opened badly,

"some things are more complicated than just . . . marriage or casual. Amber is my friend, and I do love her, but what we have is . . . it's mutually beneficial, okay?"

That at least was the truth. It got his ass out of his house, so he could avoid Nicole and any confronting feelings, and it allowed him to get a start on his bison ranch. As for Amber, it kept her safe from Davis and gave her ranch an injection of revenue.

Sure, it wasn't the kind of mutually beneficial Lark was thinking, wherein they both got orgasms, but bison were almost as good. And a lot less dangerous.

"Okaaaay," Lark said. "I guess I'm not going to understand this one, but then, I can't claim to have ever understood the two of you."

"Why is that?"

"Because you're like an amoeba that's grown together to form your own little amorphous blob, and no one can get very close to either of you, because you pour it all into each other. But you were never dating, or sleeping together."

"We're friends," he said.

Maybe it was unusual for a man and woman to stay friends for as long as they had, but the fact that so many people had trouble understanding a friendship that strong confounded him.

"Did you ever have a friend you could tell everything to?" he asked. "One who's seen you drunk, and pissed, and crying, and laughing, and never once thought less of you for any of those things?"

Lark shook her head. "No. I didn't have a lot of friends in school, you know that. I mean, Quinn is like that, but he's my husband."

"Well, I had one friend. One really good friend. And when you find someone like that, you keep them. But being a husband is different than being a friend, and I'm not geared toward being a husband."

"Why?"

Take Nicole Peterson down in the living room as the first lot of evidence.

"I'm just not, cupcake. Don't worry about it."

"Too late. I worry."

"It's my job to worry about you. No one needs to worry about me. Now, go downstairs and be friendly for me. I promise I'll be nice to Quinn later."

"And Nicole?"

"I have some things to sort through."

"I hope you sort through them correctly and come up with a solution that's not filled with asshattery," Lark said.

"I'm relieved that marriage hasn't changed you."

"Hell no. And you know what, I did go online for a few minutes in Hawaii. Just to figure out when this big gaming tournament was. Tonight, I'm going to make it rain zombie blood. Quinn will have to find something else to occupy his time."

"I love your consistency," he said.

"Thanks. I love you even when you're a growly asshole."

Cade stretched his arms out and pulled Lark into a gruff hug. "Kinder words have never been said to me."

"Aw, go on."

"It's true. I love you."

"I love you too. Now, go brush your teeth," she said. "Your breath really does stink."

"Grandpa?" Amber called up the stairs, then looked back at the bacon and eggs on the table, which were starting to congeal in a very unpleasant manner.

It was late. And by late, she meant the sun was up. She'd already eaten and had her third cup of coffee and was about ready to head to work, and there was still no sign of her grandfather.

He didn't like for her to "ride him about things" and he didn't like for her to check on him like he was "a damned child," but given that it was nearly seven, she felt like it was time to incur his wrath.

She sighed and headed up the stairs, ready to get yelled at. Whatever. The old guy couldn't go around being a more obnoxious, on-time wake-up call than a rooster ninety-five percent of the time and then one day not show up for breakfast.

She sighed and knocked on his bedroom door, waiting for a response. There wasn't one.

She pushed open the door and walked in, her heart pounding hard. The bed was empty, and the door to the bathroom was open.

"Oh shit."

She walked toward the bathroom and pushed the door open and saw him, crumpled in front of the vanity, blood trickling from his temple.

"Shit."

She knelt down and checked to make sure he was breathing. He was, but he wasn't conscious.

"Oh . . ." She stood up and ran for his bedside table. There was a phone with extra large numbers in the cradle there and she picked it up and dialed 911.

The dispatcher answered. "Nine-one-one. What is the address of your emergency?"

"Uh . . . Uh . . . 238 Sundown Road." She rattled off the address as quickly as possible while she walked back into the bathroom.

"And what is the nature of your emergency?"

"My grandfather is on the bathroom floor. And he's unconscious. And he's bleeding. His head is bleeding. His temple," she said, shaking now. "He's breathing and everything but I don't know what to do."

"Did the fall cause his unconsciousness or was there something else?"

"I don't know! I'm not a paramedic. That's why I'm calling for paramedics!"

"Ma'am, you need to stay calm."

"I need to stay calm? No, you need to panic! Don't you understand? My grandpa . . . something is wrong."

"I know," the dispatcher said, her tone still maddeningly even, "but panicking won't help him."

"Neither will staying calm, he's unconscious!"

"Ma'am, just stay calm."

"Amber?"

"Oh . . . Cade." She turned away from her grandfather and saw Cade standing in the doorway of the bedroom. "I'm in here! It's . . . Grandpa."

"What the hell happened?"

Cade barreled through the room as quickly as his leg allowed and into the bathroom. "Shit."

"That's what I said." She stood back and started ringing her hands. "I don't know what to do."

"Ma'am?" Amber heard the dispatcher's voice in her ear again. "Is someone there to wait with you?"

"Yes. Yes, yes. My friend is here. It's okay." It wasn't okay though. There was nothing okay about your grandfather lying ashen and bleeding on the floor in front of you. But Cade was with her, so it at least wasn't unendurable.

She felt her knees giving way, and then strong arms around her. He faltered, then they dipped, stabilizing when his back butted up against the wall. He tightened his hold on her.

"It's okay," he said.

"Yeah," she said. "It's okay."

"Ma'am, the paramedics are less than two minutes out."

"Okay." She hung up the phone and dropped it on the floor and let Cade hold her, his chest rising and falling against her back.

A few minutes later she heard footsteps on the stairs.

"In here," Cade called, patting her arm before releasing his hold on her. "Come on, sweetheart, let's go into the bedroom so they have room."

She went with him. Because he was so familiar. Because he was Cade, and he'd called her sweetheart, which she wasn't sure he'd ever done before with any measure of sincerity.

She sat on the bed and waited. One of the paramedics stopped to ask her questions that she genuinely didn't know the answers to, while the other two worked at getting her grandpa onto a stretcher.

"Is he okay?" she asked, even though she knew it was a stupid question no one could answer.

"We think he had a fall and hit his head, but we aren't sure what caused it," one of the men said, his tone far too gentle.

She wanted there to be more upset. More panic. Because that's what was happening inside of her, and everyone was just . . . handling it. She felt like she was going to die. Or at the very least like her insides were imploding. And everyone else was so stoic.

While she had to watch the last piece of her family go through the room on a stretcher.

"I want to ride with him," she said.

"That's fine," the medic said.

"I'll drive your car behind you," Cade said.

"Thanks," she said.

She wanted him to hold her again. And she knew that wasn't right. She didn't need anyone to hold her up. She never had. But really, really, she wanted to go back to that moment when his arms had gone around her and he'd held them both up, braced on the bathroom wall.

She was a wimp. And she couldn't afford to be a wimp right now, because her grandpa needed her. And it wouldn't do her any good to be a pansy-ass crybaby. He would be the first person to tell her that.

She rode to the hospital feeling numb. Being in the back of an ambulance wasn't interesting when your entire life was focused in on the man strapped into the gurney in front of you.

She was numb all through the hospital stuff. And Cade hung out, mainly in the waiting room, while she hovered in her grandpa's room and tried to process scary words like *contusion*, *concussion* and, the worst one, *stroke*.

Yeah, that was the worst.

"He's just going to sleep tonight," one of the nurses said, squeezing her hand and giving her a smile. Amber knew her from lunch hour at the diner. She was a chicken Caesar salad with dressing on the side, but Amber couldn't remember her name.

"Okay," she said, feeling numb.

"You should go home and get some sleep."

Amber found herself nodding and being ushered into the

waiting room. Cade was there, in a chair against the wall,
his forearms resting on his thighs, his head down.

"Hey," she said.

He looked up. "You ready to go?"

"No," she said. "But I should go home and get some sleep.
Because he's not awake and I need to make sure I get some
sleep. Because I need to make sure that I'm not completely
wiped out when he does need me. And . . . and things."

"Do you work tomorrow?"

She shook her head. "No."

"Good, then you can get wasted tonight."

CHAPTER

Eight

It was a time-honored tradition between him and Amber. Have a horrible thing happen to you, and the other one would buy a whole truckload of alcohol.

Amber had done it for him when his mom died. And when he'd found out his dad had had an affair that resulted in a child. He'd done it for her after she'd lost her grandma.

But they weren't kids now. This wasn't a job for a few 40s. This was serious business. Serious Jack Motherfucking Daniel's business.

Two hours later and he was pretty buzzed, but Amber was flat out on her back, laughing hysterically, tears rolling down her cheeks. He couldn't tell if it was from the laughter now, or if she was genuinely crying.

Probably a little of both.

"He was elbow-deep, stuck in the mare. And it's not really funny because on a contraction it can break your friggin' arm. But of course he didn't even react," she said, gasping for air. "Because he's like that, he's . . . he's a badass. He's still a badass even though he's like . . . eighty." Her laughter subsided a little. "He looked a little less . . . badassy tonight, though."

"People can recover from strokes, Amber."

"Yeah," she said, her hands folded over her stomach, her feet crossed at the ankles. He was looking down at her from his position on the couch, watching the firelight dance over her skin.

They had, of course, lit a fire in the fireplace, because Jack Daniel's had thought it was a wonderful idea.

"Yeah, they can recover," she said, rolling over onto her stomach. "If anyone could, it's him. He's the strongest man I have ever known, Cade, true story."

"Stronger than me?"

"Dude, yeah."

"I'm wounded," he said.

"Ah, yeah, whatever. Like hell you are. It's true. He's got all those grumpy old man points saved up. Crotchety old guy plus badass equals way stronger than you."

"I'm only running on one cylinder," he said, deadpan. "That's hardly fair."

"Yeah, but he's flipping eighty."

"Fair point."

She got up on her hands and knees and he couldn't help but notice the way her back dipped, then curved up to form a very, very enticingly round ass. He was buzzed, so looking at Amber's ass was officially okay.

As was noticing the way the fabric of her t-shirt stretched tight across her breasts when she straightened, still on her knees, and stretched, her arms behind her, hands clasped.

She knee-walked over to the edge of the couch and leaned forward, her chin resting on her wrists, her face right next to his thigh.

"I don't know what I'll do if I lose him," she said.

"You won't."

"You don't know that. Gramma died so suddenly. One day she was sneaking an extra stick of butter into the potatoes behind my back, and then she was just . . . gone. And

he's all I have left. They . . . I was so afraid they would get
sick of me and send me back. That they would be like
everyone else and get tired of my attitude and my crappy
music. Or of the fact that I was banging every guy at school
and sneaking them in through my windows." She laughed
hysterically at that. He didn't find it so funny. "But they
never did. They just kept me. All the way up till now. And
I just . . . I don't want him to die."

"I know," he said, resting his hand on her back, his thumb
touching a lock of silky hair. Damn, she was soft. He was
tempted to wrap a strand around his finger, stroke it a little bit.

Hell, he might. She wouldn't remember, and it seemed
like a really great idea right in that moment.

He slipped his hand over so that his palm covered the
dark wave of hair that shimmered over her back, catching
the gold from the fire. He moved his hand slowly over her,
a gesture of comfort. But he was also acutely aware of the
softness. He was saving the memory of that softness, because he'd never touched her hair like this before, and he
would probably never do it again.

Because if he was sober he would think it was a bad idea.

Sober Cade was boring.

Sober Cade was celibate for a reason. And sober Cade
would have never found out just how soft and perfect Amber
Jameson's hair felt beneath his hand.

Sober Cade lost on all fronts.

She looked up at him, a strange smile on her face, the
light from the fire dancing in her eyes now, gold flecks deep
in the brown that leapt higher when she cocked her head to
the side, stealing all that soft hair and moving it out of his
reach.

"You are . . . really sexy," she said.

His stomach tightened. "You're only saying that because
you're really drunk."

"No. I'm not."

"Baby, you're wasted."

She laughed. "I know. But I'm not just saying it." She
scrambled into a sitting position, her thigh nearly touching

his now. "I . . . I was thinking it yesterday. And the day before. I've thought it a lot of days. And especially when you said you hadn't . . . you know . . . done it, in like four years."

He winced. That truth hurt with *and* without booze.

"You know what, though?"

"What?" he asked, his throat tight.

"I haven't gotten laid in, like . . . so much longer than you."

He took a fortifying drink. "What?"

"I think, like . . . dude, Cade, I haven't had sex in thirteen years."

He just about spit out the fortifying drink. "What?"

"I was seventeen. And I was doing it with this guy. And it sucked. And I just, like . . . realized I didn't even want the guy. I just wanted to not be alone. And that's such a stupid . . . it's stupid. You shouldn't have sex because of that. You should have it because you're really, *really* horny."

She was looking at him now, her dark eyes intent on his, the flames somehow appearing more intense in them. "Right," he said.

"I'm *really* horny," she said.

"I thought you were sad."

"Yeah. But I think you can be sad and horny. I think you can be horny and a lot of other emotions."

He was a prime example of that fact right at this moment. He'd never been terrified of a woman before, but he was damn close just then.

And, he had to admit, horny.

She leaned in, her hand braced on the couch just behind his head, her hair falling forward, making a curtain around them, separating them from the rest of the world. "You know, I've barely even kissed a guy since high school. I miss it."

He could feel her breath on his face. Warm. Sweet. Enticing. A mixture of booze and Amber, and he wanted a taste.

It was a bad idea, because she was hammered. He wasn't functioning completely normally either. And there were other reasons. Valid ones. And he could think of none of them at the moment.

Because nothing else mattered but how soft her hair was. And the fact that her lips were so close, and he wanted to taste them more than he could ever remember wanting anything before.

Amber's lips.

He'd seen them turned down into a frown, stretched into a genuine smile, contorted during an ugly-cry. But he'd never watched them kiss a man.

And he wouldn't be watching now.

But he would sure as hell be a part of it.

He sifted his fingers through her hair—another chance to indulge in her softness—and he leaned in, closing the distance between them.

It turned out everything about her was softer than anticipated. Softer than anything had a damn right to be. And she tasted like heaven.

If heaven was made of alcohol, sin and lust.

And his version of it just might be.

He cupped the back of her head and crushed her harder to him, keeping the kiss firm and steady. This was just a test. Just to see.

She lowered her chin, separating their mouths so that her forehead was resting against his, their breathing heavy.

He wanted . . . he wanted to pull her top off and explore her body. Wanted to part her thighs and find out if everything about her was as soft as what he'd already discovered.

She moaned, a sweet, sensual sound like he'd never heard from her before. One that his body responded to in a very predictable, very male way.

She angled her head, pressed a kiss to his cheek, then his neck. He put his hand on her hip to try and brace himself. He had no clue what the hell was going on, but he didn't want to stop it either.

He was already rock hard. Aching. And this was the most female contact he'd had in a very long time.

She leaned back, her smile crooked, the look in her eyes a little bit fuzzy. She bit her lip, the expression one of almost exaggerated seduction, and even though his brain said it was obvious and therefore should not be sexy, his dick had another response entirely.

Obvious was right up his dick's alley.

"I wonder if sucking cock is like riding a bike," she said. "If you just never forget how."

She leaned forward again, pressing her lips to the hollow of his throat. The action, combined with her words, effectively stopped his breathing.

"There's only one way to find out," she whispered, her breath hot on his neck.

Her hand moved to cover his cock, delicate fingers curving around his erection. He let his head fall back. Let her stroke him through the denim.

Oh . . . yes. If there had ever been anything better than this, he couldn't remember it.

Better than the way Amber's hand felt on his body.

Amber's hand.

Amber.

Shit shit shit shit.

That was the other thing. The list of reasons why this was bad was so long. She was his friend. His best friend.

And her hand was on his dick.

She was drunk, she was hurting, and he was letting her . . .

He was an asshole.

"Stop," he said, moving away from her. "Stop, Amber."

"Why do you want to stop?" she asked, moving her hand over his erection. "You don't feel like you want to stop."

God almighty help him, he didn't want to stop. But she was drunk, he was halfway there, and it was the worst possible time and way to introduce sex and sexual touching and . . . and cock-sucking into their relationship.

There would never be a good time, but on a scale of terrible to Hindenburg, this was an *Oh, the humanity!* moment.

"What? So you get to be all macho and chivalrous . . ."

"Can you be macho and chivalrous?"

"Yeah," she said, taking her hand off of his body. He was simultaneously relieved and so disappointed he wanted to weep. "Because you're doing it, so it must be a thing. You're being all . . . those things and moving in with me and protecting me and pretending you're banging me and I don't even get the benefit of actual banging. My celibacy could freaking babysit your celibacy. I am practically a virgin again over here. But one who knows what she's doing." She said the last part in what, he imagined, was supposed to be a seductive whisper.

It was a little slurred. Also obvious.

And it kicked his arousal up another notch. There was something wrong with him.

"Amber, no. Not like this, okay?"

"What do you mean not like this?"

"Not with you drunk as a skunk."

She frowned. "What if I still want to suck your cock in the morning?"

"I promise that if you're in the mood to dole out any early morning BJs, I'll let you, okay?" She wouldn't be. She would sober up, she would be horrified if she remembered any of this, and they would never speak of it.

She probably wouldn't remember it, actually.

But he would.

Shit, Amber Jameson offering to suck him off would haunt his dreams for the rest of his life.

"Promise?" she asked, her capitulation ringing more warning bells than anything else that had come before. Because while sober, Amber was mule-caliber stubborn, but drunk she was a shade of common sense higher on the food chain than a good ol' redneck boy.

And that meant stubborn as hell—and no common sense.

"Yeah, of course." Arousal gave him a good, swift kick in the gut. Just to punish him further for attempting to be some kind of a gentleman. For trying to save the most important relationship in his life by not compromising it with drunken head.

A smile, one that was both wicked and pouty, curved her lips. "I really don't want to wait." Her fingers fluttered back down, caressed the top of his belt buckle.

"Amber . . ."

She looked up, dark eyes clashing with his. "Let me do this, Cade. I want this. I want you. I think . . . I think I might even need it."

He should say no. For sanity. For friendship.

He didn't say no.

She tugged the end of his belt through the buckle and released it, letting both halves fall open. He was hard, and there was no hiding it. The bulge in his jeans was plainly visible, even through JD goggles. So there was no point telling her he wasn't in the mood.

Hell, he'd been in the mood every day for four years. Every minute. Every hour. Except maybe during the weddings of his siblings and the birth of his niece.

No, even then, if a woman would have tried to tempt him into a nearby supply closet, he would have probably gone.

Four years was a long time.

A long time not to be touched by someone else. Someone who wanted you. A long time of feeling like a eunuch. Because your leg didn't work, your dick must be broken too.

Because his limp seemed to shout, *I'm dragging baggage—steer clear.*

Because he couldn't seem to bring himself to make a move on anyone for fear of rejection, and it made him feel like the horse may as well have stomped his balls into butter, because he sure as hell wasn't using them.

But Amber was making this way too easy. Amber wanted him. Amber's hands were on his fly now, unzipping his jeans slowly, the sound mingling with his ragged breathing.

Then her fingers were on his skin, low on his stomach, sliding down beneath the waistband of his underwear and wrapping around his cock.

"Hell, baby." He let his head fall back, every good intention he had, maybe every good intention he'd ever had in his entire life, leaving him completely.

He wasn't stopping her now.

He needed it.

She wanted it.

And he was too far gone.

Because nothing had ever felt as good as her fingertips stroking the head of his erection. Nothing. That first touch from another person's hand after four years of using only his own.

She stroked him gently and he gritted his teeth, trying to think of unsexy things so that he wouldn't come before she even got her lips on him.

He was close. He was that damn close.

She tugged him up out of his jeans, her lips forming an O, her eyes getting rounder. She looked up at him. "I had no idea," she said.

"What?" he asked, his voice strangled.

"That you were so big."

Oh, dammit, that was obvious too, and it was the hottest thing he'd ever heard. "I don't know if I would have left you alone back in high school," she said, squeezing him tight.

His hips thrust up from the couch, the motion completely involuntary. Seeing her, Amber, her hand on him, her face so close to him. Why was it so hot? Why was this, the worst idea in the world, the sexiest thing he'd ever experienced?

He'd had just enough to drink that bad seemed good, but not enough to erase the realization that this was very, very bad. The combination was a heady one. To say the least.

"Amber . . ."

She smiled. "Yes, Cade?"

Oh . . . his name on her lips. There wasn't anything sweeter. Yeah, they were impaired, he could admit that, but she knew it was him. And she wanted him.

That was all he needed.

"Nothing." He smoothed her hair back. She was so damn soft. And yeah, he was repeating himself, but he didn't care.

She leaned forward, her eyes still on his. His breath caught in his chest; everything seemed to freeze around them. The world outside. Hell, he couldn't even be sure the world was still outside at all. Maybe it had all fallen away. Maybe they were the only two people left, and this was the only thing happening.

Right in the moment it felt possible.

She parted her lips and flicked the head of his cock with her tongue. He curled his fingers into a fist, tightening his hold on her hair.

"Fuck," he breathed. Like a curse. Like a prayer. Like both, because this was heaven and hell, right here on Amber's couch.

"Maybe after?" she said, pausing for a moment and smiling broader. Like a cat who knew she was about to catch the canary.

Yes. Yes. Yes.

That was not his brain doing the yessing.

His brain was currently unavailable for comment.

She leaned in again, and this time, she took him deep in her mouth, humming slightly as she did, the vibrations combined with the wet suction sending a shot of heat straight to his groin that spread through the rest of him like wildfire.

He swept her hair to the side so he could see her face, the elegant line of her neck as she angled her head and took him in deeper.

It was too much. And not enough. And when she squeezed him down at the base of his shaft, the pressure combined with the slick friction of her lips and tongue, he realized there was no holding back.

It was going to be the shortest blow job on record since he'd gotten his first at the age of seventeen.

"Amber . . ." He started to pull away from her but she held him firm, continuing to stroke him with her hand while she pleasured him with her mouth.

And she pushed him straight over the edge.

He tightened his hold on her hair, rode out the storm as release raged through his body, leaving him spent, and sweating and shaking.

She pulled away from him and licked her lips. That would have been enough to get him hard again, if he hadn't just had the kind of orgasm that made him wonder if his body would ever function properly again.

She'd slain him.

"I feel better," she said, tracing a line from his stomach down to the patch of hair just above his cock. "Don't you?"

There were no words for how much better he felt. Regret would hit hard like a bite in the ass tomorrow, along with his hangover. That was a given.

But right now there was nothing. Nothing but a post-orgasmic buzz and the fuzzy edges of sleep creeping into his vision.

He needed something. A drink of water. A chance to get his pants in order. A second to breathe. "I'll be right back."

Her eyes flew wide. "Don't leave me, Cade."

"I'm not, baby," he said, tracing the line of her cheekbone with the edge of his thumb. Then he leaned in and kissed her lightly on the lips. Because right now it felt like it was okay. And tomorrow it no doubt would go back to being un-okay.

He winced against that thought. Against any thought of tomorrow at all.

"Just need the bathroom."

She nodded slowly. "Okay."

"I'll be back."

He went into the bathroom and splashed water on his face. Buckled his pants back up. And when he came back out, she was stretched across the couch, asleep like a lazy cat.

He sat on the edge of the couch and looked down at her, and he didn't think. Not at all. Because that way lay madness. And he just wanted to sleep. He wanted no madness. He wanted orgasm brain and sleep.

He maneuvered them both so that he was behind her, holding her against him. Tomorrow there would very possibly be hell to pay.

But tonight he would just hold her.

CHAPTER

Nine

Amber opened her eyes and looked across the living room, into the cold, dark fireplace. There was ash in the bottom of it. There hadn't been any ash in it yesterday, because she'd cleaned it since the last time there was a fire in it.

Oh yeah, and her head hurt like a sonofabitch.

Those were the first two things she noticed.

Then there was the heavy, warm arm slung over her waist, a large hand resting flat against her stomach. Her awareness spread out from there. The heat behind her. The solid, big body that she was resting against. And what was very surely an erect penis against her backside.

Well, this was new and interesting.

She didn't panic, because she was still fuzzy. And because the man who was holding her felt so good. How long had it been since she'd been held like this? Had she ever been held like this?

Dimly, she remembered Cade wrapping his arms around her and holding her against him in the bathroom while they waited for the paramedics.

Oh no. *That* had happened. That was yesterday and . . . and . . .

She shifted and looked behind her, her eyes level with Cade's chin. He was asleep, also fully clothed, thankfully. And he was holding on to her still.

She wiggled against him and winced when she came into contact with the penis again. It was a morning thing, not a *her* thing, and she knew that, but . . . but it made her feel strange and a little bit warm.

It just wasn't the kind of thing you should be aware of when it was attached to your best friend.

Something tugged at the back of her mind, but it hurt too badly to think too deeply, and she had a feeling she was repressing the memory for a reason.

She should move. Because she felt like she was violating Cade in some way by taking part in this early morning male ritual that he couldn't really control. And it felt a touch too intimate to be allowed.

But she didn't want to move, because her head hurt and being in Cade's arms felt good.

Because life hurt. Her grandpa was in the hospital, and she had no idea if he would recover. Because if she moved out of Cade's hold she would feel as alone as she was, and she just didn't want that to happen.

So she stayed there and tried to focus on the way his chest felt, rising and falling against her back. Just breathing with another person helped with the alone feelings. Made it seem like she was connected to earth instead of floating around in space all by herself.

Her head gave a nice, crashing throb, and she squeezed her eyes shut. Okay, she needed to get up and find the pain-killers.

She took a deep breath and sat up, bracing herself for the wave of pain it would cause and gritting her teeth hard when it hit like a tsunami.

Cade cleared his throat and stirred behind her, his arm coming around her waist again, his hand on her stomach.

It sent a shot of desire straight down between her thighs.

Strong enough that it rivaled her headache. That was strong freaking desire.

She looked back over at him and watched him scrub his other hand over his face. He wasn't conscious yet. He was probably having a buckle bunny flashback. Imagining she was one of his stacked blonde conquests from his rodeo circuit days.

She was stacked, she would grant herself that. But blonde she was not. And she'd never been one to haunt rodeos looking for the biggest . . . belt buckle.

She put her hand over his and tried to ignore the little pop of attraction that shot from her fingertips up to her elbow, spinning into electricity and spidering out through her veins to points beyond. Very interesting points beyond.

"Hey, Cade," she said, tweaking one of his fingers.

He only tightened his hold on her and pulled her butt hard against his stomach. Which was quite firm. Congrats to him.

"Cade!"

He started and blinked, then looked up at her and slowly removed his hand from beneath hers. "Good morning," he said.

"Yeah. Good morning," she said. "Well, 'cept for the hangover. And the fact that my grandpa is still in the hospital. And I need to call and see how he's doing, but . . . ow, hungover. Soooo hungover."

"Maybe we should come up with a better way to handle grief."

She arched against the back of the couch, Cade a solid lump beneath her lower back. "Are you suggesting we become emotionally well-adjusted?"

"No. I wouldn't know where to begin. I'm just wondering if we're too old to drink like that anymore."

"You seem much more chipper than I feel."

"I didn't drink as much as you did. Mainly because you drank everything."

"Meh." She paused to fully appreciate the pounding in her skull. "I did, didn't I?"

"You were a wreck, sweetheart. I don't blame you."

Again with the sincere-sounding "sweetheart." It made her feel gooey. She didn't like to feel gooey. On the way to gooeyness lay madness, or something.

She wasn't really sure if that made sense at all, but her head hurt far too badly for her to sort out basic sentences, let alone any kind of metaphor.

She let out a long breath and levered herself up off the couch, the floor tilting under her feet. "Oh, bleah." She blinked hard. "You're right. We are too old. I am, anyway. I need to call the hospital."

"Go take an ibuprofen. I'll fry you some bacon. Then you can call the hospital. It's still early, and they haven't called you, so you don't need to worry too much."

"Yeah," she said, walking on stiff legs toward the downstairs bathroom, where she knew she would find salvation in pill form.

She opened up the medicine cabinet and stared at the bottle for a full ten seconds before taking it off the shelf and pouring four little capsules into her hand. Then she filled up the cup that was sitting on the sink and took each pill one at a time while looking at herself in the mirror.

She was a wreck. Red-eyed and ratty-haired. It was probably a good thing she'd been over one-night stands by the time she'd graduated high school because she would have been doing one-nighters by default if she'd gone heavy drinking, hooked up and the guy had seen her the next morning.

He'd have been left wondering if he'd gone home with a sea monster.

My celibacy could babysit your celibacy.

She had a weird flash of memory. Of saying those words and then giggling.

Last night.

Oooohh. Had she really told Cade how long it had been since she'd had sex? Had she actually tallied it up—something she'd been avoiding doing even in her own head—and then spoken the years out loud?

She plunked her head against the mirror.

Yes. Yes, she had done that.

What was wrong with her? Oh, yeah, she'd been drunk off her ass. That's what was wrong with her.

She closed her eyes, and another flash of memory hit.

Cade's lips. Pressed against hers.

And she'd said . . . oh shit. And she'd put her hand on his . . . no. No no no.

She straightened, her cheeks flaming, her entire body prickling with heat. Oh, what had she done? Had she really, honest-to-goodness made a pass at him? Had she offered him a drunken blow job?

Wait. No.

Oh no. Oh no *no no*. And dagnabbit. And dammit. She hadn't just offered him a drunken blow job—she had given him a drunken blow job.

Pictures flashed before her mind's eye, a slide show of hedonistic indulgence the likes of which she hadn't seen since her senior year of high school.

What had she been thinking? She hadn't been, clearly. It was the drunk-off-her-ass factor. And she'd made a very, very stupid decision.

Unless you were thinking very straight and you were just drunk enough to finally go after what you want . . .

Oh, hell no. Now that path surely was the way to madness, and she didn't have to be clearheaded to know that.

She'd never had a sexual relationship that wasn't simply that: a sexual relationship. And she'd never, ever merged personal connection with it. For a reason. Her emotional issues being the driving force behind that reason.

It was why she was celibate—or . . . semi-celibate, at this point. It was because she didn't know how to do relationships. Because she needed to figure herself out. Because she just didn't have the energy.

Cade was just too important to risk on an orgasm. That was the simple fact, and she'd always known that. That was why Cade had always been friend-zoned. Even though he was hot. Even though sometimes she had small, passing fantasies about him. Very small. Very passing. Fleeting, really.

And she'd never, ever gone there with him because it was

stupid to go there with a guy you wanted to remain friends with. And stuff.

But now she'd gone there, hadn't she? In a very big way. Very big indeed.

She flashed back again, to the way he'd felt in her hand. The heavy weight of him. The way he'd tasted . . . all the way until the end.

Oh Lord . . .

At least she'd been drunk. Maybe he'd been drunk enough that he didn't remember. She could always hope.

She put her hand on her chest and leaned against the bathroom door, feeling her heart fluttering against her rib cage like a panicked mouse in a flour sack. How was she ever going to look at him again now that she'd seen his . . . and touched . . . and tasted and . . . gah!

She bit her lip and pounded her head lightly against the wall a couple of times just for good measure. Then she took a deep breath and opened the door, peering out into the hall. He wasn't there.

She slinked out of the bathroom and headed toward the kitchen, feeling awkward and weird, and shamefaced, which sucked, because she'd never felt awkward, weird or shamefaced around Cade.

When they'd been in high school they'd talked about all kinds of inappropriate things. He'd told her when he'd cashed in his V card with the older bartender at The Saloon. She'd told him that Greg Jones had the smallest penis she'd ever seen.

None of that had ever made them act awkward. None of that had ever made her feel ashamed.

Of course, talking to your best friend about another guy's penis was different than actually handling your best friend's penis. So there was that.

She'd thought the word "penis" more times this morning than in the past several years combined. Which was an odd thought, but a true one.

Maybe she was still a little drunk.

"Is my bacon ready?" she asked, heading into the kitchen.

"Not quite."

Ah, damn. He wasn't looking at her. That meant he remembered. Or maybe he just remembered the kiss. Or the offer. And his initial refusal. Or maybe he didn't remember anything.

Honestly, the odds were slim, but she had no intention of bringing up anything he might not remember. It could die a death in the annals of Cade's drunken non-memory as far as she was concerned.

He kept his back to her, his focus on the stove and very determinedly not on her.

Well, hell. Damage control was needed. How did one damage-control something of this magnitude? She had no idea. No flipping idea.

She cleared her throat and clapped her hands together. Like signaling her presence to a wild animal. "Sooo . . . bacon smells good."

"Bacon always smells good," he said. He still wasn't looking at her.

"Good enough to . . . eat."

His shoulders went a little rigid when she said that, and she felt the last hold on her very comfortable he-does-not-remember-that-blow-job-you-gave-him denial slipping.

"When it's done," he said.

"Right." She sat down at the little breakfast table with her hands folded in front of her. Her ears were burning. And she needed a coffee really, really badly. But Cade was standing in front of the coffeemaker, and that meant she would have to reach around him to get it. Or reveal her awkwardness by asking him to move.

But the alternative—sitting at the table, playing with her fingers and trying not to look at Cade's butt—meant that she got no caffeine in her system, and that was not a particularly acceptable alternative.

Particularly with the effects of her hangover wreaking all kinds of evil on her head.

She stood up again and approached Cade with caution, trying to work out what she would have done in an alternate reality where she had not stuck her hand in his pants only six hours earlier.

She would have just reached past him and gotten her coffee. That's what she would have done. She would have gotten her mug, picked up the carafe and fed her wicked addiction.

The one to coffee, not the one to his body.

She did not have a wicked addiction to his body.

One instance of oral sex did not an addiction make.

And as she was moving to the coffeemaker, she mentally decided she liked the term "blow job" better because it did not contain the word "sex" and therefore didn't seem quite as frightening in context with Cade.

But as she drew closer to him she decided she wouldn't use either term. She would mentally refer to it as The Incident, if she had to refer to it at all.

That was settled then.

She stopped just to his left and reached up behind him, opening the cupboard and taking out her favorite owl mug, keeping a side-eye trained on him as she lowered it to the counter in front of the coffeemaker.

"Coffee?" she asked.

He jumped slightly. "What?" His voice was calm.

"Do you want some?"

"Sure."

She reached up again, keeping her movements slow, making sure not to brush him with her elbow or—heaven forbid—her boob.

He could move. He didn't have to be planted so determinedly at the center of the stove. He was being all male and taking up all the space his big frame required. He could fold those broad shoulders in a bit.

So maybe he didn't remember. Because if he did, surely he would feel as awkward about physical contact as she did.

Surely.

She poured two cups of coffee and held the plain mug out to him. "Black and sugarless, I assume, in honor of last night's overindulgence."

Their eyes clashed and held, and her heart stopped for a moment.

"The alcohol," she said.

"Of course." He took the mug out of her hand and lifted it in mock salute.

She nearly said, *What else could I possibly be talking about?* But then, somehow, her inner cooler-than-thou Amber clamped a hand over her mouth and stopped her.

"Me too," she said. "With the black and sugarless, because I am all of the hurting." She took a sip of her coffee and backed away from him, edging her way back to the table.

There. She'd survived that moment of nearness.

"Sorry about that," he said, turning back to the stove. "But your bacon is ready."

"Oh good. I crave meat." She puckered her lips so hard they twitched as she tried to keep from . . . laughing? Shrieking in horror over her own stupid double entendre? "Of the preserved . . . salted"—it wasn't getting better—"variety."

"Bacon à la me," he said, putting the plate down in front of her. It didn't look particularly appetizing. She should have remembered that of the two of them, she'd actually cooked bacon before. But she'd been too busy having a medical episode over the memory of last night.

"Your bacon is underwhelming." Oh, dammit. His bacon was underwhelming. His *bacon* was quite overwhelming and was the cause of her issues this morning. His *bacon* was spectacular. The best she'd never had. A glimpse into the promised land followed with an order to continue languishing out in the celibacy desert. "What I mean is you overcooked it. It's"—she poked it with her fork—"shrunken."

She really needed to stop talking.

"However will you manage your disappointment with my underwhelming shrunken bacon?" he asked, deadpan, taking a seat across from her with his own plate of bacon.

"I shall try to manage. Imagine that it's other bacon I guess. Juicier bacon." Oh hell. That was the worst unintentional double entendre in the history of bad unintentional double entendres.

She crammed a slice into her mouth and gnawed on it until it became salty pork paste on her tongue. It really was overcooked.

"No one's bacon is juicier than mine, et cetera," he said, taking a bite, then grimacing. "Never mind. Everyone's bacon is juicier."

He was being so normal. Talking about bacon and its drippings as though it was simply that, and not an epic metaphor for a penis and its . . . well . . . drippings.

"Oh, fuck the bacon." Cade pushed his plate to the center of the table, and the plate kept going, wobbling back and forth until it tipped over the edge of the table and onto the floor.

She looked down at the tile, the plate, which was facedown, and the bacon, which had been flung to far-reaching places. She looked back up at Cade with large eyes.

"What?"

"Why the hell," he said, planting his palms on the table and standing up, "are we talking about bacon?"

She stood too, her heart hammering, ready to beg him not to pop the little bubble of lies she was living in.

"Because bacon is what's for breakfast?"

He advanced on her, that same look in his eyes that he'd had out in the driveway when she'd insulted his manhood. And then he wrapped his arm around her waist and tugged her up against his chest.

The resulting motion made him stumble. He kept his hand firmly on her back, his other hand planted on the table below them. His face was only an inch from hers, his face so close to hers she was sure he could smell her bacon breath.

"It's not what I want for breakfast," he said, his voice a low, unfamiliar growl.

Her brain was on hyperdrive, trying to meld this image of Cade, feral, growling and looking at her like he was going to devour her, with the man she'd known more than half her life.

"What is it you wan—"

Her question was devoured before she could get it out. This was nothing at all like the kiss from last night. This wasn't soft and alcohol-tinged. This was hard, firm and sure.

It tasted like black coffee and consciousness. There was no excuse for it, there was nothing to blame it on. There would be no cloak of invisibility to pull over it after.

It was the cold, sober light of day. And it was happening.

And she was letting it. She was more than letting it; she was returning it. She wrapped her arms around his neck, tangled her fingers through his hair, and kissed him harder and better than she'd ever kissed a man in her entire life.

There had been a lot of kisses—there had been a lot of men. But there had never been one like this.

Maybe that was because those other men had really just been boys. Desperate, grasping high schoolers, like she'd been.

Maybe it was because she knew Cade. And he knew her.

Whatever the reason, there had never been a kiss like this. Not on her record.

She swept her tongue across his lower lip before delving inside his mouth, tasting him deep. He growled and lifted her up against him, setting her ass down on the table, pushing her plate of bacon onto the floor.

"Hey," she said, breaking the kiss and looking down at her discarded breakfast.

"You don't need it," he said.

No, she really didn't. Because her mouth was busy.

Cade brought his lips to hers again, intensifying the kiss, biting her gently before soothing away the sting with his tongue. A little thrill shot through her. How had he known she would like that? She hadn't even known she would like that.

He parted her thighs and stepped between them, his belt buckle digging into her belly, his denim-covered erection settling against her clit. She locked her ankles together behind his butt and tugged him harder against her body as she kissed him.

He broke the kiss and gasped for air, his hands shaking as he pulled away from her slightly and started working on his belt buckle.

She wasn't going to stop him.

She wasn't going to think.

Because she needed him. She needed this. Thirteen

damn years since she'd been this close to another person. And she needed close. She needed it so bad it ached all the way through.

While he worked on his belt buckle, she tugged her jeans and underwear down, leaving her pantsless and bare-assed on the table, but she would worry about that, and potential sanitation issues, later too.

Right now, there was only one thing: need. She needed him. She needed Cade Mitchell inside of her more than she needed air. More than she needed anything else on earth.

And it felt like it had been that way forever. She couldn't remember not wanting him. Not now. It felt so much like it had always been a part of her. Like the need to eat or drink.

He freed himself from his jeans, leaving them halfway down his lean hips. He put his hand on her butt and brought her forward, nudging at the slick entrance to her body with the head of his cock.

He entered her slowly, his restraint almost killing her. But it was necessary. Because even with the great care he was taking, it hurt a little bit.

Sure, she had battery-powered devices to help weather her celibacy, but they were not Cade-size.

Oh . . . Lord. Cade.

She looked up at him, her legs locked around him, her arms around his neck. She watched his face, so familiar and so foreign at the same time. The tendons in his neck standing out, sweat beading over his forehead.

She had to look away. Had to bury her face in his shoulder while he pushed the rest of the way inside of her, because it was too scary, too real, too intense when her eyes were on him.

He thrust hard into her and brought all of her focus back to her body. To his body. Their bodies, and how much she needed this. The physical, and nothing more.

That's all it was.

Desperation; too many years, for both of them, spent not being touched.

Why not touch a little?

He flexed his hips and she gasped.

Or a lot. They could touch a lot.

She slid her hands down the front of his chest, relishing the feeling of all those hard muscles beneath her fingertips. But his shirt was in the way. She reached beneath the hem, let her fingers skim over his abs, the light dusting of hair adding an enticing texture to the hardness and heat. It was a stark reminder of just how much of a man he was.

And if that wasn't enough, his skill served as an even more potent reminder.

He wasn't a grasping, heavy-breathing teenage boy conducting a mad race to the finish line.

Cade was all man. And it wasn't only the size of his body, but the way that he used it. A man who knew that the journey was as important as the destination. Every thrust brought him into contact with the point of her arousal; every time he withdrew, every time he came back to her, filling her to the point of pain, she was pushed closer and closer to the edge.

He put his hand between them and slid his thumb over her clit, sending a lightning bolt of pleasure straight through her body. She let her head fall back and leaned forward, felt him scraping his teeth along the line of her throat, then going back over it with the tip of his tongue.

She clung to his shoulders, her nails digging into his skin through the fabric of his t-shirt. She didn't think she could take any more. But she desperately needed more. Desperately needed all of it.

This was thirteen years of deprivation come to a head. This was sixteen years of knowing and never having touched Cade, reaching a screaming, shuddering end. And it was everything she'd imagined it might be. And more. Too much more.

She gritted her teeth, pushing back at the orgasm that was building inside of her. Because she knew, beyond a shadow of a doubt, that it would break her. That it would consume her. That it might not leave anything of her left in the end.

But she couldn't hold back forever.

One more kiss. Deep, long. Cade sucked her lower lip

into his mouth just as he thrust deep inside of her, pushing her over the edge.

A hoarse scream climbed up her throat and she didn't even bother to stop it. All of her energy was given over to the intense pleasure that was coursing through her, taking her over completely. Her internal muscles clenched hard around his cock, and she felt the exact moment he let go of the hold on his control.

He froze, every muscle in his body tensing, a growl resonating in his chest, his hand tangling with her hair and tugging as he came hard.

Then there was nothing. Nothing but the sound of their breathing. Nothing but sunlight pouring through the windows and bacon on the floor.

Cade stepped away from her and turned around, adjusting his pants before dragging his hands over his hair and planting his hands on the counter, leaning forward, his shoulders stiff.

Well, it was safe to say he'd remembered the blow job.

And it was safe to say that neither of them would be forgetting this.

Even though that was the one thing they absolutely had to do. For their friendship. For her sanity.

Even while her body buzzed with an orgasm the likes of which she'd never even conceived of, even while her skin burned with the remainder of his touch, she was already working at forgetting.

There were reasons she and Cade had never done this before. And those reasons still stood. And it meant they could never, ever do it again.

CHAPTER

Ten

"Do you need a ride to the hospital?" Cade was surprised his voice still worked. That his lips still functioned enough to form words.

He'd been afraid of being permanently physically compromised after that last orgasm. And he was even more concerned about being struck dead, either by a bolt of lightning from above, or by a firm strike from a frying pan wielded by Amber.

And he deserved both.

What the hell had he been thinking?

Well, he hadn't been. Not with his head. That was a fact.

He'd just dumped his best friend's breakfast on the floor, then screwed her on the table. That was . . . wrong on so many levels.

"Uh . . ."

He turned around and saw Amber, still straightening her clothes, looking beautiful and stunned. And sad.

"Do you?" he asked. "I have to drive up to Joseph and talk to a guy about bison today. I could swing through town and drop you off."

"Yeah," she said, "that would be . . . wow. Fabulous. Great. Great and good. And . . . good." She screwed up her face. "I think . . . I think I need to go to the bathroom for a second."

"Right. Of course."

She nodded silently, then walked back toward the bathroom. And as soon as she disappeared from the kitchen he sat down heavily on a chair, his legs fully unwilling to work now.

Though, full points to his body for managing to have sex while standing. Even though it was not the time to crow over his physical abilities. Not at all.

Besides, he'd probably pay for it later with wicked, screaming pain in his spine. He felt a twinge at the base of it. Yep. It was starting already.

But it had been worth it.

Hadn't it?

He let out a long breath. It was hard to regret sex like that. Hard to regret a release like that. Easy to regret the fact that he'd possibly compromised his relationship with Amber.

That realization hit him like a bucket of river water over the head.

What if they couldn't move on from this? What if they couldn't fix it?

No, that was stupid. They were adults. They'd both had sex before. Granted, it had been a long time, but neither of them were virgins. They both knew sex could just be sex. They both knew how to detach from it.

An orgasm wasn't love. An orgasm wasn't even a relationship. It was just that—a release. And they'd both clearly needed one.

He just tried to forget the way Amber's face had looked the moment before she'd disappeared into the bathroom. Because she hadn't looked freshly orgasmed and chill. But then, he supposed he didn't either.

He didn't feel it. Which was balls. Because it had been the best damn release he'd had in his memory, and he ought to feel some sort of good feelings along with it.

But he didn't. He just felt stressed. He felt like a massive weight had been left on his chest, and breathing around it was nearly impossible. Damn reality.

He would give almost anything to go back to the moment just before he'd kissed her and undo it. No, that was a lie; if he could control time like that he would give everything to go back to the moment he'd been inside of her, and just stay there.

But he couldn't do either thing.

That meant he had to deal with the consequences. Dammit, he hated consequences. He much preferred to drink them away, or move on to another town. Ride it out on the circuit. And he couldn't do any of those things at the moment. Because his running leg was broken, and his accomplice in all poor decisions, the person who would normally give aid in this kind of situation, was the person he needed to run from.

Amber returned a second later looking pale and a little bit shell-shocked, and Cade felt like the world's biggest asshole.

"You okay?" he asked.

"Yeah. Fine. Just . . . stressed because of my grandpa."

This woman raised denial to a new art form. First, this morning, it had been all about bacon and not about the head she'd given him the night before. And now, five minutes after they'd had earth-shattering sex on the kitchen table, she was pretending all they'd done was drink coffees and stare into the abyss, saying and doing nothing.

Well. Hell.

That was probably the tactic they should take, but he would like . . . something. An acknowledgment that he'd rocked her world, maybe?

Because as petty as it seemed, his ego could really use the stroking. Four years of no sex, and the dry spell had ended in a blaze of glory, if he did say so himself. So a little bit of an acknowledgment would be nice.

"Right, naturally. Are you . . . ready to go?"

She shoved her hands in her jeans pockets. "Yeah."

"Great."

"You don't want any of that bacon?" he asked, gesturing to their breakfast, which was still on the floor.

"I'm good."

"Awesome. Let's go."

"Yeah," she said. "Let's go."

"I'm ready."

"Me too."

"Outstanding," he said, grabbing his keys off the counter. "Shall we?"

"Sure."

They went out to the truck, and Cade opened the door for her, waiting for her to get inside. "Why don't you drive your sports car anymore?" she asked, after he'd gotten in on the driver's side and started the engine.

"Because," he said, "I sold it last month."

"Why?"

"Bison," he said through gritted teeth.

"It means that much to you?"

"Yes. No. Hell, I don't know. I just wanted to do something. Something other than drive around in a sports car that shouts, 'I'm having a mid-freaking-life crisis at the age of thirty-two.'"

"Oh. Well, I just . . . usually you tell me things."

"I didn't want to tell anyone," he said, his tone grumpier than intended. But he felt grumpy. He felt grumpy that she was ignoring everything that had passed between them.

"Why not? Because heaven forbid we should know you have goals and ambitions?"

"Because I don't want to fail in front of everyone again," he said, throwing the car into gear and roaring out of the driveway.

Now he felt angry and exposed. More exposed than when he'd had his fly open in front of her.

"You've never failed in front of us," she said.

"Really? What do you call the last four years of my life?"

"You got injured, Cade. So badly it looked like you might not walk again. Hell, for a minute there it looked like you might die. I don't think anyone begrudges you this time to readjust and figure out what you want to do with your life."

"But I haven't been readjusting, have I? I've been absorbed into Cole and his plans. His life. And the truth is, I've been okay with that, because I didn't really want to want anything, but now I want to do this. And I feel committed, and he wouldn't give me the chance."

"He's a control freak."

"Damn straight."

"And you're a pain in the ass."

"Huh," he said.

"Well, you are. And the two of you together are a very poor combination. It's like this big alpha-male, there-can-only-be-one thing. You're like two stallions in the same pasture."

"Stallions?" he asked. Well, maybe she would acknowledge the fact that they'd just had sex.

"Yeah. With the testosterone and the cranky. You need your own space."

"And now I'm in your space," he said, testing things a little.

"Yeah, well, I suppose. Though, Davis hasn't been around."

"You think he just skipped out?" Cade asked. "Without even bothering to try one more time?"

He looked at her out of the corner of his eye, just long enough to catch the frown that turned down her lips. "No."

"Yeah, because if you think Cole and I are stubborn assholes, we don't have anything on Davis. He's stubborn. And pissed, because he thinks we just beat him."

"What's his deal, anyway?" she asked. "A sudden fascination with my body isn't likely."

Cade didn't know about that.

"And a sudden fascination with this hunk of dirt for the sake of it seems unlikely too."

"Well," Cade said, "ranch land is scarce, and if he has his heart set on Silver Creek, he's basically going to have to get established ranch land, unless he wants to tangle with the county over zoning and permits. He probably figures that since no one is selling, his best bet is to try and convince people to."

"I got that much figured out, actually. I guess what I don't get is: Why Silver Creek?"

Cade shrugged. "Why not, I guess."

"I guess. But he skeeves me out."

"And you were about to say you didn't need me around because we hadn't seen him in a few days."

"That's not what I was going to say."

"Like hell."

"Well, I did think that maybe you didn't need to stay at the house."

"Oh, honey, I do," he said. That brought to mind the situation back at Elk Haven, and he very much wanted to stay away from it.

He sneaked another peek at her and saw that she'd narrowed her eyes to evil, glittering slits.

"What?" he asked.

"Don't 'honey' me."

Oh, sure, don't "honey" her. Right after they'd had sex she was going to put an embargo on the word "honey."

"Sure thing, sweetheart," he said, because he wanted to needle her. Her and her sex-denying ways.

"That either," she said. "I'm not one of your buckle bunnies, Cade Mitchell."

"I never said you were." He gritted his teeth and tightened his hold on the steering wheel.

"Honey." She snorted. "Sweetheart. I have a name, you know."

"Yeah, I know it. I've known it more than half my life. Excuse me for giving you an endearment or two."

"You don't normally do that."

"Oh, that's it." He pulled the truck off the road and threw it into park. Killing the engine, he whirled to face Amber and was treated to very large, very round eyes. "Stop acting like nothing happened. It's childish to the point of ridiculousness. You're going to act like *nothing* happened? I'll tell you what happened if your memory is failing, *baby*."

"Cade, don't."

"No, Amber, you don't. I haven't touched a woman in

four years. Four years. But do you know what's worse? Having sex with a woman on a breakfast table and her going on like nothing happened. Better to just be celibate than to thrust my back out giving you an orgasm and have you act like nothing happened."

Her cheeks turned deep pink, a vein that ran from her hairline down through her eyebrows standing out. "What's the alternative?" she exploded then, her voice shrill, her hands flung wide. "To sit here and do a postmortem on the ill-advised sex that we had?"

"It's better than you running off to the bathroom and acting like all you did was sit and eat your damn bacon."

"You led the charge on that, Mitchell," she said. "You were the one who turned around with your fly done up and asked if I needed a ride to the hospital like you hadn't just screwed me near to death on my grandfather's table."

"I didn't know what else to say. But I didn't actually plan on *never* bringing it up. I think you did."

"So? This is the other option. Great, now it's out in the open. This morning we had sex. I went down on you last night. I broke sixteen years of friendship in one fell swoop of drunken skankiness."

"You weren't drunk this morning."

"No," she said, her chin thrust out, her jaw set.

"And I don't think you were skanky."

She let out a heavy sigh. "Look, I don't know why this all happened. If I could take back one thing in my life . . . Actually, it would be Greg Jones, not you, but if I could take back two things, it would be that ill-advised high school encounter, and this one."

"Well, damn, you sure do know how to stroke a guy's ego." He chewed on his next words for a moment before he decided, *To hell with it*, and spit them out. "You're a lot better at stroking his cock."

"Fuck off," she said, putting her hand on her forehead and glaring at the floor.

Regret grabbed his throat and shook hard.

"I'm sorry." And he was. He was just confused and pissed,

and he hated admitting he was confused, because men weren't supposed to be confused about this kind of thing.

But then, men weren't supposed to go having sex with their best friends either. At least his best friend was a woman; that made things a little simpler for him than it would be for some men in his situation.

At least he wasn't also questioning his sexuality. Just the most important relationship he possessed outside of blood ties.

"Look, Amber—" he started.

"I'm not in the mood to look at you," she said, her voice a growl.

"Fine, don't. But listen. I haven't felt like a man for the past four years. If you asked me what I was before the accident, I would have said, 'A man and a bronc rider.' And when I had the accident, which . . . wasn't even an accident . . . I lost one of those things. Then I discovered I didn't feel much like the other one anymore either." He rested his forearms against the steering wheel and leaned forward. "Then you . . . you touched me last night and I couldn't say no. Dammit, Amber, I know I should have told you no, but I couldn't."

"Technically you did," she said, her voice muffled. "I just didn't listen."

"Then you ignored it this morning . . ."

"I was hoping you didn't remember! I was embarrassed. Good Lord, Cade, I attacked you. I demanded you let me give you a—"

"I know. But it's not like I was too broken up about it, okay?" He shifted in his seat. "So, anyway, this morning when you didn't acknowledge it, I was pissed because . . . you stole my moment of feeling like a man again. You gave it to me, then you took it back. And . . . I didn't mean for things to go that far, but once I touched you, I couldn't stop myself."

"We've both had a lot of celibacy," she said, her voice scratchy.

"Way more than our share."

"And I guess that makes sense. Last night I was just really sad and . . ."

Amber looked down, her face hot. She didn't like the

explanation for any of this. She didn't like where the conversation was going. She didn't like the idea that he'd done that with her because it made him feel like a man. Because that kind of meant she could have been anyone.

But then, the alternative was that he wanted her, which made her feel warm and fuzzy in some regards, but also terrified the hell out of her. Because that would change their friendship, and the bottom line was she didn't want their friendship to change.

That was what she'd decided when she'd gone into the bathroom. When she'd scrubbed her face, and other places on her body, and tried to erase the evidence of their sexual encounter.

She'd decided that they couldn't do this. That they couldn't have this between them. That they couldn't have it hanging over them.

So she'd purposed to come out and act like it was nothing. Cade had started that game, after all. But now that little reprieve was over.

And the truth was ugly and painful. And it made her feel like she was being scrubbed raw.

But her own version of the truth wasn't any better.

"I was feeling really sad," she said. "I . . . I mean, I haven't done that in a long time, but that used to be my preferred method of coping."

"Sex?"

"Yeah. Because . . . because life is hard, and it's less hard when you can pretend you feel close to someone."

He frowned. "We are close."

"I know."

She could tell Cade didn't like her reasoning. She didn't really like it either. But the alternative was admitting that she'd been seriously lusty for him for . . . a lot longer than she even wanted to admit to herself, and that it had gotten increasingly intense in the past couple of years.

"Let's just . . . look, it happened," she said. "No denying it, it happened. And it won't happen again. We were both in a bad place, and hey, maybe it . . . helped something?"

"Helped some things," he said, snorting.

"Physically speaking? Yeah," she said. She wasn't going to add insult to injury by implying he'd been anything less than satisfactory. Because oh, hot damn, he'd been the best sex of her life by a wide margin—it was almost like what she'd been doing before hadn't even been the same activity.

But then, that was the difference between a sixteen-year-old and a thirty-two-year-old, she imagined.

More convenient excuses for why ten minutes of utter heaven on a kitchen table with Cade had been the best thing to ever happen to her since she'd put peanut butter on Oreos for the first time.

Actually, he was so much better than peanut butter on Oreos it wasn't even funny.

No wonder women had swarmed him like a cloud of locusts back in his rodeo days. And his high school days. At least after he'd lost it to the bartender and she'd spread it around that he was the hottest thing on two legs Silver Creek had running.

All those stories . . . they hadn't been hyperbole.

And heck, she'd had a reputation back in the day too. Sure, guys were often douchey, but the bottom line was, her sexual performance and prowess had been highly praised.

It stood to reason that she and Cade would be combustible and compatible.

They were both excellent in bed. On couch. On table. Whatever.

A slight hiatus had added no shame to their game, clearly.

"So . . ." he said. "I guess we say thanks for the orgasms and move on?"

"Orgasm," she said. "For me. You're one up on me."

Heat flared in the depths of his dark eyes and she looked away. Because now she felt like she could read his X-rated thoughts in detail, and she did not need that. "Fair enough observation," he said.

"And it will stay that way."

"Yeah, I agree."

"Because there's no reason for us to go there again. We're

both adults. It doesn't have to be a problem," she said, talking over her own uncertainty. She wondered if he bought her BS. She sure didn't. "We'll just sort of . . . draw a line under it."

"And put a gold star on it," he said.

"Yeah, okay. And we'll call it done. It happened; we can't take it back. No reason to regret a nice time, right?"

"Right."

"But there's no reason to repeat it either, because . . . well, the awkward. And because it already made us fight."

"Absolutely."

"I care about you, Cade," she said. "I don't have a lot of people left in my life. My grandma is dead, my grandpa . . . even if he recovers, I don't have much time left with him. I have you, and your family, but mainly I have you. You're my best friend. Nothing is worth compromising that."

"I feel the same way."

"So . . . the sex happened. And it won't happen again," she said.

"That's the summation."

"Great. Start your engine, gentleman. I need to get to the hospital and see my grandpa, and you have that bison appointment."

Cade let out a long breath, then turned the truck engine back on. "Okay. Let's get on with it then."

And she knew he meant more than just the day. But with life. With their relationship. What had happened . . . happened. But it was over, and they both agreed it didn't need to happen again.

So that was settled. Good. She was so relieved.

And if she kept saying that over and over, she might start to believe it.

CHAPTER

Eleven

Nicole didn't know what brought her back to the mercantile. She blamed the tractor. The little mini-tractor that she had sitting on the nightstand by her bed at Elk Haven.

She also blamed the fact that she still felt totally lost in Silver Creek, and for some reason, John had made her feel a little bit less so.

Things with her family were . . . complicated. Cole was great, if a little obviously uncomfortable with the whole thing. Lark and Kelsey were warm to a degree that made her feel a little twitchy, and Cade was . . . not around.

Because he was being completely, unashamedly self-indulgent over the weirdness that had become all of their lives.

She envied him a little. She envied him more than she was mad at him, to be honest. Because he knew it was a little bit of a freak show and he seemed to have no compunction avoiding it. She, on the other hand, felt obliged to stick it out, since she'd been the one to instigate contact in the first place.

She would really rather hide.

So she was hiding in the mercantile instead of in her little Portland apartment.

"You're back. I thought you might have skipped town."

She turned and her stomach did a little tightening thing, her heart lurching forward into her sternum. Holy cats, he was attractive. She just wanted to stare at him.

She didn't often make time for staring at men. She didn't often make time for men, period. The more disgruntled she became about her family situation, the less time she seemed to have for them. Yeah, she had trust issues out the ass. She knew that.

Which meant it had been . . . wow, *ages* since she'd been on a date. Longer since she'd done the dirty with a guy.

Okay, she knew exactly how long it had been since that had happened. Her last boyfriend, who she'd made sure was very committed. Not just to her, but to condom use. And she'd taken her birth control pill religiously, along with said condom use.

She just needed time to trust a guy before she went to bed with him. Call them daddy issues, or rather, nonexistent-daddy-who-had-made-her-unintentionally issues.

She would never be that woman. Stuck holding some man's kid. She would never be that woman who slept with a married man without knowing he was married. She had to know a guy very well before she could get naked with him.

Which was why she'd only slept with one guy.

But whatever.

And she didn't know why John and his beard were putting sex on her brain quite so much. Because he was a) a stranger and b) too charming for anyone's good. Which meant she should want nothing to do with him.

"Nope. I have not skipped town." She was starting to wonder why.

"I see. And has Cade Mitchell succeeded in seducing you?"

Her cheeks heated, a twist of nausea cramping her stomach. Ew. "Uh, no."

"I had to check. Only because I would like to seduce you. Now, Cade having seduced you already wouldn't necessarily be a deterrent, but I just wanted to know if I was headed for a fistfight or not. Also not necessarily a deterrent."

"Nice to know. But Cade has barely spent ten minutes in

the same room with me. So no worries. Also, we're blood relatives, so unless that's how you hillbillies get down over here, I don't think there's going to be any seducing going on."

"Holy shit. You're a Mitchell. I would never have known. You're . . ."

"A Peterson, actually. I don't have the Mitchell name. And I have more tattoos than most of them too."

"And piercings?" he asked.

She clicked her tongue ring against her teeth. "Maybe."

She knew guys liked the tongue ring. No guy had ever been able to take advantage of her tongue ring. Because the piercing had occurred post-breakup.

Heat flared in John's eyes, and she could tell he knew of tongue-ring benefits. Well, too bad for him. Because . . . stranger. And she was all cautious.

"Interesting. How many tattoos?"

"I'm not telling. But does this count as one?" She held out her arm and displayed her full-color sleeve. Waves and koi, and a chain of mythological creatures that wound their way from her wrist to her shoulder, where a woman sat on the edge of the beach and looked down at everything.

Looked at all the adventure she wasn't having.

She was very like Nicole in that way.

"How long did that take?" he asked, his thumb skimming over her forearm, leaving a trail of fire in its wake.

"A while," she said. "Anyway, no one gets to see all my tattoos. Some are very . . . personal." She didn't know what little devil had inspired her to say that. The same one that had spurred her into clicking her tongue ring, she imagined.

"Then I'll make that a goal," he said.

"What?"

"To count every single one of them. Up close and personal."

Amber was dreading going back to the house. She was dreading Cade coming to get her. But she didn't think she could stay in the hospital much longer either. She'd drifted around all the hospital for most of the day, absently holding a can of Diet Coke until it turned lukewarm in her hands.

Her grandfather woke up a couple of times, but he seemed fuzzy and disoriented. And he hadn't been able to talk.

Her eyes felt scratchy from all the tears she wouldn't let herself shed, and her throat ached like it was being squeezed from the inside.

Like she was being squeezed from the inside.

If one more person said "wait and see" to her today, she was going to pick up one of the plastic waiting room chairs and hurl it through a window.

She knew it wasn't their fault. They couldn't read the future. But she wanted them to. She needed them to. Every time a new nurse or anyone in scrubs had come into her grandpa's room today, her heart had stopped.

And she'd just waited for the next words out of their mouth. Afraid they would change everything. Afraid they wouldn't. That they would either say something catastrophic, or that they would say there was a terrible mistake and there had been no stroke, and her grandpa was actually just sleeping.

Neither of those things happened.

All anyone said was "Wait and see."

By the end of the day she was sick to her stomach from trying to eat hospital food and failing, and from that damned lukewarm Coke.

The phone in her pocket buzzed and she scurried out to the approved cell phone portion of the waiting area. She bounced back and forth on the balls of her feet when she saw that it was Cade, then tapped the green rectangle on the screen.

"'Sup. You bisoned, or what?"

"Uh . . . I'm informed. Are you ready to go yet?"

"Yeah. Just let me run back and tell him bye?"

"Of course."

She turned and flashed her badge at the guy who was sitting at the door that barred the waiting area from the ICU. He nodded and opened the door. She tiptoed down the hall and down into her grandfather's room.

He was asleep still, his chest rising and falling slowly and steadily. That, at least, made her feel better.

She crept in and took his hand in hers. It was rough from all those years of hard work. And it still felt so strong beneath hers.

He was her family. The first person to accept her when she came to Silver Creek, a busted-up foster kid with a plastic bag filled with old clothes and a heart filled with hurt.

She'd known this would happen. That one day, mortality would catch up with them all. But she'd been very happy to have that day as a distant idea in the future. Staring at it was a very sucky reality.

"I'm going to go home now. I spent the day here with you. Just so you know." A tear slid down her cheek and she wiped it away. Crap, she hated it when she cried. There was no point in crying. But she was doing it a lot lately.

Freaking life and its badness.

"And I'll be back tomorrow. Cade is at the house still. Keeping me safe from villains and spiders." *But not from himself.* "So you don't have to worry. He's taking care of things. Like he does. Good night." She squeezed his hand and turned and walked out of the room, the ache in her throat intensifying as more tears started to form.

By the time she was out in the waiting room again, two gigantic tears had rolled down to the center of her cheeks. Cade had come in to meet her, and she paused and looked up at him. He looked at her, his posture still, his expression that of a man who felt utterly helpless.

And then he moved, tugging her into his arms, against his chest, his hand cupping the back of her head. "I'm sorry," he said, his voice rough.

"Me too." She buried her face in his chest and inhaled his scent. And more tears rolled down her cheeks. It wasn't fair. None of it was fair. She wanted to burrow close to Cade and beg him to never let her go.

She wanted to be skin to skin with him, none of these layers of clothing between them. She wanted to press her face against his chest, feel his chest hair and heat on her cheek. And maybe that was weird, but she didn't care.

She just felt like it would make things better. But the sucky thing was, it wouldn't. It would make things worse. Because she would never be able to just lie next to him. She would want to touch him. And kiss him. And then she would want him inside of her, because it would be the only way they could be closer.

She pulled away from him, trying to shake off the bout of insanity that had gripped her.

It was a hug from a friend. And the sex from that morning was why he'd looked stiff and awkward before giving it to her.

And she was abusing his gesture of goodwill by sniffing his woodsy scent and giving in to sexual fantasies.

No more. No more. They'd gone there. And really, who was all that surprised? Everyone undoubtedly assumed they'd already done it. As much as they generally acted like friends of the same gender might, the fact remained that he was a hot guy and she was a woman of reasonable attractiveness, so . . . so . . . she'd forgotten where she was going with the justification, but she felt it was all safely justified.

But it was also in the past. There would be no more. Regardless of how good he smelled. Or how sad she felt.

"Okay, I'm ready. Tell me about your bison stuff."

He walked ahead of her, his eyes on the ground. "Well, I think I'm going to buy up part of his herd. He's looking to downsize, and . . . I'm looking to buy some bison."

"I imagine they're a little hard to come by."

"Apparently not, since I found these guys easily enough."

She opened the door to his truck and climbed in at the same time he did. "Okay, true enough. So what else?"

"They're a lot more agile than they look. Which, they look like lumbering mountains of shag carpet, so I guess that's not too descriptive. But basically, they can jump like sons of bitches and they can plow right through barbed wire without ever feeling it. So I need special fencing. High, strong. Everything on the ranch will have to be replaced."

"Do you have the money?"

"Let's just say I'm glad I sold the sports car, but yeah, I have it."

"Lots of work though."

"Yep. And it will take time. But this is my full-time job now. Bison ranching. And preparing to become a bison rancher."

"I'm sorry, it's a really funny word. Bison."

He turned the engine on and faced her, arching one brow. "Really?"

"Yes. Bison. Cade Mitchell, bison magnate. I like it."

"Or, that crazy-ass Cade Mitchell. He's turned into a bison man."

"Bison man?"

He lifted a shoulder. "Like a cat lady but with bison."

A laugh exploded from her lips, a combination of the hilarity of the image and the stress and weirdness of a day that had started with an orgasm on a table and ended in the hospital.

"Oh my gosh! That's the funniest damn thing." She leaned forward and clutched her stomach, hooting like a deranged owl. "I'm imagining people dodging you in the grocery store because you have bison hair stuck to your sweater and reek faintly of musk and hay!"

"You're a psycho, Amber; you know that, right?"

"Do they have canned bison food at the grocery store?"

"Probably not . . ."

"You need little rub posts for your bison. And you can put bells around their necks so you can always hear them coming."

"Amber, did you sneak booze into that can of Diet Coke?"

"No." She wiped her eyes and sat up. "No, I've just completely lost my mind"—she giggled again—"because today was without a doubt the weirdest day on record."

"Okay, I grant you it was weird on all fronts."

She hiccuped. "Sorry. I'm really not drunk."

"No, I know," he said. "Are you okay?" He maneuvered the truck onto the main highway and headed back toward the ranch.

Her stomach knotted up tight, making it harder to breathe, everything sore now because of the tension and because of her laughing fit.

"Yeah," she said. "I think so. I mean . . . my grandpa is resting comfortably and he might recover. So I guess that's the best it can be right now. I mean, barring a miracle. But I gave up on those a long time ago."

"Did you?"

"Well, yeah. Some people have miracles. I had a plastic bag full of all my earthly crap, so you tell me how many miracles you'd believe in if you had that experience?" She leaned her head back against the seat. "I used to pray for a miracle. For a family. For someone to love me. My mother couldn't do it. My dad never even met me. He never wanted to. Then I came here. And I had my grandma and grandpa. That felt a lot like a miracle. But . . . miracles are supposed to be easy. And perfect. And nothing about coming to Silver Creek was easy. Not so much because they were hard, but because I was."

"I remember. You were a scrungy, angry-looking little thing."

"I already had two lifetimes to your one. I don't even know how we got to be friends. I was . . . well, me. And you . . . you were this sweet little virgin country boy. You reeked of wholesomeness and innocence."

"That all changed, didn't it? Then I found out how badly life sucked too, and . . . it was just good I knew you. Because you seemed to know how to handle it already. You were just . . . unaffected by it all, and you showed me that I could deal with it."

"That's called cynicism, Cadence. Glad I could pass some of that on to you."

"I think I would have gotten around to it eventually, all things considered. What with losing my mom and finding out my dad was a gigantic dick."

She let out a long breath. "We all get around to it, don't we?"

"The cynicism? I don't know. Maybe. Maybe we don't. Lark seems to have made it through unscathed. Cole even seems to have come out the other side pretty decently."

"Ah, don't worry, Cade. I'll stay here in effed-up-ville with you. I'm comfortable here."

"Are you?"

"Hell no, I just don't know another way to be."

"Well, that's comforting."

"Why?" she asked.

"Because I can't figure it out either, and if it seemed easy to solve for everyone but me, I'd start questioning my sanity."

"You should anyway," she said, propping her feet up on his dash. "Bison man. Which could also be a superhero name, by the way. The costume would probably suck."

"You don't think it could be cool? Like a modified Batman costume? But made to look like a bison?"

"Would it have the nipples on the rubber suit, like in that one Batman movie?"

He shrugged. "If you can't show your nipples off, what's the point?"

"There's very little point at all. Your nipples are your best feature."

And that killed the flow of conversation. Mentioning your best friend's nipples after having sex with him twelve hours earlier was, apparently, a bad move.

He cleared his throat. "Thanks."

They rode on in stiff, uncomfortable silence. She watched the places on the dark road his headlights lit up, keeping an eye out for deer loitering on the peripheral, getting ready to jump out in front of the truck. It was an important job. Way more important than keeping up the conversation. So there.

Cade didn't want to hit a deer tonight, she was sure of that. So she devoted her concentration to that task. And of course didn't spot a single one.

Stupid deer. They honest to goodness had no consideration for anyone else.

They turned onto the familiar dirt driveway that led down to her grandparents' house. It hit her right then how often she thought of it as her grandparents' house. And not her house. Even though she'd lived there since she was fourteen.

Something about it had always made her feel like a visitor.

It wasn't her grandpa or grandma's fault. She realized—her stomach feeling unsettled as they pulled up to the front of the house—that it had something to do with her.

Something to do with her unwillingness . . . her inability . . . whatever it was . . . to believe that anything could possibly be permanent.

What a weird revelation to have today. But then, today had been weird, so why not? Why not a little deep, personal insight with her personal trauma and her oh-so-ill-advised sex? Why. The hell. Not.

Cade killed the engine and got out of the truck, and she just sat there, looking at the empty house—looking at it sitting there cold and empty.

Feeling weirdly like a stranger to it.

Maybe it was just because her body felt like a stranger to her too. And so did her feelings. Everything just felt wrong.

She waited until Cade had gone into the house, then she opened the pickup door and hopped down into the dusty driveway, big, sharp chunks of gravel shifting under her shoes.

She breathed in deep. The air smelled like the dirt they'd just kicked up driving in: exhaust from the truck, overlaid with pine. That at least felt familiar.

She walked up the steps and sat on the chair there, stretching her legs out in front of herself, trying to get a grip on her rioting emotions.

After about twenty seconds, she gave up, and she just let herself cry. She tugged her legs up and held on to them like it might help her hold herself together.

She wanted to go hug Cade again, but she was pretty sure she'd squandered that right about the time she'd undone his belt buckle last night.

She let her head fall back against the wooden chair rail with a thunk. It hurt. She deserved it. She'd screwed up her life. Well, no, life had screwed itself up, and she'd decided to go play in the shit-storm.

"Brilliant move, Amber. Brilliant move."

CHAPTER

Twelve

Amber woke up to the sound of boots on the front porch and a crick in her neck. She lifted her head and winced as her vertebrae cracked.

Then her expression turned completely sour when she saw the man who belonged to the boot sounds.

"I've got a shotgun in my house and I am not afraid to use it," she said, meeting Jim Davis's eye.

"You don't need to go making threats, darlin'."

"Says the man on my porch at"—she squinted at the gilt edge of sunlight around the mountains—"about six a.m. for the second time in a week. A man who, I believe, was told to stay away."

"Heard your grandpa was sick."

"Thought you'd come try to take advantage of me while I was vulnerable? Oh, you're right. I don't have any reason to worry." She stood up. "Actually, I damn well don't, because I don't do vulnerable. But you know what I do? Target practice. Get the hell off my porch."

"Where's your man?"

"Probably sleeping. But I don't see what he has to do with this. This isn't his house. It's not his porch. And it's not his ass in danger of getting peppered with buckshot."

"Take it easy, little lady," he said.

"I know you did not just 'little lady' me, you asshole."

"With your grandfather out of commission for Lord knows how long, you're going to want to think about my offer. Your position with the bank is looking pretty tenuous, and I talked to my contact there. If I push hard enough, foreclosure might become an issue for you."

"I know there's a process for that, dumbass. They can't just take my house."

"Oh, sure, maybe not. But things happen with paperwork all the time. Mistakes are made. Protocol is broken. Don't you read the news?"

"Get off my porch," she said.

The door behind her swung open and a shirtless Cade came storming out. "What do you want, Davis?"

"Trouble in paradise?" he asked.

Cade flicked Amber a glance, then turned the full force of his rage-filled expression onto Davis. "Are you here for anything more than a cordial visit? Because if this is still about selling, the answer is still no. This is turning into a bad Western movie over here."

"I was just telling Ms. Jameson here that I have contacts at the bank."

"Real interesting. So do I. I'm a Mitchell. Our blood is in the woodwork of this town. And I'm going down today with a big payment on the mortgage and a business plan. I'd say if you want to pull weight with the bank, go ahead and give it a try. But you won't get anywhere."

"I'll take that bet, Mitchell. Count on it." Davis tipped his hat and turned on his boot heel, walking back down the steps and to his truck.

"I don't know how I slept through the truck engine," she said. "I'm not sure how I managed to sleep out here, actually. It's frigging cold."

"You slept out here *all night*?" he asked.

"I didn't mean to, but yeah. Also, I hate that he takes you so much more seriously than he does me. You come out here all macho and grrr and he backs well off. I threatened to shoot him!"

"But you wouldn't."

She snorted. "You don't think I would, Mitchell? Have you met me?"

"Well, it would take a serious offense. I'd turn his face to pulp with my fist for a lot less."

"I just resent the fact that your involvement is needed. He's a villain and a sexist."

Cade laughed. "Couldn't that all fall under one heading?"

"Your point is taken." She arched her back, listening to more bones pop. "I think I'm getting old. Sleeping in odd positions didn't used to hurt this bad."

"Why were you on the porch? You know I would never . . . You know I wouldn't force myself on you, right? I get that what happened on the table yesterday was abrupt, but you seemed like you wanted it and—"

"Oh . . . shit. Cade. No, of course I know you would never hurt me! Good Lord, man. I've spent more nights drunk and generally out of my gourd with you than I can count. And you've never once touched me, or tried anything with me at all. I'm the one who pushed things the other night, okay?"

"But yesterday . . ."

"I wanted it. I hope that was clear by my ecstatic yessing. It's not that. I'm not afraid of you. I was . . . I was just sad. So I sat down out here for a while because . . . I liked the way it smelled."

"You liked the way it smelled?" he asked, his brow arching slightly.

"Yeah. Best smell in the world." Except for Cade's skin. And she'd decided against smelling him again, so the great outdoors had won.

"What about it?" he asked.

"It's home, Mitchell," she said—such a permanent word.

One she felt slightly phony using. One that made her ache. "Don't you smell that?"

He shook his head. "Nah. I don't give a lot of thought to home."

"Because you've always had one."

"Because the one I had was too hard to live in sometimes," he said, his voice rough. "Because I like being on the road better. The smell I like is the arena dirt."

"Arena dirt?"

"Yeah. It has a smell to it. When it's laid down, and after the horses and bulls have been kicking it up. The air gets all thick and heavy from the sweat and adrenaline, the dust that's kicked up. That's home to me. And I don't have it anymore."

"I'm sorry, Cade."

"Why are we all melancholy this morning?" he asked.

"Uh . . . because there's not much else to be lately? Because your leg is busted and my family is busted?"

"Thanks for the reminder," he said.

"As if you needed it."

"Not at this hour of the day."

"Hurts in the morning?"

"Yeah. Particularly after . . ." He cleared his throat.

"Sorry." She winced.

"No, don't be sorry."

"Is this ever going to not be weird?" she asked. "Are we ever going to not be weird now?"

"I imagine the weird will go away. We had sex for what? Ten minutes? We've been friends for sixteen years?"

"Something like that. On all counts. I didn't time the, uh . . . you know."

"That means all the years of . . . well, not normal, per se, but of . . . typical friendship we've had, will have to win in the end."

"You're an optimist, Cade. I didn't realize."

"Neither did I. So, you're a cynic. What do you think?"

She put her hand on her chin and tapped her fingers. "I

think we're doomed to drown in the weird awkwardness, but that's just my theory."

"I don't like your theory."

"It's just a theory. Maybe we'll get un-weird."

"I'm going with that."

"Cool. So, what about this bank run?"

"I can't make it for a while. It's early, you know? I had to get up early to save your little butt, do you recall?"

"It didn't need saving."

"Whatever. Either way, I'm up."

"Also, my butt is not little."

He stared at her, hard, tension suddenly visible from his jaw down his neck. "I have noticed that, actually."

She blinked and tried to ignore the heat in her cheeks. "Well, yeah. I'm sure. So the bank?"

"Do you work today?"

"No, this is my unofficial weekend."

"Hospital, breakfast and then the bank with me. What do you think?"

She took a deep breath. They could do this. It wouldn't be weird. They would spend tons of time together until everything felt good and normal again. That made perfect sense. "I think it sounds great."

By the time they made it to the bank, Cade noticed people in town were being increasingly odd. Someone had actually congratulated them when they'd left the diner, and by the time they were done at the bank and had moved on to the mercantile to place an order for fencing, they'd gotten congratulated four times.

"What the actual hell?" Cade asked.

"People are excited about your bison?" Amber asked, shrugging.

"I somehow don't think that's it."

"What else could it be?"

Then they bumped right into Delia, Amber's boss.

"Amber!" Delia shrieked, pulling her into a bosomy hug. "Congratulations."

"Hi," Amber said, giving Cade a sideways glance.

It was almost funny to Cade, because he knew Amber was about as huggable as a cactus on most occasions. And the fact that she was currently being squeezed like a very reluctant cat was amusing.

But he was back to the being concerned about why.

Then Delia smiled at him, her dimples deepening before she grabbed him too and pulled him into a squishy hug. "Both of you! Keeping secrets."

"Uh . . ." Cade looked at Amber, who was staring at him with wide, blank eyes. "Well, you know. Sometimes things are better when they're secret."

Logically, he knew he was not being congratulated for his performance on the kitchen table yesterday morning. But it was the only thing he could think of.

"I know, I know." Delia grabbed Amber's left hand. "Where's your ring?"

"Ring?"

Delia gave her a look that plainly said, *I do not suffer fools*, then continued, "Well, Jamie from the bank came into the diner today and she was talking about how Cade came in and paid all the missed payments on your grandpa's mortgage and got a small-business loan because he's revamping the ranch."

"What? Isn't that confidential information?"

Delia waved a hand. "What happens in the diner stays in the diner."

"We're not in the diner now," Cade muttered.

"I just didn't realize things had gotten official between you two."

"Who said they had?" Amber asked.

"Amber, come on now. A man doesn't take on a project like that unless he's making things permanent. Anyway, I'd heard that you moved in last week, Mr. Mitchell. Ain't you a dark horse?"

Cade cleared his throat. "We were as surprised as anyone."

Delia winked. "Keep me posted. See you tomorrow, Amber. And you better have yourself a ring."

Delia opened the door back onto the main street, the bell above swinging back and forth, signaling her exit with a cheery sound, which was about right for the older woman.

"A ring?" Amber said, rounding on him.

"Hey," he said, raising his hands. "I didn't say anything. You know how people are."

"So they just assume we're getting married?"

"Congratulations," John said, walking into the room and behind the counter. "I hear you're getting married."

Amber stared at him, slack-jawed.

"Yeah," Cade said, not in the mood to dispute it. Why? They were living together. They were doing so in hopes of discouraging Davis from harassing her, so what was the point of denying this particular part of the rumor. "No date set though."

Amber sputtered.

"Go look at aprons, baby," he said.

She growled. "I might go look at castration implements if you keep that up."

"It's kind of funny," he whispered.

Her dark eyes narrowed. "Your funny bone is broken."

"You need anything, Cade?" John asked.

"Fencing. I've got everything written down here." Cade pulled a folded piece of yellow legal pad paper out of his pocket and handed it to John, who read it and nodded.

"Got to special order."

"I know. But I've got some time."

"So," John said, heading back behind the counter and taking his position behind the computer, his focus on the screen, "how are you related to Nicole Peterson?"

Cade about choked. "What?"

"Nicole Peterson. She's been in a couple of times. Last time, she mentioned you were related."

"What'd she say?" Cade asked, feeling cagey. And grumpy. This was the other complication with Nicole Peterson being here. All those secrets he'd spent all those years protecting the Mitchell family legacy were going to shatter all over everything.

Everyone in town knew the Mitchells. And now everyone would know that they were really dysfunctional and screwed up, and not at all the perfect family that people had always believed they were.

And then . . . well, then what had been the point of any of it? Of keeping quiet all that time. Thinking about his mom and dad and feeling sick. Feeling like he knew the worst thing in the world but that his life depended on keeping it to himself.

At least, life as he knew it.

He'd distanced himself from Cole, from Lark, from everyone but Amber, in the interest of keeping it quiet.

And now . . . everyone would just know. Everyone would know that his mother had been cheated on. That her husband hadn't loved her enough to keep it in his pants.

Everyone would know that his dad, a man so many people had admired—himself included, until he'd had the blinders ripped away—was just a gigantic asshole who'd cheated on his wife and left a lover in the lurch with a child.

Left his kids with gambling debts and enough emotional baggage to fill the cargo hold of the *Titanic*.

But there was no avoiding it. Because whether or not he was ready, Nicole was here. She was being accepted by his siblings and she was, apparently, chatting up the townspeople.

"She's my half sister," he said, the words scraping his throat raw.

John's eyebrows shot up, and he paused his work at the computer. "Your what?"

"My half sister. Doesn't every self-respecting family have secret siblings lying around?"

John shrugged. "Wouldn't know. Though, all things considered, I imagine I do." The man's father had run off when he was only a kid, so Cade was sure he probably did. "But I've gotta say, I didn't expect those kinds of skeletons in your closet."

"My dad's closet," Cade said, "not mine."

Though the sinking feeling in his stomach reminded him

that his closet wasn't exactly clean at the moment. And more than that, that he feared he was more like the old man than he wanted to admit.

"Fair enough. I was just curious."

"Why?" Cade asked.

"Curious is all."

"Right." Cade examined the other man, unable to stop the growing suspicion inside of him. John had a reputation. The guy was a first-class dog when it came to women. Almost as bad as Cade had been back in his glory days, if you could call them glorious. At this point, it was hard for him to remember.

But either way, when it came to John and women, Cade expected the worst.

"Curious for a very specific reason," Cade said.

"And you care?"

"Hell yeah, I care."

"Why?"

"Did you or did you not hear the word 'sister' in there?" Cade growled.

"Oh, Cade, put your hackles down," Amber muttered. "Just order your fencing."

"I'll take the fencing without the questioning about a close family member, thanks," Cade growled.

"Fine," John said. "I don't need to talk to you about her. I can talk to her."

"Like hell you will," Cade said.

"Cade," Amber snapped.

"Amber," he said, "don't help me."

"Use your energy on your own piece of paradise, Mitchell," John said. "Looks to me like you need it. Your fencing is ordered. It'll be in next week. I'll give you a call."

"Fine," Cade said, stalking out of the shop.

Amber was following him, her toes on his heels. When the door shut behind them she let out a feral growl. "What the eff was all that?"

"Which part?" he asked, gripping the bridge of his nose. "I mean, there is a list of WTF to choose from."

"Uh, all of it," she said. "All of it. Engaged? And you were growling at John like he was an intruder and you were a . . . guard dog. I don't even know. And why did you let Delia think we were engaged?"

He dragged his hands over his face. "Why not? I mean, really, why not? We're doing this thing. We're living together and trying to keep Davis away, so why not? I'm on the ranch, we're working on a business thing and you know that people are going to assume . . . isn't it better to have them assume in a way that will get back to Davis in a way that might benefit us if he's asking around?"

She crossed her arms under her breasts, and he was powerless against the need to watch the motion it created in her body. Because hot damn. And that just made him even angrier. Because he should be over it. He should be able to stop ogling her like an asshole.

But he couldn't. So there that was just another little pile of awful to add to the day.

He was still obsessing about Amber's breasts.

For some reason, a completely insane memory hit him, from somewhere in the ether of his screwed-up brain. A conversation he'd had with Cole.

Women are just people, Cade. People who are worth getting to know.

People with breasts. Which means it's rare to make friends with one just to be friends with one.

And Amber?

I knew her before she had breasts, so she doesn't count.

I'm sure she'd love to hear that.

She won't.

Oh yes, such big denials he'd made about caring about her breasts.

Ha. Ha.

"And why did you lose your crap with John?"

"That was not me losing my crap," he said, thankful for the distraction from her body and from his wayward thoughts. "I think you recall me losing my crap just a couple of weeks ago in the bar. I recall punching someone out."

"Yes, I do recall that. But you know what I mean."

"Fine. Because Nicole is my sister and he just wants to nail her."

"I didn't think you were ready to deal with the Nicole-as-sister thing," she said.

"I'm not," he growled, opening the door to the truck. "I am not at all. But people are going to know now. She's here and people will know, so I have to claim her, right? The whole town is going to know about my dad. And John wants to nail her before I've even figured out where she fits into my life."

"I don't really see what the nailing has to do with you."

"You wouldn't," he said, climbing into the truck cab, not at all sure what he meant by that last jab.

"What is that supposed to mean?" she asked, getting in after him.

"I don't know," he said.

"If that was a subtle dig at past promiscuity . . ."

"You know me better than that."

"Do I?" she asked.

"Yes. You damn well better. I have never tried to make you feel ashamed for anything you've done. Just like you've never shamed me for anything I've done. That's not how we are. We're a no-judgment zone, unless the other person needs an intervention. That's how we work."

"Maybe I'm not sure how we work anymore," she muttered.

"We're going to Elk Haven," he said. "I need to talk to everyone about the fact that John knows now, which means everyone will know. And I need to warn Nicole about him."

"I'm pretty sure she can take care of herself."

"Let me do what I can do, Amber. Please."

"Fine, Cade," she said. "Whatever you need to do."

Amber felt more than a little nervous walking over the Mitchell threshold, all things considered. Considering Cade was, at this moment, the very definition of going off half-cocked. Considering the town assumed they were engaged.

Considering they'd just done . . . things, and their relationship had changed. And considering she was feeling very vulnerable because of her grandpa, and because of the things.

Even so, she was here with Cade because . . . when wasn't she with Cade?

"Hey, is anyone around?" Cade shouted when they walked in, then made his way over to the coffee bar. He grabbed a hot chocolate packet, and she had to smirk a little bit.

He was just cute sometimes. And he would hate that she thought so, but he was.

Kelsey came out of the kitchen with Maddy on her hip. "Hey," she said. "I just got a call about you."

"Interesting," Cade said, putting his hands on his lean hips and looking around. "Where's Cole? More importantly . . . where's Nicole?"

"If you're here to be a jerk, Cade, I'm not going to tell her to come in," Kelsey said, her stance defiant. "I've long been an advocate of yours, and an excuser of your occasional surliness. I love you to pieces, and you're definitely the brother I never had. But I will knock you flat if you hurt this girl, so help me."

"I'm not here to hurt anyone. I'm trying to prevent hurt, in fact," he bit out.

"First, I want to know what the heee"—she trailed off and looked down at her daughter—"eck is going on with the two of you."

Amber stared at Cade. It was his lie at this point. And it was his job to impart their engagement news.

"We're getting married," he snarled. "I need a beer." He abandoned his hot chocolate packet.

"Congratulations?" Kelsey framed it as a question as Cade stormed past her and into the kitchen.

Kelsey looked at Amber. Amber shrugged.

"Oh, don't give me that," Kelsey said, frowning.

"What?"

"You're worse than he is! I need details. I need one of you to look . . . happy."

"I feel more like I've been run over by a truck," she said.

Kelsey snorted. "Yeah, you're engaged to a Mitchell man, all right."

"Lucky me," Amber said, heading toward the kitchen.

Kelsey followed, and they both froze when they saw Cade standing there, looking at Nicole, who was sitting at the little breakfast table in the corner with her fingers curled around a mug.

"Hi, Nicole," Amber said, heading to the fridge and taking out two beers, forcing one into Cade's hand before moving nearer to where Nicole was seated.

"Hi," she said, pushing a lock of board-straight, dark hair behind her ear.

"Where is Cole?" Cade asked.

"I'm right here." Cole walked into the kitchen, taking his cowboy hat off of his head and holding it down at his thigh. "What's up, Cade?"

"I just wanted to make sure you all knew that I told John at the mercantile that Nicole is our half sister. Don't know if I should have or not, but I did. So I felt like everyone here should know that the rumor mill is going to start churning around town."

Kelsey cleared her throat loudly and made wide meaningful eyes at him.

"Oh, yeah," Cade growled, "and we're engaged."

"Wait . . . what?" Cole asked.

Amber felt guilty. She didn't really see the point of lying to Cade's family, but Cade was leading the charge, and she had a feeling that—somehow—this was all linked to male pride and his masculinity and things that she had no business undermining.

"We're getting married," Cade said, twisting off the top of his beer and grimacing, probably around the time he realized it was not a twist-off cap.

"You seem thrilled," Cole said.

"That's not what I'm here to talk about. I'm here to talk about Nicole, and the fact that this means everyone in town is going to know our sordid family secrets."

Nicole's cheeks were pink, and Amber felt increasingly

sorry for her. "It's not your fault, Nicole," she said, her voice soft. Because she knew what it was like to be the interloper. The unwanted one. The one who was just crashing the party.

A guest in her own house.

"I know it's not," Nicole said, meeting Cade's eyes.

"I know it's not too," Cade said. "But that doesn't change the fact that this is a . . . thing for us. Because the Mitchell name means something here, and if you're going to be here, we're not hiding the fact that you're our . . . you know."

"You can't even say it, but you don't want to hide it?" Nicole asked. "That doesn't make sense."

"Sorry, I missed this part in the *When Life Gives You Lemons* handbook," he said.

"Happy to be a lemon in your life, Cade."

"It's not you, specifically," he said. "It's what this means for . . . hell, Nicole, do you know I knew about you . . . I was sixteen when I found out my dad was cheating on my mom and I had to keep it a secret. I've been keeping it a secret for so long that having the evidence of it all out in the open isn't something that I'm really ready to deal with."

"I get that," she said. "I get that this has a bigger reach than I initially appreciated."

"And I wanted everyone here to realize exactly where it's reaching at the moment," he said.

She narrowed her eyes. "Why did you tell John?"

"You know John?" Kelsey asked.

"Yes," Nicole said. "I've been in his store a couple of times. We talked."

"That's the other thing," Cade said. "He's a man-whore, and I want you to stay away from him."

"Excuse me?" she asked.

"He's asking after you. I don't like it. That's why I told him you were my half sister. And I told him to back off."

She stood up. "I'm sorry, where the—" She cast a sideways look at Maddy. The little girl was holding on to her dad's knee now. "Where the heck do you get off telling a guy he has to back off of me? Maybe I don't want him to back off. You can't act brotherly only when it suits you. That's stupid."

"You don't know him."

"You don't know me!" She flung her hands wide, then slapped them down on her thighs. "Sorry, but you don't. You don't know what I like, what I might want . . . anything. And you have no right trying to make decisions of any kind for me."

"I'm keeping you informed," Cade said. "I'm not deciding anything for you."

"Yeah, I'm sure."

"Okay," Cole said. "Everyone calm down."

"Who isn't calm?" Cade asked.

"No one is calm," Kelsey said.

"And you're way out of line," Cole said to Cade.

"I'm out of line? What the hell, Cole? I am not a child in this family. I don't play second fiddle to you just because I was born two years later."

"If you don't want to be treated like a kid, don't act like one, Cade. I don't know how many times I have to tell you."

Kelsey moved across the kitchen and swept Maddy up. "I have a feeling the language is about to get adult in here," she said, walking out of the kitchen holding her daughter.

Amber wished she had an excuse to leave too.

She didn't especially want to witness Cole and Cade's inevitable explosions at each other. And that was the thing—it was inevitable. Cade had been shoved down and pushed into second-fiddle position, something Amber didn't think Cole had done on purpose. But it had happened. And for a while, Cade had allowed it to happen. Because he'd been in a fog, or something, since his accident.

But the past few weeks, or months, really, considering he'd been planning the bison thing, considering he'd sold his sports car to make it happen, he'd seemed to be waking up. He wasn't just a walking one-liner anymore.

He was a man who had goals. A man who wanted to achieve them.

She could respect that.

But it didn't mean she wanted to watch him and Cole duke it out.

"Where do you get off, Cole? Where do you get off telling anyone how to live their lives? I've watched you make a hell of a lot of bad decisions. Your first marriage being a classic example. I watched you about lose Kelsey because you were being a dick. And still you act like your word is law."

A vein in Cole's neck looked very seriously in danger of bursting. "Is that your version of it, Cade? That's convenient. I seem to recall you ran off to join the rodeo and left me to deal with everything. Left me to deal with how Dad was when Mom was gone. Left me to raise Lark while you were off—"

"That isn't fair," Cade said. "And you know it. You needed the money. I've poured more money into this place than I even care to count. I might not have been here tucking her in at night, but there wouldn't have been a bed to tuck her into if I hadn't been out counteracting Dad's gambling. He knew. He *knew,* and he took my earnings to help bail him out. To buy them a house," he said, gesturing to Nicole. "You want to talk about how irresponsible I am, Cole? You were just plowing the damn fields without a clue about what was going on around you. I knew the whole story. I was the one who was trying to keep things together without uncovering just what a prick Dad was. Without letting our family fall apart."

Cade backed away, his expression fierce, and continued. "So fine. Stand there and tell me how irresponsible I am. But I'm the only one who really knew what saving this legacy meant. Easy for you to make decisions that undermine that. Easy for you to assume you've earned the control because you were here. But you have no idea how much I've carried you over the past decade of your life. No. Fucking. Idea." He grabbed Amber's hand, and she looked down at Nicole, who was sitting there staring straight ahead, her cheeks red, then back at Cole, who looked like he was ready to hit something. "Come on, Amber," he said, starting to lead her from the room.

"Cade," she said.

"No. I'm done. If he wants to wake up and realize he's not the only person who's held all of us together, fine, we can talk. If anyone wants to pull their heads out of their

asses long enough to deal with the fact that all of this, her"—
he gestured to Nicole—"will have fallout that we have to
figure out how to deal with, then they can call me. I'll pick
up the phone."

Amber let Cade lead her out of the house. She held on to
his hand, tight, his heat and strength enveloping her hand.
She felt sorry for Nicole. She felt sorry for all of them. But
her place was with Cade. It always had been.

When they got to the truck, she turned to face him.
"Cade—"

He cut her off. He planted his hands on either side of the
truck door and leaned in, his mouth crashing down on hers.

It took her brain a second to catch up to what was happening, but her body was already responding. Her fingers
tangled in his short, dark hair, her lips parting beneath his.
She kissed him with everything she had in her.

Once her brain caught up, she kissed him even more
fiercely. With all of the years of longing that were inside of
her. With everything she'd ever fantasized about in the dark-
ness of her room. With the desire she'd had for him when
she'd been young—desire she'd stuffed way down deep because she knew she could never go there. And the desire for
him that had been growing in her ever since.

Desire borne of thirteen years of celibacy. And sixteen
years of knowing him without ever touching him until this
past week.

He slid his hands down the truck, then moved them to
grip her hips, blunt fingertips digging into her flesh. She
arched against him, and he took the hint, pressing the length
of his body against hers, the truck hard against her back, his
cock hard against her hip.

This was not in keeping with their pact. But then again,
it wasn't really against it, seeing as this wasn't sex, and they
weren't talking about the sex.

They were just kissing. Deeper and hungrier than she'd
ever kissed anyone in her life. But still just kissing.

Just kissing that made her feel like the heavens had opened
up and let fire rain down. Just kissing that made it seem like

the world had tilted on its side and everything was completely, irreversibly different.

But just kissing.

He pulled away from her suddenly, forking his fingers through his hair, swearing violently. "I'm sorry. Let's go."

Amber was still pinned to the truck. She was pretty sure she'd melted into the paint job.

She blinked rapidly, trying to figure out what had just happened. If she was still standing upright. If the world around them still existed, or had been consumed in a fiery hellstorm of doom.

Important things.

Then she realized she was just standing in the driveway of Elk Haven Stables, having just made out with her best friend. Probably with an audience from the house.

And the world still seemed to be in working order. Which was weird, because she didn't feel like *she* was in working order anymore.

"Okay," she said, stumbling a little bit and jerking the truck door open. Her legs felt like jelly and her heart felt like it was currently on a mission to pound its way through her chest. Or at least turn her breastbone into dust with the effort.

She sat down in the truck and thought, dimly, that their entire day seemed to boil down to this. Her world getting turned wonky, then Cade driving them somewhere else where it all turned wonkier.

"I'm sorry," he said again.

"I'm not bleeding. Don't apologize."

"I'm still sorry," he said. "I just am."

"Yeah, well, it's about time someone listened to you, Cade."

"I guess it's about time I said something."

Thirteen

"I'm in a bar drinking before six p.m. I feel like you should be here too. Encouraging me to make bad decisions."

Nicole stared down at the number on the business card John had given her. She really hadn't expected to call it, but here she was. Calling. From The Saloon. She was drinking a PBR and feeling generally pissed at the world. And it might just be John's lucky night as a result.

She could always just go home. Sure, she had three more weeks of leave left. But that was time she was supposed to be spending getting to know her family, and at this point, she was thinking three weeks at home staring at her ceiling would be more fun.

But then, wild sex with a stranger would be better than that.

"I even know who this is," John said, his voice warm and tempting, even over the line. "I feel like I should get extra points for that."

"Get your butt over here and you'll get a beer for that. That's better than points. That's tangible. Alcoholic."

"Oh, look, my shop's closing up early tonight and I'm headed down the street."

The mercantile was only three small-town blocks down from the bar, and it only took John five minutes between the time she hung up the phone to the time when he walked through the door.

"Hey," he said, sitting down next to her at the bar. "What's the deal?"

"What do you mean what's the deal?"

"Where has all the cagey surliness gone? Why are you now calling my number and inviting me down here to drink with you?"

She lifted her beer. "Because today sucked."

"Whatcha drinking, baby?"

"Pabst."

He snorted through his nose. "Okay. That's not a hard-day drink, if you ask me."

"Well, it's my drink of choice."

"Jack," he said to the bartender, then turned back to Nicole. "That's my hard-day drink."

"You're going to get drunk at six in the evening?" she asked.

"Hell no. I only ordered one."

"Oh . . . badass," she said, taking another sip of her beer. "You, sir, are clearly a badass."

"Clearly."

The bartender set a shot glass in front of John and gave him a coy smile while she poured some amber liquid into it. Nicole immediately felt territorial and edgy. Not that she had a reason to feel that way. But she did.

"Thanks, Chrissy," he said, tossing her a wink.

"So," she said when the bartender, Chrissy, was out of earshot. "My brother says you're a man-whore."

He snorted into his glass and a spray of whiskey shot up and sloshed over the edge. "Did he?"

"Yep."

"Let me guess . . . it was Cade."

"Yes, it was."

"Well, that's sort of the pot calling the kettle black."

"Oh," she said, feeling slightly disappointed. She was hoping for some outraged, pearl-clutching denial or something.

"I had a little run-in with him earlier."

"And I had one with him a little later. Hence . . . this."

"What did he say?"

"He was trying to warn me away from you. Because you're trying to get into my pants. And defile me. Something about my maidenly virtue. Am certain."

John snorted again, sloshing more liquid over the side. "Warn me before you talk," he said, brushing the drops of liquor off his beard. He cleared his throat. "You don't really have . . . *that*."

"What?"

"Maidenly virtue."

"Oh . . . gosh, no. But you know, he's acting like I can't make any decisions for myself. Like he has a clue what's best for me, and he doesn't even know me. We have the same dad: That's the beginning and end of it. That doesn't give him any magic insight into me, or me magic insight into him."

"You're snarky like he is."

It was her turn to snort. "Well, who isn't snarky?"

"Lots of people."

"I'm from Portland. Everything is done with a touch of irony and snark."

"Even your beer-drinking."

"Shut up."

"You're a little hipster, aren't you?"

"Labels are too mainstream," she said dryly.

He chuckled and raised his glass back to his lips. "Yeah, that's what I thought."

She looked at his hands. Strong, masculine hands. At his forearms, so muscular and perfect. Just the right amount of dark hair on them. His flannel sleeves, rolled up to the elbows. He was so hot. And yeah, so maybe he was a man-whore. He certainly hadn't denied it. But maybe she didn't care.

She'd always been so cautious. So safe. One lover. A boring job. The only interesting thing about her was the tats and piercings. And they were easy to hide. They were all for her. All things that she did to make herself feel a little more like the badass she wasn't.

"So what's the deal with you Mitchells? Exactly."

"Mmm," she said, lowering her beer bottle. "Not a Mitchell. Not by name."

"But how are you a Mitchell? I mean I know how but . . . surrounding story, please. Why are you just now here? I'm intrigued. It takes a lot to intrigue me. Or maybe not much, since I'm apparently intrigued by tattooed mini-tractor mechanics."

"Tax preparation specialist, if you please." She tapped her fingers on the beer bottle. "Okay, I know minimal amounts about my mom's relationship with Dave Mitchell. I remember him as a man who used to come and visit. I didn't know he was my dad. Not until later. And my mom didn't know his real name. His name was on the housing documents, but I don't think she ever looked at anything. He paid for a bunch of our stuff, bought a car . . . anyway, that's how I found out what his name was. And that he had a family. This was all a few years ago, after my mom died. I didn't really know what to do for a while. Then I made tentative contact, and Cole and I kept in touch . . . for money stuff. Because I was getting leaned on for the old man's debts and . . . anyway." She took another swig. "That's the story. Your standard secret bastard baby."

"Secret all right. Dave seemed . . . like a normal guy. Like . . . not the kind of guy going around making secret bastard babies."

She blew out a breath. "I sort of doubt I'm the only one. I mean, what are the odds my mom was the only special bit on the side? And he stopped coming back at some point, so . . ."

"Shit, that's a can of worms."

"A can of Mitchells!" She hesitated. "Plus, I got a call once."

"What?"

"Just . . . a phone call for a property that wasn't ours. More debt collection . . . shenanigans. For a property in Prineville. So I have suspicions."

"Did you tell Cole?"

She shrugged. "I don't know anything. And any-damn-way, I am not giving the man more bad news." She let out a long sigh and set her beer on the bar with a decisive thunk. "So . . . what do you say we get out of here and count tattoos?"

He snorted whiskey over the side of his cup. "What?"

"I'm sorry. Was I too forward? I would like the sex, if it's on offer. And I was assuming from your recent behavior that it was."

"We haven't even kissed," he said.

"Solid point. But I did just share all my family baggage with you, which in many ways is more intimate."

"Fair point."

"But I guess we'd better see how that works out before we commit to nudity." She stood and leaned against the bar, facing him. "Well?"

He stood up too. "You're sure?"

"About the kiss. And we'll see how we feel after that."

"You sound like you're deciding whether or not you want to order dessert."

"In that case, I demand to see a menu."

He leaned in, his facial hair rough against her face, his breath hot near her ear. "Well, do you like vanilla? Or do you like—"

"Chocolate," she breathed.

"Hmm. Interesting. I think there's no reason for you to choose one thing from the menu."

"No?"

"No. I don't see why you can't have . . . multiple items."

"Oh. I don't think I've had . . . multiple desserts in . . . ever."

"Oh really?"

"And I was always given vanilla."

"We really should kiss before we go deciding how many menu items we indulge in, shouldn't we?"

"Sure," she said, feeling a little breathless already.

He leaned in and kissed her. And a fire spread across her skin, went down deep and burned her down all the way to her core.

It was over too quickly. She wanted it all. She wanted more.

"What did you think?" he asked.

"Good," she said, her voice unsteady.

"You think you want to have the sex still?"

"Oh . . . yeah. I really do. You're like . . . a real live man-whore though, right? Meaning you must have an array of condoms available. Some ribbed for my pleasure, I would imagine."

He cleared his throat. "Yeah."

"Good. Because I am a stickler for safety. I'm also on the pill, as an FYI."

"Good to know."

"I'm paranoid. I think it's part of my charm."

"Sure," he said.

"Are you even listening to me anymore?"

"My brain hit a snag somewhere around the time you agreed to have sex with me. So I'm listening but my attention is compromised."

"Right."

"All my blood rushed south."

She laughed. "Wow. That's a line."

"It's true."

"I'm not used to men talking to me this way."

"Why is that?"

"Because I don't usually open the door for this kind of conversation. I confess, I'm a relationship girl. But I don't want one right now. I just want . . . to make this trip worth it."

"I see. Well, I guess I'd better work hard at making you feel like this was worth it."

"I'm sure it will be."

"I live above my store," he said.

"That is . . . so incredibly helpful."

"Put it on my tab, Chrissy," John said to the bartender, who was, weirdly, still smiling when they left.

"So, she's not an ex?"

"Not per se."

"You've slept with her though."

"Yeah. But . . . it didn't mean anything. She does. She's a good person. I like her a lot. She means something. But . . . the sex didn't."

Nicole blinked, not sure how to process that bit of information. And then she decided it was good. Very good. "That's honest. I appreciate that. I mean, a lot more than you know."

"Really?"

"Yeah, well, I'm a half-Mitchell, as I'm sure you know. And it's because our dad . . . well, he said a lot of things to my mom, and none of them were true. He said a lot of things to me, when I saw him, which was rare, and I don't know if any of them were true either. So I'd rather have you say that. Because it's honest. Because you do what you do, and you didn't lie about it. And you didn't sugarcoat it. You didn't say that she meant nothing and I was special. And I think . . . I think that's a lot more attractive than a string of BS."

"I'm not the best bet for happily ever after," he said, shoving his hands in his pockets. "But I make for a pretty fun evening. And I've never seen the point of false advertising where that was concerned."

"All I want is a fun evening."

"Then you came to the right place."

The walk to John's apartment was a short one, but long enough that Nicole was starting to get epic heebie-jeebies. Because really, only one guy had ever seen her naked. And that had been about three tattoos and several dozen Voodoo Doughnuts ago.

But John was . . . hot. Like, he was so hot. Broad-shouldered, slim-waisted, bearded, flannel-wearing hot, and she just wanted to unwrap him like a very masculine Christmas present.

So the heebie-jeebies just had to chill. Because she was doing this. Because she needed this. She needed to just let go for a minute and forget. To stop worrying and just feel.

And if anything could make her do that . . . it was this man's ass. She just wanted to keep walking behind him.

"Are you checking me out?" he asked, not turning to look at her.

"Oh, hell yes."

"Good. This is off to a good start."

"I think so."

He unlocked the doors to the mercantile, then closed them. "This way." He led her down a back hall and to another door, which he held open for her.

"Chivalry and sex. Tonight's gonna be good."

He turned then, and smiled, then he pushed her up against the wall, firm hands pinning her in place. "Very good," he said, angling his head and kissing the side of her neck. Gentle, his beard scratching her tender skin.

"Oh . . . wow." He moved away from her and went back to the door. "I think your facial hair has better moves than my ex," she said.

"That bodes well."

"I think."

He held his arm out. "After you."

"Oh . . . okay."

They tromped up the wooden stairs and into the loft space. It was dim, and open, tall windows facing Silver Creek's main street.

"This is great. Like, really—" A strong arm caught her around the waist and spun her to face him. Then his mouth crashed down on hers and she stopped talking about the view. Because all she could focus on was John's lips. His tongue. Oh . . . yes.

She chose that moment to embrace her inner vixen. The poor thing had been locked up for way too long.

She put her hands on his flannel shirt, the one that had been driving her freaking crazy since she'd walked into his mercantile, gripped both sides of his collar and pulled hard, sending buttons flying everywhere.

"Oh, wow, that was awesome," she said, leaning in and licking the hollow at the base of his throat, down in between his pecs.

He grunted and pushed his fingers through her hair, tugging hard until she lifted her head and he was able to claim her lips again.

She made a very appreciative noise that she could not be bothered to be embarrassed about, and pushed him backward, propelling them both to the couch that was at the center of the large room.

"Have a seat," she said, whipping her top over her head. She wasn't embarrassed about him seeing her naked now.

He obeyed and she reached behind her back and opened her bra, letting it fall to the floor. "Undo your pants," she said.

He arched a brow and started working his belt buckle. Shit. She was about to see a stranger naked. She hardly knew this guy and she was about to get acquainted with his penis.

Like, intimately so.

He unzipped his pants, but he didn't go pulling his cock out or anything. Which she sort of appreciated. It was her move now.

She knelt down in front of him, her heart hammering in her ears. Her breasts brushed against his thighs, sending a shock of heat and arousal through her.

"I have seriously never wanted a man like I want you right now," she said. "Ever. You are . . ." She put her hand out and rubbed her palm over his cloth-covered erection. "Oh dear Lord, you're huge."

He laughed. "Am I?"

"I've only had sex with one other guy."

"You're not serious."

"No, I am. I am short on male anatomy comparisons."

"Still, if we were doing quotes for an ad, we would just say I was the biggest you've ever seen. We wouldn't add that the comparison pool was with one other dick."

"Sure," she said, "if it makes you feel better."

She pushed her fingertips beneath his shirt and made contact with his skin. Hard-packed abs, a rough sprinkling of hair. Damn.

Then she let her hands drift down to his underwear. She took a deep breath and reached inside, wrapping her fingers around his cock and pushing the waistband of his underwear down so she could see him.

"Oh yeah . . ." She squeezed him gently and looked up at his face. He was a study in sincerity and concentration. For once, it wasn't all bullshit and charm. And it was because of her. "You know what tongue rings are good for, right?" she asked.

"I've heard rumors," he said, his voice strangled.

"Well, let's confirm them." She leaned forward and slid her tongue over his length, and was rewarded by a short curse and a sharp tug on her hair.

"I guess it works?" she asked.

"Why are you talking?"

"Don't you think this is a good time to have a discussion about feeeelings?"

The look on his face was tormented. Like he wanted to yell at her, and also agree and start telling her all his deepest emotions just so she would finish what she started. She got off on the power a little bit; she couldn't lie.

"I'm just kidding. I don't want to talk." She dipped her head again and took him deep in her mouth. She'd never been what she considered an expert on giving head, but honestly, she was feeling so giddy she was just leading with enthusiasm.

Every dip of her head was met with an appreciative groan and a tug on her hair. It was a pretty massive ego boost that a dude who was such a man-whore got off on her skill. Of course, guys got off on just the thought of a BJ, but she wasn't going to think about that.

She was officially not going to think at all. She was just going to feel.

"Okay," he said, tugging her head up. "I have to be done now because . . . I . . . I really really want to have you naked.

There will be foreplay. Later. The second time. The third time, maybe."

"Ambitious," she said.

"Yeah, I'm an overachiever in some ways. You're about to benefit."

"Oh, thank God."

"I have a serious question for you."

"Really?"

"Yes," he said, drawing her up onto the couch and somehow managing to maneuver so that she was beneath him and he was settled between her thighs. "Do you have your tiny tractor on hand?"

"What?"

"The tractor I gave you. If you don't have it, I'll be wounded."

"I do have it," she said, "but I think it's weird that you want it."

"Where?"

"My bag. Over . . . over there." She gestured to the floor about a foot away from the couch.

"I'll be back." He got up and walked over to the bag, tugging his shirt off and kicking his pants and underwear down to the floor. She admired the view. The ass was even better sans jeans. "May I?" he asked, bending over and touching her purse.

"If you don't mind the risk of touching a feminine product."

"Nope." He opened the purse and brought out the little green tractor, then he walked back to the couch and unsnapped her jeans, parting the fabric. He put the tractor on her stomach, the cold metal sending a little shock through her.

He pushed it up, and for some reason, the combination of sexiness and just freaking adorableness put her so close to the edge she thought she'd come if she shifted against his thigh. Just a little bit of pressure, and it would all be over for her.

He let it rest on her stomach while he tugged her jeans down, and her breath hitched when he got them off and stared down at her. At the most private place on her. The tractor hitched too, and tipped sideways, falling over.

"Well, damn, you wrecked my tractor."

"Sorry."

"Don't apologize," he said. "I'm just glad you had it with you."

"Don't imbue the tractor with emotional symbolism."

"I'm a man-whore, remember? We don't imbue anything with emotional symbolism. Just a second." He got up and went back over to his pants, taking a condom out of his pocket and putting it on quickly before rejoining her on the couch. The head of his erection pressed against the entrance to her body and she held her breath, waiting. Desperate.

"No," he said, pushing inside of her, "we don't imbue things with emotional symbolism." He entered her fully and his size, the amazing feeling of being so close to him, made it impossible for her to do anything but just feel. But just breathe him in. "Except for tiny tractors."

And then he started to move inside of her, the feeling beyond anything she'd anticipated, the pleasure a feeling close to pain. It was incredible. Perfect.

He hooked his hand beneath her thigh and pushed it up over his shoulder, going deeper. "Oh my . . ." Her intended blasphemy trailed off as he pushed them both higher, closer. She watched his face, the intensity, the need. It reflected her own. She felt like they were in perfect sync, both feeling the same thing. Both wanting the same thing. She'd never felt this close to anyone before. And if she wasn't so mindless with need, it might have scared her.

But instead of feeling afraid, she clung to John, and raced to the finish with him. And when she fell, he fell with her. And in that moment she was perfectly certain she would never look at a small toy tractor the same way ever again.

"Cade, can we stop?" Amber asked.

Cade looked at her from his position in the driver's seat. "To?" His first thought was maybe she wanted to park. And that made him feel like he was seventeen again. And a horny asshole. But then, when he'd been seventeen and a horny asshole, he'd never kissed Amber.

Today he had.

He had issues, and he really didn't want to go confronting them. He'd confronted enough of them today at his family home, that was for sure.

"I need milk. I just realized we're out. We can just stop at the gas station store."

Okay, for milk. Not heavy petting. That was more normal.

"Fine," he grunted, gunning it until the gas station came into view, then taking a sharp left into the driveway. "Might as well get gas while I'm at it."

He pulled up to the pump and waited for the attendant to come to the window.

"Hey, JJ," he said, when the kid came into view. He didn't

know when that kid had gotten old enough to have a job. JJ was the son of a guy he used to ride with back in the day, and yeah, the other man was a few years older than Cade, but for him to have a teenage son when Cade considered him a peer just made him feel . . . ancient.

"Mr. Mitchell."

That didn't help. "That makes me feel old."

JJ tilted his head. "You kind of are."

"Shut up, kid. Fill it up. I'll pay in the store." He turned to Amber. "I got it."

Better she wait in the car for a minute. Better he get a little bit of distance. Before his head or . . . other parts . . . exploded.

He slammed the truck door shut and, his hands stuffed into his pockets, headed toward the store while JJ got started filling the truck.

Cade pushed the door open and grimaced when he saw another local weed from Silver Creek High working behind the counter. Cade was already in a bad mood thanks to the altercation with his family, and his subsequent truncated make-out session with Amber against the side of the truck.

These kids he'd spotted being not kids anymore, and having jobs, and making him feel his age, aided by the hitch in his get-along and the pain in his back, were not helping.

He looked over in the cooler section and spotted a row of milk. He walked over and opened the door, putting his hand on the half gallon and eyeing the beer that was in the next cold case over. That didn't sound so bad.

Not bad at all.

He took the milk off the shelf and headed toward the beer, then paused at the shelf that was across from the refrigerator.

There was a box of condoms hanging there. Mocking him. A box of twelve condoms, representing twelve potential sexual encounters that he would not be having.

His body throbbed in an entirely different way.

He should grab a pack of beer. And he shouldn't look at the condoms. At all.

Still, he was looking at the condoms. And his heart was pounding hard. Because he was thinking of how it had felt to be inside Amber that morning on the kitchen table. And he was thinking about how it had felt to kiss her, less than a half hour ago, against the side of his truck.

He wanted her again.

It didn't matter what they'd said; he wanted her again. He wanted to lose himself in her. Drown in what she'd made him feel. Because it was the best he'd felt in four years. The most alive.

The most like himself.

He was having some kind of damned epiphany in the milk and condom aisle at the gas station, and he wasn't really sure what to do about it.

Except buy the condoms.

He didn't have to use them. Not tonight. Not with Amber ever. But he hadn't bought condoms in those four celibate years of his. And buying them would feel like moving on. As had his shouting match with Cole.

That had felt like moving on from something even bigger. Something that had lasted even longer. All the polite lies he'd helped his dad keep up.

He could buy beer. And that would be in keeping with the status quo. Or he could buy the condoms.

He grabbed the box off the shelf and walked back over to the counter, making a conscious effort not to limp as he did so.

He set them both on the counter and stared the kid down. He picked the milk up and scanned it slowly, then looked at the condom box and picked it up, a nervous laugh escaping his lips.

"That means you're too young for those," Cade said. And now he felt superior. Being young was overrated.

"Bag 'em," he added. Because he was not walking out to the truck with those in his hand in front of Amber. Because she would assume things. And then he might get killed by a swift jab of her car keys to his neck.

There was nothing to assume. He was buying them

because he was back in the saddle, so to speak. And that was all.

That was all.

Amber's pulse was pounding when they got back to her grandpa's house. To her house. Whatever. She was too nervous to think straight.

And far too sober.

And far too turned on from the kiss Cade had planted on her at the truck.

Far too invested in whether or not he would do it again. And if he did, what would she do?

What would they do?

She wasn't sleeping outside in a chair tonight, that was for sure. And that meant she was sleeping inside. With Cade.

But maybe not with Cade. Or maybe with Cade. She didn't know. She didn't know what she wanted. No, she knew what she wanted; she just didn't know if she should.

Well, that wasn't true either. She knew what she wanted. And she knew she shouldn't have it.

But whether or not she would let herself have it was another thing entirely.

"Don't forget to put the milk away," she said, intercepting Cade when he came through the door, putting her hand on the paper bag he was holding.

"I won't," he said, pulling away from her like she'd threatened to wipe cooties on him.

"I can do it," she said.

"I got it."

"Okay, Cade, just refrain from abusing any of my cheese when you do."

"Is that a euphemism?"

"No. You abused my cheese last time you got into the fridge. You were all agitated and you . . . squeezed it."

"That sounds wrong, Amber," he said, opening the fridge and sticking the milk inside on the top shelf, then closing it, the paper bag still in his hand.

"What do you have in the bag?"

"Nothing."

"Do you have beer?" She gasped. "You have marshmallows for secret eating!"

"No, I don't."

"You do! And you're hiding them from me. And you're going to go eat them without me."

"No," he said, holding it closer to his chest, "I'm not."

"Right, right. You have stealth sugar. I am offended by your lack of sharing. See if you get any bacon in the morning."

She felt good right now. Almost high. Because things felt silly, and like they might just be friends again. Like maybe the kiss at his brother's house hadn't mattered all that much. And like they'd be able to actually move on.

"I don't. I'm going to bed now, Amber."

"It's not even eight."

"Still, I'm tired. Burning bridges takes a lot out of you."

She frowned. "You didn't burn any bridges, Cade. You had a fight with Cole, that's all. It will sort itself out. He's your brother."

"Yeah, I don't know. Maybe it will, maybe it won't. It's hard to tell."

"No, it's not. You're brothers. It will work out."

"Things don't always work out though. And maybe . . . maybe things won't with us. I don't know."

"How can you say that, Cade? You're all each other has. You and him and Lark."

"I have you," he said.

Her throat tightened. "Yes. You do. Always. But he's your family. Lark is your family. You have to make things okay with them."

"I know."

"Nicole is your family too."

"Yeah, I know that too. But like I said to Cole . . ." He let out a heavy sigh and leaned forward, resting the paper bag on the table, one hand gripping the back of a dining chair. "There was a lot going on he didn't know about. Cole is sort of stepping into an alternate reality here. I mean, I know he's known some things for a while, but not anywhere near as long as I have. Cole idolized our dad all through the years when I knew the truth about him. When I was keeping all those secrets to try and keep our family together. I'm dealing with . . . I'm almost dealing with totally different baggage from an entirely different upbringing."

Amber nodded. "You are. You're right. And I can see why Nicole being here, and you having to deal with people knowing the truth . . . I can see why it's harder for you. He made you keep his secrets. He made you feel like it was your responsibility. He—"

"He made me understand why it was important. So things didn't change. So people didn't get hurt. He said . . . He said he knew I was the one who would understand. He knew I would help because he knew I would . . . that I'd get it."

"He manipulated you."

Cade shrugged. "Sure. Maybe. But the fact is . . . well, the facts are the facts. I spent a lot of years being resentful of the woman my father had an affair with. Being resentful of the kid he had. Because they were a part of causing my pain. And I know now that Nicole isn't at fault. But she's wrapped up in it."

"You had every right to be pissed," Amber said. "But eventually . . ."

"I know. Eventually I'll rebuild the bridge."

"Good." She snatched the bag off the table and looked inside before he could stop her, her jaw dropping, her face flaming, when she saw the contents. "Oh."

"Dammit." He snatched it back. "I told you there were no marshmallows in there."

"But you did not tell me there were condoms."

"No. Because they're mine."

"I see." She snapped her mouth shut. Then opened it again. Then shut it. She had no idea how to react. What to think. What to say.

He'd bought condoms. And he'd hid them from her. Granted, not very well, but he'd tried.

Were they for her? And if so . . . what did that mean?
And if they weren't . . .

She felt sick at the thought. That he might already be
thinking of going out and having sex with other women after
they'd . . .

No. She really didn't like that at all.

Not that she really liked the idea of him buying the box
for them either. Because they'd agreed not to talk about it.
Or do it. And yes, they'd kissed, but as she'd rationalized
earlier, that technically did not violate the rules.

The willful purchase of contraception most certainly did.

"Say something," he said.

"I'd rather they were marshmallows."

"Fair enough."

"I'm not really sure what else to say."

"Just let me go to bed."

"With a box of condoms? Alone? Do you know something about male masturbation that I don't?"

He frowned. "I'm sure I do. But this has nothing to do
with that."

"Why did you buy them?"

"Because."

"Because why?"

"Amber . . ."

"For me or for someone else, Cade? That I have to know."

"For me," he said. "Because I feel like I finally moved
on from whatever has been holding me back the past few
years. Because I feel like I'm turning a corner and I saw
them and thought, hell, I should buy them because I
might need them. And I haven't had that thought in way too
long."

"Okay, but are they purely a metaphorical purchase, or
are you planning on sneaking out your bedroom window
and going to a bar to pick a chick up?"

He frowned. "Would it matter if I was?"

"Yes!" she said, without even pausing to think. "Yes.
Because you just . . . you were just with me. And I can
handle needing to ignore it, because yeah, that makes sense.

And I can handle not doing it again. But I cannot handle you actually ignoring it, you know?"

"Not really."

"You can pretend it didn't happen, but you better damn well remember it did. You better still be thinking about it. And burning a little. And not wanting to do that with anyone else because I'm the one on your mind, because . . . because that's how it is for me. And if it isn't that way for you, not even a little bit, I'm just going to be so . . . so mad!"

She was breathing hard, her face hot, her entire body shaking. She hadn't meant to be quite so honest. Heck, she hadn't even realized that was how she felt.

But it was.

Because of course she hadn't forgotten. It had been the single most incredible experience of her life. She was certainly not ready to go and test out her new celibacy break with other men, and if he was ready to do it with other women, she was going to throw something at his head.

Possibly cheese.

"I can't win," Cade said. "This"—he held his bag up and rattled it—"this is a no-win situation for me. If they're for another woman, I'm a slutty asshole who had sex with you and am now looking for other pastures to plow, so to speak. If they're for you . . . then I'm a conniving douche bag planning on seducing my best friend again, even though I promised I wouldn't."

"Which are you? Asshole or douche bag? I want to know."

"I am a guy who thought a box of condoms might be a nice purchase to make along with his half gallon of milk," Cade said.

"Bull."

"What? Men buy condoms for no specific reason. That's why they carry condoms in their wallets. In case of a generic sex emergency."

"So which sex emergency are you planning for? One with some skank, or one with me?"

She was just pissed now. Pissed enough to smack him.

Or grab him and kiss him. Hard. And show him that he didn't want another woman—he only wanted her. She was pissed enough to tear his shirt off and lick his chest. And his abs.

Yeah, she was that pissed.

"With you," he said. "Are you happy? With you. Because I can lie to myself all I want. I can lie to you while I lie to me, but it doesn't change the fact that my cock barely twitched for the last four years." He dragged his hands over his face. "Look, I was the one avoiding sex, okay? I . . . I could have had it. And . . . and I don't even think I've ever admitted that to myself until now. Women were still up for it, but I wasn't. Because I have scars on my body, and I walk with a limp. Because I was afraid I wouldn't be as good. Because if I spent the night they'd see me hobbling around in the morning. Because if my back went out during . . . dammit. Okay, that I couldn't even think about. But . . . with you, I didn't think about it."

"I . . . thank you," she said, frowning. "I think. Are you saying the only reason you could have sex with me is that you didn't think about it?"

"Well, the first time, sure. But this time, because there is about to be a this time"—his dark eyes met hers, and her stomach plummeted to her toes—"I have thought about it. All the reasons why we shouldn't. All the reasons we should pretend it never happened. All the reasons we should never even speak of it, much less do it again. And I don't care. I don't care if it's smart. Or if I should want this. Or . . . anything. I don't care about anything right now except the fact that I want you."

"Then . . . then nothing else matters," she said, her heart pounding in her throat.

"You want to do this?"

"If there were marshmallows in the bag I'd suggest we cool things down and make s'mores. But since there are no marshmallows . . . and there are condoms . . . I think maybe we should make use of what we have."

"That's the pioneer spirit."

"So long as we don't end up dying of dysentery, I'm good with employing some *Oregon Trail* logic."

He laughed and then shook his head.

"What?" she asked.

"I don't remember ever being this turned on and this amused at the same time before."

"Good. Because this should be different. Because . . . look, Cade you and I . . . friendship is the best we have to give." For some reason, saying that made her chest hurt. "But I don't want us to just use each other to scratch an itch either. I could have done that with . . . any guy. I have done that with any guy. It's not satisfying. It doesn't meet the real need. So I'm not going to pretend you're someone else, or pretend you aren't my friend, Cade. You are. And that's why the sex is so damn good. Because you know me. Because I know you. So . . . I want us to be aware of that. In the end, I think our friendship is strong enough to add this to it. And to take it away when we're ready. Don't you?"

She didn't know what she'd say if he disagreed. What he would do. She hadn't planned on saying all that, but then, she hadn't planned on any of this. It was all true, though. She and Cade were wicked screwed up. And maybe someday he would find the right woman. But she wouldn't be his right woman.

He needed someone who knew stable. Someone who wasn't as messed up, or more messed up, than he was.

And she needed . . . She didn't know what she needed.

She didn't want love. She didn't want marriage. But she wanted Cade. And she needed him to want her—and not just for sex. She needed it to mean something.

She was done with meaningless. She was done with using guys to try and fill the emotional well inside of her that was just . . . dry. The emotional well that was her own damn problem, and not something that was going to be fixed by skin-to-skin contact with a guy she wasn't even that into.

But that wasn't what she was doing here. Not with Cade. She actually wanted him. This was rooted in genuine lust and desire—and also, she liked him. This was a first. This was the next stage in her sexual evolution.

This was the opposable thumb of her sex life.

She wouldn't cheapen it, or change it, just to take the easy way out. Just to let them both squeeze their eyes shut and chase an orgasm.

She had a vibrator for that.

Cade was her fantasy. He had been for a long time. And she'd been afraid of that, because she'd been afraid of how it might change their friendship. But now that the horse had left the barn in spectacular fashion, why not let the bastard romp through the daisies a little?

"Amber," he said, his eyes locked with hers, "you're my best friend. And I am well aware that it's you I'm looking at, and talking to, and wanting. Now please take your shirt off before I explode."

She gripped the hem of her t-shirt and tugged it up an inch, and Cade's eyes went down to that little slice of bare skin that was now on display. He was focused on her in a way she'd never seen him focused on anything, all of his attention on her. Her body.

It sent a thrill through her, a different kind of sexual thrill than she'd ever experienced with anyone else. This was desire. This was lust. Pure and wonderful and amazing lust.

She tugged her shirt up over her head and took a breath, her breasts rising in the cups of her nude-colored bra, spilling over the edges.

It wasn't the sexiest lingerie, but then, she hadn't realized anyone would be seeing it. Anyway, judging by the look on Cade's face . . . he didn't care.

"You too, Mitchell. It's not polite to tell a lady to strip down, then not give up the goods."

A smile curved his lips, and he gripped the bottom of his shirt and whipped it over his head, revealing that perfect, muscular body of his.

And she was going to look, because damn, she had permission. She finally had permission to look her fill. They weren't drunk, and it wasn't going to be a speedy, furtive and regretful encounter on the table either.

They were deciding to do this. They were committed to it. There was no rush, because they weren't trying to outrun good sense. They weren't trying to get to the point of no return as quickly as possible.

Although, in fairness, she suspected they'd hit the point of no return somewhere a few weeks back. Not in any one moment; but she just had a feeling it had all been heading this way for a while now.

She didn't quite know when, only that there had been a shift somewhere. Or maybe a thousand tiny ones. And once the last one had locked into place, there had been nothing but the inevitable.

Right at this moment, she was completely okay with that.

"You are so damn sexy, Cade Mitchell," she said, taking a step toward him, placing tentative fingertips on his chest. "Do you have any idea? I mean . . . good Lord, man. Your body should come with a warning label."

"For external use only?"

"I sure as hell hope not."

He blinked rapidly. "You're sure enthusiastic."

"I don't see the point in pretending to be otherwise. I've thought you were hot for a long time. I was celibate, not dead."

"But we're friends."

"Have you honestly never checked out my ass, Mitchell? Be warned, my ass will find a 'no' answer insulting."

"Oh yeah," he said, air hissing through his teeth when she flattened her palm on his chest, "I've looked."

"Have you been checking me out while we were hanging out alone? All this time?"

"When we were in high school . . . I shouldn't tell you this."

"Tell me," she said, leaning in and pressing a kiss to his neck.

"I used to dream about you. I hated the way guys treated you, and I never wanted you to even get a hint that I wanted your body. But in my dreams? I've had you a thousand times, a hundred ways. I've touched you. Tasted you . . ."

"You never let on."

"I was sixteen or so when I first started struggling with it. At the time it was easy to write off, and then train myself not to feel that way anymore. But still . . . still sometimes I dreamed of you."

"Tonight you don't have to dream, cowboy. You want to ride again? Save a horse and ride me." She leaned in and ran her tongue along the edge of his throat, across his Adam's apple.

"That," he said, "is cheesy. It's a cheesy song. It's a cheesy bumper sticker. But when you say it . . ." He gripped her wrist and moved the hand that wasn't on his chest down onto his denim-covered erection.

"Damn, I'm good," she said. She kissed the edge of his lips.

"You are. Lose the bra."

She backed away from him and felt a slight twinge of nerves before she reached around and put her fingers on the clasp. This felt different than any experience before. With Cade or anyone else.

She'd always been comfortable with her body, but she'd never really gone out of her way to show it to Cade. Even during their encounters so far, neither of them had been completely naked.

She released the catch and let the bra fall to the ground, her breath catching as she did so. Cade closed the distance between them instantly, curving his hand around her neck, cradling the back of her head as his lips crashed down on hers, his mouth devouring her.

She wrapped her arms around his neck, and he put his other hand on her ass, urging her to wrap her legs around his waist. And she did.

He wrenched his lips away and stumbled, bracing his hand on a chair. "Shit. No. I can't do that."

"Sorry!" She scrambled down, heat prickling her face. "I'm so sorry, I didn't think, I—"

"Forget it."

"Cade . . ."

"Seriously, let's forget it. I'll survive not being able to carry you up the stairs. As long as it doesn't terminally flip your switch off."

"Baby, you could turn the hose on me and you wouldn't cool me down. Now, I don't recommend it, but I'm just saying. I've been wanting more of this since . . . well, actually, since that night by the fire."

"You didn't get anything out of that."

She cupped him through his jeans and squeezed gently. "Sure I did. I got to taste you. Take you in my mouth. That's a fantasy and a half."

"Do you want this to be over now?"

"No."

"Then stop talking before I come," he said.

A smile curved her lips. "I should have known you'd like dirty talk."

"And I should have known you could give it good."

"Kiss me again, Cade."

He did, softer this time, cupping her face and stroking her cheeks with his thumbs. He bit her bottom lip, gently, then licked it, tracing the line of pain with the tip of his tongue before kissing all along the border of her mouth, slowly, from end to end.

"How's that?" he asked.

"Not enough. We've spent sixteen years not kissing. I think you owe me more than that."

He angled his head and kissed her deeper, his stubble rasping across her skin, his tongue teasing her lips open, sliding against hers. He held her close, her breasts pressed tight against his chest. Skin on skin.

And then she was lost. In his taste. In his scent. This was Cade. So much about him familiar, so much about him, in this at least, new.

When he pulled away they were both breathing hard.

"I think now maybe we'll go upstairs?" she asked. "But I can get there on my own two feet."

He touched her cheek, a strange shadow crossing his face. "I would carry you if I could."

"I know. But you don't have to. We'll just walk together."

She laced her fingers through his and tugged him toward the stairs. She met his eyes and she fought to hold in a giggle.

"What?" he asked.

"You. Me. This. It's sort of crazy."

"The best crazy though, right?"

"Pretty much the best crazy I can think of right now. Though, I warn you, I'm not thinking very clearly."

"I'm either flattered," he said, pulling her in close and kissing her gently, "or insulted."

"Be both—why not?"

"Can you be both?"

"Sure. I'm terrified and excited. So I don't see why you can't meld those two things."

"Why are you terrified, baby?"

"Because"—she blew out a breath—"we're about to make love."

"We did it once already."

"Yes, but this feels different."

He nodded slowly. "It is."

"Okay then. Shall we?"

"Not without these." He picked up the paper bag again.

"That would be a travesty," she said. "Since they started the whole thing."

"They deserve their moment of glory."

"They so do."

She led him up the stairs and down the hall to her room. She'd had Cade in her room lots of times, but never for this reason. It made her feel weirdly nostalgic. For a simpler time. Except they'd never had a simpler time, so that weird ache she was feeling wasn't over anything in the past. Just over things she'd wanted and given up on ever having.

Normal had never been in the cards for them.

But at least they'd had each other. Always.

And now they shared this too.

Cade cupped her chin and tilted her head back, kissing

her, and skillfully guiding her back onto the bed, one of his knees wedged between her thighs, his body hard over hers, the mattress soft beneath her back.

"So beautiful," he said, tracing the outline of one of her nipples with his fingertip, before lowering his head and retracing the path with his tongue before sucking her deep into his mouth. "I just want to look at you," he said, pulling away from her, his gaze hot, his breath making goose bumps across her damp skin.

"I wish you'd touch me too."

He gave her a very wicked Cade smile. "Feeling anxious, baby?"

She wrapped her legs around his thighs and rolled her hips slowly, the V at the apex of her thighs rubbing against his cock. "Are you?"

He cursed and lowered his head, his eyes screwed shut. "Not fair."

"No?" she asked, her voice innocent, in contrast with the movements of her body.

He lowered his head and kissed between her breasts, down to her stomach, just above the waistband of her jeans. "I feel like you're one up on me."

"Bullshit, Mitchell. You have two to my one."

"No," he said, "that's not what I meant."

"What?"

"I haven't gotten to taste you yet."

He unsnapped the top of her jeans, then lowered the zipper, slowly. So slowly. Her breath fled completely. From her lungs. From her lips. Possibly from the room.

Rough fingers hooked into the sides of her jeans and panties, and he dragged them down her legs, calluses scraping her skin.

Then she found herself completely naked and open to him in a way she'd never been in front of a man. Ever. He had her thighs spread wide, his hands planted flat on her legs, holding her still.

He took a deep breath, his chest rising and falling, before leaning in and pressing a kiss where his left hand held her leg. She shook, shivered beneath the touch. It was a kiss on the thigh, which should have been . . . nearly innocuous . . . and yet, very much wasn't.

This was a new experience.

High school boys weren't much for oral sex that didn't go their way. And there was something vulnerable about it all, so the lack of it had suited her.

She preferred to be the one going down. The one who was in control.

Her hypothesis regarding this particular act had certainly been right. Because she'd never felt more owned, more out of control, more exposed, in her entire life than she did in that moment. With Cade pinning her to the mattress, an assessing look on his face

But she wanted it this time. If she was going to be like this with anyone, it had to be with Cade. There was no one else she would let see her like this. No one else who would be allowed to hold her at his sensual mercy. Because at least she trusted Cade to catch her if she fell. Trusted him to pull back if she asked him to.

Her lowered his head and took a leisurely taste of her body, starting at her slick entrance and working his way over her clit.

She curled her fingers into the blankets, the other hand going to grab his shoulder. And she was afraid she probably dug her nails square into his skin. But that didn't stop him.

Cole continued to pleasure her with his tongue, and then his hands, sliding one finger deep inside of her while he worked her body with his mouth, pushing her closer and closer to the edge.

Every stroke was white-hot fire. And she craved release. But she also wanted it to go on forever. This pleasure that was almost pain, a hollow ache that demanded satisfaction—but one that she wanted never to end.

He added a second finger, and she flung her arm over her eyes, a hoarse sound escaping her lips, her body trembling.

A deep, rumbling sound came from Cade, a sound a man

might make when he was savoring some rich, decadent dessert. And that pushed her right over the edge.

Her climax hit hard, with the force of a runaway freight train. Speed, heat and destruction, and no way to stop it.

Her internal muscles tightened around his fingers and he swore, his face buried in her neck as she rode it all out. As she waited for her body to stop shaking.

When Cade shifted his weight and withdrew from her, he was shaking, sweat beaded on his brow. "I think we could use those condoms now," he said, his voice rough.

She shook her head. "You killed me, Mitchell."

"I'm going to be the one in danger if I can't finish this," he said, the tremble carrying all the way through his voice. It made her chest tight.

"I don't think I can come again."

"So soon?"

"Ever."

"Don't issue challenges to a competitive man, Amber Jameson," he said, reaching for the bag of condoms, tugging out the box and tearing it open. "Unlike some lesser cowboys, I complete my rides."

The husky promise in his words was sexy, even if it shouldn't have been. At this moment, everything about Cade was sexy.

He got up from the bed and undid his belt and pants, and she watched. And ogled—her internal temperature rising as his clothes fell.

She didn't feel she'd ever gotten a chance to adequately admire the man while sober.

He was spectacular. Hard muscle and tanned skin. Everything masculine and beautiful right there on one body.

Her eyes fell to the scar that ran down his left leg, from the deep groove, showing heavy muscle loss, in his thigh, down to the evil marks around his knee. From the initial accident. From surgery. A mix of both.

It made her hurt for him.

But she knew he didn't want her pity. And pity wasn't what she felt. But she didn't even want him to catch a glimmer of sadness in her eyes, because she knew it was the thing he feared most.

She looked up at his chest, then at his eyes. "You know you're sexy, right?" she asked.

"You think I am," he said. "I don't need to know as long as you believe it." He ripped open the condom packet and tossed the plastic onto the floor, rolling the protection over his length.

She made a noise that felt somewhere between a whimper and a growl.

"What?" he asked.

"I like watching you standing there with your hand on your cock."

"And as much as I like pleasing you, and hearing you say things like that, I'll be honest, I'm a little sick of my hand on my cock."

She dissolved into laughter. "Oh, yeah, I bet."

"So I'll just come over there if it's all the same to you."

"It's even better," she said.

He dropped down onto the bed, kissing her, his hands skimming over her curves. "I have an idea," he said. He reversed their positions suddenly, and she squeaked as they rolled over and she found herself sitting astride him, his shaft against her clit, her thighs on either side of his.

"I know you gave me a hard time about this before, but I think it was a pretty good idea," he said, his hands planted on her hips, his hold firm. Sexy.

She shifted until the blunt head of him met with the slick entrance to her body and she tested them both, teased them both. She was so wet it was easy to guide him inside.

When he was buried fully inside of her, neither of them could talk anymore.

There was nothing but the sound of their breathing, of skin on skin, and the rough, broken sounds that escaped their lips. She established a steady rhythm that was quickly broken by their urgency.

She met his eyes while she rode him, and her chest locked up, pressure building there, making her eyes sting, making her body burn for release. Already she was desperate for another release. But she suspected that another orgasm wouldn't do anything for the pressure around her heart.

But she would take what she could get.

"Oh . . . Cade. Cade . . ."

She found herself flat on her back again, Cade over her, still deep inside her as he thrust hard into her, claiming the control back for himself. And she found she didn't mind at all.

"Amber," he growled, his pelvis grinding hard against her, sending a shock of pleasure through her body, making her internal muscles pulse, tension expanding in her stomach.

"Come for me," he said, his words a command that she had no trouble obeying. The tension in her snapped, breaking the dam that held her together, her pleasure washing over her like a wave.

She shuddered out his name, curling her fingers into his shoulders, feeling his skin give beneath her hold. And then he followed her over, a short curse and her name on his lips.

Then he lay there on her, his weight warm and comforting. She just wanted to wrap her arms around him and hold him close. Wanted to keep him there. And that scared the ever-loving hell out of her.

"I've got to get up," he said finally.

She nodded and released her hold on him, watching as he got up and turned his back to her, tugging the condom off.

She took the opportunity to scope out his butt. Which was an epic sight. And then she let her focus wander up the strong column of his spine. The scars there were the most frightening. All surgical. Clean and methodical. Shiny pink skin that looked vulnerable against the tan, toned skin on the rest of his body.

Lines made by a surgeon's tools, necessary to try and fix the damage done to his back. A reminder that the lasting effects of the accident could be so much worse.

"I can practically hear you thinking over there," he said, tossing her a quick look before he strode into the bathroom.

"And did you hear 'Nice ass, cowboy'?"

"No, I think I heard much more serious thoughts." He

reappeared in the bathroom doorway, both his hands braced on the frame. And he was gloriously naked.

"I was looking at your back."

"Enh," he grunted, and walked back toward the bed, sitting down on the edge of the mattress.

Amber got under the covers and looked at him expectantly. He didn't move.

"Get in bed, Cade."

His eyebrows shot up. "I didn't want to make assumptions. Since sex doesn't mean cuddling."

"Cuddle me, you jackass."

One corner of his mouth lifted and he got under the covers with her, one arm going beneath her, the other over the top of her. He pulled her against his body and she pushed her leg between his thighs, her hands resting on his chest.

He put his chin on her head, his breathing ruffling her hair. Just for a moment, things felt perfect. Just for a moment, she felt like she was in heaven.

"Why were you looking at my back?"

"Your scars."

"I see."

"It's not what you think. I just . . . Cade, when I think about how close we came to losing you it almost kills me. I've lost too many people. I don't know what I would do if I lost you."

"Well, you didn't."

"Yeah, and good thing. But still, when I see it . . ."

"Then don't look. Look at my ass."

"Well, I also did that." She traced a formless pattern on his chest with her fingertips. So weird to touch him like this. Like she had the right to. They'd never touched more than friends should. They'd never crossed that friend boundary.

And now . . . now she never wanted to take her hands off of him, and as long as the all-access touching was allowed, she was going to take advantage of it.

"Are you ever going to try and find who did this to you?" she asked.

He stiffened. "I did try. I was wrong. And I almost ruined Quinn's life over it."

"You didn't do it on purpose."

"And that matters?"

"Yes, Cade, it does matter. And anyway, the guy ended up marrying your sister. I don't think he's particularly sad about how it all worked out."

"Well, anyway, I think my justice hunt is done."

"Why? Because you feel bad about Quinn? Or because you aren't sure you deserve it?"

"What the hell does that mean?"

"Exactly what it sounds like. I'm just wondering if you're not fighting for yourself because you don't know who it is you're fighting for."

"Is this the price I have to pay to see your boobs? I have to listen to your advice?"

"Don't lie to yourself—you always had to listen to my advice. You just didn't get to look at my breasts while you did it."

"That's supposed to make me feel compensated?"

"Yes."

"Okay, fine, it works."

"Does it work enough to make you consider looking into all of it again?"

"I don't think so, Amber. No. It won't make me able to ride again, so really, what's the point?"

She snuggled deeper into his hold. Because she was afraid he might start to pull away. "The point is that whoever hurt you doesn't deserve to be out there competing if you can't be."

They lay there in silence for a moment, his arms strong around her.

"Davis," he said.

"What?"

"I don't know. I think it's weird that he's here. I think it's weird that he wants this ranch. I don't see why he should care so much."

"Property is hard to come by, et cetera."

"Right. Fine. But why else?"

"I don't know."

"He's still able to compete. He was on the circuit with

Quinn and me. He was our other major competition. Though, at this point, some other young bucks have come up in the ranks, and he's still not in the top spot. I reckon he's the kind of guy who's sort of doomed to third place, because no matter who ends up out of commission, he's not a first-place guy."

"Was he your friend?"

Cade paused. "It's funny. I remember something Quinn said one time about that. About how I thought everyone was my friend. He said everyone was competing with each other. No one was really a friend. He was just the only one who didn't fake it."

"That can't be true."

"I don't think it is. I think a lot of us had a pretty genuine bond. But maybe . . . maybe it was partly true. Quinn seemed the obvious guy to point fingers at because nobody liked him. But . . . obviously the person I really had to worry about was someone who went under the radar."

"Like Davis," she said.

"I don't want to go pointing fingers wildly this time around. I still feel . . . It wasn't a good idea the first time I did it."

"Then don't point fingers wildly. But think about it, maybe."

"Think about Davis?"

"Yes. You aren't stupid, Cade. All of this is kind of wildly coincidental, don't you think?"

"Well, Quinn showed up here too."

"To nail your head to a fence post because he was pissed at you. And to nail your little sister. It wasn't a coincidence, and I'd venture to say that this isn't either."

"You raise a good point," he said.

"Is that all I raise?" She slid her fingertips down beneath the covers and stroked his length.

His breath hissed through his teeth. "I thought I was done for the night, but you're making me question that."

"If not tonight, then when?" she asked. She didn't want it to only be for the night. She wanted more. But she had no idea where more of this fit into the friendship.

"Anytime," he said.

"Really?"

"Tonight's not enough. I think we already proved that just splashing around in the water isn't going to do it. Might as well submerge."

"I know I'm wet," she said.

"Shit," he said, laying his head back and closing his eyes. "You might kill me."

"That's just the celibacy talking."

"It's not. Don't belittle it. Don't belittle yourself." He rolled over and propped his head up on his hand, looking at her intently. "You've always been a lot more important than you think."

"Sure," she said, ignoring that damned tightness in her chest. "I'm a legend in my own mind."

"No, baby, sometimes I think you're an ant in your own mind."

She leaned in and kissed him, just because she could. "I'm fine."

"Yeah," he said, "me too. A monument to emotional health."

"And a good liar."

"With a nice ass."

"There is that."

He kissed her, deeper this time, and she could feel him getting hard against her stomach. She threw her leg over his and opened herself up to him, sliding against his length, slick already, creating an easy friction between them.

He grunted and slid his shaft through her slick folds, holding her tight. "Sorry . . . I have to . . ."

"Me too," she said. "Keep going."

He did, sending streaks of white fire through her veins, pushing her closer to a release she shouldn't need, but that she desperately did. More than breathing, she was certain of it.

They rode it out together, until her restraint broke and her climax took hold. Until he froze, gripped her hips hard and spilled over her stomach.

"Fuck," he breathed.

"Yep." She rolled onto her back and stared at the ceiling, trying to catch her breath.

"Sorry," he said, as breathless as she was.

"For?"

"I usually have a little more self-control than that."

"I'm not complaining. Anyway, it's been long enough that there's not a usually for either of us anymore."

"Good point."

Her eyes started to close. "I think we can sleep now."

"We can?" he asked.

"I told you. You killed me."

"I hope you revive in the morning."

A smiled curved her lips. "I'll need a kiss from Prince Charming."

"Sorry. He's not coming. Will Busted Cowboy do?"

She laughed and tightened her hold on him. "That's actually better. A lot better."

CHAPTER

Fifteen

Nicole woke up just as the sun was peeking through the windows of John's upstairs apartment. She hadn't meant to stay all night. But then . . . they'd been . . . active all night, and then finally she'd collapsed with utter exhaustion just before four. And now it was . . . not quite six, per the clock by the bed.

She rolled over and looked at the man sleeping next to her. He was beautiful. A weird thought to have about a rough, bearded man, but it was true.

She'd never been one for flings. Now she wondered why. Last night had been just what she needed. A little cleansing ritual against all the ugly happening at Elk Haven. A little something to make her feel more alive.

More connected with another human being.

Okay, that last bit made her sound sad.

But it was true.

Still, she should maybe try and sneak back onto the Elk Haven premises, or into the diner for breakfast, so she could say she'd gone out early for hash browns or something. Anything other than the truth.

That she'd gone off mad at her half brother and screwed a guy just to exert her independence over said half brother.

She blew out a breath. That was a lie. She'd done it because she wanted John. Calling it anything else was just trying to pretend she hadn't put her lustypants on and given in to her inner hedonist with wild abandon.

Well, that's what she'd done. So there. She'd been a woman given to her passions and no logic whatsoever. No logic all over John's massive, open-plan apartment that essentially had only one room besides the bathroom, which had made it easy to experiment with different positions and surfaces, from the kitchen counter to a very conveniently heighted couch.

Every item on the dessert menu had been had, so to speak. And she was feeling fine.

The admission, even if it was a private one, offered a certain amount of freedom. Because she'd always been a little afraid of her baser, more animal-type lusts.

Because she hadn't wanted to be stupid like her mother. She'd never wanted to feel passion for someone, because that left you hurt, high and dry and with a kid you couldn't take care of.

But she'd had no-strings-attached nooky, and she felt fine. Better than fine.

She crawled out from under the covers and started a search for her clothes, doing her best not to rouse her partner.

She found her panties across the room and dangling off of a drawer-pull on his dresser. Wow. The enthusiasm had certainly been intense.

She'd dressed once after their encounter on the couch, just because walking around his place naked hadn't seemed right. But her clothed state hadn't lasted long.

She righted her undies and slipped them on, turning her back to the bed and tugging the fabric into place over her butt.

"Too bad. You stole my show."

She whirled around and saw that John was watching her, turned over onto his stomach in bed, his face resting on his folded hands.

"It's not showtime."

"Looks like it from here. And also . . . five tattoos."

"You counted?" she asked.

"Yep. The back of your neck, your sleeve, the one on your stomach that goes down to your thigh, that delicate little quote on your foot. And . . . my personal favorite." He got out of bed, completely naked in all his leanly muscled glory, and crossed the room. She swallowed hard, trying not to show just how undone she was.

He knelt down in front of her and tugged the waistband on her panties down just a little bit. "The bird."

There was a little bird right there. Well below her panty line.

He leaned in and kissed her there, and she shivered. "I got that after I broke up with my ex. Freedom or something."

"So no other guy has enjoyed this?"

"Like the tongue ring, you're the only one."

He smiled. "I'm a lucky bastard."

Not as lucky as she was.

But she didn't say that. Because that would be admitting that this had been . . . special. Mind-blowing. The best sex ever and more. He'd already said he wasn't a happily-ever-after guy and she, whether she wanted to be or not, seemed like she wasn't a happily-ever-after girl. Nothing in her life had ever indicated otherwise, anyway.

That meant she would just have to enjoy their night for what it was.

"I really have to go."

"Why?" he asked. She suspected he was now tracing the outline of the bird with the tip of his tongue, but she couldn't be sure.

All her brain could process was *OMG, HOT.*

"Because I don't want everyone to see me leave. And I don't necessarily want my family to know I went home with you."

"Why is that?"

"Because. Some things are best left . . . secret. I'm not hanging your panties out my car window to announce my conquest."

"Your conquest?" he asked, pausing in his work on her tattoo.

"Um . . . hell yes, *my* conquest. I owned you."

"Well, I won't say that's not a little bit true."

"It's a lot true."

"Either way," he said, "I don't see why you should want to hide it."

"You don't?"

"No. Are you ashamed?"

She blinked. "Well, yeah. Aren't people supposed to feel guilty about going home with a stranger?"

"I don't. Anyway, I don't really consider us strangers."

"Why is that?"

"I know your name," he said, giving her a smile that made her joints get loose.

"That hardly constitutes as non-stranger interaction, John," she said, using his name pointedly.

"You don't think? You did tell me about your family. I think maybe that means I'm not a stranger."

"I think I could talk to you better if you weren't on your knees in front of me."

He stood and shrugged. "Suit yourself."

It didn't really suit her. She'd rather have him on his knees. But there was no time for that nonsense. Even if it was very sexy nonsense.

"I just need to go." She bent and picked up her t-shirt, then found her bra, and set about to getting dressed the rest of the way. Her pants were her last discovery—they were in the kitchen sink. She turned them right-side out again and wiggled into the skinny jeans as quickly as possible.

"I'm going to call you," he said.

"Eh. You don't have my number." She pushed her hair back off her face and put her hands on her hips.

"You'll give it to me."

"Will I?"

"Abso-damn-lutely."

She growled, then walked over to his fridge and took the pen off of the magnetic notepad that was hanging there, scribbling her number down quickly. Then she gave him the side-eye. "Why do you have one of these? That is awfully organized for a bachelor."

He shrugged. "Guess I'm organized."

"Is it for phone number collection?"

"Nope. It's for groceries. I don't usually ask for numbers."

She snorted. "I guess that makes me special?"

He nodded slowly. "Yeah. I guess it does."

Something inside of her shifted, then everything tightened, like her body was desperately trying to hold all her insides together and in place. "Well. Cool. Then if you actually call the number I will feel extra special. But for now I really do have to go." She grabbed her purse off the edge of the kitchen counter, then looked down at the space of floor in front of the couch, where her tractor sat, overturned. "And, um . . . I will take this. Don't read anything into it. No imbuing it with emotional shit."

"I'll do my best," he said dryly.

"Okay, so . . . bye."

"Yep. Bye."

She snatched up the tractor and stuck it in her purse, then turned away from him, holding her hand out to the side, skimming the exposed brick on the wall with her fingertips.

Last night had been different. Last night had changed something in her.

It was too bad it wouldn't change things with her family.

She clomped down the stairs and took the exit that went straight outside, not the door that went into the mercantile. Then she shoved her hands in her pockets and started to walk toward the bar. She'd left her car in the parking lot, but that was fine. Many a drunk person had done so, she imagined. It wouldn't raise that many eyebrows.

The diner was busy, she could see that through the window, and she decided to go with "early a.m. diner breakfast" as her alibi, seeing as she was hungry anyway.

She pushed open the door and lingered in the entryway, and her heart stopped when she saw Amber, busily waiting tables. She doubted Cade's fiancée was her biggest fan, since Cade wasn't.

But then, Amber surprised her by smiling. "Go ahead and have a seat, Nicole."

"Anywhere?"

"Yep." Nicole selected a table, and Amber came over with a carafe and filled the white mug with coffee. "Oops. You don't want decaf, do you?"

"Nooo."

"Great. I'll be around in a second to take your order. Sorry I can't chat, but . . . are you doing okay?"

Nicole tucked her hair behind her ear and looked down at the menu. Her face was all hot and she didn't really know why. Well, okay, she did.

"Yeah, fine."

"Good. I'll be back by."

"Thanks." Nicole took a sip of her coffee and hoped that the unaltered brew would clear the fuzzies from her brain. Sadly, she didn't think they were entirely lack-of-sleep fuzzies. She rather suspected they were sex fuzzies, which was something she had no idea how to clear out.

Because she'd never had an experience like last night's.

She took a longer sip, until she nearly gagged on the bitterness, then gave in and added some cream and sugar.

"Is this seat taken?"

She was about to say no when a masculine hand dragged the chair out from the table and a masculine entity sat in said chair. At her table.

Her "no" response would have been contingent on his taking the chair to another location. She was not looking for a breakfast companion. She was clearing fuzzies.

But now the man was sitting.

"I was actually saving that for a giant-ass plate of bacon," she said, deadpan. "I'm hungry."

"I won't take up much of your time. But I'm curious, because I've seen you around, and I know you're staying at Elk Haven."

"I will neither confirm or deny, stranger who is sitting across from me."

"Jim Davis," he said, holding his hand out. "Not a stranger now."

Her exchange with John played back through her mind, and she knew that she really did owe him an apology for the stranger thing. Because John wasn't a stranger. They'd been skin to skin. She was comfortable with him. Comfortable enough to be naked with him.

She didn't even feel comfortable with a table between her and this guy.

This stranger screamed danger. Stranger danger, even.

She shook his hand, reluctantly, and then grabbed hold of her coffee cup and held it close to her body.

"I'm just curious what your connection is with the Mitchells."

"Why?" she asked. It was starting to become public knowledge that she was related to the family. Well, John knew. Though she had a feeling he wouldn't be spreading it around. Even so, the secret didn't seem to be sacred anymore.

"Because it's obvious you have one. I've got a contact at the bank, and I was able to see some records. For some reason, your name pops up with theirs on a few things. And your mother's name."

Her cheeks flamed, rage burning in her chest. "My mother's dead." She didn't know why she said that. Why that was the thing that came out. But her mother *was* dead, and she had nothing to do with any of the crap that was happening now. Nothing to do with this attempt Nicole was making to . . . reconnect . . . or whatever the hell she was doing, with her family.

And this stranger had no right to pry in it.

"I'm sorry about that," he said. "So is mine."

"Well, okay. But I'm still unclear about why you know anything about me."

"Let's say I have a vested interest in the Mitchell family."

That made the hairs on her arms stand on end. "Well, that has nothing to do with me. Now, if you'll excuse me, my big-ass bacon plate should be on its way, and it will need its chair."

Jim stood up and looked down at her, his eyes assessing. "Okay. Hopefully I'll run into you again."

She nodded vaguely and made some sort of placating noise, waving her hand as he walked away from her table and out the door.

That was creepy.

Amber was back at her table a few moments later. "What did Davis want?" she asked.

"You know him?"

"Yeah. He's been harassing me about buying my ranch. That's why . . . well, I mean to say, that's why Cade moved in as quickly as he did. See? It wasn't all because he was being a jerk."

"That's . . . good to know, except—what's this guy's deal?"

"I don't know," she said. "I have a suspicion, but I don't know. He was a competitor of Cade's on the circuit, and I find it . . . odd that he's here."

"Odd *sinister*? Because I got a sinister vibe." She lifted the coffee cup to her lips.

"Yeah. I find it all odd sinister. Cade is reluctant to see it because . . . well, because of a lot of things. Partly because of his own screwed-up psychology."

"I am well familiar with screwed-up psychology," Nicole said. "Given that I have some of my own."

"Don't we all," Amber said.

"I think anyone who doesn't is maybe lying to themselves. Well-adjusted is a myth."

"Clearly," Amber said, "we should hang out."

"Only if your fiancé can deal with it."

Amber frowned. "He's not my keeper. But also, I think he'll come around. He's genuinely not a jerk. What he's had is a harder life than I think anyone in his family even realizes. He . . . in so many ways grew up with a different dad than everyone else. Because he knew, even when no one else did."

She sighed. "I get that. I even kind of know it's not about me. But that does not mean it doesn't sting a little bit."

"Naturally not." Amber looked around. "I have to take your order now or my chops will get lightly busted."

"Something that will clog my arteries, please."

"Got it." Amber frowned and paused. "Also, being nosy, what are you doing in town so early?"

Heat spread from her neck to her face. "Just out for breakfast."

Amber's eyebrows shot up. "I see."

"Really. I had an early-morning craving for . . . griddle grease."

"Okay. I'm sure that's true. Who doesn't? Okay, I'm going to put your order in. If Davis starts harassing you again . . . let Cade know."

Nicole nodded slowly. "I will."

Sixteen

Cade waited outside of the diner, leaning against his truck, his arms crossed. He'd dropped Amber off that morning just because he'd been reluctant to separate from her.

He'd made some noise about needing to check his post-office box. At five thirty in the morning. And she hadn't questioned it.

It had been weird, sleeping with her wrapped around him. But it had been nice. And waking up next to her this morning had been even nicer.

He liked that they seemed to have decided to go ahead and indulge their attraction for . . . however long.

He was completely cool with that.

Amber walked out of the diner, her dark, shiny hair piled on her head, her apron bunched up under her arm.

She was beautiful. The kind of beautiful that hit a man like a punch in the gut. He wasn't sure how he'd missed that for so long.

Yeah, sure, he'd known she was beautiful. He'd looked at her figure because he was a guy, and she was a woman. He'd had serious fantasies about her in high school, excusable by the fact that he'd been sixteen and a virgin, and susceptible to an erection brought on by a stiff breeze.

But this was different. This was like seeing her for the first time. Last night, when he'd seen her completely bare for the first time, when he'd tasted her, when he'd allowed himself to linger over every detail of her body, from her flavor to her scent, the way she felt under his hands, soft, slick and perfect, well, that was when he'd realized—really, really understood—that he was dealing with the kind of beauty that a tiger possessed.

Beautiful, sleek and capable of swallowing you whole.

On top of all that, she was making him mentally wax poetic, and that was another kind of magic in and of itself.

He wanted to pull her into his arms and kiss her. Right here on the street in front of everyone. And why the hell not? Everyone already thought they were together. More specifically, people already thought they were getting married. It wasn't like the rumor was going to get any more intense than that.

Cade pushed off of the truck and started to walk toward her, moving quickly down the sidewalk. A smile curved her lips, and he felt like something in his chest lifted. Like a weight had been removed.

The last two steps were a jog, and then he pulled her against him and kissed her. Not as deep as he wanted, not as long as he wanted, because it was a public place, and if he went too far, he'd be tempted to go further.

When they separated, he looked down at her face. Her eyes were wide, her lips shaped into an O.

"What?" he asked.

"Just surprised by the greeting."

"Pleasantly, I hope."

"Yeah," she said, patting his chest. "Yeah. Very pleasant." Then she rose up on her toes and kissed him again.

"Now I'm the one who's surprised. Ready to go? We can stop by the hospital."

"Yeah, that would be good. Oh . . . shoot, I left my purse on the hook in the diner. Can you come back in with me?"

"Sure."

They walked back to the diner together, their fingers brushing. But he didn't take her hand. Mainly because he wasn't sure where that fell in the grand scheme of their line-blurring relationship.

Because kissing and sex pertained to scratching the lust itch. Even sleeping together could fall under that header, since it put lust satisfaction within arm's reach. Hand-holding was an unknown.

So he didn't.

He held open the diner door for her and she tossed him an impish smile when she walked in ahead of him. He couldn't help but smile back. And feel a little punch-drunk.

"I'm just going to go to the back."

"Sure," he said, stuffing his hands in his pockets and standing to the side of the door so he didn't block the entrance.

"Cade!" It was Delia, running across the diner, her full cheeks pink, her arms outstretched. She tugged him into a hug, and his back twinged.

"Delia," he said, wincing and pulling away.

"I just wanted to say congratulations again. And I have pie. I'm going to get you and Amber some pie. Congratulatory pie." She turned and headed back toward the kitchen, and Cade groaned internally.

"What are you gettin' pie for, Mitchell?"

Hank, the resident tractor mechanic, was sitting at a table near the door with about four of the town's other elder statesmen.

"Engaged," Cade grunted.

"Well, shit!" Hank said. "Not to my favorite waitress."

Amber chose that exact moment to appear. "Hi," she said, as if sensing she'd walked into an event in progress.

"Amber, how can you marry this lunkhead? You were going to marry me!"

Amber's face flushed pink. "I . . . well . . ." Amber was so rarely rattled that seeing it now made him feel a little rattled. "You can't marry me anyway. Because Molly would kill me. And you can't tell me you forgot about her. You've been married to her for forty years."

"His memory is startin' to go," Tom, the man to Hank's left, said.

"Well, it can't be that far gone," Cade said.

"Hey, Delia!" Hank said. "How about a round for Cade? Since he's tying the knot and all. My treat."

"Oh, no . . ." Cade said, "we've got to go to the . . ."

"Hospital," Amber said. "Best if we're sober."

"Then I'll drink to it," Hank said, his voice carrying across the restaurant to everyone sitting there having their dinner. "Drinks all around for Amber and Cade Mitchell. To celebrate their upcoming wedding!"

The room erupted into cheers and Amber ducked her head, tucking her hair behind her ear and looking like she wanted to disappear. Cade moved near her, put his arm around her shoulder. "Thanks," he said.

"Yeah," Amber said, "thanks." She offered a halfhearted wave to the people who were currently drowning them in applause and cheers.

Though it was probably mainly excitement for free alcohol.

"Let's go," Amber said, leaning in and whispering through gritted teeth. "Before they start asking for a demonstration of our love."

"Got it."

"Well, we have to go. Have a drink for Ray Jameson, if you could. There you go, Hank's buying everyone two drinks!" Cade said, framing the last part as an announcement.

"Sonofabitch," Hank said, giving Cade an evil glare that was only partially sincere.

That's what he got for being a nosy bastard.

"Sorry, man, have to go," Cade said, slapping him on the back, then returning to Amber's side, putting his arm around her waist.

This earned them another round of applause and Cade lifted his hand in farewell as he led Amber out the door. "Small-town busybodies," he muttered when they were out on the street.

"Well, I guess we have . . . Silver Creek's approval."

"I guess." He dropped his arm from around her waist, because like hand-holding, he didn't know what jurisdiction this casual intimacy thing fell under.

He did open the truck door for her though, which seemed like the thing to do for a woman you were sleeping with.

"Thanks," she said.

He watched her the whole way around the front of his truck to the driver's side. Watched her raise her arms, her graceful fingers pulling pins from her hair. By the time he opened his door and climbed inside, her hair was down, a mass of glossy waves around her shoulders, some sort of flowery scent released into the air.

And everything at the diner just faded away. Because when it was just the two of them, it wasn't about the farce. It was just about Amber and Cade, and whatever the hell was growing between them. If it was even anything. Maybe it was just sex and lust. But it was powerful sex and lust.

She was everything beautiful. He'd never in all his life wanted a woman the way he wanted her.

"You're like a perfect bite of cake," he said.

"What?"

He didn't know where that had come from. And he sure as hell didn't know where the nice, coherent thought from earlier had gone. Blown away by a floral-scented breeze, no doubt.

"Like that bite of cake," he said. "The one where the layers are joined together by frosting, and the back is frosted. So it's a little bit of cake and . . . a lot of frosting. It's the best bite."

"What?"

"I just meant that if you were cake . . . or if . . . women . . . people, were cake, that you would be . . . You're really fucking pretty," he said, gunning the engine and putting the truck in first before pulling out onto the street. "And that . . . that has nothing to do with Davis, or protecting you from him, or pretending to be engaged. It just . . . is."

"Oh."

He looked at her. She was looking at him, blinking periodically.

"What?" he asked.

"Are you trying to compliment me?"

"What the hell do you mean, am I trying to compliment you? I just did."

"Obviously. You're . . . kind of adorable when you don't know what to say."

"I really don't know what to say. Well, that's a lie, I did know what to say; it just came out in a stupid metaphor."

She laughed. "Okay . . . you're like . . . that smell in the air just before fall. When the air is starting to turn crisp in the evenings and lose the heat. And it makes you ache for the time that's passed and makes you look forward to . . . to what's ahead." She let out a sigh. "How's that for terrible?"

He tightened his hold on the steering wheel until his knuckles burned. "It was pretty damn good."

"I'm glad you liked it. It's true."

"I make you happy and I make you . . . ache?" he asked, not sure what to think about that.

"Everything good does. At least in my experience."

"Hmm."

"If you'd like, I could put frosting on my breasts."

His head snapped to the right so he could see her, and he forgot for a second to look at the road. "What?"

"I'm just saying . . . wouldn't that be a better bite of cake?"

He swallowed, his throat suddenly dry. "Technically there would be no cake. Technically it would be all icing. And skin."

She lifted a shoulder. "Semantics."

"Cake semantics."

"A minefield."

"I guess."

When they got to the hospital, he battled with the hand-holding again. He wanted to offer her something. Comfort. But that, he decided, fell under the friendship responsibility, while hand-holding did not fall under a friend gesture.

He settled for rubbing her back just between her shoulder

blades as they walked to the front counter, signed in and got their badges.

Just a little bit of contact. Just to let her know he was there.

They walked down the halls and into the room. Her grandpa's eyes were open, and one side of his mouth lifted into a smile when he saw them.

He tried to speak, but it came out garbled.

"It's okay, Grandpa," Amber said. "You don't have to talk."

Ray raised his hand in a slight wave. Cade returned the gesture.

"How are you feeling?" Cade asked.

Ray made a dismissive, slightly disgruntled sound.

A nurse breezed in past the curtain. "He's doing better," she said.

"How much better?" Amber asked. She turned and recognized the other woman as Amanda Jones, a woman who'd been about three years ahead of her in school.

"Better. He's more with it today. His mouth still isn't saying what he'd like it to, but he seems a little more with it."

Amber looked down at her grandpa, and Cade felt an echo of her sadness. They were a lot alike, him and Amber. She didn't have very many people in this world, and that meant the ones she had were special.

Not that he'd treated Cole, Kelsey, Lark and Quinn like they were at all special recently. Or, in Quinn's case, ever.

Then there was Nicole. She was family, and she had no control over her circumstances. But he was treating her like . . . well, like crap, because of all his own issues. And that wasn't fair. And it was a sorry abuse of family.

"Congratulations," Amanda said.

"What?" Amber asked.

"I heard. About your engagement. Susan at reception told me."

"I . . . I . . ." After that scene at the diner, this was really just too much.

Cade put his arm around her waist. "Oh, yeah, we're very excited."

"Ecstatic," Amber said, looking down at her grandfather,

who looked . . . happy. So damn happy. Oh, frick, how had it gotten this bad? How was it all this tangled?

Damn small towns. Honestly, it was like no one around here had their own life to worry about.

"Do you have a date set?"

"June," Cade said. "Because . . . there's something about June, right?"

"June brides are brides forever," Amanda said, her smile turning gooey. Who would have thought the town was filled with a bunch of damn romantics.

"Yeah. Forever. And . . ." Amber looked at Cade. "Ever." She tried to look gooey too, but she was pretty sure she was failing.

"Do you have a dress?"

"Yeah," Amber said. "It's . . . eggshell. And . . . butter-cream." Girly colors were always food.

"Sounds divine! Can I see your ring?"

"It's, uh . . . getting sized," Cade said. "After it gets shipped. Here. From . . . New York. Tiffany's."

She shot Cade a sideways glance. "Yeah. Tiffany's."

Amanda's eyes got glossy. "Now that really is just too romantic." Amber wanted to melt into a puddle and slither under the bed.

Amanda took a breath. "Anyway, we'll be discharging him soon. But I recommend putting him in a home for the transition.

"A home?" Amber asked.

"A nursing home. He needs physical therapy and speech therapy. It would be easier on you if he was in a facility."

"But I won't want—"

"Amber," Cade said. "If you want to take care of him, I'm sure Delia will cover for you at the diner. Hell, you don't even need the job."

"What do you mean I don't need the job?"

"I have enough to take care of you for a while. With the bison ranch getting up and running eventually, I'll be pulling in a really good income and I can support. . . ." He was about to say "us." But they weren't really getting married. They weren't really a couple. So that wasn't what he meant. Not really. "I can take care of you and Ray while you need it," he said.

"No." She shook her head. "I am not letting you take care of me. There are boundaries, and things, and no."

"You're being stubborn."

"I'm not," she hissed.

The nurse and Ray were looking at them, though Ray's eyes were starting to look a little heavy.

"Outside, Mitchell," she said.

They went out into the hall and Amber planted her hands on her hips, giving him her best stubborn face. "I'm not letting you support me."

"You need help. And you're my fiancée. So letting me help you . . ."

"You are not my fiancé!" she hissed. "You are my friend. My friend with a superman complex. But that is all. Friends don't just let friends . . . pay their way. That's not how it works."

"Friends don't usually offer to suck their friends' dicks either," he said, his teeth locked together in frustration. "I didn't realize we were playing by traditional rules."

She drew back as if he'd hit her. "How dare you use that against me?"

"Against you? Woman, I am trying to help you. And you're being damn stubborn. If you don't want him in a nursing home, let me try to fix it."

"I'm still too pissed that you said that to even move on from that point in the conversation."

"I'm sorry," he said. "I just . . . you have to let me help."

"No. I'm not going to be a responsibility to you. I'm not going to add any pressure to your venture succeeding, and I am not taking your money. I got that waitressing job as soon as I could, and I've kept it. I've helped keep my grandparents afloat with it, and I'm helping now."

"I know you are. But . . . can't I help?"

"Not like that. And not if you're going to be insulting."

"I was just pointing out that we're already doing things most friends don't do."

"Crudely. So stop it."

He bit the inside of his lip until it bled. "I am sorry," he said finally. "Because I didn't mean to make what's happened between us sound . . . flippant or cheap. It's not."

"I know, asshole. That's why you made me so mad."

"I want to help."

"Great. Then support me helping myself."

"I do."

"I can't be your project, Cade. I don't want to bear that burden."

"Fair enough."

She let out a breath. "The nurse is right though. It would be easier if his various therapies were right there for him."

"He can come back home," Cade said, "once he's feeling better."

"He took care of me, Cade, and I was never the easiest person to care for. I feel like I owe him."

Cade pulled her into his arms, even though he was sure it crossed all kinds of boundaries. Friendship ones, emotional ones . . . since she was probably still, rightly, pissed at him and his runaway mouth. "You are taking care of him," Cade said. "This is taking care of him. He'll get the best care. He'll be close to the hospital."

"But he won't be at his home," she said, her voice choked.

"Just for now."

"It doesn't feel right," she said, her voice a whisper.

"What?"

"Being in the house without him. It's his house."

"It's your house too."

"It's never felt that way. Not even knowing that I own part of it."

"Why?"

"Because I'm . . . I'm just baggage. I'm not an asset. And I keep trying to . . . make up for that."

"You aren't baggage."

"That's nice of you to say. But it is how I feel."

"You shouldn't."

"Oh. Okay. I'll stop. Wow, a lifetime's worth of baggage

is now totally gone because you just told me I shouldn't feel it! Okay, Cade, stop limping."

"Amber . . ."

"Just stop. Don't you think you've walked with a limp long enough? Get back on the horse."

Anger filled him, helplessness. And worst of all, understanding. Because he knew that there was no way she could stop feeling that way. Just like there was no way he could stop limping. Someone else had put them both here. Someone else had broken them both.

There wasn't enough Krazy Glue in the world to stick them back together. That was one reason they'd always held on to each other so tight. To keep the pieces snug—still cracked, but not piles of shattered edges.

Of course, that was hard to do when they were pissed at each other.

She didn't back down. Didn't apologize for what she'd said. But it was okay. She didn't need to. He had broad enough shoulders to take a little crap from her, especially when he deserved it.

And he'd talked his share of crap earlier.

"You know I can't," he said, shrugging.

"Neither can I."

"Okay," he said.

"Great."

He turned away from her, then back. Then he closed the distance between them, and the distance between her and the wall, until he had her pressed tightly against it, his mouth crashing down on hers.

She gripped his shirt, holding him tightly against her, kissing him back, hard and deep. He could taste her. He could taste the salt of her tears. He hated the tears as much as he relished her flavor. And he hated that he'd been a part of causing them.

Hated that there was all this turmoil and anger between them. Because he hadn't been able to keep it in his pants. Because, even hating himself for it, he still couldn't keep his hands off her.

Because he didn't know how to stop this now that it had started. Didn't know how to push back an avalanche of desire, sixteen years of lust, now that he'd set it loose.

She pulled away from him and put her head down, her face buried in his neck, sobs shaking her body. And he just held her, held her and felt like a helpless jackass. Held her and tried to ignore how much he ached to have her, in spite of the fact that she was weeping like a child in his arms.

All he could say was "Baby, I'm sorry," over and over again, and it didn't seem to make anything better. But it wasn't making it worse either, so he figured it was better than doing nothing. Or, it at least made him feel a lot more active. And a lot less useless.

When it was over, he just held her and pushed her hair back from her face, her tears leaving his hands stained with her misery.

"I'm fine," she said.

"You look real fine," he said.

"Shut up."

"I'm just saying."

"Yeah, I know." She pulled away from him and dragged her arm over her face, sniffing loudly as she did. "I'm good. And I look good."

"Damn sexy."

"Why is everything so screwed up?"

"I don't know. I'm not helping, am I?" he asked, his voice rough. "This isn't helping."

And he knew she would know what he meant. *This* was the intense sexual tension that stretched between them. The intense, impossible-to-ignore pull. The starving beast unleashed, and completely unstoppable now.

She shrugged. "I don't know if that's true. Everything seems brighter with an . . ." She looked over his shoulder and paused, and he looked the same direction, his eyes fixing on a guy sitting in the waiting area who was looking back at them. "With an orgasm," she finished on a whisper, her face turning pink.

Yeah, he supposed they were officially creating a little play for anyone who cared to sit, watch and eat some popcorn.

"I'm going to take you home now. You don't need to make any decisions tonight. About anything."

She shook her head. "No. Sorry. I can't do that. I can't leave it unsettled. I'm going to go talk to the nurse, and then I'll meet you out here, okay?"

"I can't go with you?"

"Cade, I'm going to do this by myself, okay? Thanks for being here while I had a big freaking meltdown and stuff." She took a deep breath. "But I'm going to settle this."

"You won't take my help?"

"For every reason previously stated, no. But I will take a ride home. So wait for me, okay?"

"Yeah," he said.

She was so damned stubborn. He would fix this for her if she would just let him take care of her. He had no problem doing it. She needed him, so naturally he'd be there for her. He was used to caring for people, and tying his money up in that had never been a problem.

Hell, he'd done it starting at the age of eighteen. He rode hard, worked hard and sent the money to his family. It was all fine with him. It had gotten him away and made sure debts were covered and the ranch was kept running. Win-win.

Supporting Amber wouldn't feel half as sucky as supporting his dad's lie of an existence, that was for sure.

But of course, the woman was too damn stubborn. Too damn hardheaded. Too damn sexy. He spent the next ten minutes thinking about all the things Amber was too damn.

Then she emerged from her grandpa's room, looking pale but determined. "They'll move him to the home in forty-eight hours, unless something changes dramatically either way. We have a plan."

"Great," he said.

"Oh, yeah, freaking peachy."

"Everything always is."

CHAPTER

Seventeen

Amber was asleep by nine, and Cade had a feeling a large part of that had to do with avoiding him. After the fight in the hospital, he hadn't been expecting her to jump on his body, but then, there had been the kiss . . .

Still, he'd basically been expecting her to go Orgasm Nazi on him. *No sex for you.*

And, yeah, fair enough.

But to not even talk about it all . . . that sucked. It made him wonder if things were going to go back to normal. If things were going to go back to how they'd been before they'd gotten naked together. And he really didn't want that.

Because going back to a clothing-mandatory relationship seemed like . . . a step backward. Even though it probably shouldn't, all things considered.

It should feel like . . . well, it should be okay. Because there was nowhere else for their relationship to go. There was friendship, and there was naked friendship. And if it went back to friendship, that would be fine, because . . . because.

He let out a sigh and jerked open the fridge, rummaging for a beer. He came out victorious and popped the top, tapping his jeans pocket, feeling the hard plastic lump of his cell phone there.

Amber was right. About a lot of things. And that was nothing new. But he really did need closure on the accident that hadn't been an accident. It was affecting him. Affecting his ability to move on. Affecting his relationship with his brother-in-law.

And that was as freaking Dr. Phil as he was going to get, thank you very much.

He let out a long breath and pulled the phone out of his pocket, tapping lightly on the screen before committing to dialing Lark's number.

"'Sup?"

"Hey, Lark," he said, smiling at her familiar voice, at her completely quirky, totally *her* greeting.

"What's up, Cade? You never call."

"I know," he said, lifting his shoulder and holding the phone against his face, shoving his hands in his pockets.

"Does this mean you're actually calling to tell me what I already know because of the rampant rumor weed that grows under this town?"

"Uh, no," he said, not particularly happy the rumors had made it back to Lark. He hated lying to her most of all, given the recent history of lying to her about their father, and the fallout of that.

"I thought you weren't into love and marriage?" she asked, sounding smug.

"Things change."

"Uh-huh. And quickly too!"

"Shut up, Lark, I do not need to stare down the barrel of the commitment gun and deal with your smugness too, I just don't."

"So you want to start something with me now too?" she asked.

"I see you talked to Cole."

"To Kelsey. And I'm on your side."

"What?"

"I love Cole, but he's a dick sometimes. And you . . . you

are too. But I've always felt like . . . you get me, Cade, and you always have. And I know that you're more than just the rodeo. And more than just fun and games. I appreciate what you've done for me. I don't know if Cole realizes how much you've done for him. But I do."

"That's, uh . . ." His chest felt tight all of a sudden. "That's nice, Lark."

"And I support you. In everything. In your bison and your marriage and . . . I'm so proud of you."

"I think that's my line."

"Nope," she said. "Too bad. I'm proud of you."

He cleared his throat. "I called to talk to Quinn, actually," he said.

"What?"

"I want to talk to your husband, and I don't have his phone number. So I had to call you."

"I'm kind of offended by that. I thought you wanted to talk to me."

"I'm glad I talked to you. But I wanted to talk to Quinn."

"Weird," she said. "And I don't trust you."

"I thought you were on my side?"

"That doesn't mean I trust you."

"Fine," he said, "but I have a question to ask him."

"Are you going to verbally abuse him? Because, forgive me, since you broke his nose that one time, I'm never really sure what you might do."

"Fair enough. But can I talk to him anyway?"

"Sure. He's sitting here trying to shoot zombies. He sucks at it anyway. I think . . . yeah, he just got bitten." She sighed heavily. "Quinn, I love you enough that I will have to shoot you now. Okay, here he is."

"She has you zombie hunting now?"

Quinn grunted on the other end of the phone. "Not willingly. I won't tell you what she was holding hostage to get me to agree to this."

"Better you don't."

"So why is it you want to talk to me? I know it's not to talk about the weather, so you might as well cut to the chase."

"I need to get in touch with Sam."

"My employee Sam? Sam, my right-hand man?"

"That one."

"Why?"

"Because. Because his son, Jake," Cade said, referring to the teenager Sam had adopted a year ago, "had contact with the guy who effed me up, and now I want to . . . find out what he knows."

Cade had spent three years believing Quinn was responsible for sabotaging his ride. And he wasn't the only one. The board had barred Quinn from competing, and in Cade's mind it had been a done deal. But then Jake had confessed that he was the one who'd put the spike beneath the saddle, and that he'd been paid to do it. By someone who definitely wasn't Quinn.

"So you don't think I did it anymore."

"I know you didn't. Old habits die hard. I made a habit of hating your guts and fantasizing about tying a rope to your ankle and lashing you to the back of an angry bull. That doesn't fade overnight. Plus, you took my little sister from me, and any guy who did that was going to end up in my bad books."

"Fair enough," Quinn said.

"Not really. But who said life was fair? Plus, I have it on good authority that I'm an asshole, so there is that."

"It's okay, I share the title. And people are not wrong. Though Lark makes me behave a little better."

"As long as you don't act like an asshole with her, feel free to carry on being a jerk."

"I do a lot of the time," Quinn said.

Cade was starting to like him a little bit more.

"It was easier to blame you," Cade said. "Because . . . look, I really believed you did it. I swear to God I would never have put you through that hell if I hadn't believed it down in my gut."

"I know."

"And I also know you couldn't stand by and take it. For guys like us . . . that's life. It's our whole life."

"It's less of mine now," Quinn said. "Lark and the ranch fill up a lot of space in my life. In the best way."

"I'm glad to hear that, but even so, I should never have . . . I should have been a lot more certain before I pushed with the board."

"It's over, Cade. And it's because of it that I met Lark, so . . . I'm not angry about it anymore. I'm honestly not."

"I would be. I mean, obviously. The thing is, it's not over for me. I still don't know who did this to me. I need to know. Or it's just another unhealed wound. I have too damn many of those."

"Don't we all?"

"We're a bundle of screwed-up around here."

"That's why I fit in so well."

"Put me in touch with Sam?" Cade asked.

"Yeah. Better let me tell him to call you. Since you want to question Jake, Jill will want advance warning, and I do not need that woman up my ass. I love her, but . . . sometimes the feeling isn't mutual."

"Yeah, I get it."

"I'll have him give you a call."

"Thanks, Quinn. And also, if you hide the modem, Lark will probably have a conniption fit. I learned that trick a few years back. It's the funniest damn thing I've ever seen."

"Which thing is that?" he asked.

"The box by the computer with the blinking lights. Do it when she's not looking."

"You're really not so bad."

"If I'm any one thing, it's a truly devious older brother," Cade said.

"And I appreciate that."

"Thanks."

"I'll tell Sam to call you," Quinn said. "Can't promise anything, but I will."

"I appreciate it."

When Cade hung up he felt like he might have actually buried one of the hatchets that littered his metaphorical yard.

So that was a start. Now all that was left was to deal with

Cole and Nicole, deal with Davis, find out who'd screwed up his body and his life and figure out where the hell he stood with Amber.

But he could save that for tomorrow. Yeah . . . tomorrow could take care of that other crap. For now, he would just drink a beer.

"Morning, sleepy bear," Cade said, poking at Amber's inert figure with his toe, balancing a tray of food in his hands.

"Bah snerf." She rolled over onto her stomach and stuck a hand up, waving him away.

"That's really cute, honey," he said, "but I brought you food to send you off for the day. So get your pretty ass up and eat it."

She snorted and rubbed her face into the pillow.

"Amber," he said.

"No."

"I have food."

She rolled back over and flung her arm up over her face.

"You seem like maybe you didn't sleep so good," he said. "But you went to bed so early."

She lowered her arm just enough for him to see one narrow eye telegraphing evil in his direction. "No, I did not sleep well, Mitchell," she said, her voice croaky.

"Why is that?"

"Not because of your penis."

He snorted a shocked laugh and set the tray down on the nightstand. "Obviously not. My penis was with me, in the world's most uncomfortable bed."

"It's too early in the morning for your weirdness, Mitchell."

"It's not that early, Jameson. You have to eat so you don't wilt like the delicate flower you are."

"Argh!" She sat up, her hair a mess, her expression best described as cranky. "I don't want to."

"You have tables to wait, baby. And you wouldn't, I hasten to add, if you would let me take care of you."

"You may take care of me in the form of . . . oh, pancakes! And coffee. Yes, you may do this for me."

"I know how to make pancakes. I'm at least that useful."

"Does your usefulness extend to maple syrup?"

"Yes. Yes, it does. Warmed up. Look in the other mug."

She did, and her eyes brightened. "Oooh." She poured a generous helping on the pancakes, then transferred the tray to her lap.

"Since I'm here," he said as she took a big bite of pancake and started chewing enthusiastically while he looked on, "and since you're eating my food, you've absolved me of any wrongdoing, boneheadedness and general douchebaggery, according to the fine print on the pancakes."

Her chewing slowed. "It does not," she said, talking around the pancake.

"It does. It's not my fault you didn't read the fine print."

"Asshole."

"I know. Anyway, since you're my friend again, I thought maybe we could discuss some things."

"Such as?"

"Such as the fact that I am now pursuing finding the person who caused my accident with a purpose. I even called Quinn. And I apologized to him."

"What?"

"I know. I'm having growth. And . . . things."

"Okay." She took a sip of her coffee.

"Also, I want to talk about us."

"Us?" She spit across the top of her coffee, sending a dark drop over the edge of the white mug.

"Yes. You. Me. Our friendship. And also the bit where we have sex."

"Uh-huh."

"Are we going to stop now because I made you mad?"

She lifted a shoulder. "It depends. Does us having sex mean you're going to treat me like every other guy treated me? I spent a long time not sleeping with anyone because I know I didn't have myself together enough to manage it. And because . . . because I was tired of being treated like I was less than nothing because I consented to take my clothes off with some guys. It was like . . . it was fine for them to sleep with me. Fine for them to sleep with anyone. But I had 'a reputation' and that somehow made me lower. It still makes me lower. I'm defined by it, at least as far as other people are concerned. I don't define me by it. What I've done in bed with a few people isn't the sum total of my life, but the minute I sleep with a guy . . . it is to him. And when other people find out? It is to them. You never treated me that way. But now that I've slept with you . . . you made a comment about me . . . doing things to you, and I just can't . . . I can't have you disrespecting me over the fact that I did things with you. Because you did things with me too. And it's the hypocrisy I can't stand."

"Amber, I . . . honest to God, I do not disrespect you for anything. Not anything you've done with me, or anyone else. I was pissed, so I said something stupid, but it wasn't supposed to degrade you or what we did. It was just . . . I was just pointing out that the rules have changed between us."

"Maybe that's what I'm uncomfortable with," she said.

"Well . . . I can't help with that. We can't take it back."

"I know," she said, picking at a rounded fuzzy on her quilt. "But you don't have . . . boyfriend rights. You're a friend. I sleep with. Have slept with."

"So does that mean we aren't sleeping together anymore?"

"Realistically? No. Because neither of us have anyone else in our lives and well . . . you're living here and oh, holy damn, look at you."

"Thanks," he said, shifting and then moving into a sitting position on the edge of the bed. "I think. It's hard to know whether or not I'm complimented when you talk about the inevitability of falling into bed with me with all the glee of a prisoner facing a scheduled execution."

"It's not like that at all."

"No?"

"For one thing, when I'm with you I only lose my head metaphorically. Were this a French Revolution–style execution it would be me, Madame Guillotine and literal head loss."

"You need more coffee."

"Do I not make sense?"

"No, you make a weird kind of sense. And the fact that I understand you is frightening to me."

"Sorry. I'll keep my early-morning logic to myself next time."

"It'd be better if you did."

"It'd probably be better if I'd kept my desire to suck you off to myself too," she mused.

He nearly choked. "Do you have to say things like that?"

"No."

"Then why do you?"

"It's fun to watch your face go all still and pale."

"You're a sadistic woman, Amber Jameson."

"A little, I grant you."

"So where does that leave us?"

She put her hand on her chin and tapped her fingers just beneath her lip. "Uh . . . maybe in the barn, naked, with a riding crop?"

"Not funny."

"Who's laughing?"

"I'm serious," he said.

"As might I have been." She cleared her throat. "I guess that leaves us where we've been. Sleeping with each other, at least while you're here."

"And after?"

"Don't be such a chick, Mitchell. Who needs to think about the future?" She leaned back against the headboard, her fingers curled around the coffee mug. Her dark hair was tousled, her eyes slumberous and particularly sexy as a result.

"I guess I don't if you don't."

"Back to Quinn, though."

"Yeah?"

"He's going to help you figure out who hurt you?"

"He's going to see if Sam will let me talk to his son. He knows something. I mean, I don't think he knows something he's withholding purposefully, but he knew enough to know that it wasn't Quinn who approached him, and I'm just curious what else he might be able to tell me." Cade sat on the edge of the bed and rested his arms on his thighs. "Of course, he may not want me giving his kid the third degree, which is understandable."

"Right. Sure. But he's not a child, is he?"

"He's sixteen or seventeen. I'm not really sure."

"So it's not like he's a baby. I'm sure Sam will be okay with you talking to him. Anyway, it's about your life. Your future."

Cade shrugged. "Is it? Or is it just me wanting to get my pound of flesh?"

"You're entitled to it, Cade. Don't start feeling differently now. You're entitled to a whole damn hide. Tan it, stretch it, hang it on your effing wall. It's your right. Whoever did that to you stole your career. Your passion. And he made you hurt, not just in that moment, not just emotionally, but physically. For four years you've been in pain every day. And maybe you aren't angry about it anymore, but I am. Your family is. Because we hate to see you in pain. Because you don't deserve it."

"That's nice of you to say, but who knows? Maybe I do deserve it. Maybe it's good that I'm hobbled. Hell, my dad could have used a little hobbling. Might have solved some things for everyone."

"You don't have anything to do with what your dad did, Cade."

"No? You don't think? I enabled him. I kept my mouth shut."

"You were a kid. Kids do that."

"You just said sixteen wasn't a kid," he said, giving her a sideways look. "Can't have it both ways."

"Sure I can. I'm having you as a lover and a best friend. I'm having pancakes while still in bed. I can have things both ways if I damn well choose."

"You're amazing, you know that?"

"Yes. Yes, I do." She took another sip of her coffee.

"You're going to have to put your cup down now."

She looked up at him. "Why?"

"Because I'm about to push you back on the bed and have my way with you."

She put the mug down on the nightstand and sloshed liquid over the side. "I'm down with that."

"Oh, you're down with that?" he asked, leaning in, planting his hands on either side of her head as she slid down the headboard and positioned herself so she was flat on her back.

She nodded, her teeth clamped down over her lower lip. She was so cute it was painful to look at, her dark eyes glittering with mischief, her hair spread over the pillows.

"You down with this too?" He angled his head and kissed her neck. He felt her pulse jump beneath his lips, and there was an answering kick in his gut.

"Yes," she said. "But be quick, my pancakes are going to get cold."

"Your pancakes," he said, his voice a growl, "are going to be very, very cold by the time we're done here." He gripped her thigh and tugged her leg up over his ass, settling between her legs.

"You make that sound like a good thing."

"Oh, baby," he said, kissing her neck again, "it will be. And have I mentioned how happy I am you voted for us continuing to sleep together?"

"Well, you bought all those condoms."

"You're so practical."

"I am." She angled her face and stretched upward, biting his lower lip. The pain shot straight down to his groin.

He swore incoherently. "You have to warn me before you do things like that."

"No, I don't."

"No," he said, grinning, "you don't."

"You like me to surprise you," she said.

"I do."

"You ready for more surprises?"

"Oh, hell yeah."

CHAPTER

Eighteen

Amber had been smiling for the past three weeks, nonstop. Which was odd, all things considered. Since her grandfather was in a nursing home, though, he was recovering nicely. And her crazy-ass best friend was currently building bison fencing around the property she lived on.

But then, said crazy-ass friend was also responsible for the smile.

Sleeping with Cade was . . . better than chocolate, wine, beer, riding horses and Jet Li's butt in that one movie with all the subtitles.

That was to say, it was epic.

She practically skipped down the stairs toward the smell of pancakes, which were Cade's specialty, and toward Cade, who made getting up every morning seem like a lot of fun.

Of course, getting up wasn't as great as staying in bed wrapped in his arms, but she still had a job to do.

The only thing that was getting hard was separating out their relationship. Because it was starting to feel very . . . relationshippy. She'd never slept with a man the way she did with him. Had never spent all night tangled up in blankets with a guy.

Had never woken up and brushed her teeth next to a man who was doing the same. Had never shared breakfasts and showers and all these domestic things they were sharing.

But then, she'd already decided she didn't have to sort that out at the moment. Or ever. Maybe they would never sort it out. They would have scorching hot sex while he was here, and then when he left they would never speak of it again.

That could work. That would be her temporary plan.

Her heart stopped when she came into the kitchen. He was standing at the stove, spatula in hand, his shirtsleeves rolled up to his elbows, the muscles in his forearms shifting as he flipped the pancakes.

Then her eyes went straight to his jeans. Or, more specifically, the back of his jeans. Or, more specifically, the way his ass looked in his jeans.

"Good morning," she said.

"Morning." He turned and offered her a half smile, and her heart did crazy tricks.

She really, really wished that Cade only gave her feelings in her panties. Sadly, he seemed to be giving her the emotion sort of feelings too.

And that was another thing she really didn't want to sort out.

"I left you some coffee over there."

Oh, damn. Yep, right in the heart again.

"Thank you." She moved over to the counter and picked up her mug, which contained coffee that was clearly fixed to her specifications. It was exactly the right shade. Not too light, not too dark.

She lifted it to her lips and took the first sip. Then grimaced.

"What did you put in this?"

"Just a little cream and sugar."

"Hmm." She took another sip and frowned. "I think the cream might be off."

"It tasted fine to me."

"My palate is probably more refined."

"True. For example, I have a taste for you, while you have one for me."

She lifted her middle finger and waved it in his direction. Then the bastard crossed the kitchen and kissed the tip of the offending finger.

"That's too sweet," she said, her chest getting all funny and tight.

She was a mess this morning.

"Sorry. Maybe that's the problem with your coffee. I stuck my finger in it and over-sugared it."

"Har har." She put her mug back on the counter and sat at the table.

The pancakes were good, but she couldn't motivate herself to try and finish the coffee. She would buy new cream before she left town after work.

She tried to stop herself from making googly eyes at Cade across the table. But dammit, it was hard. She was all post-orgasmic and crap.

"I'll drive you," he said.

"Are you sure?" she asked. "I mean . . . you have bisoning to do. Fences must be built, fields must be prepped, et cetera."

"I think I can take fifteen minutes out of my day to drive you to work. And anyway, I might get some pie or something out of the deal. When I show up, Delia tends to feed me."

"Yes, she does."

"And grill me about why I haven't given you a ring."

Amber groaned. "Yeah. Well, this little charade is already intense enough without adding diamonds to it. Not that I'm opposed to diamonds, but it seems like it's a bit extravagant, don't you think?"

"I'll stick to engagement pancakes."

"I'm good with that."

He leaned across the table and kissed her lips, and she felt her insides melt like whipped cream with hot syrup on top.

"I'm glad to hear it," he said.

"Well. Well. Work," she said.

"With the gentle reminder that if you'd let me take care of you, we could be in bed f—"

"Ahh! No. If I'd taken you up on that my grandpa would be here." And his near-use of a crude word for their activities had killed her gooey feelings. And made her kind of hot.

"Okay, yeah, so there would be that."

"This would not be a naked free-for-all."

"That sounds more enticing than you know. In fact, we could go ahead and make everything clothing-optional."

"I don't know if I'd man the skillet with vulnerable parts out, Mitchell."

He grimaced. "Okay, good point."

"Now, come on. I'm going to be late."

He stood and walked toward the front door, pausing at her discarded mug. "Did you want your coffee?"

She shook her head. "Nah. I'll get some at work later."

"Okay."

"I'm going to fantasize about you building fences all day," she said. "So manly."

"Then I'll fantasize about you making me sandwiches."

She narrowed her eyes, and for some strange reason, she felt her chest get even tighter from all the emotion. "Jackass."

"Yeah, but I'm a jackass who's going to get you to work on time. Come on."

"Cade."

The tone of Lark's voice over the phone sounded dire enough that Cade redirected his truck toward the house the minute he heard it.

"What's up?"

"You should get over here."

"Already on my way. What's going on?"

"A friend of yours is here at the house."

He hung up. "Shit."

"What?" Amber asked.

He'd just picked her up from work and he knew she was

exhausted. But he also knew that she would understand. "I think it's Davis. At Elk Haven."

"Why? Does he have everyone at gunpoint? You sound dire."

"Well, Lark was cagey enough that he damn well might."

He didn't. Cade was sure of that. Well, he was ninety-nine percent sure. Though Amber had now put the idea in his head. So it was there.

Which was just great.

When they pulled up to the ranch house, his theory was proven right about it being Davis. His truck was in the driveway.

"Okay, now what the hell is he doing here?"

"Nothing good," Amber said.

"I don't like that he's still hanging around here. It's been weeks, and he's still here. And now he's harassing my family."

"He was bothering Nicole a while back in the diner too," she said.

"What? And you didn't tell me?"

"I was too busy dealing with the intense, depressing reality of my grandfather's health and drowning my sorrow in multiple orgasms with you, so no, I guess in all that, I forgot to tell you."

Cade parked in front of the main house and slammed the door shut, stomping inside. Amber would follow. He knew she didn't need an invitation.

He opened the front door and stopped in the lobby area. Davis was there. And Nicole. Cole looking stressed, Kelsey looking wide-eyed. Quinn was in the corner, looking like he was just waiting for an excuse to cause bodily damage to Davis, and Lark was standing next to her husband with her zombie-killing face on.

"What the hell are you doing here, Davis?" Cade asked.

"The cavalry has arrived," Davis said.

"Are you asking my family to sell up too? I guarantee you, the answer is no here, the same as it is at Amber's place."

"That's actually not why I'm here."

"And why are you here?" Cade asked, directing that question at the room in general.

"He came to see me," Nicole said.

"What?"

"The rumor flying around town is that she's a bastard Mitchell child. I thought I might drop in and see if that was true."

"Cade and I are bastards," Cole said, "but not in the literal sense. Nicole, on the other hand, is pretty nice to be around."

"Not what I meant," Davis said.

"Oh, no, we got what you meant," Quinn said. "I think you're third-best in this room at subtlety. Which is fitting, since you were always third-best at riding."

"Who was first?" Cade asked.

Quinn shot him a look and shrugged a shoulder. "Doesn't matter."

Like hell it didn't. But Cade would let it go for now in favor of more pressing issues. "What's it to you?" Cole asked, crossing his arms over his chest.

Quinn straightened and moved to stand near Cole, and Cade did the same. He might be slightly impaired, but between himself and the men on his right, Davis could incur some serious damage.

"I thought it might be nice to have a chat with her. Since we have something in common."

"I hope you mean matching tattoos," Cole said.

"More like similar DNA."

For a full ten seconds, it was completely quiet in the room. Cade just stood, completely frozen, while he tried to sort through the implications of what Davis was saying.

There was an accepted reality he lived in. It sucked, but it was his. The one where his dad was a womanizing ass with an illegitimate child and a mistress who lived about six hours from the family ranch.

This reality, as bad as it was, only made room for one mistress. And one child.

And what Davis was saying seemed to imply that . . .

The room tilted a little bit. And then he felt Amber's fingers curling around the fabric on his shirtsleeve. And that was when he knew he didn't have it wrong. That was when he knew that was exactly what Jim Davis was saying.

That he was another bastard Mitchell.

This man who was the same age as him. This man who he'd competed against on the circuit. Ridden next to nearly every damn day during competition seasons.

This man who'd been sniffing around causing nothing but trouble for everyone he came into contact with for the past month.

This man who was a total and complete asshole.

He suddenly felt terrible for rejecting Nicole the way that he had. Apparently, random half-siblings who came out of the woodwork didn't have to be decent human beings.

"I'd ask for proof," Cole said, "but I'm not sure what you'd benefit by claiming our dad."

"Well, I want proof," Cade said. "What the hell makes you think our dad is . . . your dad?"

"I knew our dad. He even visited for the first nine years of my life. That's when, I assume, the other bastard rug rat showed up. I guess three families was a little much for him to manage."

Cade's stomach took a free fall and landed in his boots. All of his anger, in that moment, was directed at their dad. At the pain he'd caused everyone. The pain he continued to cause, even after his death.

Leaving accidental children all over the damn state. And leaving all of them to deal with the consequences.

The only consolation was that their mother hadn't known.

Which couldn't be said for Nicole or Jim's mothers. Who had obviously known all too well, at least at some point, that the man they'd had their children with had feet of clay.

Of course, the momentary stab of sympathy didn't mean he didn't think Davis was an ass.

"What is it you want?" Cole asked.

"What does she want?" he asked, gesturing toward Nicole. "More importantly, what is she getting?"

"She," Nicole said, "doesn't want anything. I was looking for family. I found the family I have left. What I'm going to do with it . . . I don't know yet. But I didn't come storming in here demanding answers either."

"I didn't read this section in the abandoned secret family handbook," Davis said.

"Maybe you should have," Nicole countered.

"Some people read. Some people act. Anyway, just thought I'd drop by and let you all know I existed," Davis said. Then he turned his focus to Amber, and Cade just about got violent. "If you changed your mind about selling, I'm here. Maybe my interest makes a little more sense now. Seeing as this place holds my family legacy and all."

"I'm still not interested," Amber said. "The ranch is Cade's. I don't need any other boneheaded cowboys on my land."

"Suit yourself." Davis turned and tipped his hat, then walked back out the door.

And he left them all standing there, on the edge of a fistfight that was apparently not going to happen. At least not today. That was disappointing. At least when Cade'd had occasion to punch Quinn in the face he'd gotten the opportunity.

"What the actual fuck?" Lark asked as soon as the door closed behind him.

"That was my exact thought," Cole said, sitting down on the couch.

Kelsey was wringing her hands and pacing, and Quinn followed suit. Lark sat down next to Cole.

Cade was suddenly conscious of the fact that his leg hurt like hell. But he had too much adrenaline from un-thrown punches rioting through his veins. He would pace if it wouldn't be excruciating. Instead he stood, Amber's fingers still curled into his shirt, like she was holding him up. Hell, maybe she was.

"That explains some things," Cade said, pulling away from her. He was uncomfortable with the idea of her being the one keeping him from tipping over. That wasn't her job. It shouldn't be.

He should be strong enough to stand on his own two feet, even if one of them couldn't bear all of his weight.

"Like why he's been circling around like a vulture?" Quinn asked.

"Yeah. That."

"And why he came and talked to me at the diner a while back," Nicole said. "I had breakfast there," she added, looking strangely guilty.

"Yeah, I remember that," Amber said. "He was being weird. He's been weird since he first showed up. I thought it was weird he wanted to be here so badly, and now it makes . . . a strange kind of sense. Clearly he's a little . . ."

"Crazy?" Cole asked.

"That's not nice," Kelsey said. "I mean, okay, he's intense, sure. But we're talking about a man who got abandoned by his father. And who was given nothing by that same father."

"In fairness," said Nicole, "I do give off a less villainous air. If I say so myself."

"You do," Cade said. "In fact, it makes me feel like a gigantic dick for being such a jerk to you."

Nicole shrugged. "It's . . . fine. I mean, it hurt my feelings, but this whole thing is a nightmare, and it's not your fault you didn't know how to handle it right. I'm not even sure what handling it right means at this point. Part of me thinks I should have just left you all alone. And then . . . some of me is just really glad I came, because I don't have anything back in Portland. I don't have family. Not even a dysfunctional one. I'm alone, and this is . . . it has been . . . so much better than being alone."

"You won't ever be alone again," Cade said. "That's one thing I can promise you."

"It's one of the more annoying things about this family," Lark said. "We take care of each other to a point of being invasive."

"It's true," Cole said. "Ask Quinn."

Quinn nodded. "Yeah. I seem to recall getting punched in the face when we first met."

"You were sleeping with my sister," Cole said.

"He still is," Lark said.

"But with a marriage license. I can deal with that."

Nicole fidgeted in her seat. "I feel . . . I had an inkling that there might have been another . . . secret our dad had. I got a call from some debt-collection company a few years ago looking for him, about a property in Prineville, and I . . . it made me wonder. But maybe there was another house. Obviously there was another family. I should have said something."

"You couldn't have known about Davis," Cole said. "It would have been a wild guess. You didn't even know us then."

"I know."

"I feel like such a jackass," Cole said, dragging his hand over his face. "How is it possible that our dad tricked so many people?"

Cade had an idea, and he didn't like it at all. Because sometimes he felt like he had the same skill. Selfishness and too much charm. Somehow, he was able to get away with an unreasonable amount of shit, and his smile had always pulled him out of it.

Inheritance from Dave Mitchell.

"He was a great guy," Cade said. "In that everyone wanted to be his friend. Or his lover, apparently. And he managed to keep it all smooth. He was good to mom, good to us. And good to all the other women in his life. But none of it was real. Or lasting."

That dug straight into his gut. Too close to him.

"You're not the one who should feel like a jackass, Cole," Lark said. "Dad's the one who lied. He's the one who tricked us. There's no shame in believing in your own father."

"Hell," Nicole said. "I loved it when he came to visit, and I didn't even really . . . know he was my dad. You can't blame yourselves."

Cade let out a sigh. "So what do we do with . . . Davis? The newest member of the Mitchell family tree."

"Bleah," Lark said.

"There isn't much you can do about him," Amber said.

"Not until you know for sure what he wants. For some reason . . . I'm not getting a snuggly family reunion scent off of him."

"Yeah," Cade said. "I'm not either."

"Our dad was an asshole," Lark said.

"On that we can all agree," Cole said, his voice rough.

"I loved him though," Lark added.

"Me too," Cade said. "And I knew a lot longer than the rest of you." That had always been the hard part. Loving the old man. Hating what he did. Hating that he'd expected Cade to be the one to keep the secret.

You understand though, son.

Yeah, sure he had. He'd said he had.

Why had his dad assumed he would? There was no good answer to that question.

"Even I kind of love him," Nicole said.

"I guess you can't help it," Cole said. "You love your parents. Even when they don't deserve it. Which is kind of a relief, all things considered," he said, going over to Kelsey and putting his hand on her stomach.

"Yeah, but, Cole, I don't have to love you if you go off and make babies with other women. You realize that, right?"

They all laughed at Kelsey's dry joke, even though it wasn't that funny. It was just nice to break the tension.

"I have no desire to be with another woman," he said, "ever. I love the old guy. But I sure as hell don't understand him."

Which was another reason why Cade had been the one trusted with some of the details. And it was why Cole was the one standing there with a wife. Why Cole was the one married with children.

One woman for the rest of your life? You and I know that's not realistic, Cade. I love your mother, but love and lust are two different things. You understand.

Sure.

Accidents happen.

His dad had said that about Nicole. Like it was no big deal. Like she was a fender bender, and not a baby.

And apparently, he'd thought even less of Davis, since

another son had never been mentioned. Never been explained.

All things considered, Cade could hardly blame the guy for being an ass. Cade acted like an ass for a lot less.

At least he'd had their dad. This house. The career he'd had.

"You ready to go?" he asked Amber. Because he needed to be with her. Just her right now, and not everyone else. And Lord knew why.

"Yeah," she said. "I don't really feel all that well."

"No surprise why," Quinn muttered.

Yeah. Who the hell could feel good after all that.

"We'll go too," Lark said.

Cole nodded. "Probably for the best."

It was unusual for all of them to split up when stuff this serious was going down. But maybe that was a testament to just how weird it all was.

"You okay?" he asked Nicole. Because probably he should, since she didn't have anyone to leave with.

"Yeah," she said. "Actually, I might . . . take a drive. Not a long one off a short pier or anything, so don't worry. I just need to . . . clear my head."

"Don't blame you," Cole said. "I think we all do. But know that you're welcome to come back here."

"I do," she said. "And I appreciate that. Actually, in some ways . . . I feel better knowing there was more than just me. That means I'm not solely responsible for ruining the Mitchell clan."

"You never were," Cole said.

"And anyway," Lark said, "you never ruined anything. It's been nice having you."

Nicole looked at him. And he knew he deserved that. "You didn't ruin anything," Cade said. "It was our dad who ruined things. We all deserved better than we got. All of us."

"Yeah," she said, "we did."

"But at least now no one's on the outside."

"Except Davis," Cole said.

"Only if he wants to be," Lark said.

"That's true. Being likable isn't a part of being family," Cole said. "Take Cade as Exhibit A."

"Hey," Amber said.

"It's true," Cade said.

Because in this whole shitty scenario, somehow he felt like he held some fault. That was the heart of it all. That was why dealing with Nicole had been so hard. He'd felt complicit, and he still did. Even now, standing here, he felt like he wasn't sure which side he was on.

Sure, he thought his dad was a dick. But he'd protected him. So his actions proved where he stood. And he didn't like it. Not at all.

"I'll see you guys later," he said. "I'm sure we'll need to have a roundtable discussion soon."

"Yeah," Cole grunted.

He laced his fingers through Amber's and led her from the house. For some reason, holding hands seemed about right. Seeing how if he didn't hold on to her he damn well might fall on his face.

Unsteady legs and a big shock weren't the best combination, it turned out.

They were silent on the drive home. All the way until they got into her house.

"Do you want to talk about it?" she asked.

"Fuck. No." He pulled her into his arms and pushed her back against the wall, bringing his lips down on hers, kissing her with every last bit of rage in him. Every bit of despair and self-loathing—and dammit, there was a lot.

He didn't want to talk. He just wanted to exorcise it all until he couldn't feel it. Until his back and leg were all that hurt, and not his head and chest.

He pushed her top up, then reached around and unhooked her bra, dragging it all to the floor before lowering his head and sucking one nipple deep into his mouth.

She arched into him, a hoarse cry on her lips. That was all the encouragement he needed.

He hauled her against him, away from the wall, and propelled them both into the living room, then he spun her away from him and pushed her down so that she was bent at the waist. She caught herself on the back of the couch, her hands clinging tightly to it.

He gathered her hair into his hand and pushed it aside, exposing the curve of her neck, the elegant line of her back.

He traced the indent in her back, down to the waistband of her skirt. To the dimples just above her butt. If there was anything more sensual than those marks, he hadn't seen it. A reminder of how soft she was. Of how different she was from him.

He gripped her hips, ran his hands down her thighs and to the flowing black hem. He curled his fingers around the cool fabric and started to draw it upward, baring her legs, her hips, her ass, barely covered by black lace panties.

"Normally," he said, "I'm not much for fashion."

"This is hardly fashion," she said, her voice choked. "This is a work uniform."

"Hush. I'm trying to compliment you." She did, which surprised him. "I like how your panties match your skirt," he said, and he felt her shiver beneath his hands.

"Normally no one appreciates those details."

"Oh, I do. Matches your shoes too."

"Yeah. I'm a fashion plate like that."

"These need to go though," he said, drawing her underwear down to her knees and taking in the view of her bare skin, her skirt pushed up, her high heels still on.

Damn.

She shifted and stepped out of the black scrap of fabric and pushed it aside with her toe. Then she started to kick off her shoes.

"No," he said. "Leave them. Then face the couch again."

He didn't know what he was doing. He didn't know why he was talking to his best friend like this. Why he was giving her orders. Why he was about to screw her into oblivion. Both his oblivion and hers.

He didn't know what gave him that right.

What gave him the right to speak to her this way, to treat

her this way. But she wanted it, of that he had no doubt. Still, he didn't know if that made it okay. If that made it right.

But right now he didn't care. Not even a little bit. Right now it didn't matter. All that mattered was desire.

And maybe, in this moment, he was finally proving it. That he was just like his father. That he really did understand. That lust was sometimes more important than common sense. Than love and caring.

Than doing the right thing.

Because how could anything be more important than this? Than Amber's bare ass, and her bent over the couch. Than her waiting for him. Begging for him with her every breath, with every needy sound she made?

There was no right thing on earth that had ever been this important.

He pushed his hand between her thighs, ran his fingers across her slick folds. Felt how wet she was. For him. Only him.

Yeah, there was nothing more important than this.

Everything else could go to hell.

He grappled with his belt buckle and finally managed to free himself before he retrieved a condom from his wallet and sheathed his length.

He pushed against the entrance to her body, the head of his cock sliding in easily. She was so tight, so wet. He held on to her with one hand, and on to the couch with the other, trying to keep himself from falling.

It was too good. He didn't know if he could last. He didn't know if he wanted to.

It would be the easiest thing to do. Just push in all the way and let go. Give in to the fire-breathing monster inside of him that just wanted to consume, and not give at all.

But that he couldn't do.

Because it was Amber. Because she was his best friend.

Because he wanted her pleasure more than he wanted his own, even now. Even in this moment.

He entered her slowly, relishing the feel of her. The sound she made when he thrust deep and hard, the little moan of regret when he pulled away.

"Hold on, baby," he said.

He took his hand from the couch and brushed it between her thighs, over her clit, as he continued to move inside of her.

"Oh, yes," she said, over and over again, the affirmations keeping time with his movements.

He leaned down and grazed the curve of her exposed neck with his teeth, and he felt her shudder, felt her internal muscles tighten around his shaft.

And then everything in his mind shattered, and he forgot about everything. About what had happened back at Elk Haven. About Davis. About his father and his anger and everything that wasn't what it was like to be buried deep inside Amber Jameson.

She was all that mattered.

This was all that mattered.

He felt her body tense, felt her muscles pulse around him, heard her harsh curse as her orgasm broke over her, and then he let go. His release roared through him like fire through dry brush, consuming everything in its path, leaving him scorched from the inside out.

Leaving him dry and cracked, and on the verge of breaking apart.

He couldn't catch his breath. And he couldn't stand anymore.

He pulled away from her and stumbled back, sinking to the floor, his leg screaming at him, his back protesting everything that had just happened.

Well, who cared. He didn't. Screw pain. It didn't matter. It had been worth it.

Hell yes. It had been worth it. Even if he couldn't walk for days.

He looked up and saw Amber adjusting her clothes with shaking fingers.

"You okay?" he asked.

"You're the one on the floor," she said, tugging her shoes off and pushing her skirt back down.

"I guess so," he said, looking around. He was bare-assed

on the floor, his clothes mostly still in place except for his pants, with a condom on. That had to be a good visual for her. He pushed himself back up. "I'll just go to the bathroom for a sec," he said, heading to the hall bath to get things taken care of.

He cleaned up and washed his hands, then made the mistake of looking in the mirror. What the hell was wrong with him?

Then he decided he didn't care. Not tonight.

Life was one giant pile of messed-up right now, so as far as where he fit into all of it? He'd deal with that concern at a later date. It could take a number.

He walked back out of the bathroom, getting his jeans and everything back in order.

"Sorry," he said. "About that . . ."

"Nah," she said, tugging her top on over her head. "Don't apologize for that. It was . . . good."

"You said that funny. Was it not good?"

"It was good," she said, her lip wobbling a little bit.

Shit.

"Are you . . . ?"

"I'm fine," she said, a tear trickling down her cheek.

"Baby," he said, walking forward and tugging her into his arms. "Amber, did I hurt you?"

"No," she said, sounding like she was barely clinging to composure, her voice shaky and watery.

"Why are you crying?"

"I don't know," she said, the sound of her misery increasing with each word.

"Don't lie to me," he said, pulling back and looking at her. "Dammit, Amber, if I hurt you . . ."

"You didn't. Cade, it was wonderful. So good. And I don't know why I'm c-crying. Maybe that's why. Maybe because it was good."

"That doesn't make sense."

"I know!" she said, her voice nearly a wail now. "It's just . . . I'm upset, because Davis . . . and your family . . . and my grandpa. And then that was so good. And I haven't had any coffee today so I think maybe I'm crazy."

"Honey, I don't know what coffee has to do with anything."

"Of course not! You had some today. I think it's why I'm emotionally unstable. You can't just quit caffeine cold turkey."

"Fair enough."

"Bleah." She shook her head and pulled away from him. "I'm fine."

"We just had sex, and then you had a breakdown. You might be fine, but I think I'm scarred for life."

"Sorry. It's not your . . . prowess."

"That wasn't my concern. I was kind of . . . rough with you, and I . . ."

"A little rough sex isn't going to break me," she said. "I've been through a lot worse."

"I don't want to be part of the worse you've been through."

"That's not what I meant, Cade. I said it . . . wrong, because how the hell do you talk to your best friend about this?"

"I don't know. That's why I'm sort of fumbling around over here."

"Fair enough. We're both fumbly."

"Right. As long as I didn't hurt you."

"Quite the opposite," she said, running her fingers under her eyes and wiping away the remaining moisture.

"Well . . . good."

"Are you okay? I'm sorry. Again. I don't have any room to be having an epic breakdown when you're the one discovering there are yet more skeletons in your closet."

"Not mine," Cade said. "My dad's."

"True. But you all kind of inherited his crap. Isn't that how it works?"

"I guess."

"Not that I'd know. Since I got nothing from my parents at all."

"This must all seem . . . weird to you. Our giant-ass family drama when . . . Sorry."

She lifted a shoulder. "No. I get it. And it's just like you said, you know? It doesn't matter what they did. Or didn't do. You love your parents. It's silly that I do. I don't even know my dad, and I'm pissed as hell at him. I never knew him, but . . . there's something in me that . . . if I ever met him . . . if I ever met him and he wanted me, even for a moment, I think I'd just run to him and hug him. I don't know why. I feel . . . embarrassed about that, really. I've never even let myself fully think that before because it sounds so lame, but . . . it's true."

"It's not lame, Amber."

"Then you loving your dad isn't lame either."

"I guess not." Though, right now, he felt like he could use a shower. He felt unclean. He felt like he'd just taken a walk in his father's shoes in the worst way. In the kind of lust that made you crazy, and made you dishonor people you cared about.

"Way not," she said. "I need to go lie down. It was a long day."

"Yeah, okay. I'll meet you upstairs. I need a shower and things. Should I bring you dinner?"

"I don't think I'll eat," she said. "I just feel weird and off. What I really want is sleep. I have to get up way too early tomorrow."

"Me too. The bison won't fence themselves."

"No. That would be far too useful. Bison aren't known for their usefulness."

"Not when it comes to using tools."

"Cloven hooves aren't so good with that."

"Yeah, opposable thumbs are a must. I'll come to bed in a bit," he said, kissing her cheek.

Cade walked toward the shower in the downstairs bathroom, stripping off his clothes as he went, not waiting for the water to heat up before he stepped under the spray.

He didn't know how to deal with any of this. Honestly, he didn't. Davis, who he had known for years now, from a distance, and who he officially disliked, was his half brother.

His life had turned into a soap opera. It was getting to be worse than a joke.

He heard his cell phone ringing from somewhere on the

floor. Probably in his pants. He shut the water off and dried off quickly, digging through his jeans pocket and answering. "Hello?"

"It's Quinn."

"Great," Cade said, tightening the towel around his waist. He and Quinn were not at the talking-on-the-phone-naked stage of their relationship. Actually, he was not at that stage of a relationship with any man on earth. "What's up?"

"Besides the general insanity?"

"Yeah, besides that."

"Sam said it was okay for you to talk to Jake. He wants to arrange a phone call for sometime tomorrow."

"I'm just out doing fences tomorrow. He can call me on my cell."

"Great. I gave him the number." Quinn paused for a second. "You okay?"

"Damn. You don't want me to talk about my feelings, do you?"

Quinn paused again. "I don't want you to, but it seemed appropriate, all things considered."

"I'm fine. I'm lying, because how the hell am I supposed to deal with . . . that."

"Look, I know Davis. I don't like him. Apart from all of the things he's been up to around here, I don't like him, and I never have."

"You didn't like me either."

"I didn't say I do now."

"True."

"I could go either way on you," Quinn said. "Davis, on the other hand . . . I don't trust him. What's his game? To come here and compete with your ranch? Put you out of business? What?"

"Do you think he's lying about our dad?"

"I don't know why he'd lie. It isn't like y'all are rich, apart from the ranch. And with so many of you, it's not like it's worth much to go in fifths on the inheritance. So I actually believe all that. But beyond that, I don't trust him."

"I'll keep that in mind."

"Or don't. I'm just putting it out there."

"No, I will."

"Good. Okay. You're good though?"

"I'm not about to lie down in front of a tractor. Anyway, Amber's here."

"Yeah."

The way his brother-in-law said that made Cade feel like the bastard had some alternate insight into what was happening with Amber and himself. Which he didn't like at all, because he sure as hell didn't have extra insight into what was happening with Amber and himself.

Except that there was some kind of engagement farce happening, and they were really sleeping together. And beyond that? He had a feeling the people they were really fooling were themselves.

"Yeah," Cade said in response. It was all he had.

Then he hung up. Things seemed to be getting slightly less awkward with Quinn, so there was that.

He tugged his jeans on, not even bothering with underwear, then stalked to the fridge on a beer hunt. He found one and went into the living room, sitting on the couch he'd just bent Amber over.

His reprieve of good feelings was over. He had nothing left to do but sit here and drown in regret and alcohol. So that was what he was going to do.

CHAPTER

Nineteen

The inside of her mouth tasted like a gym shoe.

That was Amber's first thought when she opened her eyes in the morning. Her second thought was that she was so tired, she felt drugged.

And her third thought was that the room was spinning. Which tied in nicely with thought number two.

She curled her blankets more tightly around her and rolled slowly out of the bed, trying to land softly, but not entirely upright.

Then she noticed Cade wasn't in bed. But that wasn't too unusual, since he was often downstairs fixing breakfast.

She didn't think he was though. For some reason, the bed had a half-slept-in feeling. Like only she'd been in it all night. He certainly hadn't woken her. Of course, feeling like she did now, she was pretty sure she'd fallen straight to sleep when she'd gone to bed at six and not budged once after.

Because she felt like day-old garbage. And her tongue was glued to the roof of her mouth.

She heard footsteps and looked across the bedroom, her line of sight connecting with Cade's boots in the doorway.

"Good morning," he said, not even a hint of questioning in his voice.

"Hi," she said, tugging her sheet down so she could get a better look at him from her spot on the floor.

"Are you okay?"

"I feel gross."

"Get back in bed," he said.

"No. I have to work."

"You did a tuck and roll out of bed. And you look like a caterpillar. You're not going to work." He walked over to where she was and picked her up, blankets and all, and deposited her back on the mattress. "Call in sick."

"Cade, I can't—"

"If you say you can't afford it, I'm going to tickle you."

"No! I'm weak and ill."

"Then don't say it. And stay home. And stay in bed."

"Cade, I cannnn't."

"You're really whiny this morning. Are you going to serve customers with that attitude? And anyway, no one wants a sick waitress. You'll infect their eggs."

"Cade . . ."

He took her cell phone from her nightstand and put it in her hand. "Call in sick. Imagine turning back over and burrowing back under the covers. Doesn't that sound nice?"

"Yes," she mumbled.

"Good. Do it. Everyone will survive without you."

"They will not. The café will crumble." But she was already dialing, and within five minutes had herself off the hook. And she was already drifting back to sleep.

When she opened her eyes again, the sun was high in the sky and her room was too warm for all the blankets she was still wrapped in.

She looked at the clock and nearly fell out of bed.

It was almost two p.m.

Was she sick or was she dying? Good lord, she hadn't slept this late since she was sixteen.

She stood up fast and stumbled, her knees knocking in

like a newborn colt's. Jeez. She felt hungover. And she was most definitely not hungover.

She moved into the bathroom and splashed cold water on her face, down to her neck, trying to cool off. She felt overheated, but she didn't feel nauseous anymore.

She grabbed her toothbrush and toothpaste and started trying to deal with the shoe flavor that still lingered on her tongue. Then she smacked her lips and looked at herself in the mirror. She looked like death. Like pale, vacant death.

Her eyes were flat, her cheeks gray, and her hair was hanging limp. She wrinkled her nose. Normally, she wouldn't have cared about Cade seeing her like this. After all, they'd seen each other vomit after a hard drinking night back in the day. Frequently.

But this was different. It was all different now. He was her lover, and she wanted him to see her being sexy. Not this.

Weird. Because it seemed like adding a naked element to their relationship should have demolished barriers, not erected new ones. But now she cared what she looked like for him. Hmm. An inconvenient and silly development.

She bent down and started to rummage through the bottom drawer for some floss, pushing a box of tampons out of the way. Then she froze.

Was she really that stupid? Or just that distracted? Either way . . . she hadn't had a period since before Lark's wedding.

That was going on five weeks.

And as much as she'd tried not to think about it, her first time with Cade had been sans contraception.

She'd been so deep in her denial about that, as had he, obviously, that neither of them had even spoken about it. She'd barely even allowed herself to think it.

But now, staring down at the tampon box she hadn't needed for far too long, she knew she was at the end of her denial rope. And suddenly, she had to know now.

She had to know, this very instant, if she was carrying Cade's baby.

Oh . . . holy shit. A baby. Her best friend's baby. Both of them were like the poster children for Screwed the Hell Up. How were they supposed to raise a baby? A hypothetical baby, since all it was right now was a missed period.

She couldn't just go to the store and buy a test. It would make it through town faster than a brush fire in August.

And that meant she had to trust someone. Dammit. That was the thing she was least good at. Except Cade. She trusted Cade. But not to do this.

She could call Lark. But then people would think Lark was expecting. And that would suck for her.

Amber tapped her fingers on her chin, almost grateful for this added conundrum, since it gave her an excuse to focus on the surface issue of procuring a pregnancy test, rather than actually focusing on the potential-pregnancy panic.

And then it hit her. There was no one better to send on this mission than an obviously pregnant woman.

She walked back into the bedroom and picked up her cell phone, poking her head out the bedroom door just to make sure Cade wasn't around before closing it, locking it and scurrying into the bathroom.

She dialed Kelsey's cell phone number.

"Hello?" she heard Kelsey say.

"Hi. Kelsey, it's Amber."

"Yeah. I know. Maddy, stop it!"

"Is this a bad time?"

"I'm in a grocery store with a two-year-old."

"Oh. Yeah. Well, can you get something for me while you're there and please don't tell anyone it's for me? And please don't tell Cade. And please don't tell Cole. Or Lark."

"Uh . . . if you ask me for bleach and garbage bags I'm going to get concerned."

"Prepare to get more concerned. I need a pregnancy test."

"What?"

"I need a pregnancy test. But I can't go buy one. Because then everyone will know."

"But you two are getting married."

"No, we aren't."

"What?"

"We're not really together."

"But . . . you're pregnant," Kelsey hissed.

"No. I might be."

"You just said you weren't really together. Maddy, don't pull on Mommy!"

"Well, we slept together. Many times. Are currently sleeping together . . . a lot."

"Then what the hel-ck . . . Do you mean you aren't together?"

"We're friends with . . . orgasmic benefits. Do not judge me. You have no idea how hard up I was. And there was so much alcohol . . . though, we didn't do it that night. We did it the next day. But—"

"Wait. Stop. You're just friends."

"Yes."

"And you're sleeping together."

"Yes," Amber said.

"And he lives with you."

"Yeah."

"And he's starting a bison ranch on your grandfather's property."

"Well . . . yeah."

"Do you share a bed? And not just for s-e-x?"

Amber bit her lip. "Yes."

"What part of that is not being in a relationship?"

"We are not in love."

"Really?" Kelsey asked.

"Yes! Really!"

"Honey, I think you've been in love with him since the moment I met you. And I'd bet since long before that."

Amber ignored the sharp, punched-in-the-chest feeling that Kelsey's words brought on. "Am not. We're friends."

"Bull pucky."

"I just need a pregnancy test. Not commentary."

"I'm already pregnant," Kelsey said. "What will everyone think?"

"That you're buying the test for someone who doesn't

246

want everyone to know they're buying a test. But at least they won't attribute it to the correct person."

"I'll be ten minutes."

"Okay."

Amber hung up the phone and paced until Kelsey's truck rolled into the driveway. She opened the door and held out her hand until Kelsey appeared with a bag in one hand and Maddy on her hip.

"Gimme."

Kelsey pulled the bag back against her chest. "I'm staying for this."

"No."

"I'm going to be an aunt. Potentially. I'm staying for this."

"What if Cade comes back?"

"I'll tell him we're having coffee. Anyway, you're going to have to tell him about this."

"No," Amber said, shaking her head. "There is no reason for me to have to tell him that my period was late. None at all. Because it's probably stress. Or something."

She was lying. To Kelsey. To herself. But whatever. Until the pink lines appeared, she was doing denial.

"Come in though," she growled, holding the door for Kelsey, who breezed inside and set the test on the kitchen table.

"If it's positive, what will you do?" Kelsey asked.

"I don't know what we'll do. I . . . I don't know. It wasn't supposed to be this way."

"What way was it supposed to be, Amber?" Kelsey asked, her expression compassionate. So compassionate it made her heart hurt. Dammit.

"We were supposed to go on like we always had," she said. "We're supposed to just sort of . . . make life easier for each other. Not harder. Not this."

"That's the thing though. It can't go on the way it always has, because that's not how life is."

"I don't want to hear that."

"Hey," Kelsey said, "I'm sort of the queen of dealing with the unexpected. Remember, I got pregnant with the wrong man's baby due to the shoddy record keeping of a fertility clinic. I mean . . . how do you mix up sperm?"

"It all kind of looks the same. And that's beside the point. I wanted things to stay the same. I was happy. And now I'm . . . scared. And I don't have anyone to talk to about it. Because Cade is the person I talk to. He's my go-to, and I wanted him to be the one I called in for this. But I can't. I mean . . . this morning I was worried about him seeing me looking like crap because now there's this other stuff between us, and I hate it."

"You'll get over that," Kelsey said. "Trust me. That's what happens in marriage."

"But we aren't getting married. We aren't in love. We . . . we're friends, and we can't even talk to each other about the thing that's currently scaring the heck out of me."

"Go and take the test," Kelsey said. "And then you'll know whether or not you can share this with him. Because if it's positive . . . well, then you have to. And if it *is* positive, remember, he's your best friend. And it could be worse. You could be doing it with a stranger. Trust me."

"But things worked out fine for you," Amber said.

"Yeah, even with the weirdest circumstances. So how could things not work out fine for you?"

Amber nodded slowly, picked up the plastic bag and headed toward the bathroom. It was weird. There was a time in her life when all of her possessions had been kept in a grocery bag like this one.

And now, the answer to what her future would be was contained in one.

There was a sad bit of poetry to that.

She bit her lip and headed into the bathroom. No more wondering. In just a few minutes, she would know for sure.

Cade stopped working and leaned up against the fence post, putting his phone up to his ear. "Cade Mitchell."

"Hi, Mr. Mitchell."

"Jake," Cade said. "Good to hear from you."

"I'm here too." Another voice on the line. Deeper. Gruffer. Sam, Quinn's friend and Jake's dad, Cade was sure. He'd already heard a basic confession from Jake, last year when he'd cleared Quinn's name, but at the time, none of the details he'd given had meant anything to Cade. He wondered if it would be different now.

"Great. I'm just here to listen," said Cade. "Whatever you know, Jake. Whatever you remember . . . I would be grateful for the information. No pressure." It was just Cade feeling like he was on the cusp of vindication and potential emotional healing. No pressure at all.

"I don't have a lot to say. I just talked to the guy that one time. But my dad had me look at a lineup of guys the other day. He pulled up pictures of everyone he could remember riding with. And I did recognize someone. It wasn't the guy who asked me to . . . to do it. But it was his buddy. And I'm pretty sure . . . I mean, I wouldn't be surprised if they were in it together, but I don't know that."

"Okay. Who did you recognize?"

"Jim Davis," Sam said. "The guy he pointed to was Jim Davis."

"What?" This time Cade was totally sure the ground under his feet tilted. Amber had said he should look at Davis, and she hadn't been wrong. But that was before he'd found out about Davis being a half-sibling. And then . . . well, the two together was too much.

Just too damn much.

"He was sure," Sam said.

"Okay. That's . . . good. Thanks. I don't . . ."

He looked up and saw Amber standing there, her hands clasped in front of her, her eyes wide, her face pale. "Cade . . ." she said.

He shook his head and held up his hand. "You're sure?" he said. "And sure enough that the guy he talked to was someone he was friends with?"

"Yeah," Jake said. "He was like his . . . assistant or whatever. Like Quinn and dad."

"Okay. Thanks, Jake." He watched Amber's expression change slightly, her distress turning to a kind of worried-distress that hardly seemed possible. "I need to go," he said. "There's some . . . things I have to take care of. Thank you."

"I'm sorry," Jake said. "I can't . . . say it enough times."

"Yeah," Cade said. "You can. Once was enough. I don't blame you. I never have. Don't feel bad, okay?"

"I do though."

"Don't," Cade said. "It doesn't have to shape both of our lives. Actually, it doesn't have to shape either of our lives. Let's go on and do better things, okay?"

"Okay," Jake said, his voice choked.

"Great. Talk to you later." He hung up the phone and looked at Amber, not sure what to say. Not sure what to do at all.

There was just no processing things like this easily.

"Was that Jake?" she asked, wringing her hands.

"Yes."

"What did he say?" She put her hand on her forehead. "No . . . wait. I can't know what he said. Not yet."

"Why not?"

"Because I need to tell you something."

"It's only going to take me a second to tell you—"

Amber ran over his words in a rush, while he was still speaking. "I'm pregnant."

"Davis is the one who did it."

"Oh."

"What?"

"No, you're right," she said. "That's a huge deal. I should have let you go first."

"You're what?" he asked, feeling like the world had just gone ahead and dropped away now. Just fallen out from under his feet and left him suspended in the air.

Amber tucked her hair behind her ear, her focus on the dirt in front of her. She looked . . . pale. And tired. She looked scared. It made his gut clench. Made him want to reach out and hold her, except the damn ground still wasn't under his feet.

"I think this Davis revelation is really interesting."

He shook his head. "Amber. Focus. Pregnant. What. The. Hell."

"Oh, that. Yeah. I'm . . . pregnant. At least that's what the test says. If you want to go off that. They're only like . . . ninety-nine percent accurate, and that, to me, seems like an error margin you have to consider. It's a whole percent, Cade. A whole percentage point of a chance that the test is just completely wrong."

"How did that happen?"

"Well, Cade, when a man and a woman enjoy each other's bodies very much . . ."

"Amber . . ."

"And the man fails to wear a rubber when he screws the woman on a kitchen table, sometimes that careless lust results in a baby."

"Amber. Be serious."

"I can't," she said, shaking her head, her dark eyes wide. "I just can't be. Because, Cade, if I take it too seriously, or I think too hard about any of it, I'm going to break the hell apart, and I don't know if I'll ever be able to make sense out of what's left."

He should hug her. Or something. But he couldn't move. Mostly because he still felt like there was nothing under his boots and he really wasn't sure if taking a step was an option—or if he'd just fall straight down and keep on falling.

"I don't know what to say. Which is kind of shit, I know," he said. "But . . . I don't know what to say."

"I don't either. Except . . . you know, like . . . a lot of people have miscarriages."

"Are you offering that up as a silver lining?"

"I don't know, Cade. I don't fucking know. I don't really know . . . anything." A tear slid down her cheek, and her lower lip trembled. And he knew he really needed to hug her, but for some reason his boots were still rooted to that nonexistent earth.

"Well, don't look at me, I don't have an answer."

"Oh, you don't?" she asked, her voice getting louder, shriller, and he couldn't blame her. But he hadn't been able to stop the asinine statement from coming out of his mouth either.

"No, I don't."

"Well then . . . great. So I guess we'll just not deal with it. It's in your genes not to deal with it, isn't it?"

Her words jarred him back to reality and hit with all the impact of a bucking horse. For a second he felt like he was back on the ground, getting trampled, the air torn from his lungs, the flesh torn from his bones.

Like he was bleeding out into the dirt, dying in front of millions of people on live broadcast.

There had never been another moment like that one, a moment of reckoning. When he'd stared down death and fear and truly faced what they meant. That things might be over. There was a clarity to it that had remained unmatched. Until now. Until Amber had ripped his guts out, turned his life upside down and gone ahead and said the exact thing he'd always been afraid of. The exact thing he'd never been able to say out loud.

"Yeah," he said, taking a step back. Finally his damned legs were working. "Yeah, I guess it kind of is in my blood. To leave bastard kids spread all over the place. Except, you know what? I haven't ever done that, and I'm not doing it now." As soon as he said the words, he believed them.

He'd always been afraid of being his father. That he was just like him. All charm, no substance. Able to trick people into caring, into believing he was a good guy, without ever actually backing that up.

Worse, when his father had confided in him, he'd been afraid the old man had looked at him and seen where he would end up. That if he ever tried with a woman, he'd just send it all to hell in the end.

And this pregnancy . . . it seemed to confirm it. He'd been careless with a woman who had done nothing but give to him. He'd followed his own pleasure to an end with unfixable consequences. It was worse than bleeding out in a crowded arena. It was the evidence of his weakness, right in front of him.

Except in all of his worrying, in all of his doubt, he'd forgotten one thing.

He had the control.

He had the control over the manner of man he was, and no one, not his father, not a bucking bronco, not a half brother with some kind of daddy complex, not an older brother with a god complex, could take that control from him.

Shit happened. Hell, tons of shit had happened to him. He'd lost the ability to walk straight. He'd lost the ability to compete. He'd lost his mother too soon.

He would not lose his child. He would not leave his child. And he sure as hell would never be like his father.

There were choices to make in life, and for too long, he'd made none. For too long, he'd coasted on anger and grief over a lost career. Grief over the loss of a father who'd never been what he should have. Fear that he would never be the man he should be either.

But dammit, why not?

He'd given his father a pass with his fear, and that was something he hadn't fully realized until now. Feeling like it was hereditary meant he couldn't fight it . . . and his father hadn't been able to either. But that was a boy's perspective. And he wasn't a boy anymore.

He was a man, as his father had been. His father could have been better if he'd wanted to, and Cade had to face that fact. Had to face that his father had chosen to commit the sins he had. Had chosen to dishonor his wife, to abandon his children.

To lie to a whole town, and to the woman he'd made vows to.

It was hell to realize that. To admit it.

But it was also the key to freedom.

Dave Mitchell had made decisions about how he was going to live his life. And Cade was going to make his own.

Independent from the man his father had been, independent from his fears about his own shortcomings.

He was always afraid before he got on a bronc in the rodeo. But he always saddled up anyway. And today, no matter how afraid he was, he knew it was time to saddle up.

"You just said you didn't know what to do," she said.

"That was ten seconds ago. I just made a decision."

"And what decision is that?"

"Amber Jameson, you're going to marry me."

"I'm . . . what?"

"You're going to marry me."

Amber blinked and took a step away from Cade. He had a strange and frightening light in his eyes. Determination. Determination on a level she did not want to deal with. On a level she wasn't sure she *could* deal with.

"I don't . . . think I am. I don't recall agreeing to that."

"You're having my baby."

"I'm sorry, did we fall into a time warp and go back to nineteen fifty-three?"

"You're right, Amber. I've done some stupid things. And the difference between me and my father is going to be how I handle it. I'm going to be there for you. I'm going to be there for my child."

"But Cade, we don't . . . you don't . . . you don't love me," she said, forcing the words through her tightened throat.

"What does that have to do with anything?" he asked.

"Um . . . lots."

"Yeah, well . . . my parents were in love. I assume yours

thought they were at some point. What the hell good did that do anyone? We have choices," he said, like it was some kind of revelation.

"Sure," she said. "We have choices. I fail to see why that has led to you deciding that I have one choice, which is to accept your half-cocked marriage proposal."

"Because it's the right choice," he said.

"I'm still waiting for that famous Mitchell reasoning to kick in."

"This is Mitchell reasoning. Do you not remember Cole and Kelsey?"

"You know, that doesn't make your offer more enticing. 'Well, when my brother knocked a chick up on accident, he proposed' does not make my heart skip. Even a little."

"I'm not trying to make your heart skip, Amber. I'm just saying . . . how do you want this to go? Do you want our child to have a family? Or do you want what we had? A pile of broken dysfunctional?"

"I don't know how on earth you think you and I will pass as functional."

"Because we will," he said. "Because we're not going to start out blind, or in love, or lying to ourselves and each other. Because we're going to walk in knowing full well how fragile this family thing can be. Because we'll walk in determined to live for something bigger than just ourselves."

"You're awfully philosophical about something that is a massive freaking deal."

"At least I have a plan. What was your plan?"

She let out a short, snortlike noise. "I . . . was planning on . . . being in denial for the next six months and then figuring it out after that."

"Well that's one way to go about it," he said, taking another step toward her. "Or, we can go with my plan. Which is an actual plan."

He was pissed. And it was her fault. She'd hit him low, and she hadn't even meant it. Cade was nothing like his father. Nothing at all. But she knew, with that instinct friends had about things, that it was the thing he was afraid of. So she'd smacked him across the face with it.

And now she was reaping the unforeseen consequences.

She sort of wished the consequence was just him yelling at her and not proposing. Because yelling she could do. She could yell back with the best of them. But handling a proposal? Yeah, she had no idea how to do that.

Not when half of her really wanted to marry him.

There, she'd admitted it.

Because marrying Cade would mean she had him forever. And he would always sleep with her. And hold her. And kiss her. And he would be hers.

She was forgetting why she was supposed to resist. Why she should protest.

Oh yeah, that love business. Love was A Thing. It was supposed to be The Thing when it came to marriage. But then, wasn't he right about their parents? Love hadn't gotten her mother anywhere. Her mother had ended up alone, unable to cope and, in the end, without her child. Love had gotten Cade's mother exactly nowhere too. Living a life that was a lie, even if it was a shiny one.

Cade's father, for all that he professed to love Cade's mother, had been a faithless rat. So really, what was love? Did it make any difference at all?

Or was it all really what Cade said? Making choices and sticking with them.

"I have to think about this," she said. "All of it."

"You want the baby, don't you?" he asked.

"I don't want to not have it," she said. She couldn't think about giving it up, or ending the pregnancy. She'd been unwanted. She'd been the afterthought. She wouldn't do that to a child of hers. That decision she could make with confidence.

"Well, that's . . . something."

"Oh don't be an ass, Mitchell. You can't honestly tell me you're in a place in life where you want a baby."

"No," he said. "I can't. But . . . but why not? What else are we doing with our lives, Amber? And . . . think about it. We could have this," he said, gesturing to the field. "We could have this ranch. And we can take care of your grandpa together. We can build this, build a family. And you won't have to wait tables if you don't want to. I sure as hell didn't think I would ever have a wife or a kid, but . . . but it's happening, so why not just . . . go with it?"

"It's marriage and children, not a road trip, Cade. I think impulsive isn't the approach we're looking for here."

Except she wanted it. So bad her chest hurt. And that worried her. Because if her heart wasn't engaged in this whole relationship-with-Cade-thing, it seemed like her heart shouldn't hurt. Yet it did.

"Fine," he said, his voice rough. "We'll talk about it later, but I'm not changing my mind. This is what I want."

"You're annoying."

"I know."

"Can we forget about the baby for a second?"

Cade's eyebrows shot up. "I'm not sure I can."

"I want to ask you about Davis though. And if you're okay."

He put his hands on his lean hips and looked down, his hat obscuring his face. "No, I'm not okay. The man who is, apparently, my half brother, was responsible for the accident that almost killed me. The one that cost me my career. So . . . not okay."

"Is there anything I can do?"

"Marry me."

"Cade Mitchell . . ."

"I don't know. I don't really know what to do at this point. It takes unbelievably complicated to a whole new level, don't you think?"

"You Mitchells seem to excel at that."

"At least we excel at something."

"Wish I could say the same for my family," she said. "We just excelled in splitting up."

"That's what I want to prevent," he said, the look in his eyes far too sincere. A sincere Cade was a dangerous thing to her senses.

"Let's go . . . I don't know, let's go eat."

"You're hungry?"

"Starving. I slept in till two thirty. I want a cheeseburger."

"Really?"

"Can has it?"

"You're reverting to lolcats."

"I know. Don't make me text you a graphic to illustrate. I will."

"No," he said, holding up his hands. "I'll feed you. No need to bombard me with stupid cat pictures."

This felt weirdly normal. And nothing should feel normal right now. But she couldn't say she was sorry that, for the moment at least, she felt like she was talking to her friend. Not her lover, not the father of her baby. Her friend.

Right now, she really needed her friend.

"For a bacon cheeseburger, I'll behave."

"You sure you can go out in public?"

"Why? Do I have 'preggo' stamped on my forehead?"

"No, I just thought you might be feeling . . . vulnerable?"

"I don't do vulnerable, Cadence," she said—a total lie and they both knew it, seeing as she'd been standing in front of him weeping mere hours ago. But she was pulling false bravado because she needed it.

And thankfully, he let her.

"Nah. Of course you don't. Let's go feed you."

"You have to let me out of bed eventually."

"No," John said, rolling over, his arms bracketing Nicole's head. "I don't."

"You have a store to run. It was closed. All day."

"I put a sign on the door that said I had a medical emergency."

She narrowed her eyes. "You did not have a medical emergency."

"I did. I had an erection lasting longer than four hours."

"Ha!" She put her hands over her face and scrubbed her

eyes. Really, she shouldn't find his shenanigans amusing. She should tell him he was being crass. But since she'd been in bed, naked, with him for almost twenty-four hours she wasn't sure she had any room to name-call. "You're a beardy weirdo," she said.

"And you're a tattooed city girl. My mother warned me about women like you."

"Well, no one warned me about men like you. But I still know better."

He moved away from her and laid on his stomach, his chin resting on his forearms. "How is it you know better?"

"My dad. The way my mom was about him. Men are fun, but in my experience you shouldn't get too attached to the idea of keeping them."

She extended her hand and traced his lower lip with her fingertip. She was attached to him already. And she hated that it was true. Even though she knew that there was only heartbreak at the end of it all, she was attached.

"Maybe," he said. "But if you find one who wants to keep you too, it doesn't seem like it would be all that risky."

"That's the hard part," she said.

"Maybe not."

"There's another Mitchell bastard."

"Is that why you came last night?" he asked. He hadn't asked questions; he'd just opened the door and let her inside. And then they'd spent the night in bed. When they'd talked it had been about food and music. About places they wanted to go. About hypotheticals, not about reality.

"Yes. I had to go somewhere that wasn't there."

"So you came here."

"Yeah. I feel . . . more comfortable here, actually. Which is weird. And don't run."

He laughed. "Why would I run?"

"Because. You're a commitment-phobic man-whore. I can smell it all over you."

"You smell it on me?"

She leaned in and sniffed his chest, right between his pecs, the hair there prickly against her nose. "Okay.

Metaphorically. Literally you smell like sweat, and pine and sandalwood. And it's very nice."

"I think you're the first woman to ever smell me."

"Lies. I bet the whole town sniffs you surreptitiously when they walk by you in your shop."

"Even the cowboys?" he asked.

"Oh, yeah. The women want to smell you. The men want to smell like you."

"And you?"

"I *am* smelling you," she said. "I'm the envy of all."

"Who knew it was so simple?"

"It would be more simple if I could stay here." As soon as the words left her mouth she realized how they sounded. She winced. "I mean, not in a creepy way. Just that hiding under your covers is always preferable to facing reality. Hiding under your covers with a guy who resembles a studly lumberjack is even better. That's all I meant."

"Right. Well, you can hide under my covers for as long as you want. But I will need to go down and open the store eventually."

"I could, like . . . do your taxes."

"Could you?"

"Yeah, man. It's what I do."

"That's handy."

"I know."

"What else do you do?" he asked, giving her a smile best described as wicked.

"Why don't I get under the covers and show you."

It turned out that not jumping with mad glee and accepting a man's marriage proposal killed your sex life. Who knew?

Now Amber knew.

But then, it wasn't like she was in the mood to jump on Cade's body either. She was pregnant, and freaked out, and confused. So horny was currently way down on the list. Especially since she felt like butt most of the time.

Still, Cade ignoring her, and opting to sleep on that horrible mattress instead of by her side, was a little hard not to take personally.

As, I'm sure, is your not agreeing to marry him.

Fine, fine. That was valid.

She sighed and plopped onto the porch swing, her hands in her lap, her long skirt blowing in the breeze as she rocked back and forth, watching as the sun slipped behind the mountain and melted into a gilt edge that coated the treetops.

She had decisions to make. Decisions about work. About Cade. And she didn't know which ones to make.

If she said yes . . . well, if she said yes, she would have

him. It would make her grandfather happy. It would make the town happy.

And it would make Cade . . . the most honorable bastard this side of the Willamette. So there were all the good things. Very, very good things.

Something in her chest hurt, like a piece of glass that had been stuck deep inside for a long time was starting to dislodge. She couldn't breathe past it. She could hardly think past it. She didn't know why all of this hurt so bad. Only that it did.

Only that she was more confused now than she'd ever been.

She thought she'd left that scared, sad little girl who didn't know what she wanted in life way back in high school. Had thought that by recognizing some of the stupid things she was doing to cope with her issues, and by changing her behavior, that she'd fixed all her crap.

Apparently, that wasn't true.

Apparently she'd just shoved all her crap into a little corner and covered it with a blanket. She'd done the internal equivalent of a half-assed cleaning job.

She put her fists up against her eyes and pressed hard, until she saw spots bursting into the black.

"What's up, babe?"

She looked up, the spots now superimposed over her very favorite cowboy. "I'm brooding."

"I can see that, but about what specifically?"

She snorted. "The fact that, by tomorrow, the fields will be overrun by bison. Damn bison, Cade."

Of course, the bison weren't the real issue. Or maybe they were. Bison all over the damn place. And once they moved in, getting them out wouldn't be easy. They would really just be here. Cade would really just be here.

Her grandfather's house would be his.

And then, she supposed, like her grandfather had done before Cade, she would be his responsibility, whether he wanted her to be or not.

She was like a bad penny to the people around here. Everyone cursed with too much decency couldn't seem to throw her back where she'd come from.

While plenty of other people seemed to see her for just what she was. Unnecessary, a little cheap and not your favorite thing to find in the bottom of your wallet.

Wow. She was full of happy thoughts today.

"It's exciting," he said. "It's a new beginning."

His words were laden with the kind of meaning she just could not handle right at the moment. Not even a little bit. She couldn't have a new beginning. Because for her, nothing about this was a new beginning.

And when she looked at Cade, she realized why.

Because Cade was the one person in her life who had stood with her because he wanted to. Because he'd chosen her as a friend.

She was an unwanted pregnancy that had developed into an unwanted child. Who had been passed off to foster home after foster home, people who'd had to take her because they'd signed up. Because they wanted to collect a check, or do good, or even make sure kids had someone to be with for a while. But never because they loved her.

Then she'd gone to her grandparents. Who had taken her in because what decent elderly couple wouldn't take in the abandoned, unwanted spawn of their neglectful son?

And as much as she loved them, and as much as they seemed to love her, she'd always felt . . . she'd always felt like they'd been obligated to.

And now Cade was obligated to take her. Because she was having his unintended baby. And the cycle continued.

The only person in her life who had always been with her because he wanted to be with her would now be forced to be with her for all eternity because of the baby.

And she was the baggage that came with it.

She pushed down the rising panic that was threatening to force its way into her throat and out her lips in the form of a hysterical scream.

This wasn't the time to freak out. She had to consider what the right decision was. She didn't need to give in to her hysteria. Not now.

"Yes," she said finally. "A new . . . bisony beginning. I'm happy for you, Cade."

"Well, there's still the matter of Davis, but at least this is coming together."

"Are you going to contact the Rodeo Association about him?"

"I did," Cade said.

"And?"

"They're looking into it. I think they're going to contact him first and just ask. Feels sort of wrong to do that to a guy who's probably your half brother."

"Yeah, well . . . he basically injured you for life, and he knew you were his half brother when he did it. And it wasn't enough for him to wound you and end your career. So forgive me if I don't give a rat's ass about him being barred from competition. I'd be happy to see him serve jail time. Or perhaps spend some time in a stockade in the town square. We will have bison chips to fling at his head."

"I like the way you think," he said.

She leaned back in the porch swing, and the breeze caught her hair and sent it streaming across her face. She didn't bother to push it away.

"Yeah, well . . . I'm advocating flinging animal feces at someone you hate. So naturally, at the moment, you like the way I think."

"I always like the way you think."

"Do you?"

"Yeah. You buy booze when I'm sad, you tell crude jokes to make me laugh. You enjoy bacon and pancakes. What's not to like?"

She didn't know. And she didn't know why his comments were making her feel broody and irritated. Maybe because he was making her sound like a paragon. A bacon-imbibing paragon, sure. But he made her sound like she was someone he liked because she was easy to get along with. Someone who aided in the existence of other people, rather than having one of her own.

Which was silly, but for some reason, now that she'd had

the thought, she couldn't shake it. No, Cade had never treated her like that during the course of their friendship, but that was different. That was as a friend.

He was talking about having her as a wife, a wife he wouldn't have chosen. He'd made it very clear, abundantly so, that he'd never intended to marry. That love and kids weren't for him. The only thing that had changed was that they were now having a baby.

He hadn't changed.

She hadn't changed.

Only the circumstances had. And she knew what living in that kind of situation was like. It meant squeezing yourself into the tightest, most unobtrusive little ball possible. It meant changing yourself so you weren't in anyone's way.

So that they wouldn't make you love them only to have them send you back. Only to have them decide that you weren't worth it.

Cade was the only person she'd never had to do that with. And if she had to push any more of herself down inside, if she had to transform to stay with him again . . . she was sure she would break. There was no more give left in her.

"Nothing," she said, forcing a smile. "I'm eminently likable."

"Damn straight. How are you feeling?"

"Fine," she said, waving a hand and standing. She didn't want to talk about feeling sick. Because that was tied to the baby. Which was tied to the marriage proposal. And it was all wrapped up into a little package of things currently driving her insane.

"That's good."

"Yeah. Just looking forward to those bison."

"You are not."

"Sure I am. It's not every day a woman's land is invaded by large ruminants."

"I guess not."

That shard of pure pain in her chest broke free entirely as she looked at Cade, standing there on the porch talking about his plans. Maybe it was just that very last piece of herself. The one she'd been holding back. The one that was holding her together.

The one that might destroy her to give away. But it might just be too late.

He was so beautiful, so perfect. So everything she'd ever wanted . . . but not like this.

Not when it would always be another case of charity. Another person taking care of Amber because they had to.

She couldn't marry him. She realized it right then.

She also realized she needed him now more than she ever had. Needed her friend and her lover. Needed Cade, and the position he filled in her life. A position no one else had ever had. He made her heart bleed, made it ache, made it sing. He lit her body on fire.

And he was just doing the right thing.

She wanted to scream down the walls of her grandparents' home. The one she'd never been brave enough to make a sound in.

She felt like everything, all her security, all her everything, was slipping away from her. And the only thing left to grab on to was Cade.

"Kiss me," she said.

He didn't have to be asked twice.

He hauled her up against his hard body, his fingers laced through her hair, palms covering her cheeks as he kissed her deep and long, his tongue sliding against hers, his teeth grazing her lip.

He propelled them both into the house. She expected him to bend her over the couch. To push her against a wall, or onto the floor.

Instead, he pulled away from her and held on to her hand, leading her up the stairs. He had that strange, regretful look on his face. She knew he was wishing he could carry her. But it didn't matter. Not to her.

She squeezed his hand, her eyes never leaving his, her heart thundering in her ears.

There was no question—this *was* going to destroy her.

But maybe it would be worth it.

She pushed everything aside. Everything but this. Everything but Cade.

When they reached the bedroom, he kissed her again, deeper, longer, slower. It was easier when it was ravenous. When they were both starving for each other. Moving fast, moving hard.

This hurt. This slow, careful exploration. But she wanted to revel in it. Wanted to get lost in it. Because this was the end. She felt it down deep.

It's a new beginning . . .

But not for her.

For him.

She didn't even know what her beginning should be. Or if someone like her could have a new one. She'd been born with a slate that was already written on, or at least that's how it felt. Baggage from day one.

She didn't know what a fresh start felt like.

Cade stripped her top off, up over her head, his hands skimming over her curves as he unhooked her bra and cast it to the floor. He lowered his head and sucked her nipple deep into his mouth, making a raw, desperate sound in the back of his throat.

Maybe a fresh start felt something like this. Like being touched by Cade. Having her clothes taken off, the cool air on her skin, his tongue leaving a trail of fire over each exposed inch.

Sex with Cade was like nothing else on earth. It was more than sex. It was something she'd never had before. And this was something different than every time they'd shared before. This just might be making love.

And that scared her. But not enough for her to stop.

She tugged his shirt over his head, his skin still damp with sweat from the day spent working on the fences. He smelled like dirt, and hay. Like sun and hard labor. He smelled like Cade Mitchell, and he was better than cake or fresh-made cookies. Better than bacon.

She ran her hands over his chest, kissing his neck,

desperate to touch all of him. To taste all of him. She undid his belt, his jeans, and shoved them down his muscular thighs, pushed his underwear down with them.

She dropped to her knees, pressing a kiss to his hard, flat stomach before moving lower, taking his length inside her mouth. He groaned and laced his fingers through her hair, holding her against him. She took him deeper, relishing the taste of him, the heat of him. The feel of him shaking as she pushed him closer to the edge.

"Amber . . . I can't . . ."

She slid her tongue along his length before cupping him with her palm and squeezing him gently.

"Amber," he said, his voice rough. He grabbed her arms and dragged her to her feet, holding her against his chest, his expression fierce.

"What did you do that for?" she asked, aware of how breathless she sounded. "I was enjoying myself."

"Me too. Too much. That's not what I want."

"Why not? It didn't bother you that first night."

"That's because I didn't know how much better it could be," he said. "I don't want to finish this way. It's been too long. I want to be inside you. I want to come with you."

He kissed her, propelling them back onto the bed, and down onto the mattress. They bounced a little and she laughed, because it was so intense, and sexy, and kind of funny. Because it was Cade and he was . . . everything.

He put his hand under her butt and raised her hips, testing her with the head of his cock before sliding deep inside. She arched against him, their eyes clashing. She looked away, squeezing her eyes shut tight.

Cade put his hand on her chin and turned her face back to his, but she kept her eyes closed.

"Amber," he said.

She shook her head.

"Look at me."

"No," she whispered.

"Look at me," he said, his voice rough.

She opened her eyes, pain lancing her chest when his

gaze met hers, pleasure arcing through her when he thrust back into her body.

"Look at me," he said again, keeping his eyes on her as he established a steady rhythm. Pushing her closer to orgasm, and something deeper, something that ran straight through her soul and grabbed her by the throat, squeezed tight. Made it hard to think. Hard to breathe.

She wanted to push back against the pleasure, push back against the emotion. But she couldn't deny it. Couldn't deny him.

"Amber," he said, her name a raw plea on his lips, the first wave of his climax making his voice shake, pushing her over into her own.

She held on to his shoulders, her nails digging in deep as she clung to him, tried to use his strength to hold her to earth. To hold her together.

But it didn't. It couldn't. She was breaking apart inside, slowly, completely, and being rebuilt whole. For the first time. All the little pieces of her coming together. This was the most perfect moment she'd ever experienced, and the worst.

A window into something that could be perfect. But only for a while.

She wouldn't force him to keep her. She wouldn't make him spend his life that way. She wouldn't wish it on herself, either.

She couldn't be a responsibility to Cade. Couldn't be an obligation.

Not to him. Not when she . . . not when he was so very much to her.

He rolled off of her and pulled her against his body. She rested her head on his chest, felt his heart beating against her cheek, his skin damp with sweat. And then with a couple of her tears. They didn't speak, and after a while, the rhythm of his heart steadied, and his breathing turned steady.

She lay there, awake—and started making decisions about what she would do next.

CHAPTER
Twenty-Two

When Cade got up the next morning, Amber was gone, and the bison were due to arrive within the hour.

He was a little irritated she'd gone to work without waking him, but at least they were sleeping together again. In fairness to her, he hadn't exactly beaten her door down. But he'd been trying to give her space to make her decision.

Which he thought was pretty giving, considering what he wanted to do was throw her over his shoulder, haul her upstairs and tie her to the bed until she agreed to marry him. Or maybe he'd just tie her to the bed for fun.

Though that was a separate fantasy altogether.

Or not. He could make good use of her being bound to the bed while he made her stay still and think his proposal through.

He didn't know why she was hesitating. It was perfect. They would get married, and share this house, and this ranch. She would be taken care of. They would have the family she'd never had. It was all perfect.

He made breakfast and coffee, then went outside to wait

for the truck that was carrying his new future. The future of his family.

Really, he felt like he should be panicking about this more. Like the acquisition of a wife and child should be a lot more disturbing than it was.

But no. He was . . . happy. Happy at the thought of being with her. And for some reason, ecstatic about the idea of her being with him forever. In his bed. As his wife.

Because he knew now that he would be a good husband to her. Because he wasn't his father. Because he'd decided not to be. And it was that damn simple.

Or maybe the biggest part of it was Amber. He knew he would never want another woman, with bone-deep certainty. He could hardly remember another woman. Hell, he didn't want to.

The idea of forever didn't feel so bad when he imagined it with her. Actually, it was forever without her that seemed unthinkable.

Cade spent the whole afternoon with the men who brought the bison over, getting them into the right places in the fields, and making sure everything was as put together as he thought, and by the time he was done, he realized Amber should have been home.

He ran into the house, fear hitting him hard in the chest. It was nothing, and he knew it. But he'd lost enough people in his life that sometimes his mind could only go to the darkest place first.

He took his phone out of his pocket and dialed her cell. It went straight to voice mail. He cursed and looked up the number for the diner.

"Delia's."

"Hi, this is Cade Mitchell. I was just wondering if Amber left for the day?"

"Amber wasn't here today, hon," said Delia.

"What?"

"She wasn't on the schedule. She's been sick and she told me she wouldn't be in at all this week."

"Thanks," Cade said, fear making it hard to breathe. "I'll call her cell phone."

He did, and it went straight to voice mail again.

Panic settled in his gut. He walked upstairs and looked around, walked into the bedroom they'd shared last night.

He closed his eyes for a second, then went into the bathroom and looked at the cup that held her toothbrush, and for the past few weeks, his. Only his was there.

"Shit," he said.

Then he opened up the cabinet. Her makeup bag was gone. Her hairbrush was gone. That stupid flat iron she never used was gone.

He swore and slammed the doors shut.

She'd left him.

He walked back into the bedroom, the pain in his leg shooting up into his spine. He knelt down on the edge of the bed, cursing, waiting for the pain to pass. But it didn't. It lingered. Deep in his bones, in his heart.

Amber had left him. She didn't want to marry him.

And right when he'd realized just why he thought he could be a good husband to her. Just why the idea of being with her forever didn't seem like a life term in prison.

He loved her.

He loved her, and she'd left him.

He growled and brought his fist down hard on the nightstand, the corner of the wood biting into the edge of his fist. But he didn't care. It didn't matter. The physical pain didn't matter. He might as well go ride a horse across the plains. It would only hurt his body.

Amber had cut open his chest and torn out his heart. He knew Amber. She would never yell. She would never make a fuss, or tell him to go to hell. This was just what she would do. Slip away early in the morning, with all her things in one bag. The girl who'd always acted like a tenant in the house she'd spent her teen and adult years in would pick up and move that easily.

Because she was a lot more closely related to that angry,

hurting kid she'd been the first day she'd rolled into Silver Creek than she ever wanted anyone to believe.

Pain burst inside of him like a grenade. She hadn't told him. Hadn't shared with him. In the end, he hadn't been enough. In the end, his friendship, his damned love, hadn't been enough.

He'd never wanted love. Because of this. Because of the pain. Dammit, that was the real reason. Not just the fear that he'd be like his father . . . but the fear that he'd be like his mother. In love, and so stupid he couldn't see that he was in love alone.

But that was just what had happened. Not this week. Not this month. He was sure now that he'd loved Amber Jameson since he was sixteen years old. He'd just been too scared to acknowledge it. To himself, to anyone.

But now? Now there was no hiding it. All he could do was lie there and bleed.

But at least he wasn't afraid anymore. No, he was just fucking dying.

He laid his head back on the bed, Amber's scent, the smell of that damn girly shampoo of hers, teasing him, tormenting him.

For one moment, his whole life had been together. It had all been perfect. The ranch. Getting his revenge on Davis, getting justice. Making peace with Nicole and with Quinn.

And having Amber.

But he could lose the ranch. He could lose all the goodwill between him and Quinn and Nicole. He could let Davis walk free to win the biggest damn trophy the Rodeo Association had to offer, and he'd still be fine.

The only thing he needed was Amber.

And she was the thing he'd lost.

Without her, none of it meant anything.

"I like your store," Nicole said, touching the row of small tractors she'd been attracted to the first time she'd come into the store. She had a little tractor in her purse now. She figured she probably always would.

"I'm glad to hear it," John said from his position behind the counter. "Does doing my taxes seem more appealing since you like the environment?"

"I don't know. Maybe. But then . . . I have a job back in Portland. I'm just on . . . family leave, actually. It was a family emergency, coming here to see the half-siblings I never knew. And the one I didn't even know about."

"That must have been the highlight of your visit."

She looked around the store, even though she was ninety percent sure no one else was in there. "I think the highlight of my trip may have occurred in bed. Your bed, specifically."

"That's quite the compliment," he said.

She looked at him, and she wanted to cry a little bit. Because something about this place, this town, this store, this man, felt more like home than anyplace she'd been before ever had. And she was supposed to leave it.

Go back to a desk job in Portland that she didn't like. To friends that she didn't like very much. To weather that sucked. Basically, the food was good. But her family was here . . . and then there was John.

Who was, by his own admission, a man-whore of the highest order. She was probably lucky he hadn't thrown her over for another woman already.

"Yeah, well . . . dysfunctional family reunion, multiple orgasms. It's a toss-up, but in the end I'm gonna go with the multi-Os."

"That sounds like a breakfast cereal."

"The breakfast of champions. As you've proved on a few occasions."

"So," he said, looking down at his computer, "when are you leaving?"

"Uh . . . I . . . soon."

"Don't go," he said, looking up from the computer and planting his hands on the counter, his eyes serious—shockingly so.

John was always laughing, always joking. Teasing and

flirting. Sincerity wasn't something she'd seen on him before.

"Uh . . . what?"

"Stay. Stay here in Silver Creek. Stay with . . . me."

"With you?" she asked, her heart pounding hard. "I don't understand."

"What's there to understand? You can move into my apartment and have very little privacy. I'll sleep with you and probably make you meals. And you really could do my taxes. And I'll pay you in very small farm implements. You like those. I don't just have little tractors. You could also have a tiny hay baler."

"But . . . but why do you want me to stay with you? That's what I don't understand."

"Weren't we just discussing multiple orgasms?"

"Why, John?"

"I love you."

All the air left her lungs in a rush. "You love me?"

"Yes. I love you."

She blinked rapidly, trying to decide if she was panicking or . . . if she was deliriously happy. "Can you love someone you've only known a few weeks?"

He rounded the counter and strode toward her, his eyes intent on hers. "I've not loved a lot of people I've known for years. I don't see what time has to do with anything."

"I . . . it seems like time is important," she said. "For trust."

"Do you trust anyone?"

"Yes," she said, her throat tight.

"Who?"

"You." And she realized it was true. She wasn't sure how he'd managed it, this guy she'd known for such a short amount of time, but he'd become someone she trusted. There was no one back home who fit that brief.

Not only did she trust him, she'd allowed herself to depend on him. To need him. She'd never needed anyone in her life, because in her experience, that just left you vulnerable.

But she needed him. Wanted him.

Loved him.

"You trust me?" he asked, taking her hand in his. "Really?"

"Yes."

"I think that's even better than I love you."

"Well, I think I might . . . that . . . too. But you said you were a man-whore and a playboy. And you said not to fall for you and—" He cut her off with a kiss.

When they parted, he touched her lip with his thumb. "Yeah, I said all that. But that was before."

"Before what?"

"Before I knew you were different. Before I knew you were you. It was before you let me count your tattoos. Before you told me about your childhood. Before I knew that your left cheek had a dimple."

"And those are important details?"

"They're the most important details in my whole life. Stay with me."

She nodded. "Yes. Yes, I'll stay with you. I want . . . I want this life," she said, looking around the store. "I want to live here. I want to be here. With feed and fencing and tiny tractors."

"Are you just staying with me for my store?"

"No. I think I love your store because you're in it."

"I'm glad. Because I don't think I would love it anymore if you weren't."

"That's . . . the nicest thing anyone has ever said to me. I've never made anyone's life better before," she said, tears sliding down her cheeks.

"You didn't just make my life better. I feel like you made it start."

"That is . . . way too romantic."

"You have an amazing rack."

"Oh, that balanced things out," she said, laughing through her tears.

"I'll say things like that more often than I say the romantic shit. I guarantee it."

"That's good."

He took the red hay baler off the shelf by her shoulder and held it out to her. "So, will you move in with me?"

"I will." He put the little die cast vehicle in her hand and she closed her fingers around it, happiness, belonging, home like she'd never known before, pouring through her.

She had a family. She had love. And not just in the Mitchells, but in John.

"I suddenly have so much more than I ever thought I would," she said, wrapping her arms around him and resting her head on his chest.

"Two small replicas of farm equipment?"

"Yes. And the love."

"Oh, right. The love. Well, I promise I'll keep giving you both."

"I just needed to get away," Amber said, looking from her grandfather down to her hands. "I needed to think." She'd already told him about the fact that she and Cade hadn't really been a couple. That she was having a baby. That Cade had proposed.

And that she'd run away.

"If I stay with him," she said, not sure if she was going to get an answer; not sure if she wanted one, "well, if I stay with him, then . . . I'll be forcing myself on him." Her words died out, a sob making her choke. "Like I did to you and Grandma. He'll have to take me because he's obligated to. He'll have to marry me because it's right. Because he's that good. And I just can't do that to him. And I can't do it to me." A tear rolled down her cheek. "I want . . . I just want someone to choose to love me." The words were so pathetic. She hated herself for saying them. It was such a stupid thing to have to want. To have to say. It was all so . . . sad.

"I do," her grandfather said, his voice thin.

"Grandpa?"

"I love you," he said. "Haven't I . . . told you?" he asked, his words slow.

"I know," she said. "You did tell me. It's just . . . I always felt like I . . . invaded your house, and at first I was . . . I was so bad. Because I was daring you to send me back, but then . . . but then I started to love you and I wanted you to keep me so I tried to be good. But neither of those things were me. Not the bad Amber. And not the good one. I just wanted to stay."

It was all clear then. Why she never called her grandparents' house her house, even though her name was on the title. Why she never wanted to make waves. Why she folded herself up small.

Because she'd always felt like as easily as she'd arrived, she could be sent away.

"We didn't choose to love you, Amber," he said, every word halting. "We just did. From . . . the time you were born. Strong and . . . painful. Especially knowing that you . . . weren't being taken care of. I don't think I said this when I should have because . . . it felt disloyal to your dad. And as angry as I always was with him for not . . . for not ever seeing you. For not seeing us. He was our son. And we loved him too. He disappointed me. He hurt me. He hurt you, and I still loved him. Like I love you. You don't choose love like that. It chooses you. And I would never . . . change it. It's strong. It's the realest thing there is. We asked for you, you know. When we knew, we asked for you."

Another tear slid down her cheek. "But Cade . . ."

"Is doing the right thing."

"Yes," she said. "And that's what I can't handle. I don't want to be just the right thing. I want love. I want him to love me," she said, the words breaking. "I want him to love me."

"Maybe he does."

"I'll never know."

"Then I'm sorry," her grandfather said. "I'm sorry we failed you so badly. That you never learned to see what love looked like. We didn't want to force ourselves on you. Maybe we . . . should have."

"It's not your fault that I . . . I'm broken."

"We all are," he said. "Look at me, in this damn bed. I'm extra broken right now. Does that mean you don't love me?"

"No. Grandpa, I love you. I'll always love you."

"Then I don't see what . . . being broken has to do with anything." He took a deep breath and closed his eyes. "Anyway, if I remember right, that Mitchell boy has a hell of a limp."

Amber laughed, a tear falling from her cheek and down onto her hand. "Yeah, he does."

She'd just hate to make his life any harder. If he was going to have a wife, it should be someone who wasn't so janked up.

Someone who wasn't just a little person-husk who couldn't seem to hold on to people in the same way the rest of the world did. At some point you had to ask when the problem was with you, and not with everyone else.

"Don't choose to be sad, Amber," her grandpa said.

"I don't," she said, shaking her head. "No one chooses to be sad." She wondered if he was slipping out of lucidity.

"I think you choose to be sad," he said. "Because you're scared of being happy."

His eyes drifted closed, and Amber knew they were done with their heart-to-heart. She stood up and looked down at his sleeping form.

She couldn't really leave Silver Creek. Her grandpa was here. And anyway, she didn't intend to keep Cade from their child.

But there were bison at her grandfather's house, so she couldn't go back there. It wasn't like a herd of bison was easily transferable.

She took a deep breath and walked out into the hall, scrubbing her hands over her eyes. There was one place she could go for a while. A bonus for having retained her waitressing job.

So there, Cade Mitchell.

This was the very definition of a hollow victory. But better a hollow victory than no victory at all.

She swallowed hard and dialed Delia's number. At least she'd have a place to stay tonight. As for the rest of . . . forever . . . she wasn't going to look ahead to that. Because it didn't look very good at all.

"Everything is really coming together," Cole said, looking out across the field.

Cade knew he should feel triumph. Pride, because he'd gotten all this together and was proving to his older brother that, while the financial viability of his idea had yet to be established, he could follow through with something he'd set out to do.

But he felt nothing. Nothing but that same dull pain that started at his heart and radiated out, punching him hard behind the eyes at random moments and making him see black spots. Making it hard to breathe.

Amber. He missed that woman. He missed her stupid-ass texts. Her silly jokes. Eating breakfast with her. Waking up with her. Going to bed with her. Not just the sex, but the weight of her body over his as she slept. Not just the orgasms, but the smiles. Not just his lover, but his friend.

He was just sad, was what he was. He'd give up the rodeo again, ten times, and willingly submit to being trampled by that flipping horse, annually, if he could just fix this.

But she wasn't answering his calls.

"Yeah," he said. "Everything. Every. Damn. Thing."

"Okaaay," Cole said, turning to look at him, "so not everything."

"What? Do you see the bison? They're there. They're in the field. My life's work," he said, spreading his hand grandly. "My life's work," he repeated. "Damn bison."

"What the hell happened to you? Was there a scorpion in your Cheerios this morning?"

"Nothing the hell happened to me," he said. "I'm fine."

"And I'm a purple unicorn. What the hell, Cade?"

"Can I call you Sparkles the purple unicorn?"

"If you want to eat my knuckles. And I'm being serious.

I know we haven't been getting along all that well lately, but, you know, we used to talk. So what's happening with you?"

"My whole life is falling apart. No big deal. It's happened before. Of course, when it happened before, that time I might have actually died, I didn't really think I was going to die. This time, I'm concerned I might."

"What happened?"

"Amber left me," he said. "Without even a note. And she won't answer her phone." He leaned on the fence, the wood from the top rail biting into his forearms.

"What did you do to her?" Cole asked.

"I got her pregnant."

"Shit," Cole said, leaning up against the fence. "Why didn't you say anything?"

"Because I asked her to marry me and she didn't answer."

"I thought you were already engaged."

"No. That was a lie."

"What?"

"We weren't really together. I was just . . . Davis came and he was sniffing around, and plus I wanted to use the land for this, and it seemed like a good idea to just let Davis think we were a couple. Then it seemed like an okay idea to let you think it too. The engagement bullshit was courtesy of local word of mouth."

"But you didn't correct that either."

"My pride has been stepped on every which way for the past four years. I've been nothing but a hired hand to you, and even though I know you didn't mean to treat me that way . . . I couldn't carry the bulk of the work and I knew it. So I've been limping around feeling like a useless accessory to your operation and I haven't had a damn date since that horse tried to tear my femur out. So it suited me to go with the lie. Juvenile, sure."

"Sure," Cole said. "But it sounds to me like you used a lot of the same reasoning I used when I didn't want to tell you all that Kelsey's pregnancy was the result of a clinic mix-up.

And the same logic Lark used when she ended up working for Quinn and didn't want to tell us she'd been tricked."

"Mitchell pride and stubbornness," Cade said.

"It's a helluva thing."

"We started sleeping together when I moved in. It just . . . happened."

"I'm only surprised you hadn't done it already."

Cade shot him a glare. "I didn't want to mess things up. Which is what I ended up doing. Somehow. I asked her to marry me. That's what you do when you get a woman pregnant."

"I'm having a flashback to another time and another conversation."

"Yes, I told you you were an idiot for doing the same. But the clinic knocked up Kelsey, not you."

"Didn't matter."

"I get that now," he said. "But she doesn't want to marry me. Obviously."

"Well . . . do you love her?"

"Yeah," Cade said. "I really do. And I didn't think I'd ever love anyone like this, but I do. With . . . everything." He shook his head. "I'm standing here talking about my feelings. If that doesn't tell you what a mess I am . . . then nothing will."

"Did you tell her?"

"No. I didn't realize it until after she left. And she won't answer her damn phone."

"Then you have to go get her."

"She wants to be alone, obviously."

"So?" Cole asked. "What would you have told me? You'd have told me to stop being a pansy-ass and go get her back. You'd have told me not to mess up the best thing that had ever happened to me. Cade, I can tell you honestly, having known you with her and without her, that Amber Jameson is the best thing that's ever happened to you. As a friend, and as anything else. You'd be lucky to have a woman like her."

"Sure, but is she lucky to have a man like me?"

"As long as you love her. That covers up a lot of mistakes,

a lot of flaws, trust me. But offering marriage just to make things right? That doesn't work. Trust me, I tried it, remember? I had to offer it all."

"But that's . . . hard. And it's scary."

"Sure. But if you don't do it, you're left with nothing. And that's a whole lot scarier, in my opinion."

"Yeah. I guess."

Gravel crunching under tires and the sound of a truck engine interrupted their heart-to-heart, and thank God, because Cade was going to break out into hives with all this feelings talk.

It was Davis's truck.

"You might want to arm yourself," Cade said, only half-joking.

"What did you do?"

"Well, I'm doing my damndest to get him thrown out of the rodeo, seeing as he's the one who caused my injury."

Cole's head whipped around to face Cade. "Seriously, Cade, you didn't think you owed me a phone call?"

"I told Amber," he said. "She's the only person I told. She was the only person I'd talked about the baby with. She's the only person I talk about much of anything with, and right now she's not here."

"That's the only reason you called me at all, isn't it?"

"Well, I couldn't get ahold of her to talk to her about how she broke my heart. Seriously, though, Davis might be here to kill me."

Cole took a step to the left, away from Cade.

"Well, thanks a lot," Cade said.

"I have a wife and children."

"I have a child on the way," Cade said, his throat tightening as he said it. "I'm going to be a father too, so I guess that means I better not die."

"Guess you better not," Cole said, stepping back toward Cade. "Though the mother of my children actually likes me."

Davis stopped the truck and killed the engine. He got out, and Cade was relieved to see that at least the other man wasn't packing heat.

"'Sup, Davis?" Cade asked.

"I'm here to talk."

"By talk do you mean bust my face? Because I have to tell you, there are two of us here, and if that's your intent, I will use that to my advantage."

"I'm not here to bust your face," Davis said. "I really do want to talk. Alone."

"Fine." Cade pushed away from the fence rail and gestured toward the barn. "This way."

They walked into the barn and Cade could feel Cole watching them. He had a feeling his brother would be hanging close. Older-brother overprotective habits died hard, even when you hadn't been on the best terms for the past year.

"Okay," Cade said, crossing his arms, "what's going on? And I warn you, I am in a terrible mood, so if you give me a reason to, I will lay into you with all the strength in my broken body, you hear me?"

Davis put his hands up. "Not why I'm here. I got a call from Mark Linden. He's heading up the association now."

"I know. I'm not involved anymore, but I keep up on things."

"He asked if I was the one who caused your accident."

"And?"

"I told him I was. I'm barred from competition."

Cade felt like a breeze could have knocked him down. "What?"

"It's true. And I think you know it. I was the one who was responsible for your accident."

"Why the hell did you cop to it?"

Davis lifted a shoulder and looked down at his boots. "I came here to . . . do what I've been doing for too damn long. I hated you. I hated everything you had that I didn't. When I found out who you were . . . You had everything I wanted, including the top spot on the leaderboard. I didn't want to kill you or permanently maim you. I wanted to put you out for the season. Which is bad enough, and I'm not going to pretend it's not. But look, the bullshit caught up with me, and I'm admitting it."

"Great. I'm not going to give you a medal for that."

"I don't expect you to."

"Why did you come to Silver Creek?"

"Same reason. All that unresolved shit. You all had something here and I felt like I should have it too, because if my dad hadn't run out on me . . . if he'd married my mom instead . . . well, I would have had it."

"Our dad was a prick. I can't fix that for any of us. I wish I could."

"Don't on my account."

"Oh, I don't on your account. I don't like you," Cade said, "if that wasn't clear. I've cursed you every morning I've gotten up and barely been able to move, even though I didn't know your name. I hope you know that."

"And I deserve it," he said. "Not saying that to be noble, just because it's true. I thought maybe I'd find something here that would answer questions for me. And I did. My life isn't here. And I have to stop fixating on things that are best left in the past. I'm leaving. I'm going to go buy land somewhere else and start my own life instead of worrying so much about yours. Coming and actually seeing what bad shape you're in . . . I'm not proud of it. I thought I might find answers here, but I just had to face what a huge bastard I've been. And now I just want to walk away from it."

A muscle in Cade's jaw ticked, and he gritted his teeth, shifting his weight.

"I don't really get why you never came before," Cade said.

"I didn't know my dad's real name. Neither did my mom."

"It was the same for Nicole too. And her mother. None of it all came together until the past couple of years."

"And for me, it all came together when I saw him there with you. I think . . . I think he knew me. But he never said anything. He never even smiled at me. He was my dad, and he was there to see you. And he wouldn't even look at me."

"Davis . . ."

"I don't deserve pity. Hell, at this point I don't think I deserve much of anything. Not a piece of the ranch, not a place here. I think what I really need to do is just walk away.

It's funny, I spent a lot of years hating you, and wanting what you had. And I bet you didn't think about me once."

"No," Cade said. "I didn't. But that's our dad's fault too."

"Right. He screwed a lot of things up, and I'm starting to regret stepping in and screwing up more."

Cade could feel all the anger he'd been bound up in for the last four years loosening. Falling away. He'd been angry at Quinn. Angry at a general, shadowy figure. Angry in general. And now, looking at Davis, he could see what anger did to a man. What hate did.

He didn't want any part of it. He wanted to move on. He wanted more to life. He wanted Amber. His child. A family. He wanted love more than he wanted fear. He wanted it more than he wanted anger.

He could throttle Davis. Punch him out. Press charges. Sue. But none of it would fix his injury. None of it would change a damn thing.

Cade might be crippled outside, but Davis was all twisted up inside. And Cade didn't want any part of it. It would end with him. It would end now.

So that the rest of his life could start.

"Just go then," Cade said. "I'm not pressing charges. Just . . ."

"Yeah," Davis said. "I guess that's it then."

"Yeah," Cade said. "It is."

Davis extended his hand and Cade shook it, then took a step back.

And that was it. That was the big confrontation with the guy who'd screwed up his body and his life. Knowing that guy was your half brother kind of took the rage out of it—if only because it was just sad.

Davis was a prime example of letting bitterness eat you up. Of letting it steal your chance at making relationships.

And in truth, Cade wasn't much better.

He'd let fear and bitterness steer him away from love all of his life.

If he hadn't . . . if he hadn't, he would have realized he loved Amber sixteen years ago. He wouldn't have lost her, because he would have known then. He would have told her then. He would have acted like it then.

And he would have her now.

Cade watched Davis get into his truck and drive away. And once the tailgate was out of sight, with nothing left but a dust cloud from the gravel road, Cole approached.

"So . . . how did it go?"

"He's not going to bother us anymore. Unlike Nicole, I don't think he's interested in reconciling and having Christmases at Elk Haven."

"Considering he hobbled you, that's probably for the best."

"Yeah. So, we need to figure out where Amber is."

"Why?"

"Because I'm not going to live scared anymore. I'm going to chase her down and tell her I love her."

"Then what?" Cole asked.

"Hope like hell she loves me back."

Amber peeled herself off the couch when she heard the knocking—or rather, pounding—on the door to the little apartment above the diner. It was probably Casey, the cook, with some food for her. Delia was doing her part to make Amber feel taken care of. Though "taken care of" was starting to feel a lot like "smothered."

She'd confessed the pregnancy, and her Cade woes, which had resulted in tongue-clucking and the offer of the apartment, and time off for as long as she needed.

Which just made her feel even more full of woe. Like everyone was cleaning up her messes because . . . because Silver Creekians were so damned decent.

"Coming," she moaned as she shuffled to the door.

She jerked it open and froze. Cade was standing there looking like he was ready to hit someone. And she knew that look. Because she'd seen it on his face right before he'd flattened that guy in the bar for her on a night that seemed like a whole lifetime ago.

It was certainly a whole friendship ago.

"You think you could . . . I don't know, Amber . . .

answer your damn cell phone?" He walked past her and into the room, not waiting for her permission. Just as well, since she wouldn't have given it. But it didn't really matter now.

"I was not answering on purpose. So, no . . . answering would defeat that purpose."

"You little coward," he said, staring her down, his dark eyes blazing. "You're running from a man with a limp."

"I'm running from more than that," she said.

"Tell me," he said, his jaw set, anger rolling from him in waves. "Tell me what you're running from."

"You," she said.

"Like I said . . ."

"You and your proposal," she said. "And all the damn feelings. And your well-meaning . . . well-meaningness. And feelings."

"What about me is well-meaning?" he asked, spreading his arms out wide. "Tell me."

"You wanting to marry me. For the baby."

"You think I want to marry you for the baby?" he asked.

"Well, yeah, since you proposed thirty seconds after I told you about the baby."

"I want to marry you for me."

"Why? Because I bring you booze and laughs? Because I'm your best friend and I make your life easier and it'll be convenient to have a wife and child under one roof with you?"

"Because I fucking love you, Amber, that's why."

"What?"

"You heard me. I'm sorry, did I steal your convenient excuse to run? I love you. That's why I want to marry you. Hell, woman, I don't just love you. I am in love with you. You're . . . everything. You're the sunrise and the sunset. Without you, it's all dark. It's all bad. I need you."

"I . . ." She shook her head and took a step back. She was tempted to bolt for the door.

"What? Did I take your excuse? Now, why did you leave me? Tell me, right now."

"I can't."

"Why not?"

"Because I don't know!" she shouted.

"Yes, you do."

"I'm scared," she said. It sounded so small and lame, so pathetic next to his admission. Next to the brave, beautiful words he'd just spoken.

You're the sunrise and the sunset.

I'm scared.

As admissions went, his won. Hers was just lame. But it was true. She was shaking down to her soul, and she had been for . . . for as long as she could remember.

"What are you scared of?" he asked, his tone softer now.

"Everything," she said, a sob rising in her throat, hysteria bubbling in her chest. "Everything. I'm scared that . . . that none of this lasts. I'm scared that I'll never be able to be the woman that you want, not for long enough. And once I can't do it anymore, once I can't . . . make myself fit into your life anymore, I'll be the thing that has to go."

"Amber"—his voice was rough, his eyes filled with pain—"why would you think that?"

"Because. Because that's my life, Cade. Because that's how it was with my dad, my mom. All of the foster families that took me in. And then I got here and my grandparents loved me, but I felt like I had to do everything in my power to make sure they wouldn't ever send me back."

"And with me? Who were you with me? When we drank and cussed and talked about sex and dreams? When we just sat and didn't say anything? Was that you, or was it the friend you thought I wanted?"

"That was different. You were the only person who chose me. And now . . . you'll just be someone else who's obligated to me, and I can't handle that, Cade. I can't handle the moment when it will end. When I won't be enough."

"Do you want to know why I didn't know I loved you until the past week?"

"Why?" she asked, her throat so tight she could barely speak.

"Because you were too much. Forget not being enough. You were more than I could handle, more than I could admit wanting. You were everything, Amber, and I wasn't ready for everything. I was afraid that I would be like my father, but that was bullshit. I control my actions. And I would never, ever do the things to you he did to the women in his life. I think what really scared me, what I couldn't admit, was that I was afraid of being my mother. Of loving with everything when the other person just didn't. But I'm not afraid now."

"What changed?"

"I guess I had to ask myself what I was more afraid of. The possibility of wanting it all, asking for it all, and losing it, or the certainty that I would never have you, not the way I wanted you, because I was just too damn scared."

"Obviously you found your answer," she said, her voice trembling.

"Yeah. That's why I'm here, telling you now. I love you, and I want everything. Forever, and family. Love. That real stuff. That intense, painful, wonderful, sweaty love that I have for you."

"Sweaty?"

"Come on, baby, what we have is a little sweaty," he said, putting his hands on her cheeks, his thumbs drifting over her lower lip. "That's the part that separates this from friendship. Or maybe it's just the part that adds to it. Because that's the thing—you're still my best friend. And I don't want you to change. It's you that I want. I don't want you to be anyone but the woman I grew up with. I don't want you to be anyone but the woman who knocked my socks off when I met her in high school. I don't want you to be anyone but you."

"It's so hard for me to believe that, Cade," she said, a tear sliding down her cheek. "Because so many people didn't want me. So many people didn't love me. Not me. And I stopped being able to . . . to give myself. It was too scary. So I only gave pieces. But you have all of me. And that's why I'm so scared. You're the only person in the world who has my friendship, my body and my soul. The only person who knows every dream, every fear and every desire."

He closed his eyes, his Adam's apple bobbing up and

down. "Amber . . . I'm so honored by that gift. You don't know how much."

"You realize why it's so scary, right? No one else could break me completely. You could. You have it all."

"I get that," he said, his voice a whisper now. "But I've spent half my life loving you already, caring for you. Keeping a lot of your pieces safe. Trust me when I say I'll spend the rest of my life doing the same."

"I want this so much," she said. "I . . . I love you. I do. I have. I've been running from it for so long. I told myself that I didn't want a relationship because I was working on my problems, but the thing was . . . I think a part of me just knew that you were it. But all of me was way too afraid to risk what we had. To risk myself."

"We weren't ready," he said, "but I'm ready now. And if it took this, Davis, the pregnancy, to push us there, I can only be grateful. They aren't the reason I love you, but they pushed me into realizing it faster. I don't want to marry you because you're pregnant; it just helped move things along. But that's good, because we've been dragging our damn feet for sixteen years."

She put her hands on his cheeks and closed the distance between them, kissing him deep. They just stood there, holding each other, kissing, for a long time. Her face was wet, and his was wet too; she wasn't sure if the tears were all hers, or if some were from him.

"I love you," she said, a bubble of happiness in her stomach expanding like a balloon and rising in her chest. "I love you, Cade Mitchell. You're my best friend, my lover. And I want you to be my husband. My forever."

"I love you, Amber Jameson. I know you better than anyone, and I love you more than anyone ever will."

"Forsaking all others," she said.

"In sickness or in health."

"In bison or in poverty," she said.

He laughed and wrapped his arms around her, pulling her whole body against his. "Baby, we have bison. We do."

"At my house," she said, the words coming out finally. "My house. In my town. With my man."

"All of it's yours, huh?" he asked, a smile curving his lips.

"I don't feel like a tenant anymore," she said. "I was tired of feeling like everything in my life was temporary. I'm here for keeps. I'm staking some claims."

"So, the house, the town . . ."

"And you," she said.

"I'm so glad to be yours."

"I'm yours too," she said. "Cuts both ways."

"That's fair, because you were part of making me a man who was brave enough to ask for all of this, you know."

"Me?"

"Without you, I wouldn't have been brave enough. You made me want things. Made me ask for things from life. So this is your fault, you know?"

"That seems fitting, since I think you were the one who made *me* brave."

"I think we fixed each other," he said.

"We were never broken," she said, realizing just then how true it was. "We just needed a little help from a friend."

He smiled. "I'm glad you're my friend."

"Always," she said.

For the first time, all of the pieces of her life were together, in one place. All the pieces of her were together in one place. Because of Cade. Because she loved him. Because he loved her.

And it wasn't scary. It was perfect.

Epilogue

Cade had heard a lot of people say they'd married their best friends. But he really did. It was the first wedding he'd been to in years where he didn't want to drink. No, he wanted to stay stone-cold sober for the whole thing.

Because he never wanted to forget any of it. Not even the pain in his leg.

He certainly didn't want to forget the way his bride looked. Perfect in a flowing dress that skimmed her now fuller curves, her dark hair loose, a crown of flowers on her head. She was the best-dressed woman in attendance.

Their daughter was a close second. Though Ava Mitchell, named for her great-grandma Jameson, slept through most of the ceremony in the arms of her great-grandpa Jameson.

Cade looked over at Amber, who was talking to Kelsey, Lark and Nicole, laughing as the breeze caught her dark curls.

And he couldn't just stand and watch for another second. "Excuse me," he said, tipping his hat to Quinn, Cole and John, "I have to go and get my bride. I think I owe her a dance."

He walked across the grass and held out his hand, his stomach tightening when she turned and smiled at him. It was weird how you could know someone for so long and still feel like every time they smiled at you it was the first time.

"Mrs. Mitchell," he said, "I think I owe you a dance."

"You want to dance?" she asked, looking up at the dance floor, her eyes round. They hadn't discussed dancing, for obvious reasons. But he was in the mood to dance, limp or not. And he wasn't even drunk.

"With you, yes."

"Excuse me, ladies," she said, taking his hand and letting him lead her to the wooden dance floor.

He pulled her in close, his hand on the curve of her back, the other holding hers tight.

"Dancing, huh?" she said, her face pressed into his neck, her lips grazing his skin as she spoke.

"Yeah. Every bride should dance with her husband on her wedding day."

He knew he wasn't dancing with any particular rhythm or grace, but he didn't care. Amber was in his arms. And that meant grace didn't matter. Steps didn't matter. Pain didn't matter.

The only thing that mattered was that he loved her, and he wanted to dance with her. So he did.

He felt a tear fall from her cheek and down into his tux collar.

"It wasn't supposed to make you cry," he said.

She pulled away and looked up at him, her dark eyes shining. "I can't help it. How do you do it?"

"What? Make you cry? Usually I'm just being an asshole."

"No, not that. How do you manage to surprise me after all this time?"

"It's just because of you."

"What do you mean?"

"I mean, you do something . . . You smile. You laugh. And I realize again just how lucky I am. How blessed I am. And I know I have to do something for you. To give you that feeling you give me every time I look at you."

She put her head down, her forehead resting on his

shoulder. "You don't even have to try, Cade. Because I get those feelings every time I look at you too."

"But I like to try," he said.

"Well, I like it when you try, so I won't complain."

"There's just something about you," he said, holding her close, feeling her heart beat against his. "Something that brings out the best in me. Even if my dancing is still bad."

"Are you kidding me? This is the best dance of my life."

Cade swallowed a lump in his throat and looked around the dance floor, then past that to all the family and friends that still lingered. The children running barefoot through the grass. The couples, new and old.

"There's really no chance of ever getting empty-nest syndrome around here," he said, thinking all the way back to Lark's wedding the summer before.

"No?"

"Nope. This place just keeps filling up with family."

She lifted her head and looked around. "Yeah, I guess it does." She went up on her toes and kissed him on the cheek. "I'm glad I'm making my family with you."

He looked down at her, his chest so full he could hardly breathe. "You know . . . after I got injured I thought my glory days were behind me. But I was wrong."

"Were you?"

"I was. I know without a doubt that my life with you, with Ava, will be my glory days. And they're just beginning."

Read on for a special preview of
another Silver Creek Romance
by Maisey Yates

UNTOUCHED

Available now from InterMix

It wasn't like she even wanted any of this for herself.

Lark Mitchell looked around the completely unconventional wedding being thrown in her yard and fought the urge to cry.

Which was dumb as rocks, because there was no reason to cry. Seriously, the bride was wearing a black wedding dress. It was ridiculous. And, okay, the bride was also marrying the man Lark had spent the better part of two years completely fixated on, but that was no reason to cry.

It wasn't like she *loved* Tyler. And in the year since he'd started dating Alexa, his new wife, and moved to New York, Lark had completely gotten over him.

No, this wasn't heartbreak. She was just in the throes of that left-behind kind of melancholy that she was more familiar with than she'd like to be.

She'd felt that way when most of her friends had gone off to college and she'd stayed in Silver Creek to help out on the ranch. She'd felt it all through high school when other girls had gotten dates and she'd gotten the chance to tutor cute boys in English.

Just this sort of achy feeling that other people were going somewhere while she stood in the same place.

Or, in this instance, sat in the same place. At one of the florid tables placed around the lawn. This little wedding had come to Elk Haven Stables because Tyler was once a ranch hand, and because the bride in black was best friends with Lark's sister-in-law, Kelsey.

Lark adored Kelsey, but she could honestly do without Alexa.

Which might be sour grapes. Maybe.

But damn, woman, marry a dude your own age. Tyler was in her own demographic, and he hadn't known her in high school, which helped, because as awkward as she was now . . . high school had been a beyotch.

"Hey, sweetie."

Lark looked up and saw Kelsey, holding baby Maddy on her hip and looking down at her with overly sympathetic blue eyes. "Hi," Lark said.

"Are you okay?"

"What? Yeah. I'm . . . so okay. Why wouldn't I be okay? I had a crush on this guy for like two seconds, a year ago. I never even kissed him."

"I remember how much you liked him."

"Thanks, Kels, but I'm a grown-up, as much as Cole doesn't like to acknowledge it. I've moved on. I have another man in my life now."

Because she was sure three rounds of cybersex six months ago with a guy she'd never met counted as having someone in her life. And if not, it at least bolstered her lie. She needed the lie. It was so much better than admitting she was pathetic. And that she spent most days in her room doing tech support for various and sundry people while eating Pop-Tarts and streaming *Doctor Who* through an online subscription service.

Yeah. Saying she was involved was better than admitting that.

"Oh. Do you? Because Cole"—Kelsey narrowed her eyes—"Cole doesn't know."

"No. And it's okay if it stays that way." The idea of her brother finding the transcripts from those little chats she'd had with Aaron_234 was ever so slightly awful.

Almost as bad as admitting that the closest she'd ever come to sex was a heavy breathing conversation. Over the Net. Where you couldn't even hear the heavy breathing.

The very thought made her cringe at her own lameness. It was advanced geekiness of the highest order.

At least she excelled at something.

"I'm not going to keep secrets from Cole," Kelsey said, sitting down at the table. "I mean, I won't lie to him if he asks."

"He shouldn't ask. It's not his business." Of course, Cole wouldn't see it that way. To Cole, everything in her life was his business. Thankfully, Kelsey and Maddy had deflected some of that, but then there was Cade. Cade, who was the more wicked brother. The irresponsible one. The one who should be cool with her doing whatever and finding her way in life by making a few mistakes.

But Cade was even worse than Cole, in his way. The hypocrite. She always figured it was because, while Cole guessed at what debauchery was out there in life, Cade had been there, done that, and bought the souvenir shot glass.

She'd considered ordering the shot glass online. So to speak. But she'd never done a damn thing. So all her brothers' overprotective posturing was for naught, the poor dears.

Although, Cole had nearly torn Tyler a new one when he'd suspected they might have slept together. Alas, no such luck.

She'd love to have a mistake that sexy in her past.

All she had was a greasy keyboard and a vague, stale sense of shame, which lingered a lot longer than a self-induced orgasm.

"Yes, well, you don't want to keep your boyfriend from us, do you?"

"He's not my boyfriend. He's not. I exaggerated a little. It's not like that."

"Oh, so . . . is he someone in town, or . . . ?"

"He's on the computer. He's not . . . I haven't talked to

him in a while." Like they'd ever really chatted about any-thing significant. It was more like a straight shot to "What are you wearing?"

"Oh . . . okay."

"But the bottom line is that I'm fine. With this. Right now. Alexa and Tyler are welcome to their wedded bliss. I'm not in the space to pursue wedded bliss. I have other things to do." *Like sit on your ass and shoot zombies?*

No. Real plans. To travel, someday. To have adventures. Maybe a meaningless fling here and there. In Paris? Paris seemed like a good place for a meaningless fling. Silver Creek certainly wasn't. She knew all the idiots here.

Worse, they knew her. They knew her as a bucktoothed nerd who would do your calculus while you did the cheerleader. It was a poor set of assumptions with which to begin a relation-ship, so she just never tried.

It was better than doing the guy who was doing the cheer-leader. Doing math was way less painful. Keeping it virtual was a lot less painful.

Otherwise you ended up watching the only guy you'd ever really thought you might have a shot with marrying another woman. Not that that was what was happening. Be-cause she didn't love Tyler, dammit.

But if she had married him, she wouldn't have done it in a black dress. She was a gamer geek with limited so-cial skills, but even she knew major life events were the time to drop your freak flag a little bit. Wear some lace. A pair of pumps. Ditch the Converse All Stars for a couple of hours.

Not that anyone had asked her, of course.

"I'm glad; I was a little worried about you."

Worry for Lark's well-being was apparently a virulent contagion at Elk Haven Stables. Cade and Cole had a bad case of it, and Cole had clearly infected his wife.

"No need to worry. I'm golden. I'm not in a picket-fence place right now."

"Yeah, neither was I," Kelsey said, shifting Maddy in her arms and looking pointedly at the little bundle of joy.

"Unless you can get knocked up driving by sperm banks now, I'm not going to be in your situation anytime soon."

Kelsey laughed, the motion jiggling Maddy and making her giggle. "Yeah, steer clear of those clinics, or you might find yourself shackled to an obnoxious alpha cowboy for the rest of your life."

"Already am, Kels. Two of them. We're related, which means I can't just ditch them. I'm not marrying a cowboy." She looked back at Tyler. "I'm sick of cowboys, in fact. I'll find someone metropolitan who knows that high fashion isn't a bigger belt buckle and your Sunday go-to-meetin' clothes."

"Nothing wrong with wanting something different," Kelsey said. "I guess Cole is my something different, so I can see the attraction to something you aren't used to. I still rent out my house in Portland. If you ever want to go try something a little more urban . . ."

For some reason, the idea made Lark's throat feel tight. "Uh . . . maybe another time. Cole is just getting all his social media stuff going for the ranch, and you know he needs close help with that. He's death to computers." All true enough, but in reality she could do most tech help remotely.

She would leave someday. Just not today. Or next week. Or next month. But that was fine.

"Well, that's true," Kelsey said. "But I'm not tech-illiterate, so I can help him a little. I do work on my computer, so I'm pretty familiar with everyday glitches."

"But who would optimize your blog?" Lark asked. "It's just starting to get huge."

"True. The modern world is a wonderful thing."

Kelsey was a health and wellness columnist, and she still had her column published in papers across the country, but since moving to the ranch, she'd started doing a lot of humorous posts about acclimating to life in the sticks, and thanks to her already established audience, it had become an instant hit.

And Lark was in charge of design and management of the website and its community.

Which was nice. It was nice to feel important. Nice to be needed.

"So you're really okay?"

"Yes," Lark said. "Stop giving me your wounded puppy eyes—I'm fine."

"Great. I'll be back in a minute, I have to go grab Cole."

"Neat," Lark said, reaching down beside her chair and pulling her phone out of her purse. She was itchy to check her email, because it had been a couple of hours and she hated the feeling of being disconnected.

She keyed in her PIN and unlocked the screen, her email client immediately loading about fifty messages.

She opened up the app and scrolled through the new mail. She had another one from Longhorn Properties. She'd been negotiating with the hiring manager, Mark, for a few days now. She hadn't told anyone in her family about the offer, because she knew her brothers would get all proprietary and think they had to do it all for her.

Like she wasn't smart enough to handle her own job opportunities in her own field. And yes, she worked for the family by and large, but she'd also done websites for several local businesses and had become the go-to IT tech for Silver Creek residents.

This would be her biggest deal by far. And the first time she'd be signing a contract for a job. But she was ready for the challenge.

She'd be setting up computers, servers, firewalls, and web filters at a ranch for troubled boys, and then doing a little bit of tech training too. It was a big undertaking, especially with everything she already did at Elk Haven, but honestly, she could use something to mix up her life.

Something that wouldn't take her too far from the safety of her bedroom.

She had a little bit of a complex. She could admit that.

But she'd lost her mother so early, and then her father. Cole, Cade, the ranch, they might drive her nuts—but they were all she had. All she knew. Life felt horribly insecure outside of that. Terribly fragile.

Life was safe in video games. When you had armor and you could collect health right from the ground. Along with an AK-47 to take care of anyone or anything that might threaten you.

She skimmed the email and typed in a hasty reply, asking for more details on time frame and payment, then hit send.

"Is that thing welded to your hand?"

Cade walked over to her table and sat on the edge of it, his friend Amber in tow. Amber gave her an apologetic look. She would be annoyed with Cade silently, but Lark knew if push came to shove, Amber's allegiance was with Lark's obnoxious brother.

That was one relationship she had no desire to ever figure out.

"Nope, detachable." She tossed the phone down into her purse. "Unlike your stupid face, which you're sadly stuck with."

"Very few people have a problem with my face."

"Oh, dear, the tone of this conversation is lowering already," Amber said.

He turned to Amber. "Women really like my face."

Amber's forehead wrinkled, her brows drawing together. "Do they?"

"If not my face, they like my . . ."

"No!" This came from both Amber and Lark in unison.

"My personality," Cade said. "Sick people. You are sick people."

"Yeah, we all believe that was going to be the next word out of your mouth, Cadence," she said, using a name she'd assigned to Cade in childhood to piss him off.

Her brother hopped down from the edge of the table, wincing when his foot made contact with the grass, freezing, a pained expression on his face as he waited for what Lark assumed was a wave of pain to pass through him.

"Hey," she said. "I didn't think your leg was bothering you as much now."

"It's not," he said.

"Lies. Dirty lies. What's up?"

Cade gave her a hard look. But she knew he'd tell her,

because he knew she had no problem harassing him until he did. "Nothing," he said, his tone hard. "It's nothing new. Just the same shit. It's like there's this nice little highway of pain that goes from my knee up to my spine. Not any worse."

Just not any better. Not really.

She hated that. Hated that Cade couldn't ride anymore. Hated that he hurt all the time. That day had scared years off of her life. She'd been convinced, when they'd gotten the call about Cade's fall, that he was going to die too.

That she was really destined to lose everyone she loved. All of her family. That she would be left alone.

She blinked and tried to pull her mind back into the present. Cade wasn't dead. He might be surly, and he might have a limp, and he couldn't compete in the circuit, but he wasn't dead. She really appreciated that since, as much as he drove her crazy, she needed him.

"Well, glad it's not any worse."

"Me too."

"So, want to get hammered?" she asked, not that she made a practice of getting hammered—but it seemed like it might be a good idea.

"Hell yeah," he said. "And Cole bought a lot of booze. His wedding gift to the newlyweds."

Amber's lips twitched. "You're going to get hammered drinking champagne? Because Cole bought champagne. For the toast."

"I have a talent where alcohol is concerned."

"I know," Amber said dryly. "I've held your hair, so to speak, while you puked off a hangover or ten."

Lark made a face. "Sick. I've never had a hangover."

Cade shrugged. "That's because you live timid. I don't."

"And you're all busted up to prove it," she said, knowing Cade would rather joke about his condition than say anything weighty about it.

"But I've lived. Bless me, Father, for I have sinned. Indeed."

"STFU, jackass," Lark said.

He put his hand on her forehead. "You're starting to speak lolcats. Get off the computer once in a while."

"You don't even know what lolcats is."

"Something to do with cats and cheeseburgers. Amber texts me crap like that all the time."

"At least she tries to modernize you," Lark said, shaking her head.

"How did this become a commentary on me? At least I come out into the light every day."

"Look," Lark said, holding her—admittedly pale—arm out in a shaft of sunlight. "I don't even sparkle!"

"Suspicious. I'm suspicious. Seriously," Cade said, "I worry about you, in your cave all the time. You've got to live life, Lark, or it's going to pass you by."

"Are you seriously giving me advice?" she asked. "Name one thing in your life that's organized, or settled, or . . . aspirant."

"Fun, Lark, I have fun. With real people. Outside. Look around you; it's in high-def."

"You're an idiot, and also, I have a life."

"Virtually."

And if that didn't count as having a life she was screwed. She bit the inside of her cheek. "Annnnd?"

"And maybe you should get hungover, is all I'm saying."

"But maybe have enough class not to go drinking all the champagne at a wedding to accomplish it," Amber said, somewhat pointedly.

Yeah, if Lark did that here she really would look lovelorn and pathetic.

"Then I'll hold off. Anyway, you don't know everything about me, Cade."

"Beg to differ."

"You don't."

"If I checked your browser history I would."

"Nuh-uh." No one touched her computer but her, but even so, she didn't leave certain things lying around on it. Secret shame was secret.

"Witty comeback," he said. "Witty indeed. Why don't you go talk to someone? Meet a guy."

"Right. Meet a guy. Cole would be interrogating him before a full greeting exited my mouth."

Cade shrugged. "You take the good with the bad."

"You're both mostly bad," she said, not meaning it at all.

Amber rolled her eyes. "Have fun," she said to Lark. "And catch up with us later maybe? You can help me haul his drunken ass to his room."

"I say we leave him on the lawn."

"Fair enough," Amber said, turning and following Cade down to the table laden with drinks.

Lark bent back down and took her phone from her bag, trying not to think too much about her brother and his comments. Look what "living" had gotten him. And anyway, a hangover was hardly her definition of living.

She didn't have to drink herself into a stupor to feel like she'd reached the heights.

She opened up her mail app and saw another one from Longhorn HR. She opened up the message.

The money offer had doubled, and the length of the contract was for six weeks, with the possibility of extension. And attached was the contract, to be returned as soon as possible.

She knew exactly what her answer was.

She fired off a quick reply and the promise to fax over the signed contract that night.

There. It wasn't much. It was a local contract, and she would still be able to live at home while she fulfilled it. But it was something. A decision made on her own. A step toward meaningful independence.

She put her phone back in her bag and stood up, taking a deep breath. Then she headed over toward where the bride and groom were standing, by the cake.

She was going to offer her congratulations and sincerest well wishes. She wasn't feeling quite so left behind anymore.

FROM AWARD-WINNING AUTHOR
KAKI WARNER

Behind His Blue Eyes

The Heroes of Heartbreak Creek

Ethan Hardesty wants to bring a railroad through Heartbreak Creek, Colorado, but hardheaded Audra Pearsall refuses to sign over the final right-of-way—no matter how persuasive or handsome Ethan might be. But when violence and fear stalk the canyon, Audra doesn't know who to trust—until the man she thought was her friend proves to be an enemy, and the man she resisted becomes her hero...

PRAISE FOR THE NOVELS OF KAKI WARNER

"Kaki Warner's warm, witty, and lovable characters shine."
—*USA Today*

"A must-read...Captures the imagination and leaves you wanting more."
—*Night Owl Reviews*

kakiwarner.com
facebook.com/kakiwarner
facebook.com/LoveAlwaysBooks
penguin.com

M1447T0514